T0148088

IN SILENCE AND DIGNITY-
THE
Single Mother
STORY

K A T E   O K O L I

Order this book online at www.trafford.com
or email orders@trafford.com

Most Trafford titles are also available at major online book retailers.

Printed in the United States of America.

ISBN: 978-1-4907-5337-9 (sc)
ISBN: 978-1-4907-5339-3 (hc)
ISBN: 978-1-4907-5338-6 (e)

Library of Congress Control Number: 2014922857

Trafford rev. 01/05/2015

www.trafford.com
North America & international
toll-free: 1 888 232 4444 (USA & Canada)
fax: 812 355 4082

**Over fifty million stories
One song**

Being a single parent is twice the work, twice the stress, and twice the tears but also twice the hugs, twice the love, and twice the pride.
—Unknown

To all single mothers whose story may never be told

Acknowledgements

This novel is dedicated to my lovely children—Daniella, Devine, and Denzel (the 3Ds), you are all God's perfect gift to me. A very special thank you to my son Denzel for keeping me on my feet on one occasion when I left my work unsaved while preparing dinner for everyone and he did me justice by turning off the computer. He almost made me cry! Oh how I love you all. You are my fulfilment.

And to my Achilles heel, Patrick Chinedu, my guiding light, thank you for the love, understanding, and deep friendship we have shared over the years. Meeting you is a completion of my life's story. It's so easy to love you. Thank you for a union that continues to surpass all human understanding.

I remember today and always my mother a giant of a woman. Your determination and struggle to instill in all your children discipline, hard work and the fear of God. A mother who taught me the difference between good and evil, a strong woman who taught me the importance of having an undying and unwavering faith in God. I bless you today and always.

And finally, to the omnipotent God, the creator, and the infinite one who gave this vision and revelation, my strength and redeemer. I say hallowed be your name.

The Myth, the Shame and Conquest

This novel is inspired by true life stories of different single women round the world. It talks about their silent pain and struggles, the heroic nature in which they assume the position of both mother and father because of separation, divorce, migration, absenteeism, war, rejection, teenage pregnancy, death or accident, child abuse/neglect, *xin con* or 'asking for a child', a practice in Vietnam by women veterans of the Vietnam War who had passed the customary age of marriage while engaged in the war. They asked men to help them conceive a child—a practice which was promulgated into the 1986 legitimacy of children of single mothers in Vietnam recognised under the Marriage and Family Law.

These single mums all have one thing in common, which is the fact that they may have made wrong choices in the past which they live with all their lives without being given a second chance to find love.

Prologue

Nigeria is a country in West Africa which consists of semi-autonomous Muslim feudal states in the desert north, and once-powerful Christian and animist kingdoms in the south and east, which is where the country's source of income, oil, was exploited.

At independence, Nigeria's federal constitution was formed which consists of three separate regions defined by the main ethnic groups in the country, which is the Hausa Fulani in the north, Yorubas in the south-west, and the Igbos in the south-east.

It was in 1960 when the military took over and the economic situation in Nigeria worsened and this brought about ethnic tensions amongst the three major tribes in Nigeria, which are the Igbos, Yorubas, and the Hausas. On 30 May 1967, the head of the eastern region, Colonel Emeka Ojukwu unilaterally declared the independent Republic of Biafra. As a result of this war in Nigeria, there was famine in the country and people were dying of malnutrition, kwashiorkor due to this famine.

Up to 30,000 Igbos were killed in the fighting with the Hausas and around one million refugees fled to their homeland in the east for safety.

Today, Biafra has been reabsorbed into Nigeria as the bid to secede was foiled.

This book is a story of a woman's determination to raise her children against all odds, her sufferings and sacrifices, her sorrow and inner strength and also her regrets and continuous fight to be affirmed by not just her family members but the society at large.

The characters in this novel, even though fictitious, are believable and their lifestyle is portrayed in such a way that every reader can relate with them. The characters have strong personality traits which keep the reader hooked to the book from start to finish.

This book teaches lessons about the struggles, challenges and pains endured by single parents all over the world. It is a book which gives a voice to many issues that have been officially swept under the carpet but which continues to resurface daily in people's lives.

****

Chapter One

It was early in the early 1970s, and the civil war in Nigeria has just come to an end with the military regime headed by general Yakubu Gowon making a national speech that the war had come to an end and that there was no victor, no vanquished.

Most Igbos from the eastern part of Nigeria were now returning, back to their previous place of residence before the outbreak of war which lasted for almost three years.

Chinua Onukaogu is a single mother with seven children. She had returned back to the eastern region of the country immediately before the war broke out. Despite the hardship faced during the war, she and her seven children survived the harsh conditions and the famine.

Chinua would go without food for days just so that her children could feed. She would also visit dangerous places where shell bombs were thrown by the opponents, just to put food on the table for her seven children. She sold her wrappers, her gold, and practically anything worth selling to be able to single-handedly provide for her children.

Chinua was a young pretty woman in her early thirties; despite her age, she was saddled with the huge responsibility of taking care of her seven children, three of whom she had with a very rich Nigerian businessman from the then-midwestern part of Nigeria, Bendel state, fondly called Bende'—up Bende'—by its local indigenes.

Prior to meeting Chief Mudiaga, Chinua had a rough beginning due to her poor background. She had been married off to a young man from her village with whom she bore her first four children, two of whom are twins. Chinua was married off to this young man at a very young age of fourteen years. It would appear later that her parents married her off so early because of her father's belief that it is a waste of resources sending female children to school; according to him, no matter how much you educate a female child, she will still be married off one day to a man who ends up enjoying all the benefits of the education.

Chinua's mum Nwanyibeke had ten female children; all of her male children died prematurely before they were born, and this broke her heart as she was convinced at the back of her mind that she failed her husband in that regard. Her conviction sprang from a traditional belief system which undermines the role that a husband plays in determining the sex of a child during conception.

All ten sisters in Chinua's household were married off to different suitors at a very young age while their father, upon being paid dowry by potential in-laws, used the money to attend beer parlours, drinking himself to a stupor each day. It was also spoken of on the grapevine how he used his third daughter's bride price to marry a second wife in his desperation to have a male child.

It was a taboo for female children to attend school within the household as their father thought it would be wasteful since they would end up getting married anyway. 'Training a female child in school is like throwing your hard-earned salary into the River Niger,' he would usually say whenever this topic came up.

After the civil war, Chinua's return to Effurun-Warri in the midwestern part of Nigeria was a decision she took after careful considerations of different options made available to her.

As a single mother, she suffered immensely at the hands of her other sisters during the war. She was called all kinds of names like *akwuna akwuna* (prostitute), even by her own sisters and immediate family members who were only interested in telling a single story about her single motherhood, without considering the details.

The decision to return to Effurun, therefore, was an easy decision because she understood that this was a place she called home for a long time before she returned to the east during the war, when all Igbos were advised to return to the east because of incessant killings of the Igbos in the south-east and midwestern part of Nigeria.

As the war came to an end, General Yakubu Gowon announced that it was a one Nigeria and there no victor, no vanquished.

Everyone who fled back to the east was now returning to their place of business to seek greener pastures after the war and to start a new life in a community they were used to before the outbreak of the war. Chinua was one of the Igbo women affected by the war.

****

Home coming

The Nigerian civil war aka Biafran war, which lasted from 6 July 1967 to 15 January 1970, was an ethnic and political conflict caused by the attempted secession of the south-eastern provinces of Nigeria.

This war was intensified by a conflict arising from economic, cultural, and religious tension mainly between the Hausas of the north and the Igbos of the South-East of Nigeria.

Over the thirty months' duration of the war, over one million ordinary civilians died from famine and fighting. The population of people at this time was skyrocketing despite the war and totalling over sixty million people consisting of over 300 different ethnic cultural groups with two major religions—Christianity, and Muslim religion.

Despite the religious, linguistic, and ethnic differences in the country at this time, Chinua damned all consequences and pitched her tent of survival in Effurun-Warri, which is in the midwestern part of Nigeria; despite advice by her mother to leave her children behind while she went off to test the water, she turned down her mother's request, saying that she owed her children the responsibility of being with them come rain or shine. This refusal by Chinua was by no means one of her very good qualities as she was determined that in the absence of a father figure, her children must have a mother figure to look up to for succour.

Chinua loved the culture and tradition of the Urhobo people. She did not make any attempt to master the language but she could say *migwo*, which is the general mode of greeting in the land. Three of Chinua's children were fathered by a wealthy midwestern Urhobo trader. It was difficult for her not to think of returning to a place that she now saw as home. She loved the people, the food, the banga soup and starch made out of processed palm kernel fruits served with processed cassava, dried fish, periwinkle, and snail. She also loved the Oghwrewi' sauce used in eating yam and unripe plantain. She loved the tradition and culture, the exceptionally humongous headgear, the abada wrapper and plain George matched with lace fabric which is the traditional attire worn by most people from this region.

Chinua also loved the use of pidgin English and the good sense of humour of these peculiar people whom she now considered as her people, their ability to create jokes freely through any experiences encountered by them, and most importantly, she loved the fact that returning to Effurun would give her seven children an opportunity to experience what it felt like to have a father in their lives. She could do with a never-at-home father—she thought to herself with a sigh of discontent and a feeling of hopelessness. If only fate was kind to her, maybe, just maybe, she would be happily married with her husband and children living under the same roof. In her usual 'I don't care' manner, she whispered to herself, 'What cannot be helped must be endured.'

And so, with this sense of determination to succeed despite her singleness, Chinua came back and settled in Effurun-Warri, Bendel state, or Bende'.

It was easier for Chinua to return, back to Bendel, and rightly so because Effurun-Warri had become home for her even before the war broke out. She discovered Effurun-Warri before the Nigerian civil war, when she followed her eldest sister Ujunwa to Bendel, pronounced Bende' mostly by its indigenes.

Ujunwa married a man called Amandianeze, a hard-working young man from Mbaitoli who at that time lived also in Bendel state and worked in African Timber & Plywood, AT&P, in Ugbakele, Bendel state.

Sister Ujunwa had ten children: seven boys and three girls. It was difficult to understand why she decided to have so many children, considering that her husband was paid a meagre salary while she took on the role of a full-time housewife who cared for her children and maintained the home.

It was almost as if during the period she bore these children, she was determined to impress on everyone around her that hers would be a short life lived bearing children. Ujunwa wanted to be remembered as that mother who bore different children with different behaviour and character. She would jokingly tell anyone who cared to listen that some of her children would be robbers, some drunkards, while some would be known for promiscuity. If perhaps she understood the power in words, she could have done what she did differently. True to her words, Ujunwa's children turned out very unsuccessful later in life and Chinua never stopped mentioning this to anyone who cared to listen that she would have loved sister Ujunwa to be alive to see how powerfully her pronouncements had affected her children.

Ujunwa, her husband, and their children settled in Effurun-Warri while her very hard-working husband Amandianeze, which means 'who do we avoid or be wary of', worked as a foreman in Ugbakele. He would usually visit his family in Effurun once every fortnight before returning to his base in Ugbakele. Each time he visited, he left his wife pregnant. You would often hear him boasting to anyone who cared to listen that he had brought his wife down again. 'Ekutuolam ya gbam,' he would always say to his friends each time it was announced to him that his wife was pregnant.

Rumour, however, had it that while Amandianeze was busy working in Ugbakele, his wife Ujunwa was engaged in the act of adultery with most of her husband's friends who enticed her with gifts of wrappers and laces. Each time Ujunwa was confronted with this rumour by her husband, she would deny blatantly, cursing and swearing. The last was when she became pregnant with her last child and an argument ensued between her and her husband who, on this occasion, confronted her about her infidelity, and she indiscreetly swore with her pregnancy, making pronouncements that if indeed she had been unfaithful to her husband, may she not successfully deliver her baby alive. The story has it that when Ujunwa went into labour, she bled to death—a tragic incident which, it is believed in the community, must have occurred because of the pronouncements she made by placing a curse upon herself even though she very well knew she was being unfaithful to her husband. It is believed that the ancestors may have been offended by her conduct and therefore brought about her untimely death.

Chinua met Chief Mudiaga when she came to live with her elder sister in Effurun after she lost her first husband and escaped from her husband's people and *umu adas*, first daughters in the community. Usually it is the custom and tradition of the Igbo people that when a man dies, the umu adas would plan to put the widow of the deceased through the rigours of tradition and culture.

It was typical of Chinua to rebel against this age-long tradition and custom which she thought was quite savage and barbaric. 'Shuo, dem

5

wan try me? Oghene migwo,' Chinua would say in the usual witty way typical of people from Bendel. This pattern of the use of pidgin English had become part of Chinua's daily use of words. She had imbibed it and quite enjoyed it tremendously. 'How can they put me through so much suffering over the death of a man whose death I am innocent of?' asked Chinua. 'It is even more annoying that his family members now struggle to inherit the little farmland he left behind, leaving me and my children to suffer, while his cold-hearted brother sneaks into my room each night trying to convince me on how it is the tradition that he inherits me as part of my late husband's estate, what nonsense and ingredients,' laughed Chinua to herself. Chinua always formed the habit of carving out words which soothed her each time she wanted to make light of a serious situation or incident which bothered her. The words 'nonsense and ingredients' were formed by her to express her serious concerns over the shenanigans of an archaic oppressive tradition and custom which favours only a deceased man's family while no action is carried out on the man if it is the woman that dies. The man ends up marrying the woman's best friend or sister, making it a win-win situation for the man. Chinua was in other words, a feminist to the core and was not apologetic for that in any way.

Once Chinua arrived with her children, her first port of call was chief Mudiaga's palatial home. She could not wait to show off to Chief Mudiaga how she managed to survive the war as a single parent with her seven children. This return to Effurun—back to base—was very significant to Chinua because of her insistence that she must go back with all her children when the war broke out and she single-handedly took her elder sister's nine children and her own seven children back to Umudike Umuahia, her paternal village, in confirmation of the promise she made to her mum that once things got worse between the Biafrans and the Nigerians, she would make sure she brought every one of her children and her late sister's children home. Chinua kept that promise.

When Chinua landed with all these children, her mother celebrated their safe return by slaughtering one of her white hens (okuko) as part of the celebration. 'Igba liala' nwam,' said Chinua's mum Nwanyibeke as she welcomed Chinua and her grandchildren into her wide-spaced and sparsely furnished living room. 'Your father, if he was alive, would have been proud of you.' She went on and on, praising Chinua and also calling out everyone in the traditional village manner to come see her daughter

6

and grandchildren who had returned home safely from Midwest. 'O wo' wo' o' wo' wo,' Nwanyibeke kept on shouting. 'Come celebrate with me, everyone, my generation have returned from Midwest, unharmed by the insurgents.'

'Hmm, Chinua, naram' aka' ibu wanyi' (give me a hearty handshake, Chinua, you are a woman of substance), Chinua would say to herself in praise of her determination and doggedness to succeed in life despite all her trials and tribulations.

Nwanyibeke was not the only one Chinua made a promise to before the outbreak of the war. The second promise made by Chinua which she also kept was that made to Chief Mudiaga when she took his children back to Umudike Umuahia in Eastern Nigeria.

Every attempt made by Chief to convince Chinua to stay back in Midwest Bende' was ignored. Chinua did not think she and the children would be safe as there were people who were saboteurs who gave out information to the Nigerian soldiers about where all the Igbos lived. All information given to the Nigerian soldiers led to the Igbos being murdered and slaughtered by the Nigerian soldiers.

Sister Ujunwa's husband Amandianeze was one amongst so many Igbos slaughtered during the war. He was pulled out from a ceiling where he hid upon noticing that the building where he lived had been surrounded by Nigerian soldiers upon other neighbours giving information about him to the insurgents that he was an Igbo indigene still living in their midst.

Chapter Two

The Vices and Pains of Polygamy— Love, Lies, and Deception

September 1970—home of Chief Mudiaga, Effurun-Warri, Delta state

As the fourteen-seater HiAce bus carrying Chinua and her children drove into Chief Mudiaga's compound, the driver hooted his horn uncontrollably like someone who had been taken over by an invincible spirit.

'Chinua! Chinua! Chinua!' The strong commanding voice of Chief Mudiaga rang through the silence of the still, quiet evening. The sound of the engine of the bus was still revving as the driver blasted his horn uncontrollably while all the time looking through his rear mirror to see if anyone would step out from the gigantic building to welcome Chinua and her children.

Amidst the serenity of this evening, there was the old-school music 'Sufferin' in the Land' by Jimmy Cliff quietly seeping through the window of one of the bedrooms in Chief Mudiaga's palatial mansion:

> It is plain to see we're in a terrible situation
> Sufferin' in the land
> Nearly half of the world on the verge of starvation
> Sufferin' in the land . . .

Chief Mudiaga's big mansion is a beauty to behold; it is a building constructed by foreign Italian builders and it consists of eight bedrooms, three living rooms, two garages, a separate four-bedroom apartment, self-contained servants' quarters (boys' quarters), a vast, large front garden well-maintained with hibiscus flowers planted round it, well lit-up halogen street lamps, and a six-foot-high wall with barbed wires.

Chief also loved very beautiful women and each month he was able to acquire one to his harem of women, providing them accommodation and businesses of their own so they could be independent. Chief Mudiaga had a large heart and was loved by all.

Chinua was one of the numerous women of Chief Mudiaga. She was beautiful, tall, elegant, svelte and had an oblong face with a gap in between her front teeth. Chinua met Chief during one of the many owambe parties attended by Chief years before the civil war broke out. Chief Mudiaga's fiery whirlwind romance with Chinua brought about the birth of Gwendolyn, Sophia, Mimi, and her only son.

Gwendolyn (one of the children born to Chinua and Chief Mudiaga) who at this time was quite young, could not understand the language of the white man as she started running back into the truck that brought them to Chief Mudiaga's vast premises, afraid that she would get hurt.

'Eeeeeeeeeeeeeeee, who dey drive you?' shouted Chief Mudiaga. 'Yanmiri pikin,' he said. 'Eeeeeeeeeeeeeeeeeeeeeeeeeee, you all have grown so lean as a result of hunger and starvation,' continued Chief Mudiaga. 'Where is my driver?' he further called out. 'Francis, what are you doing, get the abattoir to bring in a cow and slaughter immediately, my long-lost children have been brought back to me and indeed I must celebrate,' Chief Mudiaga joyously continued.

At this time, the whole compound was filled up with guests; there was serious celebration and activity with the music of Osadebe rending the air.

A cow was slaughtered as was customary in Chief Mudiaga's home whenever there was a big celebration. After guests retired, Chinua and her children were moved into the guest building and subsequently arrangements were made for alternative accommodation to be provided for them within the building.

Chief Mudiaga was a very wealthy man by all standards of the word *wealthy*. He was also a man with a free spirit who loved to give to the poor and the needy. He was a philanthropist to the core and also a justice of the peace (JP). Despite his wealth and philanthropic gestures, he also had a vice—women.

Chief Mudiaga also invested heavily in properties; despite his very minimal education, he was a shrewd businessman. Once there was this storyline that made the rounds that Chief Mudiaga once abruptly stopped his advances towards one of his concubines when he later realised upon taking further steps to pay her bride price, that she was an ex-wife of one of his business rivals. He could not, according to him, imagine himself eating the same food as the devil—this was the term used by him to describe this business rival.

Chief Mudiaga was not particularly what can be described as handsome when it came to physical looks, but what nature failed to bless him with in looks, he made up for with his good nature and kindness. He was quite stout in physique, with very dark shiny ebony skin, which shone even darker whenever he rubbed the olaku oil or Stella pomade all over his body when he wanted to impress a new catch.

Chief also never forgot his Saturday-night talcum powder and his Sasorabia scent which he dabbed excessively and most times unnecessarily all over his body, causing the flies to run after him in hundreds. Once, Chief Mudiaga felt insulted when during his usual hunt for a girl (twenty-eight years his junior), she asked him why he was being followed by so many flies. 'Are you an agbekpo man?' asked the chief's new female prey. 'Why are there so many flies following you and why is your calf shining so brightly and why do you have sand sticking to your calf?' she asked. It was apparent that Chief Mudiaga had rubbed so much Stella pomade all over his body that the excess cream attracted both flies and excess sand on his legs. What the chief thought would interest this young girl turned out to be a put-off, leaving him feeling rejected and angry the remaining part of that day.

After the encounter with this girl, Chief Mudiaga never arranged to meet with her again. According to him, he found her too vocal and disrespectful; he preferred his women to be subservient and submissive. 'I am sure she is raised by a single mother,' said the chief, trying to make himself happy. Despite this negative comment, he failed to see the virtues in this young lady who turned down his overtures as a show of self-discipline and moral values and ethos. Chief only told the single story of this young girl, leaving the other side of her story to be completed by posterity.

Chief Mudiaga's physical looks can be compared to that of an American war veteran, Major General Burnside, who had very notorious sideburns. General Burnside's sideburns, however, were nothing compared to the size of Chief Mudiaga's sideburns and his moustache.

The only time Chief Mudiaga ever thought about cutting his moustache *afu onu* was when he was enjoying his ofe ogbono, when faced with the dilemma of having to helplessly watch this slimy African delicacy, ogbono soup, run down his moustache uncontrollably each time he swallowed his large lump of eba down his throat with the remnant of the slimy ogbono running like a stream of mucus down his moustache and sometimes his wide nostrils.

Whenever the chief was served his favourite ogbono soup, he preferred to eat this African delicacy with his bare fingers. According to him, using his natural God-given cutlery—his five bare fingers—to demolish the okporoko stockfish and dried fish used in preparing this soup gave it an additional natural and sumptuous taste. Chief Mudiaga saw this finger-licking experience as part of his rich heritage as an African man. Anytime he was on this voyage of ecstatic experience, as he believed it to be, it reminded him of his mother—days when men were men and women were won by those who deserved them.

It was also a general practice in Chief's household that all his meals must be prepared fresh with large earthenware clay pots and firewood. Usually the earthenware pot is placed on top of a metal tripod stand while the dry firewood is put underneath the stand and then lighted up. According to the chief, there is a naturalness from the smoke emanating from the firewood which cannot be found using kerosene stove or processed gas. 'The white man has come to pollute our environment,' the chief would retort sharply each time his wives and older children tried to convince him to change the cooking regime in the household to a more modern and less stressful procedure. According to Chief, the firewood kills all the germs in the food, making it germ-free for human consumption.

Whenever the chief is served his ogbono soup with eba, Chinua would jokingly say to him in her rare sonorous joyful manner, 'Chai, chai, kamo' ga, donite, kodoronafom' (delicious food like this should not be wasted, it should be in the chief's stomach, not in the pot).

Chief would stretch out his large stocky legs, with his traditional six-yard yellow-and-blue striped onigbagi hollandaise wrapper luxuriously

11

wrapped round his very wide waist, a radio by his side, with the 'Sweet Mother' music blasting out of it and a keg of fresh palm wine served in a large calabash sitting next to him which he usually used to wash down the flavour of his favourite dish.

'Sweet mother, I no go forget you, for d suffer, when you suffer for me sweet mother,' the song dedicated to mothers was by Prince Nico—a popular African artiste. Chief always played this music whenever he was with Chinua. According to him, Chinua reminded him of his late mother. He loved her strength of purpose, her determination to succeed against all odds. 'The taste of the pudding is in the eating it,' he would say to Chinua, referring to her doggedness. One day, one of the chief's daughters corrected him, saying, 'It's not like that, it is the taste of the pudding is in the eating.'

'Shut up,' shouted Chief. 'Aproko' tafia lawyer,' he continued, leaving his daughter red-eyed in tears.

Chief Mudiaga had a vast expanse of hair lined up like a native African sponge down his temple, his nostrils, and all over his chest. He was heavily built, with a husky, commanding baritone voice.

Most times, the chief's voice could be intimidating both to strangers meeting him for the first time and to his wives and children, who never got used to the overwhelming negative effect of his voice on their personality. Once, one of chief's teenage daughters, Orona, came back from school to request for her school fees, and as she was downstairs, she heard her father's baritone voice commanding the houseboy to carry out certain house chores; immediately she started palpitating, and her heartbeat increased and her heart started beating so fast out of fear, and as she made her way through the hallway, she could no longer summon up the courage to go upstairs to her father for fear of being told off. She just stood transfixed to one direction for several minutes, not moving.

What saved the situation that day was that the chief noticed her heartbeat and immediately called in the family doctor as he saw it as an emergency. Immediately the doctor arrived, he tried to administer treatment on her while asking her about her medical history. To the amazement of everyone on that day, it was now discovered that it was because of the fear of her father that she became suddenly ill—a situation which almost affected her blood pressure. On this day, once the doctor finished attending to her, she was sent upstairs to the general children's room, where she was advised to take bed rest all through that day. She felt like a queen and thought to herself that this would be the first time she ever experienced any show of love and concern from her father.

As Chief's teenage daughter Orona rested in the children's room on that day, she dreamt that her father lived with her alone with her mum and other siblings in a tiny little mud house with a thatched roof. In that house, they ate and did everything together and she also had a one-on-one close relationship with her father who showed her so much affection, love, and respect, and there was so much laughter and joy in the family to the extent that she kept on laughing and laughing until someone patted her on the back to wake her up. When she woke up, she then realised it was only a dream and she shed a hidden tear as she never felt so loved and wanted by anyone the way she felt in that dream. She wished she never woke up from her dream.

Chief's voice was capable of joggling right-thinking adults and children alike. Chief Mudiaga's looks always scared little children. Each time he was contacted by mothers with young children, he always advised the mothers not to be worried, because he knew that his looks would definitely scare their children. He would always say to them, 'Never mind, I look ugly but my heart is beautiful, disregard my look because once you meet me, you meet money.'

Chief Mudiaga never apologised to anyone about his lucky fortune. He would go on and on about how he started from scratch, tapping rubber in the forest in order to earn a living. He would tell anyone who wished to listen about the benefits of hard work and honesty. He always used the popular saying 'Honesty is the best policy.'

Chief Mudiaga never attended high school. He dropped out of 'modern school' (high school) because of unavailability of funds to pay his school fees. He was an only child and his mother, being a single parent, worked in her farm to make ends meet. Chief Mudiaga's mother was married off to his father at the tender age of sixteen years. She was his fourth wife and led a solitary life right after the birth of her son Mudiaga. She also suffered after the birth of her son; she was also exposed to vaginal, bladder, and rectal damage. Even though she was married, she was more or less on her own as she fended for herself and her son with her husband, the chief's father, only coming around her whenever he felt he wanted to have sex with her. All her youthful years were spent working tirelessly to provide for her only son Mudiaga until she died when Mudiaga was only twenty-two years old. After his mother's death, Chief Mudiaga vowed not to ever treat women badly the way he saw his father treat his mother and the two other wives.

Chief Mudiaga was determined to succeed; he walked a long distance of over twenty miles to the rubber plantations in Pamol where he joined his master to tap rubber which was then exported. It was during the long years of rubber tapping that he met his good fortune when he was introduced to the timber business by another business merchant whom he met through his *oga* (master).

Within a period of five years of being introduced into timber business, Chief Mudiaga became very, very rich. Being an adventurous man, he also ventured into property investment, buying houses all over his immediate community and leasing these houses out at a competitive price. Most of his female tenants always benefitted from his largesse as he would not mind mixing business with pleasure.

As a person with a strong appetite for women, Chief Mudiaga would entice his beautiful young female tenants with money, expensive gifts bought from Kingsway's stores (grocery store for the elites); once they consented to be one of his mistresses, he would now cease to collect any rent from them giving them such freebies as a rent -free accommodation, eighteen-carat English gold, wrappers, Georges, and sometimes perfumes. The only thing about Chief Mudiaga's choice of perfumes was the strong unpleasant aroma. He also went out of his way sometimes by sending the very young children of his concubines who were single mothers back to school. It was quite surprising how Chief Mudiaga's business still continued to thrive despite his unserious ways of mixing business with pleasure. He seemed to be using the natural law of 'the more you give, the more you get' in his favour, albeit negatively.

Chief Mudiaga loved to sponsor anyone who showed interest in their education. He would tell anyone who cared to listen that were it not for the fact that his mother was a poor single parent who struggled to put food on the table, he would have attended Oxford University or even Harvard in the United States if given the opportunity. 'Education is the best papuacity,' he would wrongly say, with *papuacity* in place of *policy*. Chief also had a penchant for pronouncing *Oxford* as *Uxbridge*, making anyone who was listening to him wonder how these two were connected. Each time anyone tried to correct Chief Mudiaga that Oxford is different from Uxbridge, the chief would then ask in pidgin, 'Wetin concern vulture with barber?' meaning 'What business does a vulture have with visiting a barber's shop seeing that a vulture is already bald?'

Apart from not being able to attend school, another life event which Chief Mudiaga moaned about each day was the fact that despite how very hard his mother Nene (*mama* in his native tongue) worked to put food on their table, she did not live to enjoy his good fortune. 'We will continue to strongle as akperio' continues,' he would say in his deep primitive Urhobo accent again pronouncing *struggle* as *strongle*. It was very easy to identify Chief's dialect from the way he mispronounced English words; this sometimes caused him to clash with some of his very young girlfriends, who always felt embarrassed by his primitive nature. 'If you nove me, keep my commandment,' the chief would say, again pronouncing the word *love* as *nove*.

Chief Mudiaga would give excuses, to anyone who cared to listen, why he loved women. He would say to anyone who cared to hear that his love for women sprang from the fact that he loved his mother Nene so much and anytime he set his eyes on any beautiful woman, it reminded him of his mother and her beauty.

This thought for his mum also instantly compelled him to feel obliged to help any woman he came in contact with, in whatever way he can, to make life easier for the woman.

Chief Mudiaga always enjoyed giving anyone who cared to listen a running commentary on the subject of women and how he managed to conquer them despite his physical looks. 'Na handsome we go chop?' he would usually say in pidgin. 'Being handsome will not put food on your table, but hard work will.'

He would always say 'I stoop to conquer women' with a loud thundering voice. 'When my money talks, women happen,' he would joke. Chief Mudiaga also had a good sense of humour and this formed part of his many attributes which endeared him to many women in his community.

He was a leader of so many top organisations in his community, a philanthropist, and a justice of the peace. 'My appellation is concrete enough to be perceived,' he would usually say within five minutes of meeting any female.

All women in the community thronged the chief's compound daily to seek his help in one way or the other. These women consisted of married, single, separated, divorced, and would-be single women who made themselves available to him as a result of the monetary gain and his very large heart. Chief loved humanity despite his weaknesses. Notwithstanding his exposure to different women, the chief was, however, a disciplinarian and highly principled man who did not do anything which, according to him, would hurt another and so because of his principled nature, one thing which Chief Mudiaga seriously considered as a taboo was having to have any intimate dealing with a married woman, outside his ordinary willingness to assist such women. Chief came across this category of women who, even though they were known to be married and still remained married, lived their daily lives like single parents with no form of support whatsoever from their husbands.

Chief would tell anyone who cared to listen, of the advantages and detriments involved in sleeping with another man's wife. 'I have seen 'magun jazz live in my days and I will never ever have anything to do with another man's wife!' He would jokingly describe how different men of different ethnic groups in Nigeria react to another man or intruder whom they suspect has committed adultery with their wife. 'If you try an Isoko man's wife, remember that his *tolopia* cutlass is there, as he will not mind beheading you with it if he finds you with his wife,' joked Chief.

'If you try a Yoruba man's wife, you are likely to die on top of 'magun laced on her. (African voodoo)

'If you try an Igbo man's wife, be ready for a physical combat with him. If it's a Calabar man, you are done for.' Chief would go on and on, giving sermons about how not to be involved with a married woman. He knew his boundaries and his wife Chinua would always say of Chief Mudiaga, 'Onye ara na uche ya,' literally meaning 'A mad person has their own understanding and wisdom.'

A typical Urhobo man understands that once his wife cheats on him, within her childbearing age, she has his forefathers to confess to anytime she is pregnant with child, because she will go into long, endless labour pains and the child will refuse to be delivered until she confesses to the elders of the land that she has committed adultery.

'These days, however, it is said that for the Urhobos, there is an antidote and this antidote is the English language,' Chief would say. 'The white man has introduced the English language to my people which now serves as an antidote to our age-long tradition and custom which deters our wives from committing adultery. It is now believed that the culture only understands the Urhobo language and so once the adulterer communicates in English, they then do not have to make any confessions of adultery to the forefathers and so they go scot-free,' moaned the chief painfully. Chief was a very jealous man and, once he was interested in any woman, would give anything to have her all to himself. He never, at any time, wondered how his list of women, including his harem of wives, coped with the knowledge that he himself was not faithful to them. Chief kept on deceiving himself and was under a serious conviction that all women should be seen, not heard; again it was part of this belief of his that brought about his downfall.

Chief Mudiaga never stopped telling a tale of an agbekpo human waste removal man, whose wife was sleeping with another neighbour. This agbekpo man, once he got wind of who his adulterous wife was cheating with, waited for this culprit with his bucket of human waste and his broom while the adversary was returning from a late-night outing. He poured the whole bucket of excreta on his adversary, making sure that he soaked his broomstick with a considerable amount of human waste, which he sprinkled right into the mouth and nostrils of the adulterous man. Till date, no one heard anything more from this man who thereafter ran off to an unknown destination for fear of being named and shamed.

'Ah! Married women are no-go area for me oh!' he would say. 'Forget that yan, my brother, you wan try? No shaking,' he would rant on in the common pidgin English, which is a general slang used by most people from his region.

'If you are married, first leave your husband and make sure you are leaving not because of chief, then after one year show the divorce certificate before I can have anything to do with you,' he would joke foolishly. This to him is the gospel according to St Mudiaga, he would say, matter-of-factly squinting his left eye, which was always bloodshot because of constant drinking of the local gin *akpeteshi*.

Despite his strong notion and self-acquired discipline about how to handle married women, his constant strong affinity to women almost became the Achilles heel which would destroy Chief Mudiaga later in life.

Chief was reckless and became uncontrollable in his quest to create a harem of women, both those living with him and even other numerous concubines whom he kept and maintained on a constant basis.

The more Chief Mudiaga's wealth increased, the more his appetite for women increased. The moral decadence in the society where the chief found himself did not help matters. The women would throw themselves at him because they knew his weaknesses. The women would want to befriend his wives and children just to get to him, to get his attention.

Most times, innocent and genuine assistance and support from the chief were misinterpreted by these women to mean he wanted something more. Even when he innocently showed kindness to a woman, they misinterpreted his kindness and took it upon themselves to want to lead him on, understanding his weakness. Some of these women, upon having first encountered him on a one-night stand, came back months later with news of their pregnancy, which the chief would now be forced to accept by including their maintenance and upkeep in his monthly expenditure.

Chief would go out of his way to assist any woman, whether married, single, young or old. 'Hmm . . . na wa for wire road oh! Why is it that women always misinterpret a man's kindness for romantic gestures?' the chief would ask. 'Even the ones who say they are married, once you show them kindness, they want something more from you.' In his usual joking manner, he would then answer his questions himself. 'Please, I am not available,' he would say to his friends. 'I am a hunter and prefer to take the lead, that is the natural thing and the way God made it to be. An African man prefers to be the first person to initiate a relationship with a woman he wants to be with.'

'I am the head,' he would go on. 'I make the first move, and also want to be the sole provider,' he would tell anyone who cared to listen.

'I like women, but I have principles, married women, my wife's relations and friends are a taboo to me, I know when to draw the boundaries. This is my physlosophy about life,' the chief would say—this philosophy perhaps worked for him because there would have been a constant upheaval of quarrels and street fightings over Chief Mudiaga if he did not know how to draw the lines of friendship.

Chief Mudiaga also had a penchant for light-skinned women. Once there was this story about how he visited a very popular hospital in Eku where one of his children was on admission awaiting a major surgery. After seeing the doctors and confirming the date when surgery would be carried out on his child born to him by one of his numerous concubines,

Chief Mudiaga became mesmerised by the looks of one of the nurses on duty, named Maka.

The involvement with Maka later became a major reason why Chief Mudiaga's relationship with Chinua became severed—an occurrence which Chinua kept talking about till date. Chinua would say to all that cared to listen, 'This man was a good man until this possessed Maka came into his life to steal, to kill, and to destroy but she will pay for it.'

Maka was a very pretty young lady from a very poor impoverished background. Her father was a village cobbler from Obiaroko while her mother sold African foodstuff in the community market. She sold banga fruits (palm fruit), spices (*ofe aki*), spices for banga soup, ugu leaf, dry ground-up egusi, ogbono, okporoko (stockfish), abasha, waterleaf, ukazi okro, egusi bitterleaf, garri (cassava meal) amongst other typical African foodstuff / culinary items used in preparing African delicacies. Maka's mother was known within the community to supply most of this foodstuff which was supplied to her by different food suppliers. Customers also came to her from all over the country to buy what they considered her essential commodity. Essential commodity only because it was part of an age-long cultural norm for any household to be seen to indulge in eating this African food with very high carbohydrate like ground eba (cassava plant) served with either egusi soup, ogbono soup, or banga soup. These are affordable heavy meals with high carbohydrate components capable of making anyone grow quite fat. *Within the community, local delicacies are celebrated and eaten with so much joy and togetherness.* Such meals are eaten with bare fingers as it is believed that you do not enjoy its full flavour when eaten with cutlery.

This type of meals is usually enjoyed by all and sundry and has formed part of the daily menu within the community. In those days, if a woman looked too lean, people would interpret it as malnourishment and poverty to the extent that before such a woman is betrothed to a husband, her family takes her to a 'fattening room', where she is fed and groomed very well to put on weight and have feminine curves so her potential husband can have some flesh to hold on to. A lean person is therefore referred to as *kpanla*, okporoko, or dried stockfish.

It is also a cultural norm that anyone who visits, with or without a prior notification, the homes of friends and family must also be entertained with these delicacies for as long as they decide to stay. It therefore did not matter whether the host had enough to accommodate this visitor who has come unannounced. It is mandatory for this food to be shared amongst all, including the unannounced guest. This rich culture was enjoyed by both the rich and the poor in the spirit of oneness and togetherness which formed part of the heritage of the people. There is therefore a general saying 'Onye we madu kari onye were ego', meaning 'He who has friends and family is much richer than he who is wealthy.'

Another great attribute enjoyed by families is the way and manner this meal is served in a big round bowl while every family member eats from the bowl, sitting round a mat on the floor, with the usual episode of complaint from younger family members that they have been stung by soldier ants crawling on the bare floor.

The eldest member of the family takes the greatest share of the meat (either bushmeat or beef) notwithstanding that it is the youngest members who need more of these nutritive components to assist their growth. The remainder is shared amongst the children in order of seniority. Before the commencement of each meal, everyone is encouraged to wash their hands in a bowl and then for families who cannot afford a dining table, a raffia mat is laid on the floor while every member of the family sits round in a circle during this very important family dinner.

The sharing of the meat done by the eldest member of the family (either the mum or dad) is normally at the end of the meal. Children are also encouraged to drink more water to help them fill up easily.

Apart from eba and the complementary soup served with it, there are also occasions where families serve yam and palm oil as another delicacy. Usually this yam is shared amongst family members and eaten hot, either boiled or roasted depending on the occasion.

Rice as a meal is a special delicacy eaten only on Christmas days or on Easter Day, mostly a special delicacy preserved for festive seasons. However, most average families could still afford to eat rice served with well-prepared chicken and beef stew outside of any festivities.

It is due to the high demand for this food and its importance within the community that much respect and recognition is given to anyone who is involved in its sale. Maka's mother became very popular as every family would come to patronise her little corner shop usually filled with all of these condiments which had, over the years and through generations, formed part of their heritage and culture.

Despite the numerous patrons who were members of the community, Maka's mum still struggled to fend for her family as a single parent saddled with four children of her own. Her husband had left her for another woman because according to him, she was not able to give him a male child that would outlive him and bear his name. Maka's mum struggled each day to make ends meet with her four children. There was very little left for them to rely on in the form of profit after all major expenses and disbursements and so the whole family struggled each day to make ends meet.

****

Life's Choices Filled with Unexpected, Hidden Thorns

On a bright, sunny afternoon, Maka was running home from an errand for her mum, she was stopped by a middle-aged man who introduced himself as one of the principals of a popular secondary schools in the community. As this man engaged Maka in a long conversation while they walked down the footpath home, he thought Maka sounded quite intelligent for her age. As a popular school principal well known in the community, he deserved a wife not only to prove his point that he is capable of marrying a very pretty woman, but also someone who could bear him intelligent children in the future.

Principal Merenge always used to say to himself that if a child does not take after the mum, he/she would take after the dad. Maka, according to him, had all the attributes he looked out for in a future wife and she would also complement his academic achievements and intelligence. And so, the relationship between the two was quite sporadic, with Maka feeling happy that she was able to get the attention of the most intelligent eligible bachelor in the community while her not-so-young husband wanted the advantage of not only marrying a very pretty light-skinned woman who was twenty years his junior, with the additional advantage of her high IQ, or so he thought to himself. Principal Merenge always believed that something must make a man or a woman want to marry each other. Marriage therefore doesn't just happen; it is the couples that make it happen, he would say.

Despite the age difference between Principal Merenge and Maka, the relationship between Maka and her husband Merenge was sporadic. He could not get enough of her as he bombarded her with visits and

21

an offer of his services in the form of fetching firewood and water from the stream for Maka's mum just to get her approval. It was a common practice amongst young men to offer themselves to family members of their would-be spouses by offering time to serve them in their homes just to be able to get their consent.

And so in less than six months of their courtship, one thing led to the other and a relationship leading to discussions involving marriage and long-term commitment ensued.

It was this Principal Merenge who then assisted Maka to enrol in a small hospital within the community as an auxiliary nurse. She was paid 5,000 naira per month. This same principal, who at this time was known by all members of Maka's family, also promised to be responsible for funding Maka's career prospects by enrolling her to study nursing. No week passed by without the principal visiting Maka and her family with a hamper of gifts. The family already accepted his marriage proposals with Maka, formal introductions, *iku aka*, and wine carrying had already taken place, and both families were waiting for Maka to graduate from nursing school, after which her traditional marriage ceremony would be performed.

Unfortunately for Merenge the principal, when Maka was in her second year in nursing school, and also working part-time as an auxiliary nurse, she met Chief Mudiaga when he came to visit his sick child in that same hospital and the rest became history.

The relationship between Chief Mudiaga and Maka became one which was spoken about within the length and breadth of the community. This is perhaps because of the fact that Maka was already betrothed to Merenge Principal, who had been involved in sponsoring her in the local nursing school. When Merenge was informed that Maka was cheating on him, he confronted her with these facts and she immediately went on the defensive, accusing Merenge of his wild escapades and also the fact that he was twenty years her senior. 'Benfuzi, na me do you?' asked Maka during the meeting she had with Merenge. 'Is this all you have to say to me?' asked Merenge the principal. 'Ehen . . . what else?' asked Maka. 'Is it me that asked you to waste your youth?' she asked. 'So you want me to suffer all my life? How can you take care of me with your meagre salary of a teacher?'

'We will manage,' answered Merenge the principal. 'Am I a manager?' asked Maka. 'Please please pleeeeeease,' she continued, 'go look for your mate.' This was the last meeting Maka had with Merenge the principal. Every other attempt made by him to speak with her was frustrated by her as she would not hear of it.

After every attempt made to meet with Maka was unavoidably frustrated, Merenge then visited her mother's shop to express his concern. Immediately Maka's mum sighted him she screamed, 'Benfuzzi na me do you?' Merenge came into her shop, greeted her, and sat down. She mumbled a response to his greeting as if being forced to respond while she looked straight into his eyes. 'Yeeeees?' she asked. 'Ehen ma, I have come to talk to you about Maka,' said Principal Merenge. 'Which Maka?' she asked. 'My Maka.' Merenge answered. 'Your Maka? Heh heh!' Maka's mother laughed heartily. 'Please do not allow anyone to hear what you have just uttered from your mouth o! Maka is now married to a very rich chief in the city o!

'Every mouth that spoke evil of this single mother with four female children will one day speak good. I told you people that my story will one day change. Did I not?'

'Onu kwurunjo' ge kwunma.' She went on and on, narrating how she suffered at the hands of her estranged husband and how she had struggled as a single mother to raise her four children, selling foodstuff. She did not fail to also mention how people called her all sorts of names just because she was a single mother, despite not knowing her true story and what led to her being single. 'Onye ha juru oga ju onweya? Mba nunu! A person rejected by an irresponsible husband cannot reject herself.' She was referring to her husband's abandonment. She could not imagine allowing her daughter to marry into poverty by marrying a poor schoolteacher, a local champion.

'So you and your daughter did me christiana akwa?' Principal Merenge wailed while placing both hands on top of his head. 'Eh eh eh, mama mo! Mama mo! Mama mo!' He continued wailing. 'Christiana were' egom mu gba mu ngaga. So Prince Nico of blessed memory, the artiste, saw this coming, akwa?' he managed to further state none too convincingly in a melodramatic manner. Principal Merenge had a good sense of humour and always tended to bring humour into everything, including things which directly irked him.

'Please leave my shop,' Maka's mother screamed at the top of her voice. 'You are not ashamed of yourself coming to marry a girl young enough to be your first child,' she went on in ridicule.

'So now you know am old? After I have spent my life's savings on you and your daughter, now you know that I am an old man, akwa?' retorted Principal Merenge.

'Yes, you are an old man, even me that is Maka's mother cannot be married to you because you are too old.'

'Am I older than you?'

'Of course yes,' she answered. 'Old soldier turned teacher, go look for your type. My daughter Maka is taken by a man who deserves her, a man who can take care of her and her children and also bury me when it's time for me to join my ancestors. Don't come here again, your chapter is closed. Vamoose, vamoose, vamoose!' She continued screaming until Principal Merenge left in embarrassment, cursing under his breath, 'So it's because of that old married man that you and your daughter have decided to treat me this way? Is this the extent that you as a mother can go?' he asked. 'A mother encouraging her daughter to go and get married to a man old enough to be her father and at the same time a man with several wives and children.' Principal Merenge tried without success to talk sense into Maka's mum. 'Yes, leave it o, leave it o! At least he has money, not a church rat like you, I don't want my daughter and my future grandchildren to suffer the way I suffered,' continued Maka's mum.

'Can you imagine?' She went on: 'When they talk about people who are living, this one will answer "Present, sir." What does he take me and my daughter for? Is it not a woman like me that took my own husband? Upon all my sacrifices towards my husband he still left me, so what is the profit of marrying a single young struggling man who becomes rich and later abandons you for another woman?' she asked. 'No pain, no gain, no pain, no gain. No skin pain, this is me.' She went on and on.

Maka's mum continued her lecture as if trying to justify her daughter's action for not keeping her promise with Principal Merenge.

'I told them in this community that I will have the last laugh and this is my time to shine.' She went on and on long after Merenge left. She even called Principal Merenge names like Oba Nshi nahu, which literally means a person who defecates on his body. 'I and my children live for today,' she said. 'Let tomorrow bring with it whatever it chooses.' She went on and on as if trying to seek affirmation, oblivious of a customer who walked in to purchase some foodstuff from her. 'Is anyone here?' asked the customer. 'Ehen, what do you want?' asked Maka's mom as she turned to attend to her female customer who walked into her shop.

'Are you okay?' asked the customer whom she called by the name of her child. 'Huh, Mama Osy, am okay o. It's all these church rats with seven-foot-long manhood who think they can freely come and ask for my daughter's hand in marriage. I say no to poverty henceforth. Any man that cannot bring on fire, "oku" is not welcomed in my household anymore.

'Imagine this schoolteacher trying to take me and my children back to poverty. My daughter Maka is baby oku and any man who cannot weta oku is not fit to be with her.'

'Hmm,' Mama Osy mumbled in response. 'Do you think of only yourself or your daughter's happiness and future? So you say your daughter is baby oku, hot baby, and any man who does not weta oku or bring enough money cannot be with her, akwa?

'How would you then feel comfortable allowing your daughter to marry a man who has a string of women lined up and who is a serial womaniser? Is your daughter's happiness guaranteed with such a man or you are just looking at the immediate benefits?' asked Mama Osy.

'Happiness? You talk about happiness,' she responded. 'Happiness— what is happiness without money?' asked Maka's mum.

'Money cannot buy you happiness,' retorted Mama Osy. 'A time will come when you and your daughter will realise that. I will advise that now that it is not too late, you make amends and go back to Principal Merenge so that your daughter can start her life without any complication. You don't want your daughter to become an emotional wreck due to what she will suffer at the hands of this married man, do you?'

'Pleeease. What do you want to buy, international adviser?' Maka's mum shouted irritably. 'I see there are people who specialise in giving wrong advice to others while they cannot advise themselves. You once married a very rich old man after making him leave his wife and five children, didn't you?'

'Yes, I did,' said Mama Osy, almost blushing despite her very dark complexion. 'And where did that marriage leave me? I am therefore advising you as someone who has had a very bad experience in life, because of my greed and previous get-rich-quick attitude. Here I am today, still labelled a single mum without morals, battered, bruised, and full of regrets. Is this the kind of life you want your daughter Maka to live? I am one of those single parents who give single women a bad name.

I did not have the opportunity of being acquainted with a good advisor and so, getting married to a married man was one of the worst decisions in my life which I still regret up till this minute. I had so many young suitors who came to seek my hand in marriage, but I turned them down more because of the kind of friends I kept, friends who only understood the language of money. To them, money talks and bullshit happens. Where are all of them today? Some died while battling with the politics and rivalry which a polygamous marriage threw to them. Some became disillusioned once they became married to these rich men who later abandoned them for younger girls, while others like me took a decisive step on their own after realising their mistakes and walked out with their children, becoming single parents with a lot of pain and regrets due to bad decisions and choices made by them.' My life is a story of regrets, madam, and I wouldn't wish this for my enemy. If I see your daughter Maka, I will advise her not to marry Chief.'

'My sister, forget it. When we get to that bridge, we will cross it. What are you here to buy?' she asked while facing Mama Osy to attend to her needs as a customer.

'I want "ugba", "okporoko" and fresh garden eggs to entertain my guests who are visiting me from Aba.' Once mama Osy made known what she wanted to buy, she was quickly served by Maka's mum without anymore verbal reasoning relating to her daughter's decision to marry an old rich chief from the city. mama Osy left her shop with a feeling of discontentment forgetting to collect her change.

After the confrontation with Principal Merenge, every other confrontation which had to do with Maka's refusal to marry this principal was squarely addressed by her mother. People talked about her and found reasons to even address her single status as one of the reasons why she could not encourage her daughter to keep to her promise to marry the village principal despite his financial commitments towards them over the years. They coreferenced her single status with her integrity as an individual, thereby telling a single story.

Chapter Three

The Dilemma of Polygamy

While Principal Merenge was moaning over his disappointment in Maka and her mother, Maka was on the other side busy enjoying the attention and love showered on her and her family by Chief Mudiaga. She was chauffeur driven everywhere in chief's Peugeot 404 saloon car (with registration number BD 2323) by Chief Mudiaga's driver.

Chief Mudiaga would not stay one day without Maka. He spoilt her and her mother with all sorts of gifts. He also moved them to a more affluent neighbourhood while promising to buy her mother a family home as soon as all necessary marriage rites had been completed. Chief also made sure that Maka's younger sisters were placed in private boarding schools while their school fees were paid in advance. They also enjoyed the privilege of being chauffeur driven around town, to the utter amazement of everyone.

The only part of the relationship which Maka found quite demanding was whenever she had to attend social events with Chief Mudiaga, who was three times her age.

Maka also met with Chief's friends and acquaintances, whom they hung out with in the neighbourhood. She later realised that these friends also had girlfriends young enough to be their daughters, and it was the in thing amongst them as they would talk about it, laugh about it, and also encourage each other to indulge more in such practices. Maka found it quite challenging and demanding engaging in any meaningful intellectual conversation with either Chief Mudiaga or his friends. They talked about Osadebe's music and Rex Lawson's music, which she could not relate with. When it came to discussions on the politics of Nigeria, they talked about Azikiwe, Odumegwu Ojukwu and how he fought the Biafran war, they talked about some very distant history of Nigeria and their reasoning, to her, was quite archaic and preposterous.

Once during one of their numerous social outings they were confronted by one of the chief's wives, Chinua, who purposely went there to disgrace him for his continuous failure to meet his financial and parental responsibility.

'Useless old man,' she ranted, 'look at you. You are here carrying young girls old enough to be your young daughter's age.'

'Look, look, look here, I will not entertain your insults o,' the chief warned. 'After all, you are not my only wife. How come you are always the one ready to make trouble? I am a traditional urhobo man and the tenets of my tradition allow me to marry as many wives as possible,' said chief. As Chief showed no remorse over his action, this enraged Chinua the more and she then walked straight to Maka, pointing straight at her while all the time pouring insults on her. 'You little brat, so you are the auxiliary nurse from Eku hospital who has come to destroy a home that was built even before you were born. I will deal with you,' she screamed at the top of her voice as Maka watched in panic, not knowing what steps to take next. As the chief's wife moved swiftly towards Maka, she grabbed her by her collar and spat on her face. 'Husband snatcher! Husband snatcher! Homewrecker!' she raged. As Chief Mudiaga stood up to push his wife out of the premises, she hit his stomach with the sharp edge of an umbrella which she held in her hands, and the chief immediately collapsed and was rushed to the hospital by his friends.

Amidst the stampede caused by these incidents on that day, other passers-by became involved as they looked on and asked questions. 'Is that your father?' one male passer-by innocently asked Maka. 'What does it look like to you?' she retorted sharply while running off to take a taxi, which took her home that night. While running off to the taxi, Maka held her shoes in her hands and ran barefooted out of the scene of the incident to avoid anyone noticing her.

As she sat down comfortably inside the taxi, she reminisced on the pain which she saw in the eyes of the chief's wife on that day.

The memory lived with her the rest of her journey home, but despite seeing the pain of a wife who was fighting to keep her home and her husband, she, notwithstanding, made a decision not to stop, because of her greed and determination not to have anything to do with poverty the rest of her life. 'Hmm,' she thought to herself, 'if one person's relationship does not go sour, another will not be good. After all, someone took my dad from my mum and made my dad abandon me and my siblings.' She muttered these words to console herself and to make herself believe she was doing the right thing.

When Maka got home that day, she could not summon the courage to talk to her mother about her experience at the hands of Chief Mudiaga's wife. It is no use anyway, she thought to herself. 'The only language my mum understands is the language of money.' She decided not to share this experience with her mother until later. As she thought deeply of how good it would be to be married to a single man her age whom she truly loved and would have loved to spend the rest of her life with, with the two of them raising healthy, intelligent children, the tears rolled down her face as it suddenly occurred to her that her thoughts would be a far cry from reality. She was not ready to go back to poverty anymore. Chief Mudiaga was her meal ticket and she was prepared to do anything to keep it at that.

Maka preferred the tongue-lashing of chief's wife, the uncertainties of not knowing exactly what her future held, with dating a man three times her age, to being ridiculed just because she was poor. She would choose those long lonely nights of having to wait for the chief, not exactly knowing whether he was with another woman or at his family home as he would like her to believe. 'I'll choose financial stability any day and would rather be lonely than be poor.' She tended to further convince herself as she drifted into a deep sleep, with her pillow wet from hours of uncontrollable tears and sweating arising from the anxiety which such deep thoughts sometimes instigate.

After this incident and confrontation by Chinua, Maka did not have any further contact with Chief Mudiaga again until after four weeks. He was, however, in touch with her through his driver who brought in money and other expensive gifts to Maka and her family.

'Chief is not well and has asked me to bring this money for you and your mother.'

'Where is he now?' asked Maka.

'He is at home recovering, having been discharged only a couple of days back. He has strict instructions from his doctor not to be involved in any stressful work.' He was also placed on a strict diet to watch his weight and the size of his protruded stomach arising from long years of constant intake of carbohydrates and fermented beer and local palm wine.

As the relationship between Chief Mudiaga and Maka blossomed from friendship to marriage, it was thought by everyone in the community that the pace of their romance was so abrupt and intense and quite out of place. It became the talk of the town. People talked about this whirlwind romance between Chief Mudiaga and his newly found lover. He would abandon his businesses, his fatherly role, and every other thing just to be with Maka. The age difference between Chief Mudiaga and Maka in this case was also not in question. Every member of her family was very happy and they saw her as that messiah who had come to lead the whole family out of the Egypt of poverty.

While the whole of Maka's family enjoyed the luxury of his wealth and kindness, Chief Mudiaga on the other hand was experiencing a lot of problems both on the home front and in his business life. His businesses started suffering immensely from neglect. His children also felt the impact of this new woman who took over Chief Mudiaga's life instantly. Tongues started wagging and Chief Mudiaga's other wives and children and even people within the community believed strongly that Maka had used African voodoo and a spell on Chief Mudiaga.

Chinua, on her own, had another game plan, which she called the plan B of how to eradicate and purge the thought of Maka out of Chief's system. Chinua arranged with hoodlums in the community where Maka attended school, paid them, and instructed that they give her a thorough beating after stripping her naked. On the fateful day they carried out this plot and Chinua and her men struck, Chief was away on a business trip. They met Maka along a lonely footpath on her way home from school. They stripped her naked, beat her black and blue while Chinua all the time was screaming, 'Husband snatcher, red pawpaw, husband snatcher, red pawpaw.' They used blunt razor blades and scraped off Maka's hair while continuously hitting her and calling her all kinds of names. Maka was crying and wailing, 'Help, help', but no one came to her rescue because they were convinced that Maka's plot to marry Chief Mudiaga was unacceptable by them. 'See her yellow fine body,' screamed Chinua once Maka was stripped naked and her bare breast sticking out from her bra. 'No wonder my husband does not remember to come back home anymore, so this is the evil mammy water breast you used to entangle my husband, depriving his children and family from enjoying him. I will finish you today,' screamed Chinua emotionally. They made Maka sign a handwritten undertaking that she would never have anything to do with Chief Mudiaga or any other married man again. After she signed it, they left her half conscious on the motorway. Maka was later rescued by a Good Samaritan who rushed her to the hospital where she was admitted for three weeks.

If Chinua thought her actions would deter either Maka or Chief Mudiaga from continuing their clandestine activity, then she must have another think coming. Instead of warning Maka off, this action further endeared her to Chief Mudiaga, who immediately felt guilty that Maka suffered so much at Chinua's hands because of the love she had for him. He immediately sent Chinua packing out of his house, bought Maka a car and a dozen wigs to cover her shaven hair, and also started making serious arrangements to legalise his union with Maka. He kept on saying to Maka, 'Oh, you have suffered so much because of my love, I will pay you back by marrying you to shut up all oppositions to our relationship. By the way, you look even more beautiful bald, but always put on the wig I bought you, because you are not mourning my death yet and I cannot afford to have you expose a bald head as it is against my tradition baby oku, hot baby.'

Within two years of meeting Maka, Chief Mudiaga paid her dowry or bride price and instantly moved her into his palatial mansion. Maka became an authority and an institution on her own. She wielded so much power and her fear became the beginning of wisdom within Chief Mudiaga's household.

Maka would boast to anyone who cared to listen that she has chief's heart wrapped round her hands. All the chief's wives now resorted to seeking Maka's consent before they could get any favours from him. Anyone would fall out of favour with Chief once Maka made a complaint about them.

Such was the power wielded by Maka which made everyone suspect it could not ordinarily be possible for a woman to wield such powers. Little did they know that Chief Mudiaga was only enjoying a perpetual habit and Maka was only adding to his statistics of women.

Despite the seeming control by Maka, five years after she became married to the chief, he took an additional wife, and thereafter, another younger wife, breaking the silent apprehension and supposed belief by everybody in the community that he was under Maka's spell.

Despite the strong hold Maka thought she had over the chief, he took more wives even after he married her—a decision which stunned everyone and kept them wondering until his death.

When Chief Mudiaga took the second to the last wife into his harem, it became a tug of war in his household. Usually, Chief Mudiaga had this philosophy about life that women are to be seen, not heard. He was a strong unapologetic chauvinist to the core who saw woman as a tool and a weapon which should be used for his personal enjoyment and gratification. 'I love Guinness stout mixed with Peak milk,' he would say enthusiastically. 'However, I love women more, because of the naturalness of their sophistication. I love their natural oil, their natural smell and feminine idionsyncracy.' Whatever this diction meant for the chief remained unravelled. 'My appellation to women is concrete enough to be perceived,' he would further quote to himself.

Chief had this ability to use and misuse the English language whenever he pleased. He became even more eloquent once he was in the presence of a woman, especially any woman whom he was hunting to win her love and attention.

What was even more intriguing about the chief's perception of women was his belief that he owed no woman an explanation, especially when it came to life-changing decisions, even decisions that affected the future of his children. According to him, once he had been able to meet his responsibility of being a sole provider, then he did not feel obliged to discuss anything about major decisions which affected his household.

With this single authoritarian attitude, little did Chief Mudiaga understand that he was creating and preparing a lonely life for himself, filled with disloyalty, suspicion, superstitious beliefs, and conspiracy.

Once, Chief Mudiaga made a decision to buy a new car without giving any of his wives any knowledge of his plans. Also each time he took on a new adventure of adding to his harem of women, he never brought this to his wives' attention to prepare them for the new entrant into the family. This also had to do with other major and minor decisions which affected the whole family.

Once there was this story about Chief Mudiaga who bought a car and after purchasing the car from SCOA Motors (a Peugeot car, which he fondly called Pijo), he parked it right in front of his family home all day. One of his wives, who wanted to drive out of the house, then called out to know who parked his car in front of the family home. She was running late and wanted to quickly drive out and was quite furious in rage. As she tried to find out from the chief if he had a visitor, he just came out of his bedroom wearing his white singlet and the traditional six-yard hollamdaise wrapper, saying to his wife, 'The Pijo car is mine, I bought it,' to the astonishment of not just his wives but every single member of his household.

All the numerous wives who first thought Maka wielded power and control now resorted to their own tent after he married Veronica, the last wife. They became loveless, without any emotions. In place of sympathy, affection, and care, they looked out for what will be beneficial to them and their children. They called it 'my gate' and so they continuously ripped off Chief Mudiaga of his money in every possible way they could. Prices of simple things like groceries and food items were inflated. There was therefore no loyalty towards Chief Mudiaga. These women did not see any reason why they should show any level of loyalty to a man who saw women as chattels that should be used for his sexual gratification.

One of Chief Mudiaga's wives always referred to him as Mr Greedy Amukwu, a nickname linked to the size of his male organ, because of his wet appetite and penchant for changing women.

At the time Chief Mudiaga added another wife after Maka, there became a strict competition between Maka and this new woman. Maka felt threatened by this woman's beauty and thus vowed not to ever allow this woman to share her husband's bed with her without seeking her consent and permission first. These two women were also always engrossed in physical confrontations and verbal exchange of words each week, to the chagrin of onlookers and members of the chief's household.

'I told this man,' said Chinua about Chief Mudiaga, 'that women will be his undoing but he will not listen.' Chinua who now lived outside Chief's house after the whole family held a meeting and begged on her behalf for reconciliation, now visited Chief's house whenever she wanted to discuss her children's welfare.

Each time she visited and saw that Maka and Veronica were exchanging words, she never stopped laughing. 'Now the chief has finally carried the one that will bring about his downfall.' Chinua never stopped speaking about how men who are polygamous in nature always end up in their old age unloved, uncared for, miserable, and sometimes penniless because of the abandonment they suffer and experience from their wives and children. There is also a feeling of rejection, and pain experienced by the children raised within the household, because of the father not being available for them each day.

'My father did it to my mother Nwanyibeke when he left my mother and married another woman in a bid to get a male child. He suffered terribly before he died,' said Chinua.

At first Chief Mudiaga had tried hard to shield his latest wife from the fangs of his favourite wife Maka (or so people thought). The story had it that most times when Chief Mudiaga started having erectile problems, as it was believed, Maka's spell also affected him to the extent that even when he was with another woman, his thoughts still continued to be with Maka, making it impossible for him to have an erection. It was also known this time that Chief Mudiaga had a severe health condition and was struggling with type 2 diabetes and because of the constant medication, he experienced certain side effects. Looking at science and the likely side effects of the medication which Chief administered daily for his health conditions, it was difficult to relate this with the superstitious beliefs and the interpretation which was given to his erectile problems.

The whole of Chief Mudiaga's household was in awe of Maka to the extent that there was this belief that any reasonable discussion held with Chief (as he was fondly called by all) could not take place if Maka was around. All she needed do was to call Chief Mudiaga by his initial and then that would be it; he became unreasonable and uncooperative, practically driving whoever he might be having discussions with out of his presence just to be with Maka.

Another trademark of Maka was her manipulative tendencies. She knew how to work on Chief's emotions and she knew his weaknesses and that part of her which he loved so much and so she used what she had to get what she wanted from him. Once she saw any of the chief's wives having a conversation with him, she would scream out his initials 'MJ, MJ, MJ! The children's Lactogen is finished, the SMA is finished, where is the driver, MJ? MJ, please send the driver to Kingsway to buy my children's Lactogen and SMA.' Once the chief heard her voice, he lost any form of control and instantly went under the spell of Maka.

As the rivalry between Maka and the last wife continued, the older wives and concubines whom she saw as a threat also were not spared the wrath of Maka. It then became a constant occurrence within the household that anytime Maka conceived a child, she would miscarry within the fifth month. She would then fabricate all sorts of lies against the wives, convincing Chief Maka that she had been bewitched by the other wives, most importantly Veronica the last wife, and Chinua her arch-enemy.

Once she experienced a miscarriage, Maka would make all the chief's wives come to the family home to swear to an oath with a kind of concoction which is forced down the throat of each wife and concubine. Anyone amongst them who refuses to drink from this concoction or oath is believed to be responsible for the miscarriage of Maka's unborn baby. It so happened that for fear of being excommunicated from the household, labelled, or ostracised most times, all of these women took the oath and partook of these fetish concoctions prepared by a strong medicine man introduced by Maka and her mother and automatically endorsed by Chief Mudiaga.

When Maka finally started having her children, her problems and misfortune also progressed from having a miscarriage to losing her children at a very young age. After having had about three miscarriages, she had her first child, whom she named after Chief Mudiaga. She named him Mudiaga Johnson Jr. despite the fact that Chief Mudiaga already had a son who bore that name but excluded Junior from his name. And so Maka named her son Mudiaga Jr.; according to the story she told Chief Mudiaga, the birth of her son marked the beginning of their love, which was made in heaven. She was the only woman who loved the chief genuinely; the others, including the chief's first wife, who suffered with him from the start, did not have genuine love for him.

Chief's love for her also complemented and cemented the true feelings they both shared, a love which passeth all human understanding except that the humans around them believed that this love had been influenced by her African voodoo and manipulative prowess.

Chief Mudiaga believed every word which came out of Maka's mouth and never stopped telling tales to her about how he made a mistake marrying all the other wives, including the one he married after meeting her.

As disloyalty and lack of commitment is common with most polygamous marriages, despite this confession of unimaginable love,

Maka never failed to exhibit her true colours when not with Chief Mudiaga. She would tell her friends how very naive and stupid Chief Mudiaga was. 'Don't mind that old womaniser who calls himself my husband, old fool,' she would go on and on. 'He thinks he is smart, but he can only be smart with his old and local wives, not me.'

'I will scrape his head,' she would go on. 'I have to secure my children's future oh! Once this man dies, I will find one young man and marry him with my money.'

'He cannot even perform oh,' she said, referring to his lack of sexual prowess. 'The other day he almost died in my arms, panting like an old fool that he is. We' reeee' (the general Yoruba slang for madness).

Once, Maka had a misunderstanding with the chief and she ran out shouting in the streets, 'Size ogboloma, you say you go beatie me, I say na lie you talk.' This display of shame by Maka was indeed a testimony to the other wives, who never had the audacity to challenge Chief Mudiaga, except for Chinua.

The lack of loyalty exhibited by Maka was not an attribute seen in her alone. It was seen in the whole of Chief Mudiaga's household. This level of disloyalty which was the imminent disaster faced by Chief showed its face daily within the household.

Chief could not meet his matrimonial duties because the number of children he had totaled over twenty-five and still counting because some of his wives were still within child bearing age and also sexually active. Each year naming ceremonies and christening within the household would be a minimum of three. Because of this increase in the number of children, the chief could not meet his parental responsibilities any longer.

Because some of his wives were only in the relationship for their material gain, they had affairs outside the home, travelled out on long journeys with their younger and sometimes older friends and sugar daddies just to satisfy themselves because of the loneliness and forlornness they faced in the relationship.

There were also accusations and counter-accusations of infidelity by each of these wives. Some of them were rumoured to have been impregnated by their boyfriends and to have claimed that the chief was responsible. Despite all these rumours on the grapevine, Chief Mudiaga continued to boast that he knew all his children are his because they all have the traditional thin legs and calves and gap teeth which he himself inherited from his forefathers.

'You cannot have the Mudiaga blood in you without the traditional gap teeth and very thin legs,' Chief would jokingly say.

As the years progressed, and Chief became older, his priorities did not so much as change. The major love for women which many described as overindulgence or lack of control over self and lack of respect for family values, later became Chief Mudiaga's undoing.

The former happiness, peace, and love which were shared within his household became a far cry from reality. The more the women in his life increased in number, the more his life became miserable and the more his finances and businesses suffered tremendously. Once there was this story going round Chief Mudiaga's household that whenever it was the turn of any of his wives to share his bed, Maka would invoke a kind of evil spell that would reduce Chief Mudiaga's libido on each of those nights, making it impossible for him to fulfil his marital responsibilities towards his other wives. And so, like every other man who found themselves embedded in the practice of polygamy, Chief Mudiaga became a very lonely man; he became very angry, depressed, and suspicious, not trusting any of these women as he believed that the only reason why they were in his life was his money, not because they loved him. As Chief Mudiaga became older, he became more suspicious of everyone around his household. He also became too conscious of death, he feared that he could die suddenly and all his wealth would be misused by his children and his first wife.

Once he made the mistake of mentioning his apprehension to his wife Maka, who took advantage of this and advised him to sell off most of his properties while he was alive. Maka gave chief Mudiaga this selfish advice because she was apprehensive of what her fate would be if peradventure the chief died.

'I better grab as much as I can now that he is alive, my children are in the twenty-something numbers in order of seniority, I cannot afford not to acquire the best of this old man even in death,' she thought to herself.

Chief Mudiaga's children also suffered immensely from the choices he made to become polygamous. His teenage daughters decided to find refuge early at the hands of other men. In fact, Chief Mudiaga himself would suggest to them whenever they came to request for school fees, to get married as it would be a continuous waste of his money for him to train female children who would eventually get married and become the responsibility of another man someday. He would also remind his daughters not to be like their mothers. They should be submissive and level-headed.

'Don't be like your mama oh,' he would say. 'Know that with a traditional African man, women have to be submissive, don't bother about the white man inciting women to be rebellious by the creation of the word *women's liberation*,' he would say.

'Where on earth have you seen where women pour libation to our forefathers?' said the chief. 'What then is this liberation all about?' the chief, in his usual manner, always confused words as he in this case confused the words *libation* and *liberation*.

Once during one Christmas period, his teenage children from his first wife Oghale were out in the streets trying to hitch a ride, while immediately a car pulled out in front of them and as they made efforts to get into the car, they recognised their father's bowler hat and his traditional wrapper (abada). 'Ewo, ewo, ewo!' screamed Chief Mudiaga, as his two daughters ran into the streets. Chief Mudiaga then sped past as they faded into the vicinity.

When they got home on that day, it was a tug of war. 'Oghale!' he screamed. 'What my eyes saw today, my mouth cannot speak about.'

All his wives ran out of their individual rooms with their arms wrapped across their chests. 'What happened?' they all asked in unison. 'What happened? Are you all asking me? Where is the other one, who feels all about life is money, money, money? Each time I say to her, return home and take care of your children, prepare them for marriage, she will not listen.' The other wives now knew who exactly he was referring to, as they all stared towards where Oghale, the chief's very first wife was located.

'Perhaps if you were a good-enough father and spent time with them, they would not be out there in the street looking for unscrupulous men like you to spend time with,' mocked Oghale as she walked in to take a seat comfortably in the large tastefully furnished family lounge.

Oghale was the very first wife traditionally married by chief. He would not fail to tell anyone who cared to listen how he paid twenty shillings years ago when men were men, during his traditional marriage with Oghale. Oghale also came from the same tribe as Chief Mudiaga and they spoke the same dialect.

There was also this story from the grapevine which was told about how Chief Mudiaga could not resist the youthful looks of his first wife, and despite investigations being carried out on both sides to find out whether there were any reasons according to the tradition and custom why he should not marry her, reasons like whether there were any hereditary diseases in the family, any divorces, or single parenthood and also whether within the family, they had been blessed with long life. In addition, as part of the pre-marriage investigation, investigations were carried out to find out whether these couples were related either on their father's side or on their mother's side to avoid incestuous practices seriously regarded as an abomination. It was a normal practice (ome nani), and no one got married before all of this was completed.

When the chief proposed to marry his first wife Oghale, it was discovered that the chief and his first wife were related by the fact that his great-grandfather married Oghale's grandmother who, however, did not bear his great-grandfather any children, bringing about the end of the marriage a very long time ago. Despite this distant connection and relationship, the chief was able to convince all family members that because his wife was already pregnant with twins, they could carry out sacrifices to the forefathers as a form of cleansing and thereafter get married. This was exactly what was done and once the traditional cleansing and rituals were carried out and completed—a ritual which involved killing of goats for the forefathers, to appease them should they be against the union, because of the connection and link between the great-grandparents, he went on and married his wife. His wife Oghale bore him seven children.

Unlike the age difference between the chief and Maka, which was an age gap of more than thirty years (Chief was sixty-two years old while Maka was thirty-two years old), his first wife Oghale was within the same age bracket as him. She was considered the overall mother to every other person within the household. She also had a very kind heart and understood the chief's mood more than any other of his wives or concubines. She would always say to the chief, 'I will use the virtue of patience which I have been blessed with to defeat you and your numerous women.'

Sometimes Chief Mudiaga would confess to his first wife Oghale that the act of womanising which he involved himself in was not of his making and that he struggled to resist any woman. Chief would also remind his first wife Oghale how crucial it was for her not to ever leave him no matter what happened in the future. He would tell her that she was his first love and all other women in his life were *jara*, literally meaning the other women in his life were a plus.

Chief would also remind his first wife that she was the true love of his life, the wife of his youth, the one who knew him better than anyone and who understood his mood, the one whom God used to console him when he lost his mother, the one who brought him luck and good fortune that other women were now enjoying. It was also quite difficult not to believe whatever the chief told his other wives and concubines whenever he was with them alone. Chief made every woman in his life feel as though she was the most important creature in the whole wide world, therefore making it difficult to understand who he truly and sincerely love most amongst the whole lot.

The patience and understanding by Oghale, who had been married to chief for forty years, could be seen in her level of tolerance and continuous marriage to her husband despite his promiscuity.

A story also had it that during the very early stages of their marriage, Chief Mudiaga also had stints with a housemaid who was brought from Akwa Ibom state to assist with the house chores.

The product of the nocturnal relationship between Chief Mudiaga and his housemaid was never known to Chief Mudiaga until thirty years later when he became very ill and had the surprise of his life when he was visited by his former housemaid Ekaete and her daughter who, according to Ekaete, had continuously threatened to take her own life if she was not taken to her father.

Prior to the chief's encounter with Ekaete, a story also has it that Oghale his first wife once met him in their bedroom cuddling her younger sister whom she had brought to help with her young children. Immediately this infidelity was discovered, the chief apologised, saying it was the devil and that the devil used his first wife's sister to entice him. He compensated his wife and mother-in-law by sending her younger sister off to Atlanta, Georgia, in the United States to study. She now lived with her husband and two children in the States.

The silent rift between Oghale and her younger sister had since then not been healed by time. Even though she had apologised to her sister, she still felt uncomfortable in her sister's presence and not welcome to stay over each time she visited with her family.

Chapter Four

Chief's Children—the Evil Red Seed of Polygamy

There was stiff competition amongst the Chief's children. This competition started even from a very young age as their mothers each tried to warn them ahead of time of the importance of making sure that they excelled much more than their step-siblings to prove a point in the family. Everybody became quite suspicious of each other and they were always watching their backs. They spent their day setting up each other and also outsmarting each other in order to gain favours from Chief.

Most of the wives wanted their children to excel more than the others, and the children themselves, because of the environmental factors within the household, also became aware of the politics going around and took advantage of it.

Gwen was one of the four children born to Chief Mudiaga and Chinua. She had three girls and one boy. Each time, Chief Mudiaga never failed to remind Chinua how he would have loved it if Gwen was a male child. 'Are you God that gives children?' Chinua would question his reasoning. 'Leave these children alone, they all have a destiny to fulfil, whether male or female.'

'Yes, I know,' Chief would go on. 'I see a high level of intelligence and potential in Gwen, that's all.'

'All my children have potentials o,' Chinua would argue. 'Please leave them alone, this local Urhobo man.'

The relationship between Chinua and Chief Mudiaga became very strained as time went on. Chinua was not the type who could excel within an environment of diplomacy, manipulation, and lies. She was by nature a fiery spitfire, 'what you see is what you get' kind of woman. She could not cope with the lies, deception, and disloyalty which thrived within this polygamous household.

Because of her true nature which was most times misinterpreted, she always joined issues with the chief because she refused to allow him to get away with his weaknesses. Each time she was with him, there was always a lost battle and she would end up bursting in anger to buttress her dislike for his promiscuity. Chief Mudiaga on his own could not understand why Chinua failed to respect him and all that he represents—which is the fact that he is an African man and an only child of his late mother and therefore must produce more and more children through his love for women.

Chinua was the direct opposite of Oghale. Despite all of this, she had a heart of gold and would not hurt anyone. She always believed that she was with Chief as a result of circumstances beyond her control. 'Perhaps if my parents did not marry me off at an early age to a good-for-nothing man who later died, leaving me with no education or financial strength to fall back on, I would not have ended with this kind of man,' she would say to herself.

As the years rolled past, the relationship between Chinua and Chief Mudiaga became severed. Chinua, however, promised herself that she must make sure that Chief Mudiaga became responsible for the tuition fees of his children. She fought to make sure this was achieved.

Each time the children came home crying that the chief had driven them back to her for school fees, she would rage and rage and take them back to him, requesting vehemently that he pay their school fees as this was his own contribution to the children's lives.

'Did I not set you up?' the chief shouted from his balcony during one of the numerous visits of Chinua with Gwen to request school fees from him. 'I ask you, this Igbo woman, did I not set up a business for you?'

'So what if you set up a business for me? Have you asked if the business is profitable?' retorted Chinua sharply in her usual firebrand manner even before the chief finished his last sentence. 'These children have to eat, wear clothes, wear shoes and I also have to pay for their hospital bills when they are sick. The only thing I ask is that you be involved in paying their school fees and yet you complain and make life miserable for these young children. Why do you have to suffer my children each time they come to you? They will always be the last to pay school fees and yet everyone in the community knows their father is a wealthy chief. Why?'

'I don't have money. Please, this woman, I did not ask you to move out of my house with my children. There are enough women here to take care of them but when you moved out, you stubbornly moved with them. I am not the kind of father who will await the postman to deliver a parcel of money from my children in the future. I have planned my retirement. Please train your children, this woman, and leave me alone.' The chief would be on the defensive each time it came to spending money on any of his children.

'It will take you to be in your grave before you will realise what that woman Maka has done to you. You will regret in your grave,' moaned Chinua. As if in response to Chinua's words, suddenly, Maka's voice was blurring in the background. 'MJ, MJ, MJ, where are you?' Maka who all this while pretended to be taking a nap in her room, walked in with a list in her hands, requesting that Chief send the driver to buy her body cream and other toiletries for her and her children as she planned to visit her son Junior in the boarding school the next day. She then handed the chief her list, oblivious of the fact that Chinua was sitting next to the chief while having a heated argument with him.

Maka's body language could almost be interpreted to mean that she wanted to further reiterate a statement of fact to everyone, Chinua included, that she, Maka, had the chief wrapped round her finger and was capable of twisting him whichever way she wanted.

'Aha, Chinua, you can see my wife is here and I need to attend to her. I can only give your daughter Gwen half of the school fees, which is N700, go and look for the remainder and add to it.' To Chinua's amazement, Chief stood up, strolled into his room, and immediately strolled back with a bundle of naira notes which he handed to Chinua. 'How much is this?' asked Chinua. 'It's N700, I don't have more, as I said.' Chinua then threw the bundle into his face, pulled her daughter Gwen, and walked off while screaming, 'Ehen, so you don't have money but you have money to throw around town to women.'

'You have money for this evil thing.' Chinua said, pointing at Maka, who at this time was sitting with her list held out, waiting for the chief to attend to her.

'Listen, Chief,' cried Chinua, 'this will be the last time I will make my children go through this rejection from you. I will go and you will not see me and these children again. We are not slaves, we do not have to come to prostrate to you and your "queen" every time.

'As far as I have life in me, my children will finish their school, whatever height they hope to get to in life, I will make sure I work hard to pay their fees. I will change these children's surname as I do not see how it is favourable to them.

'You send your driver to their school to pick up only Maka's children and you leave the others whose mothers are not with you. You will regret this, but if what you are doing to these children is not from your clear mind, whoever has influenced your action will definitely pay for it.

'We shall not all die on the same day, we shall live to see the fruit of wickedness and voodoo,' she pointed to Maka, while using the edge of her onigbagi wrapper (an African print made in Holland which had become popular amongst African women her age) to wipe the tears from her face.

As they left the chief's compound, Chinua vowed not to ever put her children through that kind of trauma anymore. Each time these children wanted to go back to school, their father made it a bad experience for them, as they began to panic, not knowing whether he would be willing to pay their school fees before they returned to school.

On their way home, Gwen told her mum she should have at least accepted part of the money which was given, to make things easier for her, but she said there was no need as she wanted to prove a point to him, to show him how he has been callous to his own children. 'I know he is not himself. If I did not know your father when I first met him until this woman Maka came into his life, I would have said he is a wicked man. I remember him vividly as a very kind man who loved his children. He is now under the influence of voodoo from Maka. But remember my words, whether I am alive or dead, you see, Maka will pay for every trouble she brought to this family. We will not all die at the same time, someone must live to tell the story of Maka.' Chinua went on and on that day as she walked home in pain, frustration, and disappointment.

'Perhaps you should not have married him in the first place knowing he has these qualities of womanising, Mum. I am sorry, Mum, but I don't understand why anyone in their right mind would want to get married to a married man with children. You brought all of this upon yourself and now see how it's affecting me and my siblings.'

'You are right, Gwen, but then ignorance is bliss, there was no one available to me who could tell me whether what I was doing was right or wrong. Moreover, this man lied to me about his marital status, he only told me he had children from a broken marriage who are with his wife. He, however, did not allow me visit him at home as he lied that he was always on a tour due to his very busy work schedule.'

'Okay, Mum, it's fine, at least we are all learning from your mistakes and don't think anyone close to me or any of my siblings would engage in this kind of relationship with a married man. You paid the last price for us, Mum, and we are grateful to you despite all what you have been through.

'Why don't we go to Chief Rufus, his best friend, to report this injustice?' asked Gwen.

'How many times do we have to do that? Are you not tired? Leave his friends out of this as they are all birds of the same feather. Moreover, I wouldn't want you to continue to pass through all this stress as a child.

'God will provide for us and I don't mind selling my gold jewellery and expensive wrappers to make sure you all attend school up till university level. The only thing that will stop you people as my children will be your lack of interest in attending school, but once you are interested, I will make sure that you achieve the educational height you want, by struggling and working hard to pay your school fees.'

'I still insist we go either to his brother or his friend Chief Rufus to report this case so at least we would have exhausted all alternative opportunities to get these school fees paid by him. My dad pays Maka's children's school fees, he should pay mine also or is there something I have done personally to him that makes him detest me so much?'

As Gwen asked this question, she could not help the tears flowing freely from her eyes. She held her mother and continued to cry uncontrollably. 'O my daughter, sorry o! Sorry o! Ndo o! Sorry. Don't despair,' Chinua consoled her daughter. 'He has rejected us, but God, God has not rejected us. Remember the Bible version, hmm, I have forgotten the particular version, but the Bible version which says, "The stone that the builders rejected has become the cornerstone . . ."

'Gwen, when we get home, I want you to search the Bible and find me what book of the Bible mentioned this very important lesson of life.' Chinua held on to her daughter as she consoled her.

'Okay, my daughter, we will go to the chief's brother tomorrow evening then. You have left school now for three days and I don't like it. Your school exeat expired yesterday and just imagine.'

'Yes, I know, it's for a reason and I don't mind, I will be able to catch up,' replied Gwen. 'My school exeat expired yesterday, but I have to pay my school fees before going back to school and so once we see my uncle, I can leave immediately the next day.'

'I have been making arrangements with a goldsmith to pawn my English gold,' said Chinua. 'This arrangement has to be in place as I cannot continue to depend on this man to dictate me and my children's happiness. When you start working and you are successful tomorrow, I know you will replace all this jewellery for me, it's a sacrifice I have to make as a mother and the pain and reality of life I have to face as a single mother raising my children on my own. Life is not fair, but nothing in life is fair anyway.'

Birds of the Same Feather Flock Together

When Chinua and Gwen visited her uncle Mukoro the next day, it was a different story as the uncle tried to encourage her to find a suitor who could marry her. 'You are now a grown woman,' he said. 'You know your father has limited resources and if he decides to give out his money to all his twenty-five children each time they ask, how is he able to save for his retirement?' Uncle Mukoro advised. He had his neck bent to one side like someone recovering from a severe neck injury. He usually kept his neck that way each time he wanted to be difficult, earning him the nickname 'Agama lizard'.

'Your best option would be for you to get married to save your father this additional stress,' he went on. 'You can thereafter further your education from your husband's home, leaving him to bear the burden of paying your school fees. Why should a man train his daughter and then another man suddenly comes and marries this daughter, enjoying what another has already paid for?' Uncle Mukoro asked as if talking to himself, oblivious of the fact that Chinua and Gwen were with him in his living room. Chinua turned and gave Gwen a knowing look as if to say, 'I told you coming here will be a waste of time.'

As Chinua and Gwen looked on, they then heard the front door to Uncle Mukoro's living room open, and one of the chief's daughters strolled in, in her pyjamas. 'Migwo, sir.' She prostrated herself in front of her father.

'Eh vre' do'. Eeeeeeeeeeeeeeeeeeeeeeee! Jite, you woke up so early today, where are my grandchildren?'

'They are still sleeping sir.'

'Has your husband called?'

'Not yet, sir, I am still expecting his call.'

'Okay, then ask the driver to take you to Kingsway shop to do all the shopping for you and the children as soon as you are ready. Call my accountant so I can raise the N5,000,000 you requested that I should lend to your husband to support his business.'

'Migwo, we kobiruo.' Again, Jite thanked her father joyfully while rushing off to take a quick shower to start her all-expenses-paid shopping promised her by her father, Uncle Mukoro.

It was clear from the conversation that Jite, Chief Mukoro's elder daughter, only came on a visit to her father's house and was planning to return to her husband having been married to a northerner from Jos Plateau state for the past ten years. It was also not a secret that Chief Mukoro had also supported his daughter and her husband financially anytime they had a financial crisis. He had always been there for them, giving them both financial and moral support.

Jite, Chief Mukoro's daughter, also had two master's degrees acquired from University College, London.

As Chinua sat waiting for Chief Mukoro to at least make a positive suggestion as to the reason why they came to see him, her thoughts went back to his conversation with his daughter. 'You see, wise man. Another man head na pot,' she thought in pidgin. 'He is supporting his daughter whom he sent for training in the university abroad, who after completion of her education in the UK returned and got married to a young man whom she met during her sojourn in the United Kingdom.

'Despite giving his daughter the opportunity of a sound education, he still supports her and her husband each time they run to him for help, and yet, he is advising his brother's daughter who is in class 3 in secondary school to quickly find a suitor and get married. Each time I speak to my daughter about these people, she does not listen,' thought Chinua. These people don't even have the best interest of their brother at heart. You take care of your own family and yet want another to marry off his own daughter at a tender age without any strong educational qualification so they can continue to be inferior to your own children. This same Uncle Mukoro also advised Chief Mudiaga, his brother, to take my daughter to street sellers of sunglasses to purchase non-prescription eyeglasses for her when she had problems with her eyesight rather than taking her to qualified opticians to find out the problem with her eyes. As usual, his brother accepted this advice in good faith, they bought the sunglasses from the street as advised by Chief Mukoro, took it to Dr Mccoll, and upon carefully looking at the sunglasses Dr Mccoll advised that it was not possible to break the lenses of these sunglasses and then replace it with a prescribed lens. 'Chief, you are more than this, pay for your daughter's eye test, and once this is done, we shall get her prescription glasses suitable for her age which is recommended.'

As Chinua reminisced on the drama that ensued between Dr Mccoll and Chief Mudiaga, she could not conceal her delight at the way he embarrassed himself: 'Local champion, he went and bought Oyoko'meter for my daughter and was later embarrassed by Dr Mccoll.'

'Chief, my ass,' she chuckled, which brought her back to her immediate environment. As she turned, she saw her daughter already sleeping with her head laid back on the sofa where they both sat. 'Poor girl,' Chinua thought to herself, 'I don't know why a child has to go through all of this just to be in school like her mates. This has to stop, I must let my children understand that I will be with them till the end, no matter what. I will hold on to their hands and love them unconditionally by making additional sacrifices to see to it that attending school is something that should be part of a positive life experience for them, not what their father is making it look like. I am a single mother with a difference,' Chinua reassured herself. 'Yes, I am a single mum with a difference, that difference will be seen by the whole world as I make a vow to put in extra effort to make sure that my children don't lack emotionally, psychologically, and financially.'

'Uncle Mukoro, we are still here o!' she called out to Uncle Mukoro. 'Uncle Mukoro Obanshi,' she mocked, 'incontinent Uncle Mukoro.'

Uncle Mukoro at this time had already fallen asleep himself, snoring loudly. 'Uncle Mukoro, Uncle Mukoro,' she called out.

'Imagine, the things women go through at the hands of these people. I am here with my daughter to discuss an important issue about my daughter's future, all you could do is to give negative advice about finding a suitor for my daughter while your own daughters attend the best schools, both local and international,' she thought to herself again while still calling out his name. 'Uncle Obanshi—sorry, Uncle Mukoro oooooooooooooo.'

'Grrrrrrrrrrrrrrrrrrrrrrrrrrrrrr,' the heavy snoring sound continued.

'Gwen, please stand up, let's go. I have a home, I and my children are not beggars, this is why I told you I didn't want to come to see this man again o!

'You remember when your school sent you home to take care of your eye problem, this same man advised your father to buy sunglasses from street touts and then replace the lenses with a prescription from the optician. He is no good. See his pot belly filled with human waste. Please, let's go because the next thing, he will start messing (farthing). I have had enough.'

They strolled out of the luxurious living room unnoticed by Uncle Mukoro who at this time was in deep slumber. As they walked back home, Chinua wondered what kind of a man Uncle Mukoro was, and what good man would undermine a plea for a child to get her school fees paid. 'He will wake up and find out that we are gone, osondi, owendi,' said Chinua in a typical joking manner, trying quite hard not to be discouraged by this nonchalant attitude shown to her daughter by a very close family member.

The situation in Chief Mudiaga's family home did not get better even after Chinua stopped visiting to ask for her children's school fees. Most of the children living in Chief Mudiaga's palatial mansion whose mothers had left him, also suffered tremendously at the hands of Maka.

There was an obvious preferential treatment given to Maka's children who moved around town chauffeur-driven while the other children slapped home (slapping is slang used generally for taking long compulsive walks instead of commuting in a car).

These children were woken up as early as 5.30 a.m. to carry out house chores before going to school. Anytime they fell out of favour with Maka, she encouraged Chief Mudiaga to send them back to their mothers. Chief's home was also filled up with Maka's relatives who came and went as they please.

As for the first and the last wife, their presence in the family home was more or less insignificant as the fear of Maka within the household was the beginning of wisdom.

There was always a twist of fate as far as Chief Mudiaga's relationship with these other women was concerned. Once they understood their position in this polygamous setting, they decided to lead a life separate from Chief Mudiaga and his 'queen', a title now used to refer to Maka within the chief's household.

Some of the women who were highly sexually active, now started involving themselves in extramarital affairs. According to them, they could no longer wait for Chief to fulfil his role as their husband. These women would book expensive holiday hideouts, spending the chief's money visiting exotic hideouts with their secret lovers.

The women were also involved in fetish practices which meant they spent long nights and days in prayer houses, believing that this was the only way they could protect themselves from other stakeholders within the household.

The suspicion was so much to the extent that they could no longer eat from the same pot. Everyone was cooking separately and Chief Mudiaga employed cooks and stewards who specially prepared his own meals. In turn, he made these cooks and stewards taste out of every meal served him to ensure that the food was not laced with poison or charms.

Chief Mudiaga lived a life of inner unhappiness, lack of trust, loneliness, and inner turmoil due to his uncontrollable appetite for women. He would joke that before he died, as an African man, he must at least have children across the globe to meet with his compulsory mandate of being able to heal the world. He saw this as his own contribution to the universe. Chief believed that if all men were to be shared amongst women, it will be a ratio of 1:20. Even at that, he has not yet met this modest statistic.

Chief would also tell anyone who cared to listen that something definitely must kill a man. It has to be women, malaria fever, typhoid fever, armed robbers, hired killers, or stress. He joked about his reckless life, without thinking of how he hoped to spend his last days on earth if there was not one amongst these numerous women whom he could truly trust or rely on in his old age.

Chief's attitude of suspicion almost made him paranoid. Each time he saw his cooks being too close to any of his numerous wives, this would earn them a sack as he feared for his life. Chief also believed strongly in African voodoo as he was a traditionalist to the core. He knew the implication of sowing his wild oats. He knew that his numerous women were not loyal to him and strongly believed that they could lace his food with love portion out of their desperation to get his attention and money. Several times Chief Mudiaga would invite all his wives to come to his compound to swear an oath of allegiance that they would never indulge in any practice that will be detrimental to his life.

'See me see trouble o!' Chief would say. 'Women, women, women! Oh, I wish my mother was alive.' Chief would try to use the death of his mother as an excuse. 'All women want is your money. "Owo Lobirin mo" as my Yoruba brothers will say.'

Chief Mudiaga would go on and on, running his own commentary about women: 'The only woman whom you can say really and truly loves you is the woman who was there when you did not have wealth and affluence. Any other one is *jara*' (the word *jara* meaning addition or plus).

'Hmm, abeg lef meeee o,' he would say in his usual pidgin English. 'Even the ones who met you when you had nothing, they have their own hidden agenda. Something must indeed kill a man, they will not kill me, never! My mother did not kill my father, I have an immunity to their vices,' he would try to convince himself.

'This is why my friend Chief Rufus runs away from all these women once they get pregnant,' joked the chief heartily. Chief Rufus was one of Chief Mudiaga's very close friends. The story went that Chief Rufus was allergic to pregnancy and would run off once he impregnated any woman and would fail to take responsibility once this pregnancy is brought to his attention. There was a widely held belief that Chief Rufus would be determined to run after any lady who makes a mockery of his escapades and once he was able to convince her to have an intimate relationship with him and also get her commit herself to him emotionally, he then went ahead to dump her, making her chase him around town each day while he makes himself unavailable.

It was believed that there were at least five women and their family members on the row who were still waiting patiently for Chief Rufus to come and complete part of the marriage rites following the marriage introduction he made with their daughters, after visiting the parents of these young women with expensive gifts, wines, and liquors, promising them that he would be back to complete the traditional marriage rites.

Chief Rufus was another case file worthy of deliberation. He was almost believed not to have a heart when it came to matters involving women. He was also a compulsive liar who lied about his numerous failed relationships whenever he wants the attention of any new woman in his life, just to be able to convince the new woman that he is a good man.

Once Chief Rufus lied to a twenty-eight-year-old girl that he was only thirty-four years old and she believed him. There were no strict records of deaths and births during his days and so he was able to present a sworn declaration of age attesting to this false age. 'Who even cares anyway, about age?' said Chief Rufus. 'All women want these days is your money,' he managed to convince himself.

Another trick Chief Rufus used to convince young girls of his acquired age was that whenever he was with these girls, he made sure that he mentioned his mother in every sentence made by him, in a bid to make them believe he still had his mother in his life to direct him like every young person would have.

Once Chief Rufus took his escapades too far, to the extent that he married an American woman whom he met online upon checking a dating website in his bid to be adventurous.

He told this unsuspecting woman that he was thirty-four years old and that he was a prince in Africa and could not leave his father's kingdom to be with her in the States. She then volunteered to visit him in Nigeria after six months of constant contacts through telephone, email, and exchange of personal photos and text messages after the first time Yvonne (that was her name) saw Chief Rufus' photograph.

When Yvonne later visited Chief Rufus in Nigeria, he could not take her to his family home. He lied to her that because he is a royal African prince, his father's house was too crowded as people always thronged the throne each day, looking for help. He wanted some peace and quietness with her, 'super time' as he termed it. Chief Rufus then rented a two-bedroom house in the outskirts of the city, a love nest later termed by Yvonne a countryside castle. Chief Rufus paid a large amount of money to rent this house and moved in expensive furniture just to impress this Americana, as he now fondly referred to her.

As soon as Chief Rufus received the manifest and ticket confirmation from Yvonne, he travelled all the way to Lagos to receive her.

When she landed, it was all excitement for him, as he clad himself with a fez cap to conceal his bald head acquired more from old age. He also sported a pair of white ankle-length tennis trousers, white Nike tennis shoes, gold-plated wristwatch, and a white-and-blue denim T-shirt which gave him a complete look of someone who was ready to hunt a prey. Chief Rufus showed off like a peacock showing off its beautiful colours. But was Yvonne impressed? No!

Once she passed through immigration checks and out of the airport lounge, she looked out for Chief Rufus, who she fondly called Honey R.

As Yvonne came out of arrivals, she saw an old man, quite older than the picture she saw of him, waving at her and walking with a forced youthful stride towards her. She was taken aback a little bit, convincing herself that perhaps he might have sent his driver or assistant to pick her up because of his busy schedule.

'Hello, she heard him speak out as he came closer to her , 'hello', she responded in her deep, confident American accent. 'I am Rufus, your honey R', he tried to introduce himself, not sure why she could not recognise him. 'Oh! I'm sorry.' She withdrew a bit with a little backward stride.

'I'm pleased to meet you,' Chief Rufus said, stretching out his hands. 'Pleased to meet you too, Ruuuuu?'

'Yeah, Honey R.' At this time, Yvonne was sweating profusely, not quite sure whether it was due to the hot climate or due to the shock of seeing Chief Rufus in person. 'I will help you with your trolley and your luggage,' he continued. 'Thank you,' she responded.

He pulled the airport trolley from her, rolled it forward and backward to get his balance, and beckoned her to come with him as they glided through the airport down to the car park two kilometres away where they were ushered into an airport taxi, which took them to the local airport.

'I want aero contractor,' he shouted loudly at the entrance of the local airport. 'Is there any immediate flight available?' he further screamed on top of his voice. 'There are no aero contractor flights to Benin except you want to stop over in Port Harcourt, sir,' said one of the airport touts.

An alternative flight was arranged immediately for Chief Rufus and Yvonne, and within sixty minutes, they arrived at the Benin airport on board the Okada airline.

To Yvonne's bewilderment, once they touched down in the Benin airport, there was a driver waiting right in front of the airport entrance for them. From that point, Chief Rufus became a completely different person. Everything was at his beck and call. He was treated like royalty and Yvonne enjoyed this ride with a man she now called her African prince.

Once they arrived at the rented apartment in GRA Benin City, it was all party and celebration. Chief Rufus invited his friends to meet with his American princess. He was blown away by her unusual angelic beauty. He said to one of his friends in confidence in pidgin English, 'But na wa o! Dis American baby too fine o! See skin combi, see shape like Venus goddess of love, see raps for mouth' (referring to her accent). 'After dis one, I am ready to go to heaven. I don't care anymore, dis one go finish my money, dis na my last bus stop.'

All through the four weeks Yvonne spent in Nigeria, it was hard partying all the way. She could not ask for anything better in life, having suffered more than ten heartbreaks, two divorces, and three marriage ceremonies called off consecutively within a period of ten years.

'Life is a blast,' she managed to convince herself. 'It took me all these years of heartbreak and disappointment to meet my African prince. It's worth it,' she thought to herself. 'What have good looks and age or nationality got to do with it?' she tried to convince herself.

On the homefront, while chief Rufus was spending his time and money on his new found lover across the Atlantic ocean, his numerous wives and concubines suffered tremendously this period. He lied to his family that he was away on an important business trip for two weeks. Prior to this time, he acquired two different phones to enable him avoid calls from his family on the phone number they were well familiar with. He hardly took calls on this phone all through this period. The few times he picked up his family phone, as he now termed it, he hurriedly told them he was in the middle of a meeting while sounding quite abrupt and brash feigning a level of annoyance known to anyone who might have been disturbed during an important meeting. This call came from the youngest of his wives, Tega, who called to notify him that she just had a miscarriage and was on admission in hospital. 'I will call my manager now and ask him to bring you money, how much do you want? Okay, I will ask him to give you N200,000 to meet your hospital bills and maintenance. I am in a meeting, just came out to take your call. See you in a week,' he said without any show of emotion or compassion.

'I do not wish this for my enemy,' Chief Rufus' wife Tega thought to herself immediately she switched off her phone. 'Here is a man who does not know what he wants, he sees women as chattel, to be used and he misinterprets money for love. I have just called him to let him know I had a miscarriage and all he is thinking of is how to satisfy my financial needs,' she moaned. 'What then happens to my emotional needs? Eh! I have just lost a child! I wish I listened to my aunt who advised me against marrying a married man. I was carried away by the amount of money he doled out to me and my family. I failed to think of the future with this man. As far as I can now understand, there is no future with this man because he belongs to so many at the same time.'

'I am a single mother living my life thinking I am married because of a decision I made for myself based on material things and lack of planning,' Chief Rufus' wife continued in her thoughts. 'Imagine if anything happens to this man, what will be my fate and that of my children?' As chief's wife Tega thought and thought, the whole emotion filled with the loss of her child and the lack of support she just experienced, from a man who was supposed to be her husband, enveloped her. She sobbed and sobbed. 'Family planning, yes, family planning,' she thought to herself. 'The fewer children I bring into this world of uncertainties I have involved myself in, the better for me,' she sobbed.

As this thought came into her, she pressed the bedside bell, requesting to see a consultant as soon as possible to discuss the options of contraception available to her.

While the whole of his household suffered in his absence, Chief Rufus was busy gallivanting with his newly found American lover— love across the Atlantic as he sometimes jokingly called it. Chief Rufus chose to allow his family to suffer in exchange for his personal fun and adventure with his American mistress.

He could not get enough of her. 'Kweke', he once said to her, 'you will break my waist o!'

'What is *kwike*?' She pronounced *kweke* wrongly in her deep American accent. 'It is kweke, not kwike,' he tried to correct her, feeling on top of the world, never imagining that a day like this would come to pass where he found himself in a position where he was able to teach his African language to an enthusiastic American who was willing to learn his language as part of her show of love and commitment to their relationship.

'Kweke is a typical Niger Delta exclamation used when a person is overwhelmed by either pleasure or pain. In this case, I am overwhelmed by the pleasure of your beauty and graceful presence,' he said to her. 'My appellation is concrete enough to be perceived by you,' he further chipped in unnecessarily, in a bid to measure up to Yvonne's fluent use of the English language.

Despite having made an assessment of Chief Rufus' age, Yvonne did not ask about his children or wife. Each time she talked about herself and the numbers of times she had tried marriage and it did not work for her, Chief Rufus would quickly switch the conversation, afraid that she might change the topic to him.

'You know I am going to marry you,' he announced to Yvonne after three weeks of their being together. 'What do you mean you're going to marry me, you only just met me, don't be silly,' she responded, with a twinkle of excitement in her eyes. 'Is there another word used by Americans for the word marriage?' he asked her while staring directly into her eyes. 'Are you proposing marriage to me, then?' she asked him. 'I'm no longer a child,' he went on. 'I know what I want, Yvy,' (as he now fondly called her) 'you are what I want. I L-O-V-E you.'

'What? What's that?' she asked excitedly, enjoying all the attention for today, not thinking of the implication in the future. 'I just spelt out the word *love*,' smiled Chief Rufus in his usual boyish manner. 'Seriously?' replied Yvonne, laughing hysterically. 'Love you too, my African prince.'

Now there was a fifteen-year age difference between Yvonne and the chief. Yvonne only just turned fifty; she had three children who were married and in total had given her six grandchildren.

She thought to herself, if she had to travel across the Atlantic Ocean to be able to find love and companionship, so be it. 'I don't have anything to lose,' she managed to convince herself, forgetting that the time she spent with Chief Rufus meant she was investing her body, her emotions, and her time with a man whom she hardly knew was carrying a lot of baggage and cankerworms of secrets with him.

Despite not knowing if this stranger whom she met on the Internet had a criminal record or could be dangerous, she felt safe with him after having met most of his friends whom he introduced to her with all pleasure. However, the can of worms which later unfolded around this man was worse than what she ever bargained for.

Chapter Five

The Lies and Deception in Polygamy

Yvonne's visit coincided with the Christmas period in Nigeria. Christmas in Nigeria is usually a family event. It is a time when families come together to celebrate. Normally preparations for Christmas start from the three "ember" months up until Christmas Day. The "ember" months are October, November, and then December. During this period, people are seen working extra hard to acquire more funds required to meet their shopping needs for all family members during the festive period.

People prepare to either travel to meet with elderly parents and extended family members in their different villages, to spend the Christmas period with them. There are usually a lot of preparations involved. People buy bags of rice, bags of salt, onions, tomatoes, chicken, goat, and even a whole cow specifically to celebrate the festive period.

As part of the camaraderie of this season, in each family where goats and cows are purchased for the Christmas celebration, these animals are tied in front of the family home as part of showing off and then children run around, either feeding these animals with grass leaves or sometimes playing with the animals by touching or stroking them on the head.

Apart from the shopping galore, Christmas is also a period where family and friends meet and reconcile their differences and iron out family issues and squabbles; people also visit and hang out with long-time lost friends and acquaintances who travel from far and wide just to be together this period.

There are also a lot of additional religious connotations attached to this period. In Nigeria, the Christians regard it as a commemoration of the birth of Jesus Christ, and all through this period, there are different activities lined up in different churches to celebrate this season, from Christmas carols to weddings, to introductions and engagements and the opening of new homes. All of this is wrapped up as one during this all-encompassing period of celebration.

For the Christians, it is quite a big deal as it marks a commemoration of the birth of a saviour, who is Christ the Lord. It is therefore no small ceremony, but a large and quite remarkable time to celebrate. And so to celebrate this period, people are dressed in their most expensive, flamboyant attire; they attend church services, weddings parties and family celebration and use this period to hang out in clubs, bars and, restaurants.

As Nigeria is a country consisting of different ethnic groups who speak different dialects, this brings about diverse culture and practices amongst its people. As a result of these different languages spoken by its more than 160 million people, there are however three major tribes, which are Hausa, Igbo, and Yoruba tribes. And so during Christmas, you hear the Hausa-speaking people felicitating by saying in Hausa 'barka da' kirsimati', which is 'merry Christmas'. In Yoruba, it's 'E ku odun', while in Igbo, it's 'E keresimesi Oma'. During this period, you hear songs like 'Onwa December ne ruwago' blasting through the air as people are in the full mood of the season as a sign of being grateful to the Almighty for sparing their lives to see the end of another year.

Many families would organise Christmas get-togethers that will last all night on the eve of Christmas, which is 24 December.

During such gatherings, people socialise with old friends, drinking, gyrating, and eating different African delicacies usually prepared by the women. In any home where chicken is prepared, there are certain parts of the chicken which are reserved for all male members of the family. The head of the chicken and the midsection is left for the head of the family. Usually this part is specially prepared with the two chicken feet pushed across the mouth, forming a kind of design which adds to its importance.

On Christmas Day, which is the 25th December, families attend church service together to give thanks to God for the birth of Jesus Christ the Savior and also for providing for them and preserving them. Homes and streets are decorated and artificial Christmas trees are lighted up, with cards received from family and friends hung all over the body of the Christmas tree clearly showing 'merry Christmas and happy New Year'. In most christian homes, the sound of Christmas carols is heard chiming softly with most of the most popular rhythms mimed by most families– 'Away in a manger, no crib for a bed, the little Lord Jesus lay down his sweet head. . .'

An additional part of this season of celebration is the display of fireworks and banga 'knockout', which adds also to the celebration of the day. Food is exchanged amongst neighbours and it is regarded as rude to reject your neighbour's gift of food and drink.

Children also visit family and friends either with their own parents or in a group. Once they knock on the door, they are then ushered in where food and drink is served to them, and upon leaving, large sums of money are usually given to them as part of the celebration.

Some of these children save up this gift of money, which they use later towards the payment of either their school fees or other important financial needs of theirs which cannot be met with by their parents.

Part of the tradition of Christmas is the responsibility which all heads of families take on all through this period. Women enjoy the constant presence of their husband on the home front this period. It is believed that after working so hard for almost eleven months in a year, the family which consists of a wife and children deserve to be compensated by the presence of the head of the home at Christmas. Neighbours share food amongst themselves and the not-so-wealthy contribute money to buy a whole live goat or cow which they now split amongst themselves.

Another remarkable gesture of love shown during Christmas is the exchange of large portions of prepared meals amongst friends and family members. Most of this food consists of a large bowl of rice served with well-prepared chicken or goat stew, or egusi soup served with pounded yam, or banga soup prepared with dried fish or fresh fish, periwinkle, and smoked snail, served with starch. There is also another delicacy served which is Ohwo soup or hot pepper soup served with unripe plantain and boiled yam -a delicacy common among the people of the Niger Delta, where Chief Rufus come from.

It was 23 December and all of Chief Rufus' wives were gathered together in the spacious family home, discussing what suddenly became an issue of serious concern to them all—which was Chief Rufus' absence from home and their inability to contact him to make sure he was alive and unhurt.

'What worries me most about this whole sudden disappearance is the fact that he told me before he travelled that he will be away for two weeks and this is the fourth week now. We have tried to reach him on his phone without any success, his phone has been switched off.

'This 'ember month' said Chief Rufus' first wife, referring to the rush period immediately before Christmas, 'is not when this family should be experiencing this.'

'The roads are not safe and there is heavy traffic everywhere, some bad people also use this period as an opportunity to rob others. I don't understand why this man has decided to leave his family this period when most heads of family are with their wives and children,' Chief Rufus' first wife moaned.

'I pray he is all right just for the sake of his children,' she continued, 'as for me, I lost this stubborn man years ago, he is dead in my life as far as I can remember, I am just in this marriage to take care of my children and also not to be seen as one whose marriage has failed.

'I know what women who live without husbands go through in the society each day, they are judged, labelled, and viewed as loose women. Their story is told as a single story and nobody wants to tell the other side of their story. This is the pain I live with all my life, living a life of denial to satisfy societal norms and demands, living my life to please the society despite knowing the truth that I don't have a husband, contrary to the picture I am painting.'

As Chief Rufus' first wife continued moaning, she became even more philosophical accepting the fate which, according to her, life has thrown on her. Immediately, the house phone started ringing and she rushed to pick up the phone while other members of the family gazed on.

'Hallo? Hallo!' she went on; there seemed to be too much noise at the other end. 'Hallo? Yes, how can I—we help you?' Chief Rufus' wife prided herself on having qualified as an NCE and BSC holder. She was a trained teacher and presently the Principal of a girls' secondary school. She had a wealth of knowledge as an educationist. She also held several seminars and talk shows, having opened a charity whose sole objective was to prepare young girls for marriage, focusing their minds on life after saying 'I do'. She would always say to her students, 'To be forewarned is to be forearmed.'

The whole family was anxious to hear any news from Chief Rufus. 'I am Doctor Princewill calling from Eku hospital. Can I speak to the chief's wife?'

'I am the chief's wife,' she answered none too confidently, wondering which wife in particular this caller wanted to speak to. 'There has been an accident,' the voice on the other side went on. 'Your husband was involved in an accident last night and we have searched his personal belongings and found a Mrs Oviri Rufus as his next of kin.'

'Heh heh heh! Am finished o! Am finished o!' Chief Rufus' first wife yelled as the receiver dropped from her hand. 'What? What? Car crash, where, where was he coming from?' They all asked these questions at the same time as one of the children picked up the phone to ask these very many questions, only to realise that the caller had already dropped the phone on the other end. 'Oh God oh God, what do we do now? He mentioned Eku hospital.'

'Is he still alive or dead? Should we proceed to Eku hospital immediately or wait for him to call back with the full details of this car crash? I can't wait oh, I can't wait, I will call his doctor friend now to see if he knows any of his colleagues in Eku hospital. Bring my handbag from the bedroom,' she screamed at the house help who, upon hearing the shouting in the living room at this time, ran out to find out what happened. She rushed back into madam's room, grabbed the wrong handbag, and handed it to her, as she lay on the floor wailing. 'Ekpa!', fool!, she screamed out, more out of frustration than anger. 'Where did you find this bag?' she asked. 'Is this the bag I carried to church yesterday?' she asked the housemaid. 'Sorry, madam,' said the maid, as she rushed back into the room while everyone looked on. She came back in less than two minutes with a big brown handbag. 'Open it joor! Bring out that diary at the side and pass it on.'

As she struggled to find the telephone number of their doctor friend, another call came through and immediately it was a call from Eku hospital giving them the full details of the intensive care unit where Chief Rufus could be found. 'Driver, driver.' Immediately they all rushed into the 504 Peugeot saloon car, which had now become a family car. 'We cannot just all go together like that, someone has to be at home. Tega, stay back.' She pointed to the last wife. 'You have just recently been discharged from hospital, you need to rest.'

'I know, my mate, since the news of this accident I have been bleeding heavily. I will stay back to take calls from well-wishers and also prepare dinner for when you all come back.'

When Chief Rufus' first wife met with him in the hospital, she was in a stupor over the numbers of medical gadgets that were placed all over his body; she was told he was still in a coma and that they were hopeful he would come to within a couple of days, fingers crossed. They also revealed to her that he had a foreign companion at the time of the accident who was discharged the next day as she had slight injuries which were not life-threatening. She is believed to have returned back to the United States days after she was released from hospital. They thought she might be his business partner from the United States.

Chief's first wife Oviri kept vigil patiently by her husband's bedside day and night. She refused to go back home. She asked the others to return while she slept on the hospital floor each night, waking up intermittently during the night to check his progress, calling the attention of the night nurses anytime she noticed movements of his head, face, or arms.

'Nurse, nurse,' she would call quietly while walking briskly to the nurses' stand, requesting them to either check the drip or his pulse to make sure he was okay.

Five days after the chief's wife visited, he came to consciousness suddenly one early morning while she tried to dab him all over with a wet flannel. He cried out, 'Oh my God, my head, my head,' as he tried to turn his body; it was visible that he was in serious pain. 'My hand, my hand, my whole body hurts,' he now called out. 'Yve. Yve, where are you?' he asked, to the bewilderment of his wife.

'Yve? Who is Yve again, dis man? Kweke, dis man, dis man,' moaned his wife. 'It's okay, madam,' consoled one of the nurses as they tried to attend to Chief Rufus' needs, to stabilise him and make him aware of the incidents leading to him being brought into hospital; he drifted back into a coma. Chief Rufus was on and off coma until two weeks later when he started recognising people, gradually. The next couple of months became a roller-coaster show of emotions and rivalry between all of his wives as they struggled to take turns to be with him in hospital. It appeared that to them, despite the near-death incident, this was an opportunity of a lifetime where they could at least spend twenty-four hours with him, without him having to rush off to one non-existent business meeting or the other.

Christmas was not celebrated by the whole family as a result of the chief's promiscuity; his whole family suffered in anxiety and pain, and it was a bleak Christmas for all in Chief Rufus' household.

Chief was, however, discharged six months later and was taken home. He was advised by his consultants that he needed constant rest and a few daily exercises and should be placed on a strict diet which should be a combination of fruits and vegetables.

Eight months after returning home, despite walking on a health tightrope, the chief reconnected with his American lover. He became quite worried prior to reconnecting with her as he did not know whether she survived the accident which took his driver's life. They were returning from Obudu cattle ranch- a holiday resort in Cross Rivers State in Nigeria. He wanted to give his lover a treat and to prove a point that African men have got all that it takes, while leaving his family to suffer in despair.

It was all fun for chief and his American lover. As they approached Benin, Agbor road, a trailer on the opposite side of the road lost control and rammed into their vehicle, killing the driver instantly while the other two occupants were brought out by Good Samaritans who took them to the nearest hospital, where they were administered with first-aid treatment to stop their bleeding and later taken to Eku hospital, where a major surgery was carried out on Chief Rufus.

'Ol' boy, I really want to go to the United States, said Chief Rufus to his friend Chief Mudiaga. I miss that acata babe seriously. I have been seeing her in my dream even when I was told I was in a coma. I feel strongly that seeing her alive will serve as a therapy for me.'

'Ol' boy, relax o!' advised Chief Mudiaga. 'What will you tell your other wives you are off to the United States for?'

'Of course medical check-up,' Chief Rufus answered abruptly.

'Hmm, if dis okpe'ke' na Naija babe now, our people go say she done give you egbele' korkormiyo,' Chief Mudiaga said, referring to a love charm.

Two weeks after Chief Rufus had this conversation with his friend, he kept on calling his lover on the phone every other day, telling her how he missed her and wanted to be with her.

Arrangements were made by Chief Rufus and Yvonne, his American lover, who waited for him at the airport in Houston, Texas, to pick him up. Immediately Chief Rufus was picked up, she drove him straight to her seven-bedroom house in Sugarland, Texas, a nice posh suburban area in Houston, Texas. As usual, a trip meant to last for a couple of weeks extended into months. Chief Rufus followed his lover to the States recklessly, abandoning his whole family, leaving all that he had behind for a new life of fun and adventure in the States.

He arranged with Yvonne to have his visa extended and subsequently like a bolt out of the blue, he proposed formally to her and later married her in her local church to the amazement of more than five hundred guests who attended the strictly by-invitation-only event.

His marriage to this American woman was a society wedding, and a lot of money was spent during the wedding. The story goes that after the wedding between Chief Rufus and his American wife, he became quite demanding and unreasonable and also stupidly confided in his cousin that the only reason why he married this American was so that he could get his green card; at least that would save him from having to queue up at the American Embassy in Nigeria to apply for a visa.

Chief Rufus' pet name for his American wife was Acata. When he met his American wife, he told her he had been painstakingly unlucky with women. He told her he had so many women stalking him because of his good looks. He told her also that these women came after him because of his money and the fact that he was from a royal family and the first son of a king. He went on to boast to this new catch, 'When you meet me, you meet money.' As is customary with most womanisers, Chief Rufus told dozens and dozens of lies until he started believing himself that indeed this was the true account of events in his life.

Papers were filed for Chief Rufus as the spouse of an American citizen and he was later issued a green card.

This marriage built upon lies and fabrication started experiencing cracks eighteen months later. After their second anniversary celebration in church, Chief Rufus made up stories about why he needed to travel back to Nigeria urgently. His father 'the king' was seriously ill and wanted to see him.

He returned to Africa, earning him the popular name Ajala Travel. It was almost as if Chief Rufus' reckless lifestyle made him live a life filled with emptiness, lies, and deception. He hurt so many women whom he came across either while doing business or as part of his daily escapades. He hurt his first wife badly despite sacrifices she made in their thirty-five years of marriage. He abandoned her eight months after surviving a ghastly accident and relocated to the United States, lying to the whole family that he needed medical attention abroad.

According to stories told on the grapevine, Chief Rufus had more than twenty children who were scattered all over, and yet he did not involve himself in their lives; neither did he have a relationship with them. Unlike Chief Mudiaga who was a kind-hearted and caring man, Chief Rufus was the typical playboy without any heart or emotions. He was so self-centred to the extent that he sometimes used women in his life for his financial gain, as clearly depicted in his comments to his friend when he mentioned that the main reason why he married Yvonne was so he could acquire the American green card to save him from having to apply for a visa each time he travelled to the United States.

****

There is a far contrast between Chief Mudiaga and his friend Chief Rufus when it came to physical looks. Unlike Chief Rufus, his friend Chief Mudiaga could not be described as a particularly handsome man; He, however, had his way with women. What he lacked in looks, he gained with his kindness and gentleness. He had a very thick upper lip and, in the middle of his lower lip was a deep scar which, according to his first wife, he acquired when he had a fight with another neighbour whose wife he tried to take over when this neighbour travelled.

Women were one of the many Achilles heels of Chief Mudiaga, and his love for the company of women was far more addictive than that of American major general Benjamin Hooker. And so it was that if anyone wanted any form of favour from Chief, as he was fondly called by all and sundry, they would wait until he was with one of his numerous women and, once he was approached, consider it done. Chief also had another nickname, 'talking na do', which means in general terms that once he promised anyone a favour, he carried it out meticulously without failing. Chief was a jolly good fellow, and so Chinua was one of the numerous women who fell for his charm, his boisterousness, and his ability to bring forth fire—meaning, in pidgin, he provides for his numerous concubines and wives alike.

Chief Mudiaga never failed to remind his friend Chief Rufus how he might end up living a miserable life in his old age, because of his unkindness to his wives and children.

'Na who go bury you, my brother?' he asked Chief Rufus. 'How do you mean?' replied Chief Rufus. 'I mean, don't you want to be celebrated by your wife and children in your old age and also when you die?' asked Chief Mudiaga. 'Hmm, my brother, forget all this your sermon,' Rufus would say. 'How you take better pass me? We dey the same category na, the only thing be say, you dey use your money to wan buy love from your children and your wives, abeg go find out from a diviner to see the hearts of all these people wen you take near yourself. Dem no love you at all ooo, na your money dem like.' Chief Rufus was a hard-core unrepentant womaniser. He would go on about how he planned to have children all round the nations of the world. According to him, women needed that help because they were lonely. There was nothing wrong in him helping them to fill that loneliness and to help them procreate. If he left them alone, who would help them? He would always say foolishly. 'I am helping them,' he would try to convince himself. If anyone reminded him about sexually transmitted diseases and the disadvantages of having multiple sexual partners, he would shout out loud, 'Something must kill a man abegi lef me,' meaning 'leave me'.

Chapter Six

In Silence and Dignity, Strength Is Made Manifest

The aftermath of the war had left many in abject poverty and lack, Chinua was one of the many Igbo women who suffered great financial loss as a result of the war. She had lost her property in Effurun-Warri, which was at this time regarded as abandoned and her former job was also taken from her.

With seven mouths to feed after the loss of her first husband, with whom she had a set of twins, and with her four additional children being fathered by a polygamist never-at-home traditional chief cum father, she was left in the hands of fate, and the peril and scar experienced by her from this heavy burden of single parenthood coupled with the fact that society saw her as a failure. Society called her unpleasant names like loose woman, rebellious woman, asewo, akunna, kunna (hooker), and never do well, who cannot raise successful children, because of her family circumstances.

Chinua's children also suffered the same fate as their mother. They were exposed to all kinds of derogatory abuse both within the community they lived in and also amongst extended family members and neighbours who knew of their mother's circumstance.

It was also even more painful because Chinua's family circumstance was only viewed as a single story by everyone, including her family members despite the fact that she was not given the opportunity to prove herself otherwise.

'I will stay focused to raise these children that God has given me. I will prove to the world that something good definitely comes out of Nazareth,' Chinua always used to say to herself. Once, her daughter Mimi came home crying profusely, saying that one of her classmates made a derogatory comment about children raised by single mothers. 'What happened?' asked Chinua. 'Er, erm, er, er!' Mimi tried to speak up in between sobs. 'I cannot understand what you are saying if you continue to cry,' snapped Chinua in her usual impatient way.

'My friend Ego and I were playing outside the front of our classroom during break hours and suddenly, we disagreed over who takes a turn first in the game of jorokoto. I was surprised when we started arguing and she said to me, 'This is what happens when you make friends with children raised by single parents.' I walked off and ran into the classroom feeling really embarrassed and thinking that would be the end of this argument; however, at the end of school day, Ego rushed at me with some of her other friends who were much taller and bigger, shouting all kinds of unprintable words about me and my mum.'

'Is that why you are crying?' asked Chinua. Looking sternly up at Mimi, more because she did not want to encourage her daughter to grow up feeling inferior or less of a person just because she had a single mum. This was the strategy adopted by Chinua to deal with any such confrontation experienced by her children, in a bid to make them confident and strong. 'There are always battles to fight in life and so I do not want to raise weak children,' she would always say to herself. 'Go and undress and wipe your face with water in that bucket, and then come have this delicious jollof rice specially prepared for you. Time will tell, and you will have the last laugh when you are successful tomorrow.' Chinua tried to encourage her daughter.

'Maybe your friend prefers that you are an orphan without a mother and a father,' chipped in Chinua. 'If your father decides not to be part of your life, others have to be there to take care of you and I do not see how that is a bad thing anyway. I am always here and that is more important than anything anyone says to you.'

Chinua was not perturbed by the circumstances in which she found herself, or if she was, she never showed it. She was quite hard-working and despite her perceived background, so to say, she had boundaries which, according to her, must not be overstepped by friends, family, or neighbours in the community. She was not interested in any form of self-pity; neither would she allow anyone to undermine her or take undue advantage of her situation because she was a single parent.

Chinua believed in the dignity of a woman. She believed that a woman is an achiever, a trailblazer, and pacesetter. She would raise children who bore these qualities whether she was married or unmarried. Society might have perceived her as someone who had failed because she was a single mother; as much as she could not tell every individual she met her personal story and how she came about becoming a single mother, she would, however, work hard to change her children's stories.

She left home early in the morning and came back late at night selling jewellery, traditional coral beads, women's abada and George, women's shoes and bags, and housewares. She would travel sometimes long hours on the motorway to neighbouring towns like Onitsha and Balogun Market in Lagos to buy the merchandise, which she sold at a minimal profit to cater for her young children.

Chinua's determination and zest to succeed in life was indefatigable. She became unstoppable as her business grew from strength to strength until she was able to purchase her own shop where she would now leave her merchandise all locked up safely as against having to move them to and fro in a wheelbarrow which she borrowed from the nearby market master.

Chinua was solely responsible for the upbringing of her seven children. One of her daughters, Uloma, did not return with her to Midwest after the war. Uloma had, against the will of her mother, absconded with an army officer whom she met in Umuopara village during the civil war.

This army officer was later killed during the war, leaving Uloma with a young son, Kelechi. Chinua's first daughter, who loved men in uniforms, later became lucky as she was fortunate enough to meet and marry a colonel in the Nigerian army who rose through the rank and file in the army and later attended courses in Sandhurst, United Kingdom and others in the School of Policy and Strategy studies in Jos Kuru, and also other courses in Jaji Kaduna state which saw him through a rapid career progression, later earning him a very befitting post as a military administrator.

Uloma's marriage to a top military officer can hardly be said to be a happy one. She experienced serious domestic violence in her marriage to her husband. However, Uloma vowed never to make known her ordeal to her extended family members, firstly because her single mother was against this union and secondly because she would not want to end up as a single mother like her mum, in a society where this status is seen as more or less like a taboo. 'If I was lucky enough to still get married after having my son Kelechi, I will be a fool not to remain married. Who else will take me? – especially with my son and my size 22? Haba, my husband has tried o,' Uloma would say to herself, sighing in contentment.

On several occasions, Uloma was beaten black and blue by her husband, who became very authoritarian and narcissistic as the marriage continued having problems. The main problem faced in this relationship was her husband's infidelity and drunkenness, which were condoned by Uloma over a long period of time. Whenever close friends tried to talk to Uloma to seek help before she got killed, she would hear no such thing. According to her, she would remain married even if it cost her her life because she did not want to be labelled a single mother. 'I know what my mother suffered at the hands of people when we were growing up just because she is a single parent,' Uloma would tell anyone who cared to listen. 'Even women whose husbands were never there for them or who were living separate lives from their husbands, called my mother names just because they were covered by the cloak of the word "marriage." The taboo of single parenthood will not take place in my family twice,' moaned Uloma.

Despite Uloma's strong dislike for the name *single parent*, after being married to her husband for fifteen years, one day something drastic happened which almost cost her her life, leaving her hospitalised for three months. Her husband never came to see her in hospital; neither did he allow her children to visit her. The eldest of her children, Kelechi, born from a previous relationship, would sneak out through the back house to visit his mother in hospital. Once Uloma was discharged, she decided never to go back to her matrimonial home, leaving her with no other option than to reunite with her mother, who at this time assisted to rehabilitate her through counselling sessions in church, as a result of the long-term physical and emotional abuse which at this time had left Uloma an emotional wreck.

In a bid to stay married despite a threat to her life, Uloma condoned her husband's promiscuity for years until she took ill again months after moving in with her mother and was advised to carry out a blood test. After several treatments for malaria and typhoid proved abortive, a test later changed Uloma's life and the lives of other members of her family forever.

The period Uloma reunited with her mother Chinua gave her enough time to reflect on her mother Chinua's life and all what she went through just to survive with her seven children, one of whom had sickle-cell disease due to the fact that Chinua and her first husband had the same genotype—AS.

Chinua dropped out from school and so lacked the needed skills to take up any white-collar well-paying job. She had to battle life as a single parent in order to make a livelihood for herself and her children.

Her situation meant that she was left with the burden of child-rearing single-handedly—a job purposed for two people, was now handed over to her to take on single-handedly which is to raise seven successful children, nurturing them, guiding, directing, setting a good example, teaching and sharing their pains, fears, and anxieties, counselling and admonishing, and moulding them into successful individuals. Whether Chinua understood these roles is quite uncertain, however, for years she carried this burden of life with so much dignity and grace. Waking up as early as 4 a.m., preparing breakfast for her young children, preparing the evening meal, making it easy for when she returned in the evening, and then making sure the children are dropped off at school before setting out to her shop. Because of the epileptic shortage of supply of electricity, it was also important for Chinua to see to it that her children are fed with freshly prepared meals all the time, and so she formed the habit of cooking fresh meals every other day to make sure that her children would not be malnourished.

As a single mother, Chinua could not afford to be sick. Once she had malaria fever and was quite ill to the extent she could not open her shop during this period. She, however, was able to still manage to prepare lunch for her children, awaiting their return from school. She also self-medicated by visiting her local chemist man, Mr Uche, to purchase Fansidar and Nivaquine tablet and local purgative called iba shurrup, made in Aba, which she administered on herself as treatment for her malaria fever. Sometimes, Chinua also gathered lemongrass, plantain leaf and banana leaf, orange fruit, pawpaw leaf, and other herbal plants at the back of her compound which she boiled for about one hour and then covered herself with a wrapper while sitting in front of the bucket, inhaling the hot steam from this herbal concoction for about thirty minutes, after which she used the water to take a warm bath. It is believed that this herbal alternative cures malaria fever and is quite potent.

Once, Chinua used these herbs to treat her son Ejikemuwa, who later collapsed from the high potency of this herbal treatment and was rushed to Eku hospital, where he was admitted for two weeks because of his crisis arising from his illness as a person living with sickle-cell anaemia. This was a tough period for Chinua as she had to close up her shop for two weeks having to shuttle between the hospital and her home to make sure that the other children were all right. She later got some assistance from a Good Samaritan neighbour, NK (short for Nkechi), who attended the same church as her.

'I said it that that man brought me nothing but pains,' said Chinua when her son was discharged from hospital, upon his return home. 'Now his family wants to kill the only son that bears his name just to wipe his memory off the Guinness book of records,' she joked. 'Such wicked people, it must have been when I had this boy that they changed his blood under the guise of circumcising him,' she argued innocently, not understanding the intricacies of her son's condition, rather blaming it on superstition. Ejikemuwa had several crisis, more because of the condition of living than any other thing. He was exposed to mosquito bites. There was very little balanced diet with seven mouths to feed; he was always anaemic and the only likely nutritious food Chinua could afford was beans. Despite Chinua's strong personality, each time she watched Ejike, as he was fondly called, writhing in pain, she broke down and cried, praying endlessly for God to recompense her suffering and spare her son's life.

Chinua would go on for days without food to see to it that her children ate three square meals. She would usually say in her native Igbo language, 'Unu rie, erie lam' meaning 'Once you all are satisfied, I am satisfied also.' Such was the extent of the strong love Chinua had for her children—a love which doubled for the fatherly love missing in their lives.

Chinua could not afford a housemaid even on a temporary basis to assist her at home like most average families would do. She had the rent to pay, the children's books, school uniforms, hospital bills, Sunday clothes for church, and in addition, she made sure that at the end of each year, in December, all her children were given two brand-new clothes and two pairs of shoes, one for the Christmas celebrations and the other to be worn to church on the first Sunday of the new year.

Chinua loved BATA products. She would not purchase her children's shoes from anywhere other than BATA and Lennards—two high-quality department stores that had a good reputation for stocking quality children's products. All her children's clothes were also purchased from Balogun Market and they had to be ready-made.

Once, one of Chinua's sisters thought she was doing the children a favour. She brought second-hand clothes for Gwen and Mimi, as a gift in Chinua's absence. When Chinua came back on that day, immediately her daughter Mimi ran to her, she smelt the aroma which is affiliated with preservatives used on second-hand clothes brought from abroad. 'Hmm,' Chinua exclaimed, 'where did you find second-hand clothes?' she asked her daughter sternly. 'Aunty here brought it for me,' Mimi joyfully pointed to Chinua's sister. 'Come on, take it off,' she angrily shouted to Mimi. 'We don't have much in this home but we strictly don't do *okrika* second-hand clothes in this place.' She looked at her sister scornfully.

Chinua had five sisters and they were against her returning to the midwest after the war. They did not understand what stake she had in a place where her elder sister's husband was murdered during the civil war. Despite trying so hard at the beginning to advise the elder sister's husband to return to the east as the midwesterners had started pointing out to the Nigerian soldiers where all Igbo-speaking residents lived, Chinua's brother-in-law Amandianeze—a bullheaded self-opinionated man who hated Chinua with a passion because she was a single parent, could not see himself taking advice from Chinua, a common single parent without a husband, according to him.

And so, Amandianeze refused to listen to Chinua's advice to return to the east, a decision which later cost him his life.

The story has it that Amandianeze, Chinua's brother-in-law, continued to stay back in the midwest until his home was raided by the Nigerian soldiers and he was dragged out of a ceiling where he hid himself and shot to death. His corpse was never found and till date his death was an incident which broke Chinua's heart every day.

One good thing which came out of Chinua's doggedness and determination as a survivor is the decision taken by her when the war broke out. All thanks to Chinua, the children of Amandianeze, her late sister's children, were smuggled by her single-handedly and returned, back to her mother in Umuahia before the Onitsha bridge was bombed and it collapsed, and all roads leading to the east became blocked by the Nigerian soldiers.

In addition to her determination to succeed, Chinua had a fiery temper and would tell you as it is without caring whose ox is gored. She called herself Okpata aku (which literally means a maker of wealth), oka ome, and ijele Nwanyi. This quality of Chinua became part of what helped her to succeed in raising her children single-handedly. She was not cut out for self-pity; neither was she ready for any form of mediocrity. Chinua had a lot of praise names for herself, and each time she remembered any of these praise names, it made her happy and gingered her on, as you saw her majestically walking like a gazelle that she truly is.

Chinua had this belief that no man could ever tie her down or make her feel worthless like they did to her mum and her sisters. According to her, what a man can do, a woman can do better. She would tell anyone who cared to listen that if God did not think women were worth it, he would have left Adam alone in the Garden of Eden. Women indeed have a vital role to play in the whole world. Despite this seeming Thatcher-like, iron-lady nature, Chinua was soft on the inside. She also had her own feminine part, which sometimes came to play during her quiet moments. She longed for genuine relationships as a woman, she wanted to love and be loved, she wanted someone she could call her own and vice versa, but where did she go wrong? She seldom asked herself.

She felt she was misunderstood; nobody gave her a chance to prove herself. She was labelled a rebel and a woman of easy virtue; she was mocked despite being a victim of circumstance. Who in her position would abandon her children? What woman in her right senses would not stick with her children to give them a proper upbringing when all else had failed?

Chinua's five sisters were married with their own families and could not be bothered about what happened to her. One of the sisters also married an army officer who was very promiscuous and was a never-at-home father to both his wife and his children. Each time Chinua had a clash with her sister Njideka, Njideka always referred her to the issue of her being a single parent in a bid to ridicule her. Each time, Chinua never minced words in trying to remind her sister that if marriage was like the one Njideka was in, then she preferred not to be married at all. She called her sister's marriage 'trophy marriage'.

Chinua's sister Njideka and her army officer husband lived two separate lives. They lived under the same roof but led two separate lifestyles. It was more or less a marriage of convenience. They grew apart over the years, more because the husband was hardly around as he was busy jumping from one five-star hotel to another four-star resort, his favourite hideout being Concorde Hotel Owerri.

There were accusations and counter-accusations of infidelity between these couples who never cared about flaunting their shameful lifestyle within the full glare of their neighbours, family members, and friends alike.

There was a general trend where Njideka went on long weekends away from her matrimonial home in hideaway motels and guest houses. Neighbours, friends, and other family members never stopped talking about Njideka's double-standard life or what ordinarily can be classified as hypocritical lifestyle.

The lifestyle Njideka and her group of friends lived was something which became a common and popular trend in their community. There was a complete moral decadence and a drastic drop in family values and ethos to the extent that anyone who was not involved in their madness was termed a *mugu* or *ode*. It was the in thing.

The African and most importantly Nigerian values which were observed in the days of our forefathers and which used to be the norms and commendable behaviour within the society had been exchanged with sexual immorality in and outside marriage. There was a lack of love, dishonesty, and lack of the fear of God, almost to the extent that anyone who did not involve themselves in this act was seen as a JJC, Johnnie just come.

In this community therefore, the folk stories which teach 'if you sow good, you reap good, and if you sow bad, you reap bad or evil', which usually prompted moral sanity, healthy living, and the general African virtues which are a way of life had been swept under the carpet.

And so, such was the society which was more or less a morally decadent society, a society which upheld the philosophy of 'anything goes'. Njideka was part of this world of decadence where all that mattered was wealth, affluence, sexual prowess, and survival of the fittest.

Among Njideka's group of friends, they called it an antidote to long-lasting marriage. According to them, cheating on their husbands with younger men helped them to live with the heartache and loneliness they suffered each day from their husband's infidelity. What is more intriguing about this group, however, is the fact that they were fully involved in their daily religious practices. They sat in the front of their churches as they were elders, deaconesses, and scarily, counsellors to younger women. Their lifestyle can be equated to what is played out in the soap series *Lekki Wives*.

Despite being married, Njideka had loose morals, lacked discipline, and more or less acted like an *oku elu*, a high-maintenance woman who uses the marriage institution as a cover to perpetrate her obnoxious conduct. Njideka also had other fake side to her—which was her Christian faith and devotion to church activities. On first contact with her, she would recite more than ten different bible verses and quotations, to the extent that anyone would wonder why all of this was not put into practice by her.

When she was not away on her long weekend trips with her numerous rich boyfriends and sugar daddies, she was committed in attending church meetings and involved herself fully in offering her service and time to her church and her community. Njideka was a totally different person when in her church environment. She also had a sonorous voice and sat in the front pew among elders of the church. She was one of the most powerful power brokers in church, always coming out to give testimonies and doling out offerings each Sunday.

When not socialising with her numerous boyfriends outside her matrimonial home, Njideka would cling to her King James Version Bible reading through and through and taking notes in what seemed a rather sketchy-format handwriting. She never made one sentence without backing it up with a quote from the Bible. She also quoted the portions of the Bible that teach against adultery and fornication. It is therefore so amazing that despite this level of Christianity portrayed by Njideka, she continued to cheat on her husband with other men and did not see anything wrong in her actions. Perhaps she tried to justify her actions with the fact that her army husband also cheated on her with younger girls and other married women. Yet they were seen together in high-profile gatherings, chairing sensitive ceremonies with their children and others who saw them as mentors.

The lifestyle of this couple, even though not discussed by either of them, suited them and they carried on. She called her husband Ichoku, parrot, carved out from his ability to convince any woman to grace his bed.

Each time Njideka had a fight with her husband, he used his army boots to kick her, and punched her mercilessly. She would then call him all sorts of names like Ogbunigwe Biafra and Usu (bat). It is therefore surprising that despite the dysfunctionality of this family, they still remained a pair, seen as husband and wife within their community, to the chagrin of everyone who knew them and to the utmost confusion and bewilderment of their children.

Once, one of Njideka's female children vowed never to get married or to have any children of her own. When asked why, she told her teacher that she was scared that all men would behave like her unfaithful father, and she would not want to have children and later be labelled a single mother like her aunt, Mama Bendel—a name which they all fondly called Chinua.

One weird attribute Njideka and her husband had in common and definitely enjoyed together was the ability to deceive everyone around them that theirs was a successful marriage. Even though they had separate rooms and didn't do things together, the first thing she mentioned to everyone who cared to listen is the fact that she has been happily married for the past thirty-five years.

To Njideka, success in marriage is all about staying married, building and acquiring expensive houses and flashy cars, and being able to afford yearly holidays, expensive designer clothing, wristwatches, and perfumes. Njideka never cared about the impact her lifestyle and that of her cheating husband had on their children. Once it was brought to Njideka's attention that her daughter Ulari vowed never to be married. She laughed and waved it off as youthful exuberance, which would wear off once she met her very wealthy prince charming who would sweep her off her feet. Ulari responded to her mum, saying, 'It's all about money, isn't it, Mum?'

'Biko zuzuru puo rim,' retorted Njideka, meaning 'Please move out of my way with your foolishness.'

In confirming the general saying that two cannot work together except when they agree, Njideka's husband of thirty-five years, despite knowing that he cheated on his wife and vice versa, adored her in the presence of her family members and friends. He organised surprise birthday parties for her once every two years, a ceremony which sees them displaying a feigned show of affection, love, and warmth to everyone who cared to watch.

There is also a high level of notoriety and lies which embeds such celebrations as Njideka's husband celebrating his wife's fortieth birthday consecutively for over a period of five years non-stop, to the amusement of their friends and family. During the last fortieth birthday celebration, Chinua was told about how her sister celebrated her fortieth birthday five different years in a row. They made sure anyone invited to the last birthday celebration was not included in their next guest list.

Upon hearing this, Chinua laughed and murmured to herself, 'These people, you see these people, there is no difference between the two. They know what they are doing! How can Njideka who is older than me now celebrate her fortieth birthday? Then how old am I? How old is her first child? How old is her husband? Nde ashi,' meaning untruthful people.

'And yet on Sunday, these same people will pick up the Bible and sit at the front of the church. Church leaders need to preach against such acts of hypocrisy amongst Christians, but who am I to speak? I am a single mother, with a single story.'

Chinua hated hypocrisy. Despite not being married, she frowned on this lifestyle of her sister and her friends. She would sometimes refer to her sister in these words, 'There is an Igbo aphorism that says an elder does not stay at home and watch a goat tied to a stake suffocate to death. My children must be taught there are no shortcuts to wealth and affluence, other than hard work and persistence in prayer. Being married is good, but my children must be taught to understand that the choices they make in choosing a life partner can make or mar them for life. If they must be married successfully, I must from this time teach them how to strategise themselves to meet the kind of man who will live with them for better or for worse.'

And so with this in mind, the virtue of chastity and the love and fear of God, even though considered archaic, were what Chinua taught her children. Chinua was a gem of inestimable value undiscovered by the society within which she lived just because she had a label on her, a label of a single parent.

Being a complete opposite of her sister Njideka, Chinua (despite her single status) was more honest in her dealings with people, and a person who could be described as 'what you see is what you get'. Chinua's genuine and straightforward lifestyle made her find her sister's behaviour as appalling and disgusting and she never failed to express her dislike and disapproval, saying to her sister Njideka that *ripu ripu* (maggot) and *chinchi* (bedbug) will definitely fall off her sister's nostrils upon her deathbed because of the indecent and deceitful life she lived.

Njideka was also the complete opposite of their mother. Nwanyibeke was subservient to her husband, and she carried the role of a mother whom everyone had access to when things go wrong. Despite her husband's notoriety and betrayal with her best friend's daughter, she still remained faithful and submissive to him even after he left her to start a new life with his second wife immediately after she bore him a son named Chiboy.

There was a general family story told about how their mother Nwanyibeke (literally meaning a white woman) was called white woman because of the light colour of her skin—a common attribute of women who come from her ethnic background. Nwanyibeke had six female children for their father, who was worried about not having a male child who will inherit his compound; according to their father, this childlessness of his, despite having six female children, made him a very sad man.

Coming from Igbo land, which has little gender-sensitive culture and in his quest to fulfil the Igbo culture *Omenala ndi igbo*, he decided to betray his first wife by clandestinely sleeping with a family friend's daughter, Amaka, who later bore him a male chid called Chiboy.

Chinua's father had this overbearing male chauvinistic character of domination, oppression, and marginalization even within the domestic ambience of his home.

Having a son after a long time, according to him, meant a lot because he now had a man to take his place and continue with the family lineage when he joined his ancestors. On the other hand, while Nwanyibeke, his wife, kept on moaning over this betrayal by her husband and her friend, Chiboy's mother was overjoyed as the birth of her son will definitely entrench her love in her husband's heart because having a son means that nothing can take her away or uproot her from her husband's family.

During the naming ceremony of Chiboy, their father made a vivid statement that his female children would soon be married off and also that having female children is like tending and caring for other people's vineyards while yours is unkempt and hopeless. He ended his valedictory speech on that day by saying it would have been *nso ani* (an abomination) if he died without a male child.

As a result of this outward show of preference, it was with this mindset that Chiboy grew up thinking himself to be superior, more important, and indispensable within his household—a behaviour which caused a serious rift between him and his older half-sisters till date and which also severed their relationship.

The severance in relationship between Chiboy and his sisters if seen as a thing of concern cannot be compared to that experienced between Chinua and her sisters because of the fact that she is a single parent.

When Chinua returned to the midwestern part of Nigeria, she further severed her relationship with her sisters in the east. She could not cope with them, she would say each time she was asked why she did not remain in the east.

'Ah, you know these people and the way they reason. 'Being a single parent to them is like a taboo, yet some of them live a life of deception even though they are married, they are not married. Ndi ononadi acho di,' she would say literally meaning women who continue to chase male admirers even though they are married.

Something, however, happened which brought Chinua close to her sisters again after a very long time. The relationship with her sisters was further rekindled after several years when she started having dreams and trances which, according to her, were from their late father warning her of impending calamity which would befall the whole family if he is not accorded the necessary *ome ani* (tradition) which will enable him to be accepted by the forefathers in the land of the dead. According to Chinua's dreams, her father's spirit had, since all these years, been roaming around in the spirit world, unable to find rest because the tradition and custom of his people had not been carried out and completed by his children.

Chapter Seven

An Accepted Custom and Tradition of the Igbos in South-East Nigeria

According to Chinua, at first she thought this dreams were mere nightmares. Even when she mentioned it to her children, they made a joke out of it by nicknaming her Joseph the dreamer.

One of Chinua's daughters, Mimi, said to her when she tried to share her experiences in the dream with them, 'Hmm, madam de madam,' as Chinua was fondly called by her children, 'how can your late father, who has been gone for over thirty-five years, now suddenly start appearing to you warning you to perform a certain ritual in line with tradition and custom to enable the Ndi Ichies to accept him in the land of the dead? Where then has he been all these thirty-five years? Are you sure you don't have malaria fever or typhoid fever?' It is a common belief that when a person has constant dreams and nightmares, it may be one of the symptoms of malaria fever.

'Alika,' as Chinua fondly called her, meaning 'slim one', 'I am not a baby, you know. When I say something, believe it. You know as well as I know that all this traditional belief and superstition is not something I encourage myself. I have zero per cent tolerance for fetish practices, but in this particular case, it is true,' said Chinua.

'Let me tell you, do you know that as I was shopping yesterday in the market, I took a walk down the main market stairway, and something unknown to me prompted me to look back, and as I gazed, I saw my father wearing one of his favourite Ekpe masquerade attire, beckoning to me. In a flash and as I stared deeply, he vanished before my eyes.

'Hey, hey, hey, I find it difficult to believe, but you see, this custom of my people is real and sometimes I wonder where this custom and belief and Christianity come into play. I say this because a lot of people have died, ignoring this custom of our people when asked to carry out the *omenani*, the tradition of our people. Their deaths are believed to have come about because of the fact that they ignored this tradition, claiming that they are now Christians and cannot indulge in pagan practices.

'For example,' Chinua further explained, 'we know of a lot of these people who, having failed to properly bury either their mother and father, years later unknowingly attend funeral parties of their friends and acquaintances' mum or dad and thereafter they died suddenly, having been seen eating and drinking at these funerals when it is forbidden to do so because of the fact that they are yet to carry out the traditional customary rites involved during the burial of their father, and as such, it is believed that Ndi Ichie, the forefathers in the land of the dead, got upset and strangulated them.

Despite Chinua's unwavering faith in Christendom, she however wanted desperately to pass on the message received from their late father to her sisters, notifying them of recent occurrences where she had been told in the dream to join hands with her siblings to perform the traditional burial rites (remembrance of their father to enable him join his ancestors). Chinua went on to say that each time she saw their dead father, he always asked her questions about why he had been left in the cold in the spirit world because of their refusal to perform his burial rites.

Chinua immediately arranged visiting her sisters and her mother in the east to notify them of this message. Once she met with them, she passed on the message to them, and instantly, they believed her because it was their custom. They were also grateful to their late father, thanking him for giving them enough time to the extent that he took it upon himself to warn them in advance before striking without warning. There were some families who, according to them, their late parents would strike them dead once this tradition and custom is not carried out within a reasonable time frame.

This tradition involved the killing of cows and other pomp and pageantry. In line with the traditional ethos, the dead are normally accompanied by cultural music and dance and other rituals which are normally transported to the ancestors with cannon shots, usually seven cannon shots which, according to their belief, are a noise of merrymaking to alert the predecessors of the coming of the dead person who at this time is ready to meet and join them.

There is also a widely held belief that where the ceremony is omitted, this disrupts the dead relative as they go halfway and would now come back in visions as ghosts to disturb the living until such a time as the complete send-off ceremony, namely burial rites, is completed.

This Igbo tradition is so strong and powerful that many Igbo traditionalists would prefer to go down to hell with their ancestors than to be separated from them on account of baptism preached to them by the missionaries who preached hellfire.

Once arrangements were put in place, Chinua and her five sisters all travelled to the village with their children and grandchildren to carry out this very important funeral rite. As the ceremony continued in Chinua's village, there were certain traditional rites which were expected of a first son to carry out. Chiboy their half brother had also been informed of the importance of such a ceremony, and everyone was expecting him to come to the village to perform these traditional burial rites which would enable their dead father join his ancestors successfully.

On the day the ceremony proper was to take place, everyone waited for Chiboy to come home. But he was nowhere to be found. No one received any message from him notifying them of his whereabouts.

It will be seen as a taboo if this ritual is not carried out and so in the absence of Chiboy, they needed a male child who could stand in the gap. A unanimous decision was made to make a choice amongst themselves to use one of their male children to carry out these traditional rites. They consulted the services of diviners to set things right. Chinua's most senior sister Chituru, who had a son older than Chinua's son, gave one excuse for her son's non-attendance and inability to carry the masquerade Ekpe. The second sister also refused to release her son and advised that they wait for the right person to carry this out.

In a usual naïve and vibrant manner, Chinua gave up her only son Ejikemuwa aka Tega, who was a fearless young man in his twenties and who touched so many lives with his fiery strides and physical good looks and ability to warm the hearts of women.

And so, despite being a maternal grandchild, Ejikemuwa was used as the sacrificial lamb to carry out his maternal grandfather's funeral procession and also the beheading of a gigantic he-goat which symbolised the end of an era for the grandfather who was a member of the "Ekpe" masquerade.

Ekpe Masquerade/Festival

Immediately Tega was presented to the whole clan as the chosen one who would carry out all the traditional rites befitting for a person of their late grandfather's status, there was a frenzied air and silence amongst everyone. There was fear and apprehension considering that Tega was only linked to this clan through his mother Chinua. Most of the villagers had strong belief in paternal rights as this was a patriarchal society. Another concern was Tega's young age; also there was fear about the dire consequences of being booed, flogged, and jeered if peradventure Tega failed to properly carry out the traditional rites, the shame and disgrace which awaited not only him but the whole village if he was not able to behead the he-goat in one go. If this did not occur, there were implications to that, as he would be beaten severely by the youths and also seen as an abomination, where further rituals and traditional cleansing would have to take place simultaneously to cleanse the land of the abomination caused by his inability to cut off the head of the he-goat in one go. This would also mean that all neighbouring villages will make a mockery of Umuigwu village for the abomination done by them, by their failure to behead the sacrificial he-goat instantly and drop the beheading cutlass. If on the other hand, Tega successfully cut off the he-goat in one instance, the head of the goat is picked up by the youths who are members of the masquerade who hold this goat head high up in the air while everyone chants the traditional 'ekpe . . . heee, haaa, heee, haaa, heee, haaa' while running round the market square, rejoicing over the success of this ritual. Chinua, however offered herself and her son, partly out of her naivety which sprang from her staunch belief in her christian faith that you give to Caesar what is Caesar's and to God what is God's. She strongly believed that this practice even though have pagan connotations, cannot in anyway have any detrimental effect on her son Tega. Normally palm fronds are tied round people's legs and waists while the Ekpe masquerade dances round in the market square, with women keeping distance for fear of being molested and flogged.

It is important that Tega carry out this ritual as part of the commemoration in remembrance of his grandfather's strength and powers during the days when he used to be the head of the masquerade.

Despite not being the eldest in her family and despite the fact that her older sisters had male children whom they could bring forward to perform this ceremony, they did not offer their sons, perhaps because they understood the spiritual and cultural implications of this pagan tradition. Chinua, however, offered herself and her son partly out of her naivety which sprang from her staunch belief in her Christian faith.

She believed that volunteering her son to participate in this masquerade ritual would save her family the shame of not doing the right thing expected to complete these traditional rites; she also believed that it was only an activity meant to increase authenticity of the whole ceremony. In her usual kind manner, Chinua did not want her family to be jeered at by members of her late father's clan. 'There are male children in this family, we do not lack male children,' she spat out in her usual way. 'In the absence of Chiboy taking over this role as my father's son, we do not lack male children, we are called battalion soldiers and must therefore provide a male child to complete this ceremony successfully,' said Chinua.

Little did Chinua know that this would be her undoing. Her sisters, who were more exposed to spiritual village practices and voodoo, intentionally refused to bring their own sons forward even though their sons were older in age than Chinua's son Tega.

Chinua and her son later paid for their naivety because months after this ceremony, her son Tega died in mysterious unexplained circumstances.

Soon after this ceremony came to an end, Chinua's stepbrother Chiboy, appeared from nowhere in the crowd. When asked why he failed to come earlier, knowing the rituals which needed to be carried out on that day to give their father a safe transition and landing in the spirit world thirty-five years after his demise, Chiboy gave excuses that because he still lived in Maroko, a downtrodden waterlogged area of Lagos, his house was flooded and he became homeless, making it difficult for him to leave Lagos immediately to proceed to the funeral.

When Chiboy discovered that the main ritual which their late father was known for had already been performed by Tega, he became very bitter and was spoiling for vengeance.

Chiboy's stepsisters nicknamed him *opara iberibe*, worthless son, a name they enjoyed calling him in a calculated bid to show that even though they were females, they turned out better than their stepbrother Chiboy despite their late father's preference for a male child.

'If not for the fact that we have respect for the tradition and custom of our people, we would have left him to hang outside there in the land of the spirits. He would have waited for his so-called male child Chiboy to raise enough money to purchase all the cows and additional condiments needed to successfully complete this ceremony,' fumed Chinua, cursing under her breath.

It was not clear till date whether Tega met his untimely death from his mother's lack of diplomacy in involving him in a tradition which was gradually fading out from the strong pagan belief and which was contrary to the beliefs and ethos which Christianity has embraced.

A Mother's Silent Pain

'Water, water, water,' called out Tega, who at this time had been ill for close to two months, six months after he joined his mother and other siblings to attend his grandfather's funeral.

'Why do you want water?' asked Chinua.

'I want water, water, my throat is dry,' groaned Tega.

'Okay, wait for me to get you water. I'm happy that at least you are now requesting to drink water. Since three days ago, you have not eaten or drunk anything. Anything you take in, you have brought out.'

'Tega, Tega, Oghenetega, Te -ga . . . ga . . . no, no no, don't do this, Tega!' As Chinua gave Tega the water, she noticed his eyes suddenly rolling as he took a sip and instantly breathed his last.

'Tega, Tega, don't leave me, heh, help, who will help me? Where do I run to? They have finally killed my son. Evil tradition and customs have killed my son.

'Heh! Since I involved myself in the tradition and custom which is alien to my strong belief as a Christian, I have not recovered from its heat,' moaned Chinua. 'I was told that once I pass on the message received from our late father which should be sent to my sisters and extended family and all traditional rites carried out and completed, things will turn around for me. This is why I do not believe these fetish archaic traditional practices,' she went on.

The blood of Jesus had taken over all these satanic practices, she tried to convince herself. 'Since I came back from this so-called funeral, my business got burnt, I became very ill, my daughter had a ghastly accident and now the death of my son. How do they want me to believe their lies anymore?

'Henceforth, I will run into my God for he alone can save, not tradition and custom.' Chinua wailed and wailed over the loss of her only son born to Chief Mudiaga. She refused to be consoled. And so, this was how Chinua lost her son Ejikemuwa Tega.

After the death of her son, there were suspicions of foul play as rumours started going round that Tega might have been killed with voodoo by relatives who became envious that he successfully performed the traditional beheading of the goat's head which was the main ritual carried out by his late grandfather as the head of the Ekpe masquerade. Some of the story has it that the whole family might have misdirected themselves by allowing a grandchild, Tega, to carry out these traditional rites which should have been the sole prerogative of their father's direct son Chiboy. Till date there has not been any proof of why or how Tega lost his life, only insinuations arising from traditional superstitious beliefs.

Tega was more popular in death than in life, and because of his popularity, the whole Umuigu village, upon hearing of Tega's death, mourned him sorely. They prepared to give him a befitting burial while at the same time forgetting that Umuigu was only Tega's maternal home and so his corpse could not be brought back there. Tega's remains were buried in Effurun-Warri, which was his paternal home.

Marriage by Proxy—An Age-Old Tradition of the Igbos

Tega did not die in vain; he already had a son from a woman married to him under the native law and custom. This woman was traditionally married to Chinua's mother, using Tega as a male member of the family in order to fulfil the traditional rites and custom. This marriage of Tega to this woman was another tradition and custom which is practiced amongst the people of south-east Nigeria.

Chinua accepted that her son Tega should be betrothed to a young woman who would live with Nwanyibeke (his grandmother). The main role of this young woman would be to take care of Tega's grandmother and, at the same time, conceive and bear children within the community who would look after and inherit their grandfather's home upon the death of the grandmother.

'Mama is growing old, we will need a wife who can take care of Mama and also be there for us to cook and cater to our needs when we visit the village,' said Chinua.

It is part of the Igbo custom and tradition for family members to come together and marry a wife whom they term a 'family wife'. Usually such a woman stays in the family home in the village and takes care of all family interests, be they farmland, houses, cooking, fetching water from the stream, tending the family farmland, and seeing to it that the family home is not empty when other family members visit from the city.

Such a tradition is mostly practised when there are no male children in the family to secure their lineage. This tradition, custom, and practice is encouraged to make sure that any child born by this woman becomes the first son of that family and also the head of the family, who engages in carrying out any traditional rites and customs required of that household during ceremonial gatherings or traditional masquerade celebrations. The birth of a male child is an important part of a typical Igbo family.

Chinua and her sisters were later introduced to the young lady when the whole family, upon noticing that their mother Nwanyibeke was becoming quite ill, needed help with daily living. They then came together and made arrangements to take a wife for their mother. They visited Mbaino several times, and once all the gifts and traditional rites involving marriage became complete, they then brought Tega to see her. Immediately she caught sight of Tega, she liked him. She did not stop giggling from one end of her mouth to the other like a Cheshire cat all through that day. It was obvious she liked Tega.

Upon setting eyes on Tega, Chinwoke—that was her name— excitedly asked, 'When am I going home with you?'

'Mbanu,' retorted Chinua. 'Isi Mgbaka, please wait and let us complete the marriage rites before your clitoris starts itching you, pour hot water on it to calm it down, this is the problem when a girl is not circumcised, she becomes easily sexually aroused. God will help us o! My son is still too young,' she mumbled to herself.

Tega was a likeable young man, a ladies' man, and loved by all family members. It was just as if his life played itself out completely while he was still alive. Tega never lived under the same roof with this young lady whom they married for him. He, however, slept with her just for purposes of procreation; such was the tradition. Chinwoke was the family wife and would remain so. Her children would also bear the name of Chinua's late father to preserve the family name.

Despite officially marrying Chinwoke, her bride price was not paid by Tega; it was a contribution from all members of the family. The tradition allowed Tega to marry a wife of his choice later and also bear his own children if he chose. Chinwoke and her future children belonged to the whole family. Prior to accepting to follow his mum's family to Mbaino, the whole process was explained to Tega and he accepted it more out of the excitement of being seen as the superman in his mum's family than being able to understand the future implication. He was, however, asked to cooperate by making sure that he slept with this lady and impregnated her—which he did, and they later had a son together called Chidera, which means 'what God has decreed'.

On the night when Chinwoke met Tega alone in the village, she could not wait to have him all to herself. He was himself intrigued by her sexual prowess, considering she was a village girl. She was quite proactive and participated in all the sexual moves introduced by him.

At first Tega wanted to use the condom but she refused. 'Are you not my husband?' she asked him. 'I want to feel your gbangus,' she whispered into his ears. 'What is gbangus?' he asked her, already aroused by her touch and the wriggling of her tiny waist. 'It's size ogboloma,' she said.

'Size ogboloma, size ogboloma?' He got the message and could not hold in his laughter. 'Ha ha ha ha!' His laughter lingered round the whole of the bedroom.

The result of this first meeting with Chinwoke was seen a couple of months later as she became pregnant. The whole family was very happy, screaming, 'Epe' he ha, he ha, he ha!' Chinwoke's pregnancy was affirmed by different gifts from all members of the family. Gifts of wrapper, lace, shoes, and jewellery were bought for her. She could not believe her luck as everything worked according to plan. She thought to herself that Mother

Nature was perhaps compensating her for the death of her mother and her sister, the two most important people in her life, who died during childbirth. 'Hmm . . .' she heaved a sigh of relief and mumbled under her breath, 'Perhaps they did not want to live, that is why they died.'

Once when Chinwoke was around twenty-eight weeks pregnant, Chinua visited from Effurun. Immediately she saw Chinwoke in her heavily pregnant state, she fixed her eyes on her, like someone who had seen a ghost. 'This girl's waistline looks too tiny for a woman who is seven months pregnant, I hope her cervix will be wide enough to bring forth the unborn child.' In response to this, her sister reassured Chinua that Chinwoke was okay and there was nothing wrong with her waist or her cervix.

Two months later, while in hospital to deliver her baby, Chinwoke died on the same night she had her son Chidera, bringing to an end the hope of finding someone who would look after the family estate in the village.

The death of Tega was not the only grave mistake which was made by Chinua because of her naivety and openness of heart. Once when Mimi, one of Chinua's daughters, was in secondary school, Chinua allowed her to visit her uncle whom she had been estranged from since the death of her first husband in Enugu, and it was agreed by both parties that once the school holiday period was over, Mimi would be released.

When Mimi visited her uncle Ozumba, his wife of over twenty years requested and managed to convince her uncle that there was no point for Mimi to return to her mum Chinua. These two plotted together on how to frustrate any efforts made by Chinua to take Mimi back.

When Chinua came to pick up her daughter as agreed, she was not allowed in by the gateman.

Chinua knocked and knocked endlessly without any response from the inside. Just as she stood wondering what might have happened to her daughter, she sighted movement from the opened window. Someone was peeping through the glass window. Chinua cursed and cursed, 'Otolo gbagbukwa unu.' (May you all be infected with diarrhoea.) She further demanded that if the door was not opened, she would call the police and inform them that her daughter had been abducted.

At this stage, the door was now flung open and Mimi's uncle came out raging, asking her, 'What do you want from us? Do not step your foot here again. My daughter' (referring to Mimi) 'can be taken care of.'

'Thank you for the little job you have done so far by taking care of her, but if you had allowed us all this while, maybe it would have been easier for everyone involved,' he ranted.

'Usu,' screamed Chinua. 'Bat that is being controlled by a woman, so this is your plan with your wife, eh?' As if this verbal exchange was not enough, Chinua rushed through the gate, which was at this time opened to allow another guest to drive in.

As she approached the main entrance door, she met with the mai guard, who now tried to stop her from gaining access. 'Udele, vulture,' she went on, 'if you don't leave my way now, I will remove the remaining hair on your vulture-like head.' She pushed the mai guard to one side, rushed at Mimi's uncle, and grabbed him by the loin. 'Where is my daughter?' she screamed at the top of her voice. As she screamed, she punched him even harder, while still asking to know where her daughter was kept. At this time, Mimi's uncle was rolling on the floor helpless while the male guest who drove in had alighted from his car trying to pull off Chinua's hands from Ozumba's groin. 'Ewu, mbgeeeee! Goat!' she screamed. Immediately all of this noise intensified, they all heard the strong, commanding, innocent voice of Mimi saying 'Stop, stop, Mama, stop, I am here now, let's go!' Chinua turned around and saw Mimi her daughter holding a small travelling bag, staring at them. She looked gaunt and emaciated.

Immediately Chinua caught sight of her daughter, she jumped up from where she was holding down Ozumba, ran quickly to where Mimi was standing, and embraced her while using part of her Nkpuruoka wrapper to wipe Mimi's face. 'Hey, see how lean you are,' she cried. 'They have not been feeding you, I suppose, and yet they want to take you from me. Never—none of my children will be used by another family as their housemaid. Never!'

'Mama, come, let's go,' cried Mimi. 'I don't want to visit this family ever again anymore. Thank God you fought to find me. I was told I will never go back to you again,' cried Mimi.

This time, Uncle Ozumba's wife had already called her husband's DPO friend who quickly sent a lorry-load of police officers with their van to visit the compound and arrest the child abductor according to the story told him.

'Move, madam, I say move,' commanded one of the police officers. 'Move to where?' asked Chinua, pushing her bare chest forward. 'Before you move me, please let me tie my wrapper tight to cover my nakedness, or do you want to expose my nakedness?' she further asked.

'I am Sergeant Chukwujeku of the central police station Enugu, you are under arrest for suspicion of child abduction, child molestation, and failure to allow reasonable access by child's family. You have a right to remain silent. Anything you say will be used as evidence against you in a court of law . . .'

'Okay now,' shouted Chinua. 'Police wayo! Child dis, child dat, including failure to allow my own child to be exposed to hunger and starvation, abi? Make we go see your DPO then. Where is your moto?' asked Chinua. 'Moto ke,' answered the police officer. 'Madam, you go have to pay for taxi that will take me and you and your daughter to the station. Our van is filled up, as you can see. You have to also . . .'

'So you came to arrest me over an allegation which you have not investigated, you have made several counts on my head without telling me how you arrived at these counts, now you want make I still pay for taxi wey go carry you to police station. I no go anyhere again gbam!' At this time, Chinua spread her legs wide, while digging both feet into the bare sand in a bid to firmly resist any further use of force by the police officers.

'What did you say?' asked the police officer. 'I said you will need a trailer to move me out of here since you did not provide a vehicle that will take me to the station after my arrest.'

Immediately, the police sergeant sprang into action by pulling out his handcuffs. 'You must have to put that on me first,' shouted Mimi. 'My mother has not done anything, leave her alone. She is a helpless woman without a husband who has single-handedly raised her children and yet rather than the society supporting her welfare and that of her children, you are trying to oppress her and steal her child from her, wicked people!'

Chinua and Mimi were finally taken to the central police station in Enugu were they met with the DPO himself and statements were taken from Chinua and Mimi, her daughter. Upon carefully considering the whole story, the DPO made a decision to release Mimi to her mother Chinua. He also sent a police vehicle to take them back to the park while at the same time handing his contact details to Chinua to call him anytime. 'I was raised by a single mother myself,' he said to them. My mother raised me and my four siblings and I know what she went through as a single mother after the death of my father. I will therefore not sit here and watch anyone maltreat or disrespect any single mother based on a single story,' said the DPO.

Chapter Eight

The Single Story

I do so admire those who are alone
Alone to raise a part of their future
To the child's birth to the age of teen
To be taking care of an adolescent . . .
—Unknown

Chinua suffered so many setbacks within the community she lived, because of the single story told about her. During this period, single parenthood was something given all kinds of interpretation, and so in place of support and affirmation, single parents were mocked, called names, and relegated to the background. Nobody wanted to associate themselves with them or their children. Once someone mentioned that he or she lived with her mother, all eyes would thereafter focus on them and they were seen as a bad influence within the community where they lived.

This was a far cry from the strict organized marriage and courtship structures people in the community were used to. It was therefore more or less like a collective responsibility where single parenthood was being averted as it was seen as a taboo.

Chinua was a widow who lost her first husband; after her husband died, tradition and custom demanded that she marry her husband's brother in order to continue with the family lineage. She revolted and ran off to find a better life for herself and her three children from first husband.

She became labelled as a person with questionable character because she met this tragedy of life. In a desperate bid not to remain single, she met with a married man who promised to assist her and love her. She fell for him in her naivety and later had four additional children for this man who again abandoned her. She became single once again upon discovering that she had gone into this relationship with Chief Mudiaga in a bid to find love and affirmation by a man. During the period she was with Chief Mudiaga, she thought she could fill that loneliness and emptiness she felt all her life, but unfortunately, this was not to be.

Chinua found herself becoming a single parent during an era where traditionally, marriage was taken seriously as a holy, sacred, and holistic part of life and living and also in an era where traditionally, Africans were carefully guarded and guided, and they promoted and supported marriage mainly by implementing a set of significant customary laws, values, taboos, and norms. Single motherhood therefore at this time was seen as something which threatened the rich traditional African culture and its concept of family.

Chinua was amongst the single mothers at this time who were labelled incomplete and unfulfilled. This labelling came not only from people who did not know her true story and circumstance, but also from family members whom you would expect should be a bit sympathetic, having known that she was once married but unfortunately became a widow upon the death of her husband.

To Chinua's sisters, she could not attain the full status and accomplishment which was realized in marriage. She was therefore a source of concern and ridicule to her family members, they avoided her like the plague and she did also the same as a way of avoiding what she later saw as a shame.

Each time Chinua visited her family home in the village, she was not allowed to have a room to herself just like all her other sisters. She would share the guest room with the guests and her children, being denied any privacy whatsoever, while her other sisters had a whole wing of the building and enjoyed the comfort and privacy needed during their stay in the village. Chinua suffered ridicule and social condemnation also amongst her peers. She became a family shame.

Chinua's family were even more lenient to her in terms of hostility; they did not adopt name-calling as other single mothers were called witches, persons who engaged in sorcery and were also believed to cooperate in malicious magic, and persons of bad omen—these were dehumanising and depersonalizing accusations and counter-accusations levied against single mums. During this era, so many of these single mums were taken undue advantage of, by men who played on their vulnerability, promising them marriage while at the same time exploiting them both financially and emotionally as they ended up leaving them broken-hearted.

Others died and sometimes they were banished from their communities because according to traditional belief, they represented evil in the society.

In African society also, it is believed that single mothers have something wrong with them or that they must have done something very wrong which is preventing them from getting married.

It is also believed within Christendom that these problems of single motherhood have spiritual inclinations and may be a foundational or generational curse.

With this attitudinal mentality therefore, it was unfortunate to find oneself in this state of single parenthood as the one which Chinua found herself. This is because this single status dictated Chinua's social organizational networking and her much-desired deep familial interpersonal relationship.

According to her family members, Chinua did not deserve anything good. Any good thing that came to her must be taken away from her; after all, she was only a common, morally loose single mother whose moral decadence, according to them, was the only explanation behind her single parenthood.

It was so easy for Chinua's sisters to forget that she was once married, before her husband had died. While mourning her late husband and carrying out the traditional burial rites, she was forcefully raped by her late husband's elder brother who accordingly told her that she now belonged to him according to the traditional Igbo rites and custom of inheritance.

Despite not getting any help from extended family members, Chinua understood where she was coming from. She never tried to live in denial.

She reminded herself every day of her travails and pains and also her hope for a victorious life at the end.

It was with such high hopes that Chinua lived each day, and this hope was something which changed her life's experience forever.

Chinua never stopped reminiscing on her past life and the journey so far. She remembered how she was forcefully raped by her late husband's elder brother during the period she was still mourning her husband. She remembered the pain, the loneliness, the false accusations made against her that she killed her late husband; she remembered how she befriended a local transporter who ran a transport business that travelled to the midwest after she confided in him and begged him to assist her to escape with her children to a destination where her late husband's family could not trace her.

She remembered how she wanted to get away as far as possible to a place where they could not locate her. Suddenly the thought of her eldest sister Ulari, aka false hope, came to mind. 'Ulari, false hope, has to give me hope this time around,' thought Chinua sarcastically. She remembered how she reconnected with her sister Ulari, who accommodated her and her three children. 'I want to go far away from these people to a place where they and their funny oppressive tradition cannot reach me,' she said.

Nine months after her husband died and while still mourning, Chinua took her children and ran off to meet her sister Ulari in Effurun-Warri.

The journey to Warri was a very long, winding one; despite all of this, Chinua was able to make the journey with her three children through the help of a sympathiser who happened to be a transporter.

Chinua would never forget how she first met Chief Mudiaga, who took both sisters out to shop in one of the exclusive shops in the town. This singular gesture of kindness from Chief Mudiaga brought about a serious feeling of envy and jealousy from Chinua's elder sister Ulari, who did everything possible to ruin her relationship with Chief Mudiaga.

She would go behind Chinua and continue to say all kinds of negative things about her to Chief Mudiaga. She would say to Chief Mudiaga, 'Haba Chief, Chief, Chief, how many times did I call you? Do you not know that involving yourself with this single mother will bring bad luck to your business? Chief, have you asked her why no man wants her? This should send a message to you . . . Blah-blah, blah!'

Ulari's hatred for Chinua did not just stop with her attempts to destroy her relationship; she also made sure that she made life unbearable for her sister, who later, upon Chief's suggestion, moved out of her sister's house.

The antagonism faced by Chinua did not stop with only family members. Her children suffered the shame also. At this time they were already growing with the societal notion being put into their heads that indeed there must be something wrong with their mother, which is why their father died.

It is only a mother who knows who the biological father of her children is,' said Chinua to her second daughter Mimi. 'Who is my father then, Mum?' questioned Mimi. 'Don't be silly,' said Chinua. 'What do you mean, who is your father? Whose name do you bear?'

'I have heard several times in the community how you were unfaithful to the man you call my father when he was alive,' Mimi stuttered. 'Who are my father's relatives and why have they never asked after me and my siblings?'

'Please do not stress me up, I have had a very bad day today. You ask too many questions. When you get older, you will understand everything once it is explained once and for all to you.'

Whenever Chinua had such conversations with any of her children, like the one she was having with her daughter Mimi, it further reminded her of her pain, her frustrations and inner suffering as a single mother.

She not only faced being called names within her immediate society, but from her own children who, because of that same lack of affirmation extended to them because of their mother, now unconsciously decided to hit back at her.

'Why is it that everyone has a single story of me?' she asked angrily. 'I have to be careful with the friends I make each day, because I am single, for fear of being misinterpreted.'

Chinua was also isolated by her married friends and sisters alike, most especially her sister Njideka, despite Njideka's promiscuity and the lack of commitment to marriage vows by her and her husband. This singleness which had become a never-ending pain to Chinua also indirectly affected her children as they were not expected to be married to certain people, because of the sin of being born to a single mother.

Once during a Christmas period, Gwendolyn, one of Chinua's daughters, attended a marriage ceremony with some of her schoolmates and whilst enjoying the rhythm and dancing of atilogwu dancers who graced this beautiful marriage ceremony, she stumbled into one of their neighbours, who asked her in a sarcastic manner, 'When are we coming to your home to eat and drink over the marriage of you or any of your siblings? I do hope you people will not turn out to be like your mother.' This comment, coming from an older woman whom Gwendolyn had a lot of respect for and looked up to, affected her so badly.

She felt like an outcast and immediately she left the marriage ceremony running home and crying into the night. That same night as Gwendolyn slept, she had a dream that she was in a strange land, a white man's land, and during this sojourn to the white man's land, she met a young, vibrant man who later became her husband and with whom she bore several female children. As she tried to have the third child in that dream, she discovered that the child was also female after having a scan which had fully confirmed that the baby she carried was a boy. She cried and cried in the dream and then later woke up with tears rolling down her eyes as she realised it was only a dream.

Gwendolyn became quite withdrawn after this encounter. She bottled up emotions and shut down. She felt rejected. She decided, however, not to be a burden on her mother, because her mother had done so much. She did not want her mother to see how vulnerable she felt each time this issue of being raised by her alone was mentioned. She felt it was her fault that she did not have her father in her life. She, however, saw her mother as a survivor, despite her flaws. She wanted to grow up fast; she wanted to be successful and to be able to take care of her mother for all the sacrifices she made by single-handedly carrying out a job meant for two people. 'If only society will understand my mother's role rather than judge her,' she moaned. 'If she abandoned me and my siblings the way everyone did, I wonder what would have become of us all.'

It was with this mindset therefore that Gwendolyn started carving a niche for herself into the future. This dream would later form part of the motivational transgression leading her to travel outside the shores of her country, looking for freedom, actualisation, and living with purpose.

Chinua also suffered this level of discrimination even in her local place of worship. Despite her willingness to be a committed church worker, she was never appointed or given a defined role. Several times, she was faced with the dilemma of seeing her children bullied in school and called all sorts of names by their mates, names like 'children of the woman without husband, the man-eater, seven man body.'

Once she visited her son's school to make a complaint about bullying, and she met with one of the parents, who made cynical remarks about her, warning others to please keep an eye on or their distance from Chinua's children. These were the kind of cynical comments which Chinua and her children faced each day of her life. Comments like 'like mother, like daughter' and 'Nne ganu' which literally means an old maid who ends up being married to mum, were not uncommon to her.

Because her children wanted identity to cover them in the society, she made sure she included their father's name as their last name, for identity and security. Despite the stigma which was contributing to her low self-esteem, she shouldered all the burdens at home, social and economic.

Her loneliness and pain, however, produced for her a determination and desire to succeed, to prove to the world that something good can come from nothing, as she would like herself to believe. Chinua's perception of how she was seen by the society heightened her anxiety, leading to serious health problems later in her life.

Chinua was the kind of person who has a big need for acceptance and belonging in her immediate community, and so she kept her self-discipline and dignity. She was desperate to be accepted, making her an easy prey in the society.

She had this self-conviction about her that she would have been better than most of the so-called married women if given an opportunity like her sister Njideka. She never stopped making herself happy by saying if all marriages were like that which her sister Njideka and her husband involved themselves in, then she would rather remain single. She believed strongly that Njideka and her army husband were not good role models of what marriage should be, as they kept on defiling their marriage bed and their marriage vows.

'I think this marriage thing is part of luck,' Chinua would say to anyone who cared to listen. 'If not luck, then what else can it be?' she would ask while giving examples of some bad neighbours who treated their husbands very badly and yet still considered themselves married.

Chinua always felt guilty and had a feeling of regret for past mistakes, despite most of these not being her fault. She sometimes made herself happy by justifying some of her actions which were due to financial constraints leaving her to shoulder all economic burdens at her disposal.

'Rather than see me through school, my parents married me off at a very young age to a man who lacked vision and direction. On top of it, he decided to die to give me a bad name,' said Chinua in her typical matter-of-fact way.

Chinua would always remind anyone who cared to hear of the significance of single ladies like Tabitha (Dorcas) in the Bible and also the Samaritan woman who later became a great evangelist. She always told people that God loves the humble faithful woman and that obedience and faith in God would lead her to receive God's blessings. The many wounds Chinua had as a single mother were enormous.

She felt invisible and ignored by the whole world despite the enormous role she played in raising her children. Despite the lack of significance given to her role as a single mother, she did not look back, and she was strong and resilient despite the societal labelling.

She had goals and was determined that her children must succeed. She must not make the same mistake her parents made. Her children must not suffer what she suffered.

She imbibed values of hard work and sacrifice within her community life which was somehow denied her because of the way society viewed her as a single parent. She was resilient and unstoppable and continued to forge on.

She woke up very early every morning getting her six children ready fir school, giving instructions to them to return to her market stall to meet with her once they closed from school. Apart from this task, she kept with her responsibilities as a petty-business person. Chinua had the additional task of making sure that she met her customers' needs by constantly keeping a happy face, attending to them when they came into her shop to buy their clothing, jewellery, beads, or other additional wares which she sold to meet her very tight budget.

Finance was a major part of the daily struggle for Chinua and her children. She would go without food and new apparel, unlike her contemporaries, just to be able to buy her children's schoolbooks, school uniforms, and other household needs.

Several times, as it was common, she had also confronted personal challenges that led to physical fights and verbal exchange of words, where her opponents did not fail to remind her of her single status.

A particular encounter was when she had a fight with a regular customer of hers, who owed her some money over a long period of time and refused intentionally to pay up. On this day, this customer (Mama Nneka) turned up at her stall and requested that a particular George (a handwoven material worn by women for special occasions like parties, naming ceremonies, and church services) be sold to her on credit. Because of the constant demand for credit, Chinua had this bold signage in front of her shop which read 'MR & MRS CREDIT, NO CREDIT TODAY, COME BACK TOMORROW', meaning she had a policy of not selling her products on credit.

As soon as Mama Nneka mentioned that she intended to take this lace George on credit, Chinua shoved her to one side and pointed directly to the sign she had, reminding Mama Nneka that she was not ready to sell her a wrapper on credit.

Mama Nneka then stated, 'You are not happy that I come here to ask for your wrapper, don't you know you are an equivalent of an Osu, an outcast whom no one should have nothing to do with because of your single status? This is why you ran away from the east where you come from, because you are an Osu and you know very well that if you were in the east, you will be treated like the outcast that you are.'

Immediately Chinua heard this, she grabbed this lady by the scarf on her head. 'I will remove your *gele* from your hair as this is what covers you from looking like a vulture,' said Chinua. 'I will teach you that vultures are even treated more like outcasts than the so-called man-made Osu that you are referring to.'

And so, on this day a serious fight ensued between these two women and they were later separated by passers-by and neighbours, however, not without Chinua insisting that the money owed to her be paid immediately.

She sprang towards Mama Nneka with a piece of wood, hoping to hit her immediately to teach her a lesson. She, however, dodged this instantly, as she was fast, to the extent that it looked as though she saw that blow coming. She halted the blow with a balancing blow to the side of Chinua's chin. Adrenaline was rushing; in the distance, some passers-by had stopped to watch upon hearing noises coming out from the shop. This was prime-time entertainment.

The fight grew even trickier as it looked as though both women were giving each other a run for their money. They had mastered each other's antics and could anticipate each other the same way. They were too well matched, both of them fast, hearts thumping in their chests, and sweat coated their skin. Then Chinua finally got through; she moved in for an attack, coming at her opponent with the full force of her body, using the advantage of her 5' 11" height and strong build. She was so strong that Mama Nneka stumbled from the impact; she did not waste the opportunity but she further dragged her to the ground. Behind them, people were clapping. The fight was finished, but the remains of the adrenaline and the animal intensity lingered on in the minds of these two women and other onlookers for a long time.

Chinua fought like a man and her second nickname was Oputa Obe Igirigiri; fighting was part of Chinua's therapy. When she engaged in a fight, it gave her a buzz, especially when fighting with men. Once when she engaged in a fight with a man called David during a village meeting organised once every month amongst people who came from her ethnic group, as a way of keeping in touch with each other. She pulled this man in the groin, and he collapsed on the floor, begging her to leave him, and she made him vow instantly that he would never call her *asewo* or prostitute again because she was a single parent.

Chinua always thought the only way she could show that she valued herself was to fight to be treated with dignity like every other woman. She usually had this to say: 'Sometimes I feel sorry for some of these people who give married people a bad name. They deceive themselves, saying they are married and yet they go about cheating on each other.' She would argue, 'The men cheat on the women, the women cheat on the men also. Most of the children born to these cheating women are not biological children of the so-called men they call their fathers. Who exactly is fooling who? One day the wind will blow and the anus of the cheaters will be exposed.'

After long painful months of overbearing name-calling by a neighbour, Chinua asked this man whose wife was caught cheating on him, 'Is it paining you then that the woman you call your wife is cheating on you? John today, John Bull tomorrow, blackie is giving birth to mulatto. It means that she too is a prostitute just like me according to your definition of who a prostitute is.'

Chinua would always say to her opponents, 'I am going into this fight with you, with a backup.'

'Which is better?' she would ask, 'Me, Chinua that is a decent single parent who became a single parent out of necessity and bad luck or you that pretend to the world that you are married, and yet you go all out there looking for other men to sleep with, pretending to go on a business trip while you seek getaways to meet with your secret lovers.'

Chinua would always profess a form of godliness as she managed to convince herself that she was even more morally upright than some of the married people she came across who only portray this status of being married and sticking to one man, one wife, just to meet the societal norm and practices, while behind closed doors, they involved themselves in all kinds of infidelity.

She never stopped telling her female children of a couple she knew who, even though they were married for twenty-five years, kept on cheating on each other. The story had it that some of the children of the man were not his biological children as a very wealthy, popular doctor who had a clinic was involved in this woman's life during the period she bore her last three children while still married to her husband. The whole secret was revealed when one of the children took ill and a test was carried out which finally confirmed that this man was not the father of the child, leading to several other of the children's paternity also being exposed. That family was destroyed as a result of this scandal.

No day passed without Chinua encountering all kinds of societal disapproval of her status as a single mother, and she continued to fight her way through life to survive in the midst of this non-acceptance of her person.

Despite the inner struggles covered with an outward boldness, Chinua was a kind-hearted person. She smiled politely at everyone when she was not under pressure and also performed random acts of kindness. She was also an uninhibited person who did what she felt was right within her immediate community. At the same time she was in touch with some reality beyond anything negative, she had a free spirit and was never afraid to express herself in any form. She was also witty, spontaneous, and funny and a person who was considerate of other's sensibilities and was respectful to others. More importantly, her children were her life and she would do anything to protect them against any seeming harm.

Chinua also had a strong faith in God and believed that whatever she did not get from God by being blessed with a good man, she would gain from her children. She attended the nearby community church and was fully involved in church and community work. Chinua's unrelenting faith in God and His supremacy over all was one of the main avenues through which she gained her strength and hope.

In describing her uncompromising faith in God, Chinua would tell anyone who cared to listen of how once she was confronted with the dilemma of having to part with her rooster which a herbalist (native doctor) had requested should be killed and used as a sacrifice to appease the gods once when her father took ill.

According to Chinua, she pretended as if she was tagging along with this traditional medicine man, who unsuspecting, left his medicine box (akpa ogwu) within her reach. Chinua destroyed every single object and figurine inside the medicine man's wooden box and set it ablaze, challenging that his god should prove himself by killing her if truly the medicine man's akpa ogwu was potent enough.

Of course, she lived to tell the story as she outlived this con medicine man who, according to Chinua, could not afford a rooster and wanted to con them out of a rooster the whole family had saved to be slaughtered during the Christmas period.

Chinua's unwavering faith in God was contagious, taking into consideration that her father was a member of a traditional masquerade group called Ekpe.

Apart from being a member of this group, Chinua's father was the leader of the group and carried this masquerade during each yearly festival which took place on 1 January every year. These traditional practices involved different pagan practices of calling on the gods to preserve them through the new year and to make them fruitful and provide them fruitful harvest.

The responsibility falls on whoever it is that has been chosen to carry this masquerade called Ekpe. Prior preparations involving pouring of libation, and chanting of war songs and the wearing of raffia skirts and other regalia carefully prepared by the masquerade keepers. On the day the masquerade comes out, there is a particular function which must be performed to complete this period of celebration. People come from the cities and other neighbouring villages to watch the performance and different families prepare different delicacies like ugba, (igbo name of the fermented African oil bean seed, a traditional condiment generally produced by natural local fermentation in homes as a small family business prepared with "okporoko"-stockfish and "Nkwobi"- a classic delicacy originating from South Eastern region made with cow leg cooked and smothered in thic, to mark this great occasion. During this period also, people who come from the cities use this as an opportunity to show off their wealth to the onlooking villagers, and it serves as an opportunity for bachelors to make marriage proposals to their intended wives and pay bride price or what they call *iku aka*, wine carrying, introducing themselves and their intentions, leading to ceremonies of engagement and to subsequent marriages.

This Ekpe festival is also a time when people visit the village to show off the wealth they have acquired within the last twelve months. They are dressed in different beautiful, expensive regalia like abada and George or akwete.

Normally women run into hiding once they hear the sound of the masquerade passing through. The main climax of the occasion is when a he goat is tied and kept in the market square and the masquerade Ekpe is now asked to cut off the head of this he-goat. The trick is that the masquerade is not allowed to cut twice the head of the goat. It must be decapitated once and once this is carried out successfully, the head of the goat is thrown up amidst a frenzied screaming and shouting and more gyrations of dancing which completes a celebration leading deep into the night.

Once the goat is successfully decapitated by the carrier of the Ekpe, you will hear the shout of jubilation 'ekpe heee, haaa, heee, haaa . . .' and this rendition goes on and on in the spirit of the celebration.

There are certain significant pagan practices which take place during this celebration; most Ekpe festivals are carried out during iri ji—new yam festival. This ekpe climaxes with the severing of a goat's head with one stroke of the machete (an art not to be undertaken by the weak or careless as there is a price for failing in the task and a reward for success).

There are also other practices Chinua's clan is involved in, like Okonko, which is a similar pagan practice where membership is accomplished in two stages, which are *ida iyi* (immersion in stream water) and *ikpu ulo* (homecoming).

As a member of this group, you are entitled to participate fully in matters that have to do with keeping law and order within the village, e.g.

in land disputes, resolution of sacrilege, and any decision on how to deal with other societies and nearby villages.

Another feature of this Ekpe festival is the war dance called Ikpirikpe Ogu, with the ishi Aja (three sacred heads on a platform which is not put down by the carrier until after the Ekpe festival). The carrier of this Ekpe is not allowed to speak during performance of this task and usually has a palm frond (*omu*) placed around his mouth to prevent him from talking and keep onlookers aware of the role that he is barred from talking.

There is usually a procession through all the compounds, called Ama, within the clan before its arrival at the main market square for the climax of the ceremony. To participate in these pagan practices, you have to be initiated. It is believed that it was meant for warriors and strong people in the community.

Despite its pagan undertone, masquerade in the south-eastern part of Nigeria is used to honour the dead and pray to the gods for a successful planting season.

The members wear masks to hide their identity from the rest of the village. The mask is also worn to represent the spirit of the dead community member. By wearing this mask, one who performs the masquerade is thought to have spiritual powers that are conducted through the mask. How far this is true remains unknown.

Despite their pagan undertone, masquerades in South Eastern Nigeria are a major form of entertainment. Chinua was one of the firm believers that these masquerades are a form of entertainment and nothing more.

Chinua also believed in women empowerment and made sure that every newly married young woman introduced to her within the community had access to her business premises once they showed interest in learning a trade. She would always call any woman who depended solely on her husband lazy; she preached the gospel of self-actualisation and financial freedom, thereby earning her the nickname madam de madam.

When Chinua turned fifty, she carved out diction in front of her stall which read,

> PRAY for
> Single parents
> Their journey requires the strength of two
> But is carried on the shoulders of one

Chinua had an ability which lay with her good qualities and positive contribution within the community where she lived despite being labelled a woman of easy virtue. She used these seeming imperfections positively, making her a hero.

Another thing Chinua did in her community was to assist young married couples whenever they had new born babies and there were no elderly family members to help them to bath the baby, pierce the ears of a female child, or help with the circumcision or treatment of the navel / umbilical chord of the newborn baby to avoid it getting exposed and infected. She also helped families with the bathing of the new mother. Such bathing skills, involved Chinua having to properly massage the nursing mother with very hot water which is left to reach boiling point, and then a large flannel is gradually dipped into this hot boiling water which is now dabbed all over the lower abdomen, back and the head of the new mother. This practice is believed to help detox the mother and allows for free blood circulation to avoid internal bleeding. Usually when the abdomen of the new mother is massaged, congealed blood usually flows freely from her vagina. This practice is continued every single morning and evening for as long as a period of 3 months to make sure that all after birth is purged out of the new mother to avoid any form of internal complications.

Chinua would travel the nooks and crannies of the community to assist these women and their husbands in order to lessen the plight they faced in their inexperience of handling the new addition in their home.

She never stopped telling the story of how her mother was a local midwife who worked tirelessly to assist women in labour to make sure that they deliver their babies safely. She would use *ori*, the traditional snake oil, to massage both mother and baby and would also see to it that the new baby's navel healed naturally by making sure that it is kept dry for days to avoid contamination.

Issues of circumcision for male children were also arranged on behalf of these families to assist them, and the afterbirth was always taken away by Chinua and buried on behalf of these families to help them as all bloodstained clothing of the new mother is also washed and ironed by Chinua. Chinua would also prepare pepper soup, the spicy soup prepared on behalf of new mothers which, according to the general belief, helps new mothers to recover as it flushes out the remaining blood which may be inside of the woman, as a residue. She received numerous gifts from these new parents who came in to show their gratitude.

Chinua also carried out certain traditional rites and practices on young mothers who experienced prolonged labour. Once she was called, she ran to the hospital and then recited some incantations, calling the baby to come out and also speaking to the baby, notifying it that a lot of beautiful clothes have been bought and that it will be missing a whole lot if it refuses to come out.

Also, Chinua progressed with an additional practice of pinching of the mother's feet twice, encouraging her to push out the baby when she was asked to.

Once these traditional rites have been performed, it does not take long before the baby is born and everyone joins to rejoice at its birth, with Chinua running out to get the new mother a big bottle of Odeku, the traditional name given to Guinness stout. It is believed that Guinness stout is medicinal and helps to replenish the lost energy and strength which the pain of childbirth may have caused any new mother. It is also believed that Odeku helps to stimulate the mammary gland of the new mother, causing enough milk to be produced for her new baby.

Such was the in-depth involvement and impact Chinua had within her community despite the labelling; she still contributed positively in her community which sometimes made her indispensable. Because of her carriage and strength and positive contribution and village wisdom and her interest in making sure that every woman who came within her reach must be empowered to be financially independent.

Chapter Nine

Diamonds Come in Small Packs

Another good attribute of Chinua, outside her beauty , was her high IQ and the ease with which she remembered events and happenings. If she had been educated, she would have been a good historian as she remembered every single history relating to the unwavering Nigerian political system and the incessant history of coups and counter-coups.

Part of Chinua's pastime is to sit with her children and the neighbours' children and then she would tell them the story of the Nigeria/Biafra war and the subsequent history of coups and counter-coups. Chinua understood what it meant to spend quality time with her children. Sometimes even when she felt sleepy, she still managed to sit with them to tell them stories that would help them understand their history.

Chinua would remember vividly how she used to walk miles to 'attack market' during the war, to fend for a living. She would also passionately speak about her late father, for whom she had so much respect and admiration despite his unfaithfulness to her mother.

While telling her story, Chinua would pause and say, 'Oh, if not for that my mother's bad friend, my father would still be married to my mother today and possibly still be alive. This bad woman and her daughter ripped off my father, made him sell off all his properties in Enugu and, after squandering the money, abandoned my father, giving him conditions on how and when he could see his only son Chiboy.'

According to Chinua, her father died early as a result of the heartbreak he suffered at the hands of his second wife, whom he married in the desperate bid to have a male child. She would say to anyone who cared to hear that her father was a legend and a warrior who stood for any cause he believed in. She took after her father and did not have any regrets at all.

'Where are my children of Africa?' Chinua would call out. 'Gwendolyn, Tata, Mimi, Tega the Urhobo boy, Nwa Chief, where are all of you?"

'I am in the mood today,' she would call out. 'I need to tell you people a story of your country Nigeria.' She would go on and on.

'I made a good sale today. I deserve a cool bottle of Odeku beer mixed with a bottle of Fanta. One of you go get some drinks, let's all drink and be merry,' she would say with an unusual spark in her eyes filled with sorrow and a form of distant aloofness and stillness which did not show the happiness, joy, and satisfaction which she wanted her children to believe existed.

She would unwrap money tied away at the edge of her wrapper. 'Buy Fanta and Coke for everyone here and then one big Odeku for me.'

She would always start her story by saying, 'In those days when men were men and women were won by those who deserve them'. She would have preferred a night out with a real man. She would then say, however, she prefers the role of mother, and being given the opportunity to be a mother and carer of her children, whom she adores, she has no regrets.

Once Chinua's Odeku mixed with Fanta was served in her large metal cup, she would then take a long sip while making funny sounds saying, 'Ekwensu na Ndi irom Ntoi', meaning 'Woe unto the devil and my enemies'.

'Do you know that the first Nigerian national election took place in 1964?' she would go on. At this time, all eyes would be fixed on her. 'This election involved a lot of *ojorro* and *wuru wuru*,' she would say in pidgin English, meaning that the election was marked by boycotts, malpractice, and violence.

'The sojas,' in Nigeria, referring to the military, 'they have always been hungry for power.' She would go on and on, reminding her children of how Major General Aguiyi-Ironsi, an ethnic Igbo man from the Eastern Region came to power in 1966 as a result of a military coup.

'Aguiyi was my brother,' she would go on, 'but I don't think that coop' meaning *coup*, 'was necessary. It cost him his life as he was killed a few months later and Gawon' meaning Major General Gowon, 'came to power.'

When Gawon declared no victor, no vanquished after the war, he continued to enjoy power and delayed handing over to the civilians through election. There was a 'coop' again in 1975, and Muritala, referring to Brigadier Murtala Ramat Mohammed, took over Gawon; this same Muritala was killed a year later and Obusonjor, meaning Olusegun Obasanjo, took over government.

What Chinua lacked in pronunciation, she gained by her ability to remember very important events like the Nigerian political history.

Chinua had a penchant for pronouncing things her own way, be it a person's name, appellation, or even inanimate objects. She would pronounce sugar as 'suga', virgin as 'vargin', prick as 'prig', nutmeg as 'gun nut', 'diginity' for dignity. She always said education gives a woman 'diginity', instead of dignity.

'I don suffer o!' Chinua would always say.

'I don try as a woman also, I tried even like a man well well. If una no praise me,' she would say, 'I go praise myself.' She went on in the usual pidgin English which was the means of communication used by most people within the community.

'Hmm, hmm,' Gwendolyn, one of the children sitting next to Chinua exclaimed, using her right hand to shut her nostrils. 'Who mess?' she asked in pidgin English, meaning 'Who farted?'

'Shut up,' Chinua would say. 'You don't speak when an adult farts, just pretend it's the smell of perfume,' she would go on. 'Smell of perfume?' Gwendolyn retorted. 'Yes, smell of perfume.'

At this stage, the smell had enveloped the whole room where Chinua and her children sat while they all listened to her story. Each one of her children would then suddenly start standing up. 'Huuun, huuun, disgusting like rotten egg.' Amidst laughter and embarrassment, they would all disperse from this interesting gathering, bringing a once-enjoyable evening with their mother to an abrupt end.

'Where are you people going now?' Chinua would want to know. 'What is driving you people?'

'Una papa,' she would say, referring to their father, 'una papa nor dey mess?' She would go on in pidgin English, 'You children have missed the best part of my story tonight, I will reserve it for another day. Now, Gwendolyn, go put hot water on fire and start preparing eba and bring out the egusi soup from the cupboard and warm it. It's time for dinner, tomorrow is another day.

'Hey,' Chinua would exclaim, 'what is today's date? Is today Monday or Tuesday? What month are we? Onwa Mbu, Onwa Abuo, Onwa Ife Eke, Onwa Ano, Onwa Agwu, Onwa Ifejioku . . . grrrrrrrrrrrrrrrrrrrrr' a snoring sound from Chinua, clearing her throat, 'Onwa Okike, Onwa Ajana, Onwa Ede Ajana, Onwa Uzo Alusi . . .'

Referring to the traditional Igbo calendar, she would go on: 'Eke, Orie, Afo, Nkwo . . . grrrrrrrrrrrrrrrrrrrrrr.'

'Madam de madam,' Gwendolyn called out cynically. 'Liquidator,' Chinua responded in between snores. *Liquidator* was the word used by Chinua to describe Gwendolyn. Chinua had this feeling that of all her children, Gwendolyn would cause her much grief, pain, and monetary loss. Gwendolyn was the one who would run away with boys, get heartbroken, and then also perform badly in her academics.

Gwendolyn would retake her exams and always repeat one class each year while her mates were being promoted to the next higher class. Chinua was convinced in that her daughter Gwendolyn was an "Ogbanje" and her beloved late aunt "Ogbeyanu" meaning a maiden who can never be betrothed to the poor. Chinua loved her aunt Ogbeyanu, who died in mysterious circumstances and whose physical attributes Gwendolyn exhibited.

According to Chinua, Gwendolyn was conceived immediately after the death of Aunt Ogbeyanu. Aunt Ogbeyanu had unusual characteristics just like Gwendolyn; she had great physical beauty, fastidiousness, and a high level of unreasonable demand for attention each time within the family. Several times, Chinua had been consulted by family members who suspected that Gwendolyn was an Ogbanje child (repeater child who dies and keeps returning to be reborn to her parent).

They kept advising Chinua to stabilize and disengage Gwendolyn completely from the Ogbanje band, but she refused to be involved with any such fetish practices, saying that this belief was totally and completely nonsense as there is no such thing as Ogbanje or reincarnation.

She would therefore not be involved in an elaborate pagan ritual in which her child would be required to dance to frenzied pagan music while a concoction in a medicine pot is placed on her head, after which she would then reveal the place where the object of the oath has been secreted, which is then excavated or otherwise exposed, and then the child recovers.

Gwendolyn was also the only child of Chinua for whom she fought every male bachelor who was her neighbour, as they tried to woo Gwendolyn to have an intimate relationship with her.

Chinua never stopped reminding her female children that once they were touched by a male, they would automatically get pregnant. Touching in Chinua's interpretation meant touching any part of her daughter's body. According to her, you do not have to have direct sexual intercourse with a male to get pregnant. Once he touches your hands, you get pregnant; her daughters believed this myth and that helped to minimise any teenage pregnancy or promiscuity.

The incident of religious violence experienced by Gwen when she was in high school affected her so much that she became almost frigid. Years after this incident of rape, she still could not come to terms with her ill luck—a term which she used to refer to herself each time she faced any struggle or challenges in her very short life.

Her experience made her feel inadequate and so she shut down from fear of intimacy, guilt, a feeling of inadequacy while at the same time, she understood that you can't love somebody without being truthful to them.

Gwendolyn yearned so much for that father figure to provide for, nurture, and guide her.

She was not confident her mother was capable of bringing all of these to the table: the emotional relationships between her and her father, the feeling of pain and anger. It's like you get the heart and the wallet; she wanted so much to strip off her ego and inner desires, fears, and insecurities so that all that was left was happiness.

Despite this seeming power play between Chinua and Gwendolyn, their mother-daughter relationship was infinitely easier despite Gwendolyn's lack of academic achievement.

Gwendolyn's traumatic life journey, however, brought on a mild depressive state as she gradually experienced a spiral of events in her life. She silently continued to feel low, stopped seeing friends, and continued to feel worse each day. She tried to deal with this problem alone without discussing it with anyone. She was most times extremely tired and had a loss of interest in life and even her personal hygiene. She had mood swings and suffered a low self-esteem due to early life experiences. All of these were unknown by friends and family because of lack of knowledge and understanding. Gwendolyn was to face this demon alone later in her marital life when it presented itself in full circle after the birth of her first child.

> Yes, I am a single parent,
> No, my parents aren't raising my child.
> Yes, we will exist.
> I am your parent, you are my child . . .
> —Unknown

Torn Between Two Cultures

Good character is the life of right conduct—right conduct in relation to other persons and in relation to oneself (Palmer 1986)

'If the culture and tradition of a people perish, the people also perish.' This was Chinua's daily quote to her children. She tried to raise them to understand the custom of her people. Chinua taught her children a lot about life. She spoke to them mostly about how compulsory it is to have an intimate relationship with God. She taught them about marriage , friendship, disappointment, hope, faith, managing finance, business, about relationship with others, kindness and ability to give to the needy.

Chinua taught her children about the virtues of goodness and the vices that come with being bad.

The strife between Chinua and all Gwendolyn's male admirers was also a source of tension between the two.

Each day, Gwendolyn discussed her mother's overprotective nature with her friends. 'I don't know why this woman will not let me be,' said Gwendolyn to her bosom friend Judy Anne. Judy Anne had become a very close buddy of Gwendolyn over the years. She felt comfortable being with her and jesting with her.

Judy was a Londoner whose parents were of African origin. She was sent to attend high school in Nigeria, from the age of eleven years. This was the in thing now for most African parents in diaspora who preferred their teenage children to attend school in Africa in order to have a taste of the African culture and be able to imbibe some African discipline and the variety in culture. The children became familiarized with the African culture and also seized the opportunity to know uncles, cousins, nieces, nephews, and grandparents and to grow up in an environment where morality and good character were relatively regarded as a watchword.

It is therefore in a bid to acquire these progressive traditional African values like obedience and respect for elders and at the same time imbibe the duty and obligation to care for parents at old age rather than dumping them in nursing homes, community orientation, good moral character and behaviour including ability to cook and tidy up that Judy Anne was sent back to Nigeria to live with her maternal aunt and her uncle.

Once Judy Anne tasted the rich culture of the Nigerian people, she kept on returning to Nigeria at every opportunity made available to her. Judy decided to do a twelve-month gap year in Nigeria after she graduated from the university.

Judy Anne's aunt whom she lived with, happened to live in the same neighbourhood as Chinua and her children.

Judy's parents were convinced that this African culture could be better learnt by living with and observing the people of that society through interacting with them. Judy's parents lost one of their sons, Judy's brother Ryan Ugochukwu, to a sad incident, an unexplained knife attack on his way home after a night out with friends, against his parents' wish.

Ryan hated his African name Ugochukwu and would always say to his parents, 'Don't call me my African name in the presence of my friends.' Each time Ryan made this comment, his mother never failed to remind him of how important it was for him never to forget his roots.

Each time Ryan had a heated argument with his dad about his group of friends and the incessant drinking, smoking, and partying rather than being focussed on his university education, he would become quite agitated.

On this particular day in question, Ryan held the collar of his father's shirt and pinned his father to the wall; he refused to let go despite his mother's pleadings. He kept on screaming, 'I hate you, I hate you, I hate you.' The neighbours called the police, who then asked questions, more about Ryan's safety and where he should spend the night before returning him to his home when peace finally returned.

The disrespectful way Ryan held on to his father's shirt and the physical attack on his father was never addressed. His father kept his cool, stoically wondering what had come over his son. This incident happened days after another black family had their two daughters taken into foster care by the social services, because of what they called neglect arising out of the fact that these girls wore partly wet clothes to school and the school contacted social services to report what they observed.

Judy's parents were part of the people who fought to make sure that these children were returned home and the necessary parental support given to their parents so that they can cope with the challenges of parenting and working full-time. It would appear, upon carefully carrying out their investigation, the parents of these two children had housing problems which they needed to be resolved to enable them properly take care of their children in an environment which was conducive and habitable. Once the support needed by this family was provided, the children settled in and family life sprang back to normal, thanks to the intervention of Judy's parents and other concerned neighbours who supported this family and made sure that they attended all conferences and meetings fixed by Social Services to safeguard these children.

Judy's father never stopped telling anyone that cared to listen how in Africa it was a whole community that raised a child with the support and help of friends and family acknowledging the enormous task.

When this incident occurred in Judy's family, Ryan was taken to the home of his dad's younger brother, who at this time lived around Catford. A couple of days later, he returned home and refused to say a word to his father while his mother tried to advise him about his behaviour and how everything done was for his own future good, and to protect the family name and his future.

Judy's mum always used to say to Ryan, 'We are only trying to save you from yourself. Everything we are doing to help you is for your own good.' Ryan would sometimes say to them, 'I hate you, I can't wait to leave this house.'

When Ryan went out clubbing a week after his confrontation with his dad, unfortunately, he never made it home alive. Ryan was stabbed in a London nightclub while arguing with another gang member in a bid to show the superiority of their gang over the other.

The investigation into Ryan's murder was even more traumatic than the news of his death itself. The killers were found, and during investigation, they confessed that they were members of a rival gang within another estate who wanted to prove their supremacy over the gang which Ryan belonged to. These young lads were sentenced, a sentence which would never bring back Ryan to life.

******   **********   ******

Ryan's death was traumatic and his family became uncontrollable and full of regrets as they had turned down advice from other family members to take Ryan back to Nigeria years ago when they first noticed a drastic change in his behaviour. It was not until Judy's family had a very bad experience with Social Services that they made a decision to change things for good.

They felt the system dictated the pace at which they could raise and nurture their children. They did not feel supported within the community; they thought the family counsellors dictated to them how to raise their children. The system failed to set boundaries for children, to save them from destroying themselves. The system encouraged positive reinforcement for negative behaviour. They had also communicated with other parents who felt disappointed and betrayed by the lack of support from Social Services.

Judy's mum always used to say, 'My children must be brought up with a serenity and softness which is love and a bulletproof strength in their soul. They must be unbreakable in a beautiful way, not a lost way.'

Judy's mum was not alone in her plight. It was the same story everywhere. 'There is a popular African saying,' she would always say, 'it takes a village to raise a child and a community to keep the parents sane.' She would lecture anyone who cared to listen to her, by saying, 'What is experienced by Africans in diaspora is a completely different norm where a child tells the parent, 'Shut up, I hate you' just because there are no boundaries set. Rather than support us, by providing help and assistance to us in the community, on how to successfully raise our children to be responsible adults and at the same time not to forget their African culture and roots which is their history, we feel rather victimised by the system, which sends conflicting, negative messages to our children and tries to separate our family by inciting the children to be disrespectful through conduct, encouraging families to be separated and undermining the importance of parental control and guidance, which is detrimental to family cohesion and the mental growth and moral development of our children.' Judy's mum would speak passionately about this area of interest to anyone, on the bus, on the tube, in church or even when she goes shopping in Asda, Tesco, or Aldi. Once you said hello to her in the store, she managed to engage you, non-stop speaking on these mind-blowing issues about how she would have loved all her children to imbibe her African culture as part of their heritage.

'In raising our children in diaspora,' she continued, 'we must not lose our African cultural heritage, we must not lose our cultural identity as Africans,' Judy's mum would always say.

When her family was brought to the attention of Social Services, she felt quite betrayed by the way her case was handled. 'We want to be with our children,' Judy's mum once screamed out to one social worker who visited her home unannounced. 'We are Africans, we have a history and a culture, we are taught to respect our elders and to have acceptable behaviours which we use to set boundaries in order to make our children productive in our society. Our culture cannot be undermined just because we are in diaspora, our children must be encouraged to imbibe our culture, to understand their roots and their heritage.' She went on and on.

'We love our children enough to set boundaries for them so that they become useful members of the society where we live,' continued Judy's mum. 'All my husband and I want is your support in being able to do that, rather than trying to incriminate us. You cannot love my child more than me,' screamed Judy's mum. Unknown to Judy's mum, her screaming was all the time interpreted to mean that she was aggressive, and because of her aggression, she was deemed not to be a fit mother.

After several meetings with the social workers, a parental class was introduced to her and her husband. Her husband blatantly refused to attend this parental class as he could not understand why after over eighteen years of raising his children, he was suddenly seen as someone who lacks parental skills. 'These people lack understanding of my family need,' he once muttered. 'I don't understand what I stand to gain from attending such a meeting,' said Judy's dad angrily. 'Never mind, I will attend,' said Judy's mum, 'and once I find out the intricacies and it becomes interesting and useful, then you can join me.' She tried to prompt her husband reluctantly, not sounding convincing herself. Unfortunately despite showing interest in attending this parental class, months after it was mentioned to her, she never received any help as to where and how to achieve this. She felt betrayed and undermined, thus causing her to wonder in what way she and her family had been helped by the system which once made them think they were there to help.

As Judy's mum tried to discuss her concerns with a confidant, it then dawned on her that a lot more families were suffering in silence all over, because of the lack of support received from the system which pretended to want to be involved in their family life. There were stories of several children taken into care who ordinarily would have been assisted and supported within the enclaves of their family without having to find another family for them, thereby destroying them both emotionally and psychologically through neglect and abuse suffered in foster homes. Judy's mum met women who were also given alternatives to leave their matrimonial homes rather than assist the family by offering the desired help and support for the family, depending on the intricacies of what their problems were.

The stories shared by thousands of families in diaspora who had lost their children to the system, because of carelessness which ordinarily would have been avoided were they properly guided, supported, and given a second chance, taking the interest of the children into consideration and understanding that the best place suited for a child is within the home environment.

This was the situation in Judy's home which later prompted a visit to Africa in a bid to allow the children have another perspective of life.

During a family vacation in Africa, Judy's parents never stopped reminding her that for the culture of a people to flourish, the people must possess the appropriate character and the moral foundation to cultivate and sustain it. They went on to inform her that there must be loyalty to that culture and tradition which must be instilled in the people at an early age. If all parents in diaspora instill that culture in their children from an early age, perhaps that will bring about a better attitude towards parenting, where the children will from the start understand what respect for elders is, and also the importance of honouring parents rather than abandoning them in their old age.

Upon hearing this lecture about culture and heritage over and over again, it was therefore out of curiosity and a love for something different and more challenging that Judy Anne accepted to remain in Nigeria to continue her education.

'I am excited about this idea,' she said. 'I will definitely enjoy the experience—the warm weather, the people, the community and the extended family members. Please, Mum, say yes, I don't want to go back to England. I can enrol in September and start school immediately since Aunty is the head teacher of one of the most prestigious, sought-after private schools in the community.' It took another three years after Judy Anne had continued to live in Nigeria, returning home to England during school holidays and breaks, before she met Gwendolyn in church and the two of them struck up a friendship immediately despite the age difference. The relationship was cordial at first until Judy Anne's second return to Nigeria during her gap year.

Judy Anne was twenty-two years old when she returned to Nigeria. Having sat for her GCSE and passed with very high grades, she went back to London to acquire a university education.

She looked physically older than her age due to her very tall svelte build, a physique which she inherited from her mother. She returned to study in one of London's best universities after her GCSE in Nigeria. She studied sociology and anthropology and, after qualifying with flying colours, decided to take a gap year which she decided to spend in Nigeria.

Gwendolyn, on the other hand, was nineteen years old, had sat for her GCSE more than three different times and, upon failing on the third attempt, was almost giving up when she was encouraged to try again, an attempt which saw her coming out with flying colours. These two young people, despite the disparity in their background and their intellectual ability, enjoyed each other's company each time they met, either in church or outside the community.

Gwendolyn gained admission into Bendel State University to study English and at the time she graduated of University and had gone for her National Youth Service and back, she was reconnected with her childhood friend Judy Anne, who at this time had returned to Nigeria for her gap year. Judy Anne called her gap year 'my twelve months of renaissance and eureka', meaning a rebirth of a classical interest in African culture and heritage.

What Judy Anne learnt during this twelve-month period would assist her in her life's journey despite the struggles, trials, and temptations which she later battled in her life as the years rolled past.

Chapter Ten

One afternoon as both Judy Anne and Gwendolyn sat outside the verandah of Gwendolyn's house, these two young women from two different backgrounds decided to compare notes.

Gwendolyn felt quite comfortable talking with her Londoner friend Judy. There was always this ease she felt each time she was with Judy. She saw her as her sister from another mother. She also imagined in her mind's eye that Judy's father in London would be her imaginary father whom she hoped to reunite with someday when she travelled to London.

'What a great family reunion that day would be,' she often thought to herself, hoping that a day like that would one day come.

Gwendolyn still felt the pain and rejection of not being fortunate enough to have her father in her life. She always blamed herself for this, despite not clearly being able to convince herself of the reasons for this self-blame. Each time she was with her friends and they talked about their fathers, she tried as much as possible to avoid any eye contact with them. This topic had become a demon which Gwendolyn chose not to fight, despite having a fighting spirit. 'I will continue to forbear this demon,' she would say to herself. 'I am a survivor, I have survived all these years without a father, I will live without him, thinking in my mind that he is dead.' This was Gwendolyn's way of overcoming the rejection and sadness she felt knowing that her father was not in her life.

'I don't know why this woman won't leave me alone,' moaned Gwendolyn.

'What woman are you referring to?' asked Judy.

'Who else? My mother. Am I not of age? I am a grown woman and yet this woman will not allow me to have relationships. I will one day run away from this house so I can feel free to be myself.'

In response to Gwen's remarks, Judy chuckled and then replied, 'Do you know why my parents brought me back to Nigeria to study when I was in high school? They believe life in the UK is a bit too wild and that children have too much independence and are too exposed to all sorts of technology like the Internet, iPad, and iPhone.' My parents seriously believe that exposure to these gadgets, if not monitored, exposes children to all kinds of information which people their age should not be exposed to.'

'Since coming to school in Nigeria, I have come to realise that there is still little difference between the two. The world has become a global village and children in Africa are able to access information on the Web just like every other developed country. What every child needs therefore is good parenting and supervision irrespective of whether they are in school in the UK or in Nigeria.

'I wish I could convince my mother then to take me back to the UK, I miss home. I miss the weather and the feeling of safety and security which people take for granted in the UK. I thought then to myself that you only have to dial 999 and the police will be at your doorstep to save situations. I thought the system worked and that was my comfort zone, however, despite all of the systems put in place, upon reflection, I can at least say sincerely that there is a great difference in raising children in these two different worlds. The opportunity given me to visit Nigeria exposed me to a different environment, making me appreciate my life and people around me better. Before I visited Nigeria, I thought I could do anything and get away with it. It was also difficult for my parents to set boundaries because they could not understand why, as Africans, they could not speak to their child or raise their child the African way. Looking back now, I feel really guilty about what my siblings and I put my parents through, but thank God that we were all given a second chance to change from our ways after the death of my brother, God rest his soul,' said Judy.

'The environment in Nigeria is different for good moral education and the discipline instilled into children by not only family members but all members of the community. Moreover, my living in Nigeria has helped me a great deal to be better person. I have value for education, which consists of not only good character but intellectual capabilities which has been instilled in me.

'I am now educated both in mind and in morals. Before now, I knew nothing about Africa—my heritage—other than the distorted and negative views the Western media houses have about the African continent. Had my parents not taken the bold step to allow me the opportunity of an appropriate and realistic information about Africa, I would perhaps not have been able to learn this rich culture and would have continued basking under a negative euphoria,' continued Judy.

'I know about a lot of my dad's friends who came to the UK in the '60s, who never went back home or took their children home to Africa because of the new lifestyle and foreign culture they acquired, abandoning their own culture, for that of the white man,' emphasised Judy as she gesticulated with her hands. 'Some of them later got divorced or lost their wives after their children who by now had become so westernised to the extent that they never came round to visit or care for them. Some of these men died after living a very lonely and forlorn life while some who never had a family in the UK but acquired considerable wealth lost all their estate upon death, because of the fact that no information was given about their next of kin, allowing the state to take over their personal assets upon their death. Such people may as well have had family members in Africa who could have inherited their wealth if they kept steady contact with their home in Africa and if they had also imbibed that culture of visiting home when they were younger.

'I remember a certain middle-aged man who used to attend my parents' family meeting, he lived alone all his life, ate alone and died alone. A story has it that on one fateful evening, this man was eating alone and as he cracked the bone of chicken which he ate, he choked on the chicken bone and could not save himself by quickly calling an ambulance because he lived alone. His corpse was discovered weeks after, it was noticed that he had not been seen around by anyone and his phone also stopped ringing as his battery ran down. He lived uncelebrated and died uncelebrated because he abandoned his progressive traditional African values.

'Judy, are you sure you are truly twenty-two years old?' asked Gwen. 'You are a historian and quite detailed, in just less than fifteen minutes, you have taken me through all the stories told you by your father and also other personal encounters or experiences you have enjoyed by having access to two different rich cultures which you are fortunate enough to be part of.'

'Huh huh,' mumbled Judy Anne, 'what do you reckon?'

This time, the conversation had now shifted to Gwendolyn and there was a silence on Gwendolyn's side. 'Why are you suddenly quiet, Gwen?' Judy fondly used a short form of Gwendolyn to refer to her older friend. 'I actually drifted and you don't want to know what is on my mind,' Gwendolyn replied.

Gwendolyn was actually feeling lonely and empty inside of her each time her friend Judy mentioned her mum and dad who lived together as a family unit in the UK and whom Judy shared a close relationship with.

'One of these days as you plan to return, I will travel to the UK with you,' smiled Gwendolyn. 'Is this why you look lost?' asked Judy. 'Not really,' replied Gwendolyn, 'there is a whole lot going on in my life, I can't seem to place it. Since turning twenty years of age, I have continuously felt this emptiness which I cannot place and I strongly feel that I need someone to fill this emptiness outside my family.'

'What?' replied Judy. 'Do you know what that means?'

'Of course I do!' Gwendolyn continued moaning. 'Are you a virgin?' asked Gwendolyn.

'Me a virgin?' retorted Judy. 'No of course, these days there are very few virgins my age.'

'What?' retorted Gwendolyn sharply. 'How come your mum and dad allowed you to be deflowered?' screamed Gwen rolling her eyes down and up with her hands over her mouth and a look of surprise over her face.

'No, my mum and dad did not allow me to be deflowered, I allowed myself to be deflowered. You don't want to know what else I got myself into. I got into a gang and smoking of weed and street fighting and all sorts at a very young age. I was always getting into trouble even though I did not lack anything. My brother also died from this uncontrollable lifestyle. I was my own boss and became uncontrollable, not sure if it was the open-door policy of the system or just plain influence from my friends. Our teachers could not control us because they were so scared of us to the extent that sometimes I pitied them.

'On the home front, my mum and dad were never there. They worked full-time and had a particular target to meet as far as societal echelon was concerned. They were chasing the pounds. They could afford expensive holidays for me and my other siblings, expensive clothing, and luxury cars, however, they hardly have time for me and my siblings. Because they were hardly there, they left us in the hands of child minders, after-school clubs, neighbours, and friends.

'I remember vividly when in school, I was almost raped by a family friend's husband when upon short notice, my mum requested they pick me from school when she could not meet the 3.15 p.m. closing hour and then she quickly phoned her friend and the husband to please pick me up with their own daughter, since we attended the same school. The only thing that saved me from this beast of a man was the fact that I had already been educated by my mum about the possibility of such things happening to any teenage girl my age and the precautions I should take.

'On that day, I ran off screaming out of the house once I was able to free myself from the wicked grip of this man whom I had to deceive into believing that I needed to use the toilet. I then ran non-stop to another neighbour, shaking and dumbstruck, pointing to the direction of this man's house. The female neighbour whom I ran to then called my mum and dad, who left everything they were doing and rushed down to my rescue.

'Thank God for neighbours with African values, even though I was not expected, as I knocked on the door, they opened it up to let me in. And their kindness saved my life.

'I don't really remember quite clearly what happened after that incident, what I remember is that my parents confronted this man and his wife, and threatened them with the police.'

'Hmm. I thought it was only me ooooooooo,' chipped in Gwendolyn, giving Judy a light slap on the back as a mark of emphasis. 'You need to see the endless street fights my mum engages in, each time a male shows an interest in me. She fights like a man, with so much determination as if her life depends on it.

'Once my mum pulled the penis of one bachelor who, unknown to her, I had started a relationship with. Once my mum got wind of this clandestine relationship with this apprentice man, she became so furious, she sprang into action like a lioness, waited for this neighbour when he was on his way from work and unsuspectingly attacked him from behind while consciously pulling his scrotum, bringing about a temporary loss of consciousness to this man who was later rushed to the hospital. My mum never regretted her action till date. When questioned by the police, she told them that indeed she justified why a 'peter file', meaning *paedophile*, like this man should be castrated for trying to spoil the child of a hard-working mother like her who struggled to raise her children single-handedly without any support.

'My mother was released by the police officers and all charges against her were dropped after cautioning her not to overreact again if she found herself in such a situation in the future. Typical of my mum not to take the advice, as she went about telling everyone who cared to listen how this male neighbour has a very tiny penis and was not worth her daughter's attention and love. She kept on calling this man 'earthworm', referring to the size of his manhood, to his embarrassment and shame. The man moved out of the neighbourhood to an unknown location, because of the shame and embarrassment he suffered upon encountering my mum.

'Hmm,' chipped in Judy, 'your mum was lucky to have gotten away with that conduct oh. In the UK, she would have been charged with GBH.'

'Ha ha ha!' laughed Gwendolyn. 'This girl, you will kill me with your *okpokpo oyibo* Queen's English. Which one is GBH?'

'Oh, GBH?' said Judy. 'It's an abbreviation of grievous bodily harm. If it was in the UK, the state would have prosecuted your mum as there is zero tolerance for such antisocial behaviour, notwithstanding that this man may have been at fault by trying to woo and deceive you into having an affair with him considering your age difference. That would have been investigated also and your opinion sought as to whether you are ready to press charges against this man, since you were already over eighteen years of age at the time this incident happened,' said Judy.

Judy continued to analyse the differences she has experienced in the two societies she was exposed to. 'What I have noticed since starting school in Nigeria is that there are loads of things which usually are taken for granted in people's conduct and their social interaction with one another. Take for example, I noticed that in Nigeria, adults who are over twenty-five years of age and sometimes even adults in their forties still continue to live with their parents under the same roof, unlike the UK, where young people prefer to leave home at a very young age of eighteen to twenty-one years, in their quest to lead an independent life away from their parents.' Judy continued in her narration: 'Looking at both cultures now, there are certain practices in the UK that I would rather not accept, and same goes to what is seen as acceptable in Nigeria.

'Now my question is, why do grown-ups in this country still feel that their parents are obliged to them both economically and otherwise?' asked Judy.

'Maybe due to the economic situation in the country and the lack of access to social housing and other benefits which ordinarily the government should have been able to provide for them to make them independent of their parents whilst trying to find a job.

'More importantly, there are no jobs available in Nigeria and so, you see a young graduate returning home after the National Youth Service job hunting each day while still depending on their parents for accommodation, feeding, and clothing. This is a normal situation in this country.

'There are some parents who also take pride in keeping their children around them for some selfish reasons, using this as a tool of control,' laughed Gwen. 'Such parents encourage their children to get married and continue to live with them while procreation takes place within the household. There are also some parents who become overprotective of their children to the extent that the female children become frigid from the negative stories told about men and women and from failed relationships experienced by them.

'I know of some of my mum's friends who have never been married all their lives and never had children, and when they are asked why this is, you will be shocked at their response.

'You won't realize how incredibly hilarious and bizarre your upbringing might have been until you compare it with others.

'Aunty Ogbeyanu is one typical example of a woman who lived her life without planning or strategising. I found the courage to ask her why she was not married despite being such a beautiful woman with good manners,' lectured Gwen.

'I was shocked at what she told me. Hear her. "Gwen, Gwen, I like your courage o! My dear, I would have loved to be married if I had good advisers around me. My mother was exceptionally overprotective because of her ignorance and selfishness—she did not mean bad, but unfortunately, she kept on warding off all my suitors. From the time I was eighteen years old, people started approaching my parents, seeking my hand in marriage, and each time they came, my mother would turn down their proposals, saying they should please stop distracting me from getting a good education. There were also suitors and their families from abroad, who wanted me to relocate with them and then continue my education abroad. I remember one of them particularly offered to write an agreement indicating that once all marriage rites were completed, he would make sure I continue with my education once I join him abroad. Hmm . . ."

'She paused again and continued, "My mother refused and banned this man and his family from ever setting foot in her compound again. When he tried to contact me, I then lied to him that I have a phobia for flying and what will then be my fate if the plane crashes and I am found inside ? ;what will I then tell my God that I am on a voyage to meet with a man whom my mother does not approve of?

"'Gwen, women are like flowers," continued Aunty Ogbeyanu. "I know it because I have experienced it," she went on with a very sad gaze in her eyes. "At first I thought to myself it will get better once I graduate from the university. Unfortunately it took a different turn at this stage. My mother also puts down certain criteria as to the kind of man I should marry.

I found out that I was wiser, (or so I thought), more sophisticated and financially stronger than most of my contemporaries. I could not stand any struggling man. As a result, I resorted to sugar daddies, married men who were capable of meeting my financial needs. I changed these married men like anyone would change their knickers. I thought I was enjoying my life. It was a wild, wild life," continued Aunty Ogbeyanu. At this stage, her voice was shaking and filled with emotions.

As Aunty Ogbeyanu continued with her story, she said, "I stuck to the literal meaning of my name as I swore that no poor man is worthy of my love. At the age of thirty, I was controlling a six-figure bank account, had a fleet of expensive cars, and also started separating myself from not just following any married man but intentionally looking for the super-rich married men who could hook up with me not only for fun and sex but also for business proposals. As my biological clock kept ticking, my appetite for money and material things grew enormously. I became so materialistic and covetous that I could not be seen hanging out with just anybody except the who's who in the town where we lived, and beyond."

'Aunty Ogbeyanu continued, "I befriended politicians, governors, senators, legislators, and even presidents. I felt I was invincible and boasted to anyone who cared to listen that no man can resist my beauty. I also broke many homes and one thing I found quite amazing is that these same men who left their wives because of my relationship with them ended up leaving and dumping me for other women, sometimes my very close friends or younger relations. It became like a case of dog eat dog. A few times I attended church and sought counselling, and I found myself seducing the head of the church in my desperate bid to become the first lady or church mama, despite not having the spiritual ability to be a pastor's wife.'

"'One thing I regret so much," continued Aunty Ogbeyanu, "is the fact that my mum kept on encouraging my escapades each time I came home to visit her. She never told me that what I was doing was wrong. She encouraged this frivolous lifestyle perhaps because of the booty I handed to her upon any visit.

"'I bought my first home at the age of twenty-five years, two years after my graduation from the university—a home bought for me on my twenty-fifth birthday, from one of my numerous rich fellas. I also spoilt my mum with the booty acquired from these money-miss-road pot-bellied men who never get satisfied with one woman and who, at the back of my mind, I saw as money-spinning machines who should be used and dumped.

"'In my craving for more wealth, I met with some very wild females who came from either the same poor back ground as me or even from a more impoverished background and who from day one have sworn that the poverty they suffered at home while being raised is the last they will ever experience in their lives. This group of wild girls were a bang, they would party all week and all night with these married men jumping from one luxury hotel to the other. They carried money in Ghana-must-go bags. They wore all named designer labels. Their fear of poverty made them desperate to the extent that they would even say 'I do' to any of these rich married men if peradventure they proposed. These girls travelled round the world with these men and were spoilt with all kinds of expensive gifts like Rolex wristwatches, Dolce & Gabbana handbags, Louis Vuitton designer bags, Givenchy, and Yves Saint Laurent shoes and bags. The least expensive gift would be a bottle of White Diamonds expensive perfume from Elizabeth Arden. Once, one of these men bought me a perfume, Anais Anais, and upon handing over this perfume, the first thing he callously said to me was that he hoped the two of us would not end up like Ananias and Sapphira in the Holy Book of life, as if indirectly confirming our indecent involvement with each other."

'Aunty Ogbeyanu continued to tell of her experience of life thus: "It may also interest you to know that some of these girls whom I called my friends were also from very rich homes but their foundation and upbringing were corrupted. They watched their parents involve themselves in extramarital activities, mum cheating on dad and dad cheating on mum. It was like Armageddon! Some of them were also so worldly wise as they copied their parents' lifestyle of lies, deception, and greed in any relationship they find themselves."

'Because their mums and dads involved themselves in deals and contracts which encourage bribery and corruption, back-stabbing, and all kinds of shady deals, they therefore in the same manner allowed the love of money to dictate their happiness. Their worship of money and material things became a way of life because of the dysfunctionality of the parents which badly affected them to the extent that they no longer believed in relationships based on love.

"'I remember one of my friends saying her mum advised her never to start life with any man who is poor because there is no benefit when the man becomes rich, he will still cheat and maltreat you anyway, so what's the point?" According to her mum, men have very poor memories when it comes to remembering favours done to them by a woman. It's better to marry a wealthy man and enjoy his wealth with your children because all men cheat anyway, said her mum.'"

Experience—the Best Teacher

"'Just like me," continued Aunty Ogbe, as I now fondly call her, "my group of friends work in oil companies, as top-flight bank executives, chief executives of their own business conglomerates, while some of them are self-employed business owners warming up to politicians for political posts and major government contracts.

"'At thirty-two years, they did not have a clue as to the importance of marriage. They became older than their age in their outlook and mentality to the extent that we found younger men boring and not having anything to offer. We had a name for them, drawback, meaning time-wasters.

"'At thirty-five years, there were some among us who got married by accident, or so we thought then, and because of the lifestyle they lived, they met very rich young unmarried guys whose means of livelihood were shady. They were into drugs, fraud, 419, hired killers, and all kinds of fraudulent businesses. They called themselves international business men, importer, and exporter. If you make the mistake of enquiring from them what they import and export, you would be gobsmacked."

'The police always visited their homes and their husbands were in and out of prison, leaving them to live alone with their children in the big empty mansions for years on end, living a life full of uncertainties, fear, anxiety, and insecurity—the same insecurity they feared which they thought money would buy them, they ended up empty at the end more than they were in the beginning.

'"Some of these friends of mine were even worse off as the married men cum sugar daddies later abandoned them with their children after their wives found out about their escapades, leaving them to become single parents by greed." Aunty Ogbeyanu's account of escapades with her friends was quite detailed and thought-provoking.

'She continued, "There was this rumour about one of these my friends, Iyabo, who married this sugar daddy thirty-eight years her senior. This man spoilt her with all kinds of expensive gifts, bought her a mansion in Ikoyi with maidservants and menservants at her beck and call. She was later found sleeping with the younger male business partner of her husband Alhaji El Amin, who upon carefully carrying out a DNA test to confirm the paternity of the three children whom all this while he was made to believe were his children, was distraught with grief and disappointment when he discovered that these children were not his biological children. Alhaji El Amin instantly seized every single possession of Iyabo and kicked her and her three children out.

'"We later heard on the grapevine that all three children were fathered by Alhaji El Amin's young business partner named Idrissa Farouk who, according to the grapevine, would not accept parental responsibility when confronted with this discovery; he screamed and shouted, 'Dan buruba, dan iska kowai, I cannot marry you fa iyabo,' he said in his typical Hausa accent. 'I can buy you Fathpinder,' meaning Pathfinder SUV, 'but I love my wife and children.'

'After this discovery, Iyabo was left with the tax of having to care for her children on her own. This incident also affected her children tremendously, as they witnessed disagreement, rejection, anger, and most importantly, the divorce process, which brought about so many traumas for the children.

"'As the children grew older, they became hurtful in their words as they felt betrayed by their mother. She, on her own, started being aggressive towards her children in a passive way by playing the blame game. She used dismissive gestures to talk down on their biological father, whom they desperately wanted to have a relationship with, but who unfortunately refused to have anything to do with them. I can go on and on telling of these life experiences faced by young women and which I don't want you to experience at all.

"'Now, Gwen, do you now see why at fifty-plus, I am still not married?" asked Aunty Ogbe. "This is because the decisions you make today in life will live with you in the future," she went on. "My advice to you, Gwen, is to strategise."

'She went on, "You see, the way you have started your life, you have to prepare and plan everything, including marriage, to be able to achieve it. You have to desire marriage just the same way you desire to attend nursery school, primary school, high school, and university, which you intend to achieve. Always put marriage in your list of plans also if it is important to you. What I and my friends did not have was good parents, good mentors, and good advisors, she went on and on.

"'Have you realised that marriage is the only school in life where certificates are issued even before you have graduated?" she asked. "This is because marriage is very, very important. The second mistake I and my friends made, apart from the fact of not having a good mentor whom we looked up to, was that we did not desire to be married. We were too worldly, vain, unreal, and artificial. We were too materialistic and had grandiose ideas of what kind of husband we should be married to.

"'We thought money could buy us happiness, we thought we had the whole world in our pocket and never thought time was passing us by. At forty-five years of age, we were still seen in clubs and five-star hotels sneaking in with one man or the other, stealing what did not belong to us.

"'We looked down on all our male contemporaries who were struggling at that time as we saw them as losers. We were too fast for our age, too worldly and too opinionated about who we were and what we wanted out of life. We thought we would never grow old, we thought all the rich men would continue to run after us. But lo and behold, we later realised how stupid we were because, as we grew older, the sugar daddies grew older and their own priorities also changed. They also grew apart from us and as they amassed wealth over the years, their desires for girls younger than us increased before our eyes and so we suddenly realised that our appointments with these sugar daddies were no longer important to them, they no longer felt enthusiastic about picking up our calls, they would give excuses with their wives and children and how it was suddenly now important for them to spend time with their wives and children.

"'In all of these, we lost out big time because we were not smart enough to have our biological children, forgetting that our biological clock kept on ticking. More importantly, because of societal demands and self-proclaimed religious upbringing even though deep inside of us we knew we were not holy, we did not think it will be acceptable for us as Christians to have children outside matrimony. We were the biggest hypocrites in town! We did not want to be laughed at, neither did we want to be rejected by any super-rich Prince Charming who was likely to propose, because of the fact that we had one or two children outside wedlock. We could not afford to take that risk at all, we wanted it all, not seeing that this game of ours was a lose-lose situation.

"'When we turned forty-five years old, I remember another friend of ours, Aisha, took a giant stride by stooping so low, or so we thought, to marry a man she met at her cousin's fortieth birthday bash. It was a whirlwind romance and these two became a pair and a thing of ridicule amongst our gang of elite friends. Six months into their relationship, wedding bells rang and we could not believe it. Aisha married this younger guy who was a teacher in a secondary school. She did everything possible to polish this guy to make him presentable to her group of elite friends. She even lied to her friends about his career, saying that he was an Oxford University graduate. She tried to make that guy what he was not and five years down the road, as she struggled to and fro from one obstetrician to the other, desiring frantically to conceive, this guy went around sleeping with anything in skirts, including their housemaid.

"'Once another friend of ours stumbled into this guy in a hotel lobby thinking he came with his wife. Immediately this friend tried to introduce herself by warming up to him, Mr G. He snobbishly pretended to be oblivious of the friendship between her and his wife. Presently as I speak, Aisha and Mr G have separated and she has filed a lawsuit against him for trying to swindle her of over £3.5 million of her hard-earned life's investments."

'Aunty Ogbeyanu continued, "This is a life we chose for ourselves, now we are all suffering the loneliness that such a life brings. Don't get me wrong, we have relationships and flings here and there, but there are no commitments to the relationship and sometimes you find yourself being emotionally drained, knowing that you had a choice to do the right thing but chose a different path just because of the love of money. There are so many ifs, Gwen. 'Had I known' is always a brother to Mr Late," she stated philosophically. "In all of this, the fact remains that my friends and I were not only foolish, but we were also unlucky because we had no good mentors or people to look up to." As Aunty Ogbeyanu continued with her story, her eyes moistened, and I could feel the emotion in her voice, an emotion which showed someone with so many regrets.

"'I have learnt not to judge single parents like your mother Chinua," Aunty Ogbeyanu went on. "Your mum is a disciplined woman but may have been unlucky in her relationships with men. She may have also become a single parent out of necessity of circumstance, not by choice. Seeing how she has struggled single-handedly to raise you and your siblings, I guess if given a chance, she would have been a devoted wife and mother.

"There are women who are married but still morally loose, they deceive themselves everyday just happy bearing the name "mrs", while leading their lives as if they are single. Some of these women are afraid to be seen as having failed, because of societal demands of being seen as married. Some also live in denial as their other half is hardly ever around, they carry on like they are married in principle but single in reality." A time spent with aunty Ogbeyanu is worth the while as she is a woman filled with experience of life.

"'I have my misgivings about women who claim to be married and yet carry on a single lifestyle daily," Aunty Ogbe went on. "Some of them pretend a lot. They live a double-standard life even with their wedding rings on. They have now formed a cliché were they try to retaliate to their husband's infidelity by also becoming involved with both younger and older male friends outside their marital home in a bid to measure up with their husband's infidelity. They are everywhere," she said, "in churches, when you go shopping, in the mosque and even in your children's school. So tell me, which is better, when it comes to morals: a single parent who works hard to fend for her young children, who carries herself with dignity and finesse each day and yet society names her immoral, or the so-called married parent who works under a cover of being married and yet defiles her marriage bed all night long? Tell me.

"'One thing you must know Gwen is the fact that in life, we learn our lessons every day," continued Aunty Ogbeyanu. "Sometimes you win, sometimes you lose. Make hay while the sun shines, so strategise!" she emphasised.

"'Once you are out of university, start planning your marriage by desiring to get married. This is the mistake most young girls make. They don't plan their lives. What you don't desire, you don't get. Be careful also how you relate with people around your school environment, your workmates, and even at the bus stop, you never know who can recommend you to be their brother's wife, friend's wife, or cousin's wife.

"'I remember the last relationship I had, which was years ago. I was heartbroken from the fact that a guy whom I rejected at school, saying point blank to him that I can never marry a poor man as my name depicts, now became the guy whom I was introduced to on a blind date. I had forgotten completely about how I mistreated this guy, but like they say, an elephant never forgets. He remembered me. However, he was now a very wealthy, affluent, and notable entrepreneur whom any girl would want to die for. The first thing this guy said to me once we met was 'I remember you! Oh wow! How are you? I recall our university days, you were one of the girls who kept us guys determined to work really hard. Thank you for rejecting me way back then, you are my best inspiration, perhaps if you did not, I would not have thought of working so hard in order to succeed. Now I am here with you. Oh the life of a woman. Now my priorities have changed. I wish I could still see that spark I saw twenty years ago, but no, all I see before me now are lines of regrets, loneliness, and remorse. I'm sorry if my words hurt you, but hey, what would you like to drink? We are still buddies.'

"'Hmm, Gwen, after my encounter with this guy on that day, I went home that night crying myself to sleep, not only because of what this guy told me that day but because of the mess I found myself in. This same guy knew of my escapades, my runs, my insatiable appetite for money, and the fact that I was an undesirable element who can never be wife material. I am a product of my society, a society that worships money. Perhaps, if I was lucky enough to be married, I could have carried that same lifestyle to my matrimonial home. Who knows?

"'Being a good wife is about having respect for the relationship, it's about commitment, it's about love, compassion, and reliability. I do not have those qualities, Gwen, and this is because relationships with the opposite sex don't mean anything to me. It's all about money, that's all.

"'Gwen, I have accepted my faith. My only regret is the fact that I was not wise enough to bear children before I clocked fifty. Now I live a lonely life, all thanks to my mother of blessed memory. How I wish she was alive to see the seed she has sown in me which has germinated into loneliness and a desperate, forlorn life.

"There are young women like me all over the world Gwen and sadly, it has become an acceptable practice not commonly frowned at. Please don't be like me o! I learnt the hard way but it was too late," she moaned, sounding quite melancholic.

"'Now hear this, Gwen. On a final note, something happened which got me thinking of the path I chose. When I turned thirty, there was competition amongst these rich men to organise a heavy birthday bash to mark my thirtieth birthday. I could not change the venue or be at three different parties at the same time," Aunty Ogbeyanu continued. "As I tried to juggle the complication which I called life at that time, there became a serious personal confrontation between two of the married men who thought to themselves that they owned my life. The two men fought between themselves physically at the car park, in the presence of onlookers. One of them who was quite loud, commanded his driver to dole out two trunks-boxes filled with crisp notes of naira and dollars. He then slapped the other several times on both cheeks with this crisp naira notes while chanting, 'When my money talks, your bullshit happens, when my money talks, your bullshit happens, dis baby Oku is mine. I will buy this baby's love with money you cannot spend.' Upon hearing this, I became so annoyed as I thought that was quite bizarre, as he inferred by this rude statement that I am a chattel who could be sold and bought with money.

"'Now you know my story, Gwen, I hope you learn one or two things from it. Don't go down my route, okay? I'm off to Bible study, all of this is vanity.'"

'Judy, hmm,' continued Gwendolyn, 'after this lecture from Aunty Ogbeyanu, I saw life, men, money, and relationships differently.' I decided

I must strategise, plan, and achieve henceforth my set goals for life which are to get married, settle down, have children, and also have a career.'

****

Chapter Eleven

The Unspoken Anguish, Rejection, and Anxiety of a Child Raised by a Single Parent

'Yours is good now,' said Gwen to her friend Judy Anne. 'At least you have both mum and dad whom you look up to.'

'Hmm, who told you?' retorted Judy. 'Don't be deceived, are they always there? Just immediately before I was brought back to Nigeria to study and learn some African culture and manners, there were times my mum and dad would be heard talking in hush-hush voices, not wanting me and my siblings to know that they are quarrelling. They would call themselves all types of unprintable names like bitch, thief, loser, drawback, adulterer, etc. I used to wonder why two grown people choose to make themselves so unhappy by living together. My parents are not religious people by any standards, I say this because if they were, they would not be married and still feel comfortable cheating on each other. They are just mere churchgoers, who never spend time to read the Ten Commandments, which says "Thou shall not commit adultery." They are just churchgoers who attend church to fulfil all righteousness. So I thought to myself, if they were fearless and bold enough to want to cheat on each other, why continue to live together, deceiving themselves and making the whole world believe that they are such a happy couple and their marriage is made in heaven? Once, I heard my mum accusing my dad of never being supportive despite all the contributions that she, my mum, has made in the family. My dad was always on the move, visiting friends and sometimes travelling outside London where we live, to work in Birmingham.

At the mention of the name Birmingham, Gwen now turned around and asked, 'Where is Birmingham?' pronouncing it as Barmengham.

'Huh?' answered Judy in between chuckles. 'Birmingham is the second largest city in England, it's approximately 125 miles from London, two hours' drive. We are, however, not sure whether our dad's claim of working away from home is genuine. My mum was not interested in finding out as I later learnt during her series of telephone conversations with a mutual childhood friend of my mum, who tried to introduce my mum to a lifestyle of how to stay married and be unfaithful. You will kill yourself or age in time while trying to monitor these men, relax yourself, she said and do what others do to retaliate.

'According to my mum's friend, who we nicknamed Ms Finicky, this is the new lifestyle for all twenty-first-century married women whose husbands are Casanovas. I have also heard my mum's friend saying to her that there are also people who profess to be quite religious who, however, indulge in such acts notwithstanding. Such women live a double-standard life. They attend church, and are quite involved in activities and church work, but outside the church, they live a completely different lifestyle contrary to the tenets of their Christian faith. They live like the modern women in the Nigerian soap series *Lekki Wives*.'

As Gwendolyn listened to this detailed account of how unhappy some so-called married couples could be and yet still portray to the outside world that all is well, she never ceased to feel amazed and also arrived at the conclusion that indeed there are different strokes for different folks and no single human being has it all. Here she was thinking that she was being raised by a single mother, she was busy admiring her friend whom she thought had everything that life could offer, a home in the UK, a mum and dad who are in holy matrimony, a very nuclear and closely knit, respectable family; little did she know that this so-called closely knit family were not as close as they were portrayed to be. Every family has its history and storyline, her mum would say.

Family Lies, Deception, and Regrets

'Judy, I don't mean to judge you now because you have revealed this family situation to me,' Gwen went on, 'but do you know that my mum always uses this Bible verse to remind me that whatever we sow on earth, we will reap?'

'What Bible portion?' asked Judy.

'Galatians I 6: 7–9,' Gwen quickly replied. 'This verse of the Bible has been my watchword because of my mother. Even though my mother is a single parent, she taught me that God is the omnipotent and the omniscient and that God sees all human hearts. My mother taught me that the relationship between husband and wife does not involve just the two of them alone, but also involves a supreme being who is God and whom these couples are accountable to.

'Despite being looked down on within the community because of her single status, she has strong moral values and convictions. A no-nonsense woman whose principle is that every woman should live their life with a dignity of purpose, irrespective of what challenges they face each day.

'My mother taught me a lot of good things in life that will help shape my life for the better. My mother Chinua also taught me that being faithful to a marriage does not only involve being able to make the other party happy and keeping to your marital promise, but also being able to keep God's commandments. Sometimes, I am forced to want to question where she got the experience of what a good marriage should be, seeing she is not married herself. She always responded to me, saying that the path between good and evil is a narrow path, you either know it, or you don't know it. You don't have to be married to be able to know the difference between what is good and what is bad. The difficulty in not knowing what is good and what is bad is that if you make the mistake of getting involved in a marriage relationship with a man or indeed a woman who does not know the difference between what is good and what is bad, how would you raise credible children? Whether single or married, you must know the difference between good and bad, as being single or being married does not change your perception of life. This is Chinua's philosophy of life.

'I can go on and on about what my single mother taught me,' continued Gwen. 'She taught me that a commandment is a mandatory thing and is not optional. She taught me that the reason why people feel so comfortable cheating on their husbands or their wives is that in the first place, they think their actions can only affect their spouse, without thinking of their children and God's commandment, which is the ultimate.

'There is this song my mother used to sing to us to buttress her philosophy in life whenever she is happy and it goes: "You will reap just what you sow, you will reap just what you sow, in this world, even in heaven, you will reap, just what you sow."'

As Gwen continued in this uncommon and unplanned close and intimate conversation about life and relationships, with Judy, her friend, she suddenly felt really close to her and decided for the first time to express her fears, worries, and anxiety to her.

'Judy, you don't know what it means to be rejected, do you?' Gwen asked her.

'What do you mean?' she retorted. 'Rejected?'

'Yes, rejected. Every day of my life, I have this sudden feeling of rejection. Anger and regret fill my mind. I regret not having my father as part of my life. I regret not knowing him. I wished and longed that he was part of my life. I wished he was there to send me on errands or even teach me more about life and godliness. I wished to hear his voice. I wished he had been the one picking me up from school. But no, instead, he left everything to my mother.

'Maybe it was my fault he left, maybe my mother could have coped more if it was not for me, maybe I will end up like my mother. Maybe, just maybe, no man will want to be associated with me just because I was raised by a single parent. Maybe I will continue to be a thing of ridicule just like my mother, maybe, just maybe,' moaned Gwen.

'If only they know what efforts, energy, zeal, and determination my single mother Chinua puts into her work every day,' Gwen wailed. 'If only they know she is carrying out work meant for two people all by herself. If only they know she has a heart of gold, if only they know the advice she gives to me each day about how to live a life of godliness.

'My mother taught me how to love myself, how to love the world, and how to live in peace with everyone. She taught me how to be prudent with money, my time, and my work. She thought me to love and cherish people. She taught me how to give even in the midst of little. She taught me that the best form of relationship, which stands the test of time, was one where both couples start together from scratch when the man has nothing to his name,' continued Gwen. 'She also taught me not to take whatever does not belong to me, be it money, material things, or otherwise. She taught me self-respect and how holy a matrimonial bed should be and I have seen her despise any woman whom she knows in the community to cheat on her husband.

'Judy, how can such a woman not be a hero? Why should such a woman be classified as less honourable than her married female counterparts just because she is single?' asked Gwen.

'It beats my imagination also, Gwen,' replied Judy. 'I have seen your mum work so hard. I have seen the passion, the love, and the commitment in her. She carries out the double task of both a father and a mother. She commits her time, her money, and her life to not only you, Gwen, but to your other siblings. Indeed, your mum should be your number 1 hero, Gwen,' enthused Judy.

'Why do you fret? Why do you dare have a feeling of rejection? Are you crazy? Without mincing words, I will give up my plastic mum for yours if mums can be swapped,' Judy Anne went on angrily. 'My own mum lacks integrity, the fear of God, shame, and dignity,' said Judy. 'I'm sorry I have to say this, but this is the truth. My mum and dad are living a lie,' she went on.

'My aunty here in Nigeria, even though she still claims to be married, her husband is hardly supportive, she does everything herself, while they both have different agenda and structure to their life. I never see them doing things together. Each day, my aunty just consoles herself by saying, "I am still here because of my children, I don't want any woman to raise my children for me."

'Gwen, there are so many single and married mums and dads all over the world today, they live together but live separate lives. They do not support each other financially, emotionally, and otherwise. I actually thought it was more common in the UK until I experienced my aunt and her husband doing the same thing.

'Coming back to my mum, Gwen, one thing you do not know is that I dare not bring any man home who is not a president's son or the son of a minister or a retired army general. My mum will not accept anything less as a future son-in-law. She particularly warned me on this trip that I should not bring disgrace to the family by getting myself entangled with any riff-raff all in the name of a relationship. That is my mother for you. It all cuts across, Gwen. I would rather be single and have integrity rather than be married and still live an adulterous life, God forbid,' spat Judy Anne.

'Do you know, just last year, a family friend of ours who lives in Streatham in London had a problem with her husband, whom she continually accused of adultery. This same woman all the time made people feel sorry for her; according to her, she made her husband rich by introducing him into merchandise trading. One of the twin children of this woman took ill and needed blood and both parents offered to donate their blood to save his life. First of all, it was the father who came forward to donate and once the hospital ran a series of tests, it was discovered that the man is not the biological father of the twin children. The whole family was torn apart. The man was crying like a baby and the children were too young to understand why their dad was crying like a baby. This discovery brought about further tests carried out on the older children, and lo and behold, both the children and the man they have called father for two decades and more were distraught when the DNA results came out negative. Tears and more tears were shed, and the whole family was torn apart just because of the selfish action of one single member of this family.

'Right now as we speak, this woman is in a mental home as she could not cope with the shame which she brought on herself and her family. Her children and husband are estranged from her till date and don't want to have anything to do with her. Talk about people who claim to be in holy matrimony.'

Judy's story also reminded Gwendolyn of other close family friends of hers who were quite wealthy and lived in an exclusive suburb in the GRA. There was news on the grapevine that husband and wife lived separate lives even though they are still living under the same roof. This particular family also enjoyed all necessary social life together as they attended wedding functions and engagements together. Once it was reported that this husband and wife travelled abroad on the same flight, with the husband in the first-class cabin while the wife and children were checked into the economy class of the same airline, to the surprise of the cabin crew on board the plane.

'Gwen, I need to run home now. I have learnt a lot from my discussion with you tonight which will help to shape my thinking and help me to change my attitude, not to be too hard on myself.'

'Before you go, let me quickly tell you,' chipped in Gwen quickly. 'One of the reasons why my mother hated Inno, one of my male admirers, is that Inno is an apprentice who spent time with one of his cousins, working for them with the hope of being established in business, by either being set up or given money or tools with which to make a living.' (This practice amongst the Igbos is called "Idu Uno" meaning settling an apprenticing to enable him to own his own business after years of service to his master.)

'Another reason why Chinua despised Inno is that there is rumour going around that he and his cousin whom he lived with are Osus—a group of people whose ancestors, it is believed, were dedicated to serving in shrines and temples for the old deities of the Igbo and therefore were regarded as belonging to the gods.'

Amongst the Igbos, relationships and interactions with anyone classified as an Osu were forbidden. Most times when Chinua tried to discourage her daughter from having anything to do with this young man, the first thing she mentioned is the fact that he was an Osu, an outcast. This labelling, however, did not in any way deter Gwendolyn, who went on to remind her mother of her professed Christian faith and how everyone is equal in the sight of God. Gwendolyn also reminded her mother of how she felt being labelled promiscuous just because she was a single mother.

'Thank you, Judy, for being yourself and coming into my life,' said Gwen with a sparkle in her eye.

'You're welcome, I'll run along then and speak to you later,' replied Judy.

Chinua would tell stories about how the Osu people and their ancestors were an abomination to the whole village. When she told a story, be it on marriage, politics, life, the history of the Igbos and their different festivals and masquerades, she left an indelible mark in the hearts of her listeners.

Chinua started her stories without any preambles or formal introduction. Once she told her children about the Nigerian political class. While sipping her well-prepared pepper soup and her usual bottle of stout mixed with soft drink, or fizzy drink.

'In 1979, after election, Shagari of NPP came to rule us after he won election. He stayed until 1983 because he won another election second time,' continued Chinua historically. 'These khaki boys, meaning military men, came back again when Buhari took over power through military coup in 1983. God catch Buhari oh! Chinua would go on excitedly. 'Because another one whom we call Maradona, meaning Major General Ibrahim Babangida, took over power again through counter-coup,' pronounced 'kanta coop' by Chinua, referring to the counter-coup in 1985. 'Maradona promised to hand over to civilians in April 1990, but when he became power drunk, he continued till 1992, even though all arrangements were in place to carry out this promise of handover. Another coup was attempted in 1990 but they failed o! This was the Gideon Orkar coop,' meaning the Gideon Orkar coup.

Chinua would go on and on about a particular story and would not rest until she had given a detailed account of incidents. Hear her.

'The election of 1992 was so funny and kwonkios,' she would go on and on in her colloquial language. 'There was rigging and rigging and rigging, and because of this, the presidential election was postponed. In June 1993, Abiola won but his election was annulled by Babangida the master coup plotter, "Oye Isi" coop. Babangida gave the reason that there were election irregularities. Are you people listening at all?' Chinua would ask. 'Yes, we are,' answered her children.

She would go on to state how an interim national government (which she called kabu kabu government) was established by the Babangida's administration, who went on to convince the Nigerian people that transition to civilian rule could not be completed by August 1993; he was however forced to resign and Chief Sonekan became the interim president. After a couple of months, Mr Sonekan resigned and this was how Mr 'who the cap fits'—referring to General Sani Abacha's political campaign of 'who the cap fits' when he was in leadership of the country.

'How did you manage to remember all these dates and events?' one of Chinua's daughters, Ugoh, would ask her, and she would say, 'Hmm, I went to school o! I attended a missionary school called Ovim girls' school and I was one of the top girls in my class.'

'Why did you then drop out from school?' prodded Ugoh. 'It was one bad day like this: I saw one of our missionary sisters staring at me with her eyes moving tick-tock, tick-tock like a pendulum, and speaking Queen's English. I became really afraid of her eyes and additionally as I could not understand her English I felt intimidated and could not cope with the grammar. I immediately ran away never to come back ever again to school, a decision which, till today, I still regret,' Chinua explained to her daughter Ugoh amidst laughter by all present.

'Ehen, as I was saying, you see that stubborn man,' referring to Ojukwu, 'that stubborn man . . . Oh, my good brother-in-law, De Chuks,' or brother Chuks, 'he died in the war as a result of his stubbornness, I advised him to return with his kids to the east when there were serious rumours confirming that the Igbos in the South were at risk of getting killed. De Chuks refused to listen to me because I am a single mother, whose words are of no consequence. Oh! May his soul rest in peace and may he never be foolish again in his next life. Amen,' continued Chinua to herself.

'War! War! You see war!' Chinua would exclaim, 'War is not a good thing oh! We lost lives and we suffered, both old and young. Women were raped, children had kwashiorkor because of malnutrition, but I made sure that my children did not suffer from kwashiorkor. I would trek miles and miles and miles to Umuahia attack market, looking for things to buy and sell to people who were not ready to take the risk.'

The only thing capable of stopping Chinua once she was in a mood to tell stories was sleep. As she told this story about Nigeria and about coups and counter-coups, she jumped to another experience she suffered because of being a single parent.

On that day, Chinua also told of an incident which she suffered as a single parent when she returned to the east during the war. She was subjected to humiliation by her family. There was an incident which involved a big fight in her family when they gathered her and beat her. She believed that the mortar and pestle used to hit her must speak to the ancestors on her behalf; she then threw it into a pit latrine—an act which is forbidden in the Igbo culture and which caused another serious problem for Chinua and her children. Despite being a woman of courage, strength, and indefatigable character, Chinua could not boast of overpowering the existing culture and tradition of her people.

Chinua was also known to use popular slogans as her watchword to connote her sufferings.

Once she gathered her children together and narrated to them how she was maltreated by her late husband's family and the immediate community after her first husband died. 'These people are not good at all,' warned Chinua.

'What people?' asked Mimi, one of her daughters. 'Mum I thought you invited us to tell us a story, ehen, now!' Replied Chinua, 'Tori no dey pass tori now' (referring to the story).

'It's not good to have a father who does not value girls o! My father felt it was a waste of time to train girls in school, and so at the age of fourteen years, I was married off to this village man without ambition, education, or vision,' Chinua would always say sarcastically to anyone whom she thinks is not working hard enough—see, see, see, you no get ambition, education or vision.

'Now this man made me suffer so much, he could not provide for me and the children. The annoying part was that I had three solid girls for him, which helped to annoy him the more. I wanted financial support, direction for my children, and physical presence. But no, none of this was available. He failed to see anything good in me, just like himself. He was a drunkard and came back home drunk most of the time while I struggled with my petty trading, selling foodstuff as I did not want my three children to lack anything.' According to Chinua, most of her struggle was not for herself, but for the upkeep and maintenance of her children.

Education was also paramount in her heart as she was determined that despite anything, she would continue to trade to raise money to train her children up till Yoruba City level (Chinua's pronunciation of *university*). Chinua worked tirelessly all day and all night, not minding her husband's laziness. She would always say to her first husband, 'You are my punishment for being a woman, but I will turn my life around, through my suffering.' Did she? Yes, of course she did.

Chinua's first husband did not, however, live long enough to witness her successes in life as all three children and the additional four children fathered by Chief Mudiaga were single-handedly raised by Chinua. They later became qualified engineers and medical doctors residing both in Nigeria and in the diaspora.

Chinua never stopped telling the story of how she was subjected to the rigorous and savage custom of Igba Nkpe (widowhood rituals in Igbo land). Chinua would moan about the fact that despite the fact that her first husband was the laziest man she ever came across and never contributed financially to her life, his family still managed to convince themselves that they owned her and her small business.

Upon the death of her first husband, an opportunity presented itself for the other male members in the family to increase their holding of the scarce and inelastic commodity which was the only parcel of land owned by her late husband.

Because they also wanted to acquire Chinua's petty business, one of them, whom Chinua called Mbe (translated into 'Tortoise') forced Chinua to have a sexual relationship with him while she was still in mourning. Chinua was dehumanised and humiliated by the religious rituals, superstitious sanctions which were geared towards oppressing her physically, emotionally, and psychologically.

When her first husband died, any widow in Chinua's position usually became more amenable to keeping silent over this form of oppression, but not Chinua. 'Ta!' she screamed in rage, on one of the numerous nocturnal visits of Mbe to her mourning room. 'How dare you? You call yourself a man! If you come close to me again, that thing you call prig,' meaning his male organ, 'I will chop it off, roast it, and make sure you eat it for breakfast.'

Chinua recounted that apart from these incidents, she was also ordered by elders in her late husband's community to explain the cause of his death. Apart from this, she was also commanded to give an account of the business which according to them, their late brother opened for her with his money.

They asked for her husband's passbook and savings book and other valuable items. Each time they requested these from her, she responded to them, 'Search me. Are you laughing at me? Search me. Are you laughing at me? Search me,' until they got tired of asking her and finally stopped in anger and frustration. Chinua would mutter to herself each time they came and went, 'Nde Oshi thiefs, Ole Jinkoliko'.

During that same meeting, they also demanded a list of his investments, property, land, and money in his account. She advised them to ask him—meaning the dead husband. This infuriated them the more and they vowed to deal with her.

Every day during this mourning period, she would go into traumatic wailing, immediately beating her chest, flinging around her arm and then falling down, while the other women in the community *umu ada* would surround her immediately and restrain her and request her to sit down on the ground, while they sat around her. This was the custom practised by widows in her community.

Chinua never stopped talking about how one of the women almost suffocated her with the oozing smell from her mouth and armpit. Each time she cried and wailed, she would look straight into this particular woman's face and scream, 'Eh, these people want to kill me the way they killed my husband eh, eh eh, huh,' she tried to pass on this message to the woman who was oblivious of occurrences at that point in time.

'Why did it take you people so long to announce his death?' asked Chinua. 'At the end of the day, he was not a titled person, why the special arrangement?' she would ask.

One major thing which Chinua also noticed is the fact that all deaths within the community were always ascribed not to illness or lifestyle, but to either family members who were jealous and covetous or to jealous friends who are enemies of progress. Death therefore is not taken with stoicism and resignation; there is always intense wailing, weeping, and hysteria generated from this sad occurrence.

Chinua also gave an account of how her hair was shaved and how she was instructed to cry every morning and evening for four days, after which she was told she had an option not to cry or to cry again.

In the morning she was taken to have a cold bath and to continue wailing, shouting, and screaming her late husband's name. 'Putty,' she screamed on, 'Putty, you smeared me with Putty.' Chinua screamed, blinking her eyes to force tears out. 'What on earth is Putty?' asked one of the women with her. 'Putty is the new name given to my husband,' Chinua lamented. 'He smeared me with Putty both in life and in death,' screamed Chinua, an answer which left this woman reeling with uncontrollable laughter.

The last four days after the burial were horrendous and she had to mourn an additional three months. Most of this pan-Igbo custom was not carried out through and through by Chinua who claimed to be born-again Christian. This self-proclaimed Christian faith and belief was frowned on, and she was later excommunicated from the village and no one would speak to her. For over a period of 8 months, no one bought from or sold to her. They also asked the spirit of her dead husband to deal with her. Chinua's response to this segregation was 'Fa . . . fa . . . fa . . . fa . . . fa . . . Fowl! According to Zebrudaya Okorigwe Nwogbo of the village headmaster fame.'

The decision to segregate Chinua was a combination of so many things. She was placed in the room beside her late husband's body, in the same room where she was asked to wave flies from perching on the corpse. The quality of her crying was also judged by the patrilineal daughters (umu adas).

Chinua would brace up herself and still have something to say to the umu adas despite her vulnerable state. 'Umu ada, your tyrannical powers did not work when that Mbe was alive,' she screamed. 'It will not work when he is stone dead. What have you not accused me of? You accused me of causing the death of Mbe, oh, Mbe, You feel it did not show on me that I lost Mbe, forgetting I did not just lose him now, but years ago.' Apparently she was referring to the neglect and struggles she experienced even when her first husband was alive.

'I am Ocho Nma,' she would go on. 'I have also found Jesus' (finding beauty and Jesus).

'You say I should not bathe for days because I am mourning, what about my hygiene, and cleanliness?' she asked. 'You denied me the little basic comfort which I worked hard to bring myself and my children, I cannot even wash my '*akwa-mkpe* (mourning clothes)

'I have stopped my business now for months because of Mbe, are these not enough sacrifices? I cannot go to the stream or the market or even our farmland. Now you feed me with broken and old plate fit for an enemy. Tufia kwa! Enemies of progress,' cursed Chinua.

When Chinua was taken to the marketplace as part of this ritual, at the marketplace she sat down and opened four different packs of empty green leaves. As she opened them, rather than saying 'I have sold out evil luck, and may evil and bad luck be far away from me', a normal practice, she went on to carve out her own niche statement thus: 'Mbe, pa pa pa Mbe Lewe Ayan Nelu Mbe, may I not go through this again, Chinua Ntoi, Ntoi. (Meaning 'Good for you, Chinua, for accepting this archaic practice.')

'I have sold your bad luck away from me and my children. May I and my children not be subjected to this humiliation or savage custom ever again. May these children become great and be heard for great things ooooo!' she screamed out loud to the amazement of onlookers, who wondered in their hearts what amazing strength of character Chinua had.

According to Chinua, when her own father died, he continued to appear to her everywhere in the form of apparitions and in a dream complaining that he was not at peace yet and not yet been accepted by his dead ancestors. She held several meetings with her sisters, also did a lot of travelling, which brought a little unity between her and her estranged sister. The whole family finally performed certain rituals before the spirit of their father finally rested.

Chinua never failed to express her feelings each time she experienced any form of oppression. She was a feminist to the core and was not ashamed to say it loud. This also severed her relationship with Chief Mudiaga, who found her too forward, and outspoken without diplomacy. She said things as she felt them, not minding whose ox is gored. 'I don't give a tinker's cuss,' Chinua would say most of the time after she had lashed her opponent.

Life's Simple Truths

'Chief! Chief!' called his wife Maka. 'Where are you?'

'I'm at the verandah,' answered the chief. As she proceeded to join her husband, she met Chinua and her daughter, who came visiting to request school fees and maintenance money. Immediately Maka sat down, every other conversation with the chief became futile. He suddenly changed, would not want to engage and would not want to compromise or negotiate how Chinua's need will be met, with that of her children.

'Chi chi, I done finish with you,' the chief said in pidgin English. 'You and your daughter done take my time the whole of today.'

'What do you mean? You have not answered us and yet you say you done finish with us,' replied Chinua in an angry tone. Suddenly they now heard another voice from the back of the room calling, 'Chief, chief, my baby's Lactogen has run out, I need four dozen from Kingsway stores. Please send the driver to quickly get some.'

'I will straight away.' As the chief responded to Maka's request, he called out to the driver, 'Driver! Driver! Driver! Ooooooooooo. Where dis stupid driver, I sure say e don dey sleep somewhere under the stair case. Driver!' he screamed at the top of his voice, oblivious now of Chinua and her daughter sitting close to him.

'Oga, sir, madam,' replied the driver as he ran upstairs to the chief.

'Where you dey since I dey call and madam dey call?'

'Sorry, sir, madam!' replied the driver again in pidgin. 'Come on, run to madam and ask her what she wants you to get from Kingsway store. If you like sleep there or take my car go do kabu kabu, idiot!'

'No, sir,' retorted the driver as he ran off to Maka chief's favourite wife.

'Ehen, Chi chi, make you come back some other time, you hear, I don tire.' He was referring to Chinua, who all this while continued to sit at the verandah, waiting to be attended to, oblivious of the drama between the chief, his driver, and his small wife. 'Come o, wetin you just talk dis man? You want make I come back again? Wetin dey worry you sef?' echoed Chinua. 'E be like say the thing wen dem se do your head dem don go renew am. Useless man, you no go remember wetin you do yourself until you enter your grave.' Chinua went on and on, spitting fire and brimstone in her usual acidic tone when things with Chief were not going as planned. 'I go go change dis children name. Make I know say na me alone follow train dem.'

She went on in her normal pidgin English. 'You know fit suffer dis children every time dem wan go school, you call yourself big man and yet you no fit bring Oku.' 'Oku'-fire is the usual slang used when someone is not meeting a financial obligation.

'Oghene!' shouted Chief. 'Dis woman, dis woman, wetin? Na only you born for me?' Chief went on, 'If I begin throw way my money to all my thirty-nine children, how I go fit take care of myself wen I don old? Make una go marry, tell your children to go marry.' Chief was advising his female teenage children to go get married to save him the stress of having to see them through high school.

What was happening in Chief's household is typical of every average family home where polygamy is a konk Nigerian tradition and tolerated amongst the women and the men alike. The consciousness of the average Nigerian man, especially those raised in the cultural setting like that of Chief Mudiaga and Chief Rufus, his friend, has not changed.

The moment an average African man is able to achieve some measure of success materially, there is always the tendency to let go of the inhibition that Christianity or education imposes on them; you immediately find them marrying numerous wives. There is also some percentage who are challenged by their Christian faith, who choose an alternative by finding a way around it. Instead of publicly marrying numerous women, they keep many mistresses and concubines, invariably because they are under this false notion that an African man is an African man.

They believe that it is more a cultural issue and this is why even when they attain a level of westernisation imbibed by an average African man in terms of his academic qualification, exposure, dressing, among others, when it comes to marriage and things relating to women, he remains an African man in his consciousness.

And so within the Nigerian cultural context, it is permissible for a man to have more than one wife. Men are given free rein to have as many wives as possible, but when it's a woman, it becomes a taboo. However, once this happens, loyalty to the man now becomes divided and questionable as the different women take turns to get financial favours from the man in question just to be able to give their children the best. The man who is supposed to be the head of the home now suddenly becomes a lone ranger.

This is exactly what is experienced in Chief's household, where turns are taken by the wives to cook for him, and also to warm his bed. Despite all of this, he still sees several chains outside, a habit which makes anyone start to wonder how exactly he acquired his sexual prowess.

He is never one to worry about having an intimate father/son or father/daughter relationship. Children belong to their mothers, especially when they fail to succeed.

Chinua faced the challenges of daily life with wisdom, wit, dignity, confidence and courage. She is a typical example of a single mother by chance, not by choice because of the death of her first husband.

What men like Chief don't recognise, however, is the fact that the more women they get themselves involved with, the more they expose themselves to dangers of sexually transmitted diseases, lack of love and commitment from this chain of women, likelihood of being involved with a woman who may use charms and additional spiritual powers which may lead to his early death or serve as a tool of control, making him function only within her control.

This is the general belief in Chief's compound, as his other wives and concubines strongly believe that one of his wives, Maka, has him wrapped around her finger, having used African magic/voodoo to make this possible. Chief would do anything to please this particular wife, Maka.

Maka controlled his time, his money, his cars, his properties; she had serious undue influence over him, and there was this general belief that if you wanted to engage in any positive talk with Chief, you were better off doing that when the wife was not around. The fear of Maka is the beginning of wisdom in Chief's household. All her children are chauffeur-driven to school, while other children within the same household take public transport to the same school attended by her children. Once, one of the chief's children who attended the same boarding school as Maka's son was left to walk back home during a school holiday, while Maka's son was driven home by the chief's driver.

'Are you truly my father?' This was the resounding question asked by Rona, one of Chief Mudiaga's sons who was left to walk home while his stepbrother was picked up by the driver and driven home.

'Oghene! How dare you come into my sitting room and ask me that stupid question? Have you ever tidied up this sitting room for me before?' asked the already enraged Chief Mudiaga. 'Why should I?' retorted Rona. 'Are you truly my father? The children whose mum you love so much and whom you think deserve your love should tidy up your living room for you,' replied Rona struggling hard not to be tearful.

'One day, all of this will stop. I regret the day my mum introduced me to you as my father,' shouted Rona, who at this time was sweating heavily after having walked over five miles to return home. Chief stood up instantly from where he was sitting, properly adjusted his wrapper—the traditional George wrapper which most men with traditional title like him usually tie around their waist.

'So you are sitting there telling me you cannot tidy up my sitting room, aren't you? Go back to your mother. I have told you, go back to your mother! Your mother dumped you with me here, running around with other men to satisfy her insearchable appetite for men. I took you in, you this ungrateful child, and this is what I get, huh?'

This time, Rona had already stood up in fear before his father got to him. He ran to the entrance door, panting, 'Yes, leave my mother out of this. If you were nice to my mother, perhaps she would have been here to take care of me, so leave her out of this. I should have not been born at all because you hated me from when my mother conceived me to the extent that you advised her to abort my pregnancy, wicked man. Perhaps you value all those who use African voodoo to turn you into a zombie. That is what you prefer, isn't it?' This time as Chief approached the door, Rona ran as quickly as he could into the bedroom he shared with his other three stepbrothers. He quickly shut the door, with the bolt which was behind the door, while at the same time screaming and shouting, 'Zombie way na one way oh, ajoro jara, joo! Zombie way na one way oh, ajoro jara joo!' from an old song by the late Fela Ransome Kuti.

As Chief Mudiaga returned to his room, he briefly pondered what his son Rona said to him. 'Voodoo? Voodoo, silly boy, he has been also brainwashed by people, this is what you pick up from these silly lazy women in this house, isn't it? I am voodoo myself, every voodoo partaker in this household including your gallivanting mother shall be exposed and disgraced. Yes, they shall be exposed and be disgraced,' the chief tried to convince himself.

As Rona was now changing into his casual clothes in the boys' room, he went into deep thought and reflections of the happenings around his father's house. 'Polygamy, polygamy, polygamy,' he thought to himself. 'How did my mother find herself in this kind of situation?' he thought angrily. Now I am the one who is suffering the after-effect of her past decisions to involve herself with a married man. 'Why do I find myself in this kind of situation?' he mumbled to himself. 'I blame my mother anyway, even though she knew this man is a womaniser, still went ahead to involve herself with him. How can a father show so much preferential treatment to some of his children and then allow others to suffer just because their mothers don't live with him?'

As Rona stared and gazed into the ceiling in the children's room which he shared with others of his stepbrothers, he immediately noticed tears flowing from his eyes. 'Maybe it's my fault,' he thought to himself. 'Who knows, maybe my dad hates my mum because I was born.' In that deep thoughtful state, he found himself drifting off into a deep sleep instigated more by hunger, tiredness, and a feeling of hopelessness and insecurity. As Rona drifted into slumber, he dreamt that he was reunited with his mother in a peaceful home where he lived with his mum and dad and other siblings where love, togetherness, and contentment reigned supreme.

In his dream, his father showered him with so much love and affection that he became so determined that when he grew up, he would only marry one wife, whom he would be faithful to and he would love his own children exactly in the same way, knowing that this indeed is what is required of all parents.

Rona also promised himself never ever to be involved in polygamy; neither would he love his children unequally since this brings about sibling rivalry. He was determined to succeed in life and to be a prosperous father and husband providing for all members of his household and, most importantly, having a deep, lasting father/son and father/daughter relationship with his children.

Rona's dream world was abruptly cut short by a bang and a scream, 'Orona! Orona! Orona!' He hated it when his stepmother called him his name in full. At this stage, he heard his stepmother's shrill, annoying voice cutting through his make-believe world. As he jostled out of his dream, he then realised he had been dreaming. 'Oh what a world!' he muttered. 'I have been dreaming,' he said to himself.

'This wicked woman, this woman,' he cursed under his breath. Her children are there; she will not send them on errands. The housemaids are there; she will not call them. What is she calling me for now?! 'Orona!' he heard the more determined voice. 'Now I am in serious trouble.'

'Ma!' he screamed back. 'Come here immediately!' his stepmother called out in a more commanding tone than was necessary. Rona then strolled sleepily into his stepmother's bedroom, a room which served as her closet and private meeting place when she wanted to be away from Chief, her husband.

'Ma!' Rona replied again, as he stood right in front of his stepmother. 'Waaah,' mimicked his stepmother. 'Did you not hear me calling you all this while?' she asked him. 'No, Ma,' he replied. 'I was sleeping, Ma.'

'You were sleeping?' asked the stepmother.

'Yes.'

'What time is it now?' she asked. He then turned round to stare at the wall clock opposite where his stepmum was sitting. 'It's past four o'clock, Ma.' he replied. 'Past six o'clock and you are sleeping?'

'Yes,' he answered. 'Have you washed the dishes in the kitchen?' she asked. 'It's not my turn, Ma!'

'Whose turn, then?'

'It's your son's turn, Ma!'

'My son?'

'Yes, Ma!'

'Since when has my son become your slave in this house?' she asked further.

'So I'm the slave, then. Is it because my mother is not here? You are against me sleeping, and yet your sons are there sleeping. Your driver picked up your sons from school and left me walking home, and yet you don't see anything wrong in it. Your sons have had ripe plantain and beans for lunch and yet I have not eaten. Now you want me to wash the dishes after them. Have you asked me whether I have eaten,' Rona asked, staring into his stepmum's face with tears rolling down his eyes.

As he threw this challenge to his stepmother, she stood up and walked straight through the throughway into Chief's lounge. 'Chief!

Chief! Chief!' she screamed. 'Chief! Where are you?' She usually called him Chief when she wanted to compel him to do something drastic. 'Chief!' she screamed out.

Immediately, Chief, who at this time was having a nap, woke up, stretching himself in the armchair where he was lying down. 'Chief, have I done wrong to accept you and all your baggage?' she asked. 'When will all of this end? I receive insults from your numerous children, their mothers, and even your girlfriends.'

'What is it this time?' asked the chief. 'What else, it's Orona o! If you see the rubbish that was coming out from that little boy's mouth, you will not believe it. Orona poured all kinds of insults on me just now, just because I asked him to wash his own plate which he used to eat.' she lied. Immediately the chief stood up and rushed straight to Orona's room. 'Orona! Orona!' he called out frantically. 'Today you must leave my house. I have had enough of you. Pack your things and leave.' At this time, Orona was already in the kitchen, washing up dishes which Maka's children ate with earlier that day. There was no leftover food for him; he looked in the fridge and saw old stale bread, which by his calculation had been there for four weeks. He took a bite from the bread, which tasted stale, and as he tried to return the bread to the position where he found it for fear of being accused of binning it without permission, he suddenly heard his father's voice calling out his name.

Orona froze in fright and stood still, thinking of the next move. At this time, he heard his father threatening that he must leave. Suddenly, he summoned up the courage and ran upstairs to confront his father by telling him his own part of incidents leading to this false accusation by his stepmother. Chief was not interested. He was busy packing all Orona's personal clothing together, saying, 'Enough is enough,' in his traditional gravelly voice. 'You must return to your mother today.'

'Okay, no problems, I will leave,' said Orona in an emotion-laden voice. 'I will leave but before I leave, I want you to listen to my side of the story so at least you get to know the truth.'

'I don't want to hear anything,' screamed Chief in his thundering, loud voice. 'Which part don't you understand?' he asked, 'Before I open my eyes, pack your things and return to your mother.'

As Orona packed his clothing into a Ghana-must-go bag, he wept so loudly and his body shook in a spasm as he was filled with the emotion of a child destroyed by polygamy. Rejection, hatred, and revenge filled his heart. He also hated his mother for putting him through all of this. 'When she knew this man was married in the first place, why did she go ahead to have a relationship with him?' he asked himself—a question which he had asked himself more than a million times with no answers.

A lot of women need to check themselves when making choices in life. The choices we make today affect a whole lot of people in the future, including our children. Orona thought through all of this as he packed his things. 'I was not there when the two of them were enjoying their clandestine relationship as secret lovers. I was not there when he used to take my mother to isi ewu and pepper-soup joints, spending money on her and keeping late nights away from his wives. Now I get to suffer all the pains and rejection even though I did not ask to be born. Na wao!' Orona packed his things and moved back to his grandmother's home, a movement which took place without a bump because Orona's grandmother was quite pleased to have him back. 'See how lean you are,' she said, immediately he entered her sparsely furnished living room. 'I knew your father is not wise enough to see the handwriting on the wall. 'That woman called Maka, you see that woman, anyway, I may not be alive on her payback day, but at least I am sure she will definitely pay for all the grief she caused so many people since she came into Chief's life. Drop your bag, go in the kitchen, and have some jollof rice. I actually had it in my spirit that you will be here today, didn't know it was something permanent anyway.'

> I don't know how to
> Speak up for myself
> Because I don't really have
> A father who would give
> Me the confidence or advice
> —Eminem

Chapter Twelve

BFF

'I will really miss you, Judy,' grinned Gwendolyn. 'So you are finally leaving tomorrow.'

'Yes of course and I thought to stop by to greet your mum while I say my final farewell,' mumbled Judy Anne in an emotion-laden voice. 'You are my best friend forever,' said Judy abruptly while hugging Gwendolyn tightly. 'I really enjoyed every moment spent in Nigeria, the friendships, the new families formed, the warmth, the laughter, and most importantly, I cannot forget the delicacies prepared by your mum Chinua, her very delicious jollof rice and nsala soup prepared with fresh fish and uziza leaf.

'My mum should be on her way now, just wait a bit, she will soon be here. What do you have in your hands?'

'Oh, this,' said Judy, 'it's just little bits and bobs which I brought as my parting gift to you and your family.'

'Bits and bobs?' Eh ya! Thank you so much,' laughed Gwendolyn heartily. 'Ehen, when are you coming to take me? I hope our friendship will not end here. I need to come visit you in that London, so you can show me a bit of your culture also. I think I could do with a bit of that Eliza's snow, I know it will soothe my moods.' Gwen was deliberately sounding quite funny.

'That won't be a problem,' answered Judy. 'Once I get back, I will arrange to see how I can invite you to come and visit me in the UK, at least to meet my parents.'

'I plan to set up a registered charity once I get back to the UK,' said Judy Ann enthusiastically with a sudden spark in her eyes which only passion and commitment can bring about.

'My vision is to see to it that most parents in diaspora encourage their children to visit their home country at least once every twenty-four months, to enable them to understand their roots and where they are coming from. This move will also help them to imbibe the rich culture which the African community provides. I will also use this charity to raise funds to assist families who cannot afford such trips abroad but who have shown an interest in learning a bit of the African tradition and culture,' continued Judy Anne. 'In addition to this, my charity will be a platform where families in diaspora who are in need are assisted when they are being threatened with a court order involving their children being taken away by Social Services. A lot of African families have lost their children to the system, because of situations in which they found themselves which ordinarily, if managed properly and with appropriate advice and support given, would have brought about positive changes in their family. We will provide the support and awareness that such vulnerable families need in order to be able to get their children back, and after they have gotten their children back, help, support, and assistance will be in place for them, to see to it that these children settle fully into the family—which is being able to bond again emotional and psychologically with their parents and being able to understand boundaries of respect and family values in order to create a safe and stable family unit where peace, love and mutual respect are practised by all.'

'Whatever informed this vision?' asked Gwendolyn.

'Did I not mention to you that I lost my elder brother because of carelessness and lack of the necessary support and proper counsel and parental support by the system who claimed to be helping my family?'

'Oh no, no, no!' screamed Gwendolyn. 'I was not told the story in detail! What happened? Please lead me into it,' begged Gwendolyn, with tears rushing down her face. She loved Judy Anne so much that anything that affected her also affected Gwendolyn. 'What happened to your brother, Judy?' At this time, Judy herself already started crying, and as tears rolled down her eyes, she walked towards Gwendolyn and the two young women held each other in an emotion-charged room. They were grieving more for the imminent fact that Judy would be leaving in what seemed like a couple of hours and then over a hidden grief which Judy had kept inside of her all these years.

'I lost my brother, my sweet brother, because of these stupid people,' she moaned. 'If they had given my parents the support that they needed rather than encouraging my late brother to do as he pleased, all in the name of failure by my parents to understand his moods properly, maybe, just maybe, he would be alive today. My parents were discouraged from setting any boundaries, they interpreted their desire to set boundaries as abuse and blew these actions out of proportion, giving my late brother an opportunity to do as he pleased, which eventually led to his death.

'Oh God! Oh God! Oh God! Help these innocent children whom the system allows to do as they please while at the same time ruining their lives. Lord, let my brother's death not be in vain. Let all organisations who work with children be genuine in their approach, putting the best interest of every child at the forefront. Lord, please remove all vindictive social workers who tell lies and fabricate stories against families and encourage families to be separated and disunited just because they want to be seen as carrying out their work. Let the pursuit of each social worker working with children be for the welfare and best interest of children and their families rather than for their own selfish professional and egoistic gain.

'Oh God! Oh God! Oh God! Save our children from homewreckers, liars, night marauders, and scavengers who abuse the powers given to them to protect children and families, who would rather destroy homes and take children away from their families and encourage homes to be destroyed by inciting hate and lies.' As Judy cried and cried, she held on tight to Gwendolyn. Despite not understanding the extent of Judy's grief and half of what she was on about, Gwendolyn knew she had never seen Judy in this vocal display of emotion before. She had also not seen this religious aspect of Judy before, making her understand that this indeed must be something which had affected Judy and her family deeply. 'Amen, Amen, Amen oh!' mumbled Gwendolyn as she sobbed along with Judy.

> Nobody can give you wiser advice than yourself.
> —Marcus Tullius Cicero

Judy later sat down and narrated her family ordeal at a time when her late brother Ryan Ugochukwu was trying to discover himself as a teenager. The incessant disagreements and shouting between Ryan and his parents, the constant disrespect shown by Ryan, his drinking habits, late nights clubbing, etc.—all of this lifestyle was not addressed by the system when her family was brought to their attention.

'There was nothing put in place to help my brother, in form of counselling or mentoring to help him change his life. All that was provided was constant harassment by Social Services, who arranged meetings upon meetings, contacted my brother's school notifying them that my family had been abusing my brother physically even though upon police investigation there were no traces of abuse.

'They have this notion about African parents and their parenting skills, interpreting every effort made by the parents to set appropriate boundaries for their children to be a show of aggression. Because they have this negative notion about African parents, once a complaint is brought to their attention, they find it difficult not to be biased once a complaint comes through to them.

'Rather than help this family by giving them the necessary parental support and counselling to settle the scores with their children, they immediately spring into action, ignoring the child's bad behaviour and also making up all kinds of stories to separate the child from his or her home by blowing the incidents out of proportion.

'In their desperate effort to save a child from his or her family, they fabricate lies using social workers of the same ethnic origin to carry out this nefarious conduct. These social workers forget to look at the acteus rea and the mens rea of the parents by at least putting systems in place to monitor how things can be resolved amicably within the home front, failing to understand that a couple of years down, if this bad behaviour complained about by parents is not checked and corrected properly, it may end up destroying the child and the society they live in. In my family's case, it was that same thing my parents complained about that ended up killing my brother.'

'What is going on here?' asked Chinua, Gwendolyn's mum, as she pushed her way through the front room door. As she took in the sight of Judy, she called out, 'My pikin, why are you crying? Come, come, come, dooooh! Don't cry, my daughter!' She approached Judy and embraced her, using her abada wrapper to wipe her face, and touching her lovingly on her hair. 'Le Ntutu.' She spoke in Igbo, her mother tongue, admiring

Judy's natural long hair. 'My son's wife,' she continued, 'who made you cry, my beautiful daughter?' she continued.

'Mum Chinua,' as Judy fondly called her, 'nothing, Ma. I was just narrating a story to my friend Gwendolyn about an incident which happened to my family years ago,' replied Judy. 'It's okay, Mum, I'm fine now. Mum, I will be travelling back to the UK tomorrow, just to let you know, and I brought a small gift for you.'

'Hmm, you mean you brought a gift for me? You see why I call you my son's wife,' replied Chinua. 'Come, come and sit on my lap, my daughter.' Chinua carried Judy on her lap while stroking her continuously on her hair.

'Wetin you buy for me, my daughter? Eeeeee, eyeeeeeeh' (a tradional shout of jubilation amongst the Urhobos which she had imbibed) Chinua always enjoyed screaming in the traditional Deltan way whenever she was overwhelmed with joy.

It was past 7 p.m. Judy had been served food—the traditional jollof rice which she had become accustomed to now, and loved dearly. Chinua also put some in a plastic bowl which was given to Judy as takeaway to take to London the next day. 'My daughter, let me pray for you before you go,' Chinua said. 'The Lord will go with you, he will bless you, you go get good husband wen go love you, as you cough, your husband, go leak your feet, he go love you sotey, you go tire. You nor go suffer alone like me to raise your children. We go dey hear good news about you oooooo! No forget us ooooooo, get up my daughter, God done bless you already,' prayed Chinua.

'Amen, Mum Chinua,' Judy answered her prayer. 'Thank you, Ma.'

'Oh, Gwendolyn go really miss you more. Bye-bye o, greet my friend Queen Eliza for me ooo! Remember us o!' Chinua continued in the usual Deltan pidgin English known amongst people of this region.

'Gwendolyn, Gwendolyn,' Chinua called out, oblivious of the fact that Gwen was standing right behind her. 'Gwendolyn, see your friend off.'

'I'm here, Mama,' said Gwendolyn. 'Aha, did you not see me? Have been here all this while now. I wanted to give you time to greet Judy. She has been waiting for you.'

As Gwendolyn and Judy stepped outside into the dark night on Judy's way back home to do her last-minute packing, they chatted and chatted and Judy promised to be in touch and to invite Gwendolyn over soon to the UK.

When Judy Anne got home that night, she met her aunty sitting quietly by her favourite couch. 'Aunty, Aunty!' she called out. 'You okay? Why are you sitting all by yourself? Is Uncle not home yet?'

'No, my dear. He is not, quite typical of him though. The earliest he has come back home every day is 1 a.m. the next day so I'm not surprised. Judy I will miss you so much, you have been my niece, my friend and confidante,' she said. 'Notwithstanding your young age, you speak with much wisdom and understanding. I have really enjoyed this last couple of months spent with us. I will really, really miss you, my darling,' continued Aunty Amaka. 'Now that we have a little time, let me give you a bit of advice. Have you finished packing just yet?'

'Not really, Aunty, but I will give up anything for this advice coming from you and then later I will go and tidy up my bits and bobs,' Judy answered in her traditional British fashion.

'Come sit close to me, the walls have ears. Judy, you are growing into a very pretty young woman. This advice I want to give you, if you take it, it will guide you in life. You have been part of this household for over five years now, the most recent being this last stay with us. Thank God for the experience which you will be taking home with you, especially in the area of marriage and relationship. My daughter, it is good to desire to be married because what you don't desire, you don't get. Desire to be married at a young age so that as you work towards it, you strategise, prepare yourself, know who you are and what you want so that at the age of twenty-five years, you are in a serious relationship leading to marriage and at least between the ages of twenty-seven years and twenty-eight years, you are married and in your own home. Be careful not to rush into marriage just because you want to satisfy societal norms and practices.' Aunty Amaka went on. 'Marriage is not an easy venture. Planning to be married and getting married to the right person, makes it easier. Please make sure you marry a man who has the fear of God as this helps to minimise the risk of maltreatment. The way the heart of a man works is quite different from the way the heart of a woman works. However, a man who has the fear of God, once married to you, understands that his loyalty and obedience to you is motivated by not only his love for you but also his love and fear of God.'

As Aunty Amaka continued with her wise counsel, she almost sounded as if she was talking based on past experiences of life. She became quite emotional and tearful.

'Judy, do not marry a man who does not have the fear of God o! It's important,' she went on. 'Aunty, how do I know when a man has the fear of God, then?' Judy asked. 'Aha,' exclaimed Aunty Amaka, 'you will know by his fruits, which is why it is important to have enough time to prepare for marriage by strategising yourself for marriage at a very early age so that you will have enough time to observe a man during courtship. It is not possible, though, to know everything about a man during courtship. However, you will have time to at least observe his likes and dislikes, his religious beliefs, his family values, and the way he treats you and other women, whether he respects and values you. Do not rush into marriage based on the end balance in a man's bank account o. Your happiness and that of your future children matters a lot. Once you make the mistake, that is it. Remember, you cannot change a man once you accept him and his shortcomings, be sure to live with it once you get married. A man who gets distracted by the sight of anything in skirts—this is a sign that he will not be faithful to you in marriage. If you accept him thinking he will change later, you are only deceiving yourself, my dear. He will not change o! Be ready to have several lonely long nights spent alone waiting for this man to come home. Be ready to share him with your friends, other women, and the public. He will not change. If you think you can cope, fine. It means you have an exceptional tolerant character, which may be a virtue. If, however, you cannot take it during courtship, don't aspire to take it during marriage because he will not change.'

'In rounding up, Judy,' continued Aunty Amaka, 'look out for a man who truly loves and adores you as a woman, not a man you love more. You will know by the way he treats you when you are sick, the way he frets around you to make sure you are okay, the way he reacts to you when you are unhappy, he makes sure you are happy, and when something happens to you, the way he makes sure he fixes things right to make sure you are happy. Money, my dear, does not dictate happiness. However, money plays an important role in a relationship. Be sure that whoever you want to be married to has the same vision and aspirations as you. Make sure you two are on the same page o! Marriage is not about money, love, beauty, and sex o! There is more, my dear. Marry someone whom you can walk through the journey of life together, someone you can grow with, a man you will have one voice with in raising your future children, a man who will be your partner in progress.

'There is no such thing as Mr Right o! You only know you have found Mr Right after you are sure that you are on the same page when it comes to paying bills together, building your future together, and raising successful children together.'

'Now you are scaring me, Aunty,' Judy quietly whispered.

'I don't mean to, my dear. You can make it, you passed through nursery school, secondary school, and university, you even left the comfort available to you in the UK, just to have a taste of life in Africa. I know you are a strong woman, you will succeed in marriage. Just be very prayerful and trust God. Judy, the bad thing about a man who is a womaniser is the fact that as he continues to move from one woman to another, he may end up one day in the hands of the wrong woman, who is desperate enough to destroy him, his marriage, his children, and his business. Several men and their households have been destroyed by the fact of their promiscuity leading to a destruction of their homes, their businesses and careers, and even their children which eventually led to their untimely death.

'This is my advice to you Judy, don't end up the way I have ended up o! I have ended up with a man who is never at home. I am a married woman but indirectly, I am a single parent. I raised all my children on my own. This man whom I call my husband has never been there for me and my children. One thing you must know is that I am not alone in this struggle. There are loads and loads of women out there who still remain married to their promiscuous husbands just to satisfy societal demands. They live under the same roof with these men they call husbands while they lead two separate lives. The man does his own thing while the woman does her own thing. In the past, the women just remain patient waiting for these men to come and be with them while the men go around sleeping with girls young enough to be their daughters. However, times have changed. The women now have a better strategy to deal with their frustrations and loneliness. They now sleep with younger men whom they spend their husbands' money on. Some of them also sleep around with men who are wealthier than their own husbands in a bid to get contracts and all kinds of favour. Judy, there are so many broken homes and dysfunctional families these days in our community, it's such a pity. All of these could have been avoided if the men and women took the time to understand why they are entering into a marriage relationship and being able to marry the right person by making an informed choice.

'Judy, you see these husbands and wives still living a plastic life together. The women say they do it for their children, and the men do it to prove a point to others that they have been married for so long—which is part of their success story. Some of these men have stopped sleeping with their wives for reasons best known to them as they involve themselves in all kinds of occult practices and engagements just to belong in the society. Before I forget, the fact that you helped a man in his time of need does not necessarily mean that he will remember your kindness tomorrow when things are well with him. It only takes the grace of God. Look out for a man who is appreciative of you and a man who has the fear of God. A man who appreciates and loves you will also appreciate any kindness and support you have shown to him in the past and this will make him stick with you forever.'

'The spirit of kindness, love, and appreciation is very important in a relationship. Judy, look for a man who is quick to say "I am sorry" and not be ashamed of it, knowing that his ability to say "I'm sorry" when he is wrong makes him more of a man not less. Marry a man who knows and understands your mood. An affectionate man who knows when you are unhappy, when you are in a bad mood, and when you are stressed out. It may be advisable to support a man in his time of need but you must be sure that he is a man who will appreciate your kind gestures in the future, not a man who, after you marry, now switches roles, expecting that you have to provide all the financial support all through the lifespan of the relationship or does not feel he owes you any role of being a husband who should take care of you and your children. Judy, I, your aunty, I am a living example of a woman who supported her husband financially all the time and every time to the extent that my husband does not feel obliged to me anymore financially. He searches my wallet every day for more money even when he has. He feels I should be the one giving to him, not the other way round. I spoilt him. Each time, he says to me, "I don't have, I cannot kill myself for you." This has been the practice in this home which I have grudgingly accepted. So I don't want you to have the same experience. If a man does not have, support him, but the man should know that it is his place to provide for his wife and children and be apologetic and remorseful if he is not able to do just that.

'Judy, I wish we had enough time to discuss fully in detail about life, love, and relationships. One thing you must remember is to make a wise choice, and you have enough time to do that if you start to position yourself in time to find your own man. When you rush into a relationship because you feel time is no longer on your side, you may end up making the biggest mistake of your life.'

'Thank you, Aunty, I will remember this day. Thank you so much, Aunty Amaka, this advice is the most important thing I will be taking along with me to the UK. Thank you so much. Thank you, thank you, I'm so grateful,' Judy said with her voice now laden with emotion. 'It's my pleasure, replied Aunty Amaka, who at this time saw how touched Judy was after her advice and, in order not to break down, took a youthful approach to share an awkward high-five with her niece Judy.

'I need to rush and finish my packing. I have an early busy day tomorrow,' Judy stood up, hugged her aunty with a kiss and rushed off into her room to finalise her packing.

It was already past twelve midnight, and as Judy hugged her aunty and retired back into her room, they heard a sound of the lock opening. It was her aunt's husband. He strolled into the living room casually. 'Welcome, Uncle,' said Judy politely.

'Huh hum,' replied her aunty's husband. 'Welcome o,' said Aunty Amaka to her husband grudgingly. 'I hope you remember my niece is travelling back to the UK tomorrow. Are you still able to drop her off at the airport?'

'Yes, of course but be sure to fill up my car as I don't have any money for that extra expense.'

'I don't mind o.' Aunty Amaka went on, 'As far as it's my problem, I have to solve it. Please let me know how much it cost to fill up your tank as far as you take this girl to the airport in Benin early in the morning.'

'Goodnight, Uncle,' Judy chipped in. 'Goodnight,' he responded grudgingly, having noticed now that all this while, Judy was standing and eavesdropping on the last conversation between him and his wife. There was this look of embarrassment all over his face. This made Aunty Amaka happy. 'Ehen,' she whispered, 'he has embarrassed himself in the presence of this little girl, shameless stingy man,' she thought to herself.

'When it comes to anything that concerns me, you never have money. I have been married to you for thirty years now, when have you taken time to make any financial sacrifice on my behalf?'

'Why does it have to be me alone who makes the sacrifice? Every time I have a need, I have to solve it myself and yet I have a husband. Do you have glue attached to your hand? What is the difference between me and the so called single parents out there? I don't feel supported and loved by you at all. There is no affection, no support, no love.'

'If after thirty years of being with you, I still feel this way, should it not be a thing of concern to you?' asked Aunty Amaka. 'Na wao! People wen no marry dem dey complain, people wen marry dem dey deceive themselves,' she began to speak cynically in pidgin.

'What will you do to satisfy the world? Osondi owendi!' she mimicked a popular saying in Nigeria. Aunty Amaka always had a way of adding humour to her pain; maybe that was how she had been able to cope with her husband's miserly nature and other excesses for thirty years. 'Am off to bed oh, see you tomorrow. I will put on the alarm for 5.30 a.m.' she spoke to her husband on a final note.

> When we honestly ask ourselves which person in
> our lives means the most to us,
> we often find that it is those who,
> instead of giving advice . . .
> —Henri Nouwen

On the other hand, when Gwendolyn returned home after seeing Judy off, she found her mother Chinua crying and holding something that looked like a card. There was also another pack containing two simple sets of earrings with a matching chain with the inscription 'To Mummy Chinua, my hero!'

'Oh! Is that why you are crying? You don't know how very highly people who know you closely place you within the community,' said Gwendolyn.

'Oh, this girl has killed me o! Me, a hero, a hero!' (Chinua pronounced *hero* as *euro* in her usual controversial manner.) 'Hey, God I thank you for letting me see today. For once, it took a beautiful girl from Obodo Oyibo to make me know that I am valued despite the fact that I don't have a husband. I have lived my life thinking that nobody values me, nobody cares. This girl has made me have value for my life. I am thankful to you, O Lord,' cried Chinua.

She tried on the jewellery, looked at herself in the mirror, and continued to cry. She lay down on her bed that night, drifted off to sleep and dreamt that a beautiful princess visited her from a far country and offered her a beautiful bouquet of flowers. She woke up the next morning with an additional spring to her walk as she raced down the footpath on her way to her stall to meet with her customers.

Chapter Thirteen

'This one that you are up early this morning, where are you off to?' asked Chinua.

'Have you forgotten that it's today Judy is going back? I want to follow her to Lagos at least to see her off and then I will hang around for sometime in Lagos to find a job.'

'Aha, how come you did not tell me of this plan about following Judy to Lagos?'

'Mama, I told you now, you must have forgotten,' replied Gwendolyn.

'Please turn on the light ewo. Nepa has taken the light already. These Nepa people sef. Have you ironed what you will wear?'

'Yes,' answered Gwendolyn, 'I did that yesterday.'

'Let me quickly take my shower, I'll be back. I have packed a few things in that travelling bag you gave me for Christmas, that's the one I will use.' As Gwendolyn rushed to take her bath, her mother went into deep thought about life generally. In her heart, she prayed for her children not to have her kind of luck. She felt she had not been lucky with life. She prayed that as Gwendolyn was setting out to Lagos, she would be favoured. 'I know that once she is favoured, she will come back to help me and other of my children'.

'Mama, mama, mama,' Gwendolyn tapped her mum on the shoulder, 'What are you thinking about?'

'Oh, sorry, my daughter, did not know you have finished your bath already.'

'Yes, I have.'

'Where is that your body cream?'

'Which one?'

'How many do you have? Okay, check that my drawer by my bedside.'

Gwendolyn escorted Judy to the airport in Lagos, they exchanged email addresses and other contact details, cried while waiting for her flight to be announced, and once all of that was done, Gwendolyn returned, back to another of her friends' houses in Ikeja, Lagos, in search of a job. Her friend's name was Yewande Cole.

Yewande Cole was a long-time friend of Gwendolyn. She came from a middle-class family from Lagos state. They attended university together. Unlike Gwen's, Yewande Cole's parents lived together until the father's tragic death when she was in high school.

Unlike Gwendolyn's, Yewande's mother became a single parent because of a tragic incident which happened when Yewande was in high school. Yewande was an only child, and after her father's tragic death, her mother had never found any true love again, though she had continuously kept steady relationships which ended shortly after they began. Yewande's mother often compared every man she met with her late husband, sometimes mistakenly calling them Baby Tee, a pet name which she fondly called her late husband.

As Yewande introduced her friend Gwendolyn to her mother, immediately Gwen knew that she would enjoy her stay with this very happy family who happened to have something in common with her— being named a single parent without stopping to find out what brought about the circumstances of single parenthood.

After all formal introductions, Gwen was shown her room upstairs and she and Yewande chatted deep into the night until they were reminded by Yewande's mother about how early their day was the next day and about the traffic in Lagos Island, where Yewande worked as a bank executive.

'You look so beautiful in your blazer and pants,' Yewande's mum said to her as she looked at herself in the mirror while Gwen waited for her to get ready. 'Thanks, Mum, I'm learning from you how to be smart and elegant.'

As Gwen and Yewande, her new host, approached the car, which was a gift from a friend on her twenty-fifth birthday, Gwen noticed a passport photo which fell out from the pigeonhole of Yewande's car. She picked it up, and she stared at the photo of an elderly man standing close to Yewande. Yewande quickly snatched the photo off her hands, jokingly saying, 'Curiosity kills the cat, shh.'

As they sped through the heavy traffic from the third mainland bridge to Lagos Island, the music of 2 Face, 'African Queen', was blasting through the air as they sang along joyfully.

Then suddenly they stopped in front of the most gigantic building Gwen had ever seen in her whole life, as she looked at the bold inscription in front of this large glass building: SILVERLINING BANK PLC. They entered through the reception, with the security men exchanging pleasantries and respectful glances at Yewande as they strolled into her private exclusive office.

'What are you staring at?' asked Yewande as she sat down to work while Gwendolyn sat to the side of her office, close to a bookshelf. 'What! Okay, this,' replied Gwendolyn casually, 'the same man whom I saw in the photograph with Yewande was walking through the glass window casually while everyone at the foyer stood up to pay obeisance to him. He must be a very important personality, Gwendolyn thought to herself, but how did he now snap a very close and intimate photo with Yewande?

'Hmm, Lagos na wa, I swear!'

During lunchtime, Gwen met with a few of Yewande's colleagues who were bank executives, they all had lunch together, and there were exchanges of complimentary/business cards and telephone numbers.

Yewande also made some introductions and pressed some buttons to assist Gwen to find a job; she had with her a well-structured CV which she was ready to forward upon requests from any potential employer.

The day, however, went so fast, and lo and behold, it was closing hour and they drove back home at about 6.30 p.m. with the very heavy Lagos traffic slowing down smooth movements here and there until they got home at 10.00 p.m., tired, worn-out, and grumpy.

And so the days spent job-hunting in Lagos ran into weeks, weeks ran into a month. A month turned into months, and Gwendolyn was losing all hopes to get a job. The very few interviews which she attended, she was told after to meet with some executives privately to discuss further. She was not used to their inappropriate sexual gestures and hated their guts and confidence. She could not stand their pot bellies and constant talk about their children who were schooling abroad. Once she met with one old chief who was a prominent politician. She happened to be introduced to him through another friend she met through Yewande.

This chief, as is the practice in Nigeria, also had this arrogant attitude of 'nothing goes for nothing'.

He invited Gwen to lunch and she accepted, trying to keep an open mind as much as possible. Immediately she got to the popular restaurant, it suddenly occurred to her that she would be left alone with this man in an exclusive part of the restaurant reserved for high-calibre members of the society, just like himself.

She walked straight to the reception as already advised by this chief and was chaperoned to the reserved area, where she sat down comfortably and was asked immediately what she wanted to drink. 'Er, chapman!' she said as quickly as she could remember. She was not yet used to the sophistication and luxury that the city of Lagos has presented to her since she came to live with her friend. 'Are you sure?' asked the waitress. 'We have a list of choice wines, we have choice spirits and liquor, we have Italian red and white wine, there is also Bloody Mary and chapman, cognac and of course, apeteshi local gin.'

Gwen's thoughts had suddenly drifted off from the environment where she found herself. It had been six months since she left home on a job hunt to Lagos. 'Only God knows how my mother Chinua and my other siblings are coping right now,' she thought to herself. 'Rather than give me a job, all these men have put me through for the past six months is all kinds of sexual harassment. What kind of a country is this? Who then will help children of poor people in this country? After my mother as a single parent suffered day and night to see me through school, there is still no hope of getting a job in order to help my other siblings. When will this chain of struggle and poverty be broken? What kind of country is this? Where is the hope for the common man? People like my mother, who is a petty trader, what hope does she have towards retirement and pension when a child she has suffered and trained with her last savings cannot even find a job after graduating from the University.

'Aunty! Aunty! Aunty!' Gwen suddenly felt the bartender tap her on the shoulder softly to bring her back to reality. 'Oh,' she sighed, 'I'm so sorry, have had a very long tiring day. I just drifted off,' retorted Gwen. 'Is my host not yet around, then?' she asked. 'No, ma'am,' the bartender replied. 'Ma'am, I was actually telling you the different drinks and liquor we have while you are waiting for His Excellency.'

'His Excellency?'

'Yes, His Excellency,' said the bartender. 'Oh, pardon me. I remember requesting a glass of chapman.'

'Yes, you did, ma'am, but I just thought you might want something more serious than that. Do you want some chewables, then? We have fried snail, fried turkey, fried fish, nkwobi, isi ewu ugba—'

'No, thanks, I would rather wait until His, erm erm, Excellency turns up,' she said.

As Gwen waited and sipped the cold chapman drink which had now been served by the bartender, she looked at her wristwatch and it was past four o'clock in the evening. She had been there for over three hours and there was no sign of His Excellency.

'Oh my God, how will I pay for this drink if this old man does not turn up? See me see trouble o! This rich men are so rude and mannerless, and they have no regard for anyone, including young women like me,' she cursed under her breath. 'How can you stand up anyone, no phone call, no messages, nothing?'

As she brooded over this delay, suddenly she saw a young man who later introduced himself as the manager of the restaurant. 'Hello, ma'am, my name is Nicholas, Nick for short, I am the manager of this prestigious restaurant. I have a message for you from His Excellency. He says to tell you that he will not be able to meet with you today because he needed to be at a very important board meeting outside the state. He has asked, however, that you relax and feel free to order any food or drinks that you want and when you are ready to go back home, we have a registered taxi available to take you home.'

Gwen stared at this man in disbelief. 'What?' she actually uttered her disbelief before she realised that. 'Oh! I see. Okay. No worries,' she said. So what next? 'Yes, madam, as I said, you are free to order anything, and once you are ready to leave, let me know and I will call a cab to take you home, ma'am.'

'All right! Very well, then. Give me some time, I will get back to you in a jiffy.'

As the restaurant manager walked off respectfully, Gwen took time to compose herself. She was fuming and cursing and hissing. 'Can you imagine? He did not even have the courtesy of calling my number to cancel the appointment. All these money-miss-road rich men in this country, they do not have any respect or regard for women o! They actually think that the world revolves around them because they are the best thing that happened to the world. I don't blame this man at all, thank God sef,' she thought in pidgin, bringing herself down to the grassroots.

'How I for manage follow this man comot here after this lunch sef with him big over-bloated belle? That thought alone has haunted me all afternoon. At least he saved me that embarrassment. O God, I wish I had a father! Now I really miss my father! That man who my mother has three children within Delta, only God knows whether he has been assisting my mother, as at the last time they had a quarrel when my mother visited his house to request for school fees. On that day, my mother Chinua vowed that on no account will she put her children through the trauma of having to beg for school fees months after other children have resumed school.'

'Today is the last time you will go and ask that wicked man for school fees again,' raved Chinua. 'No more. Enough is enough. What is it? Anytime my children want to go back to school, they have to cry and suffer and beg for money and be disgraced and returned home by the school. Every time this man will be disgracing my children, exposing them to ridicule and embarrassment. No more of this pain for my children, I will sell my gold and wrappers to make sure my children go to school just like every other children. I will also change their name and they will cease from answering to this man's name, to save them the additional shame and embarrassment they will have to suffer just because they bear the name of a rich man and yet they are not able to pay their school fees.'

As Gwen thought through the role of her mother as a single mother, a motivator, and a strong fighter in the life of her children, she suddenly became quite sad; she put her head down and started crying. In order not to be noticed, she quickly stood up and rushed to the ladies' to wipe her tears with a cold splash of water. Once she had freshened up, she walked towards the reception, beckoning on the manager to let him know she was now ready to leave.

A cab was called immediately for her and she was chauffeur-driven back to what she now called home—her friend Yewande's family home in Ikeja, Lagos.

It was almost 6 p.m. at the time she got home. She was not expecting anyone home at this time since it took Yewande close to four hours to get back home from Lagos Island because of the heavy traffic.

Gwen could not wait for her friend to come back home so that she could share her experience. She took time to change into her casual clothing and decided to lie down on the bed to reminisce on the happenings of the past couple of hours.

As she lay down in deep thought, she briefly recited Psalm 121, which she had become used to over the years. 'I will lift up my eyes unto the hills from whence cometh my help . . .'

Gwen immediately drifted off into slumber, and as she slept, she dreamt that she was home with her mother and her siblings. She dreamt that she earned a very fantastic job in an oil servicing company in Lagos called Halliburton. She later built her mother a big family home where all single mothers who were struggling in the community would come share their experiences and support each other, eat, sleep, and pour out their hearts.

As she continued in the dream, she saw herself blessing these single mothers by washing their feet and saying to them, 'Well done, unsung hero, well done, unsung hero!' As she washed their feet, they were touched by her kindness and cried out loudly because of the affirmation she accorded them. She cried also with them, with tears rolling down from both eyes, soaking her pillow.

Suddenly, she was rudely woken up by her friend Yewande. 'Madam, how are you? How did your lunch with His Excellency go?'

'Oh God, you disrupted my sweet dream.'

'What dream?' asked Yewande.

'Oh dear, oh dear, I wish I did not wake up from this dream, it was so sweet.'

'You wan try? If you no wake up na wetin go happen.' Yewande spoke in pidgin English to bring home her point: 'Abeg come yan me jare' (meaning 'Come and give me a gist of your escapades earlier today').

'Nothing, nothing o,' replied Gwen. 'You will not believe it. That old man stood me up, he did not turn up. Can you imagine? He did not have the simple courtesy of even calling to cancel. All he did was to send the manager of the restaurant to me, imploring me to eat, drink, and when ready, be taken home by a chartered taxi. Na wao! Na so una dey do for dis Lasgidi?' (She was referring to the slang name by which the city of Lagos is known to all.) 'I don't get it at all,' she continued, putting her hands over her mouth while blowing out air from inside her mouth.

'This bad habit, you've still not stopped it?' asked Yewande.

'What bad habit? Oh, you mean the one I use to smell my bad breath in the morning?' Gwen asked. 'There is nothing I hate like a bad breath, you know me now,' continued Gwendolyn. 'That is my formula with which I check if my breath smells. There is nothing like a clean, fresh breath,' she laughed while this time forcing herself to stand up from the bed.

'His Excellency must have been caught up in a meeting or maybe something came up that he could not call you up before going in for his meeting. Is that why you are annoyed and looking like someone's new wife who caught her husband cheating?'

'Why won't I look like that, Yewande babes? Do you know it's been six months now that I left home in search of a job? If not for the kindness and support of you and your mother, what would have been my fate by now?

'I keep hoping and hoping that I will be invited to an interview, which is the normal thing after applying for a job, but no. Rather, all these old sugar daddies keep doing is to invite me first for lunch. Na wao! I don't get these people at all.'

'As you were driving into Lagos, what did you see written in front of the three statutes at the entrance of the city? Is it not "This is Lagos"? Not "Welcome to Lagos!"

'Lagos is the more you look, the less you see, and so open your eyes well well o! A million girls will want to be in your shoes today and will not mind being stood up a million times by one of the wealthiest business moguls in the country. His Excellency is a power broker and a mentor to so many, an owner of a business conglomerate. Chill o! My sister, don't be naive, shine your eyes, I say again and again,' Yewande continued her rather vain lecture.

'It's one thing to be beautiful, it's another to be favoured. The fact that this man in his busy schedule even remembered to send you a message through the restaurant manager, and arranged a cab to take you home, it all means you have been favoured by him.'

'Na wao! I really don't understand you Lagosians o! I thought we were on the same page,' said Gwen with a look of astonishment in her eyes. 'So you are even supporting this man abi?'

'No, I'm not supporting him, I'm only telling you what is obtainable. This is a society that respects wealth, affluence, and position so much to the extent that you become almost insignificant if you don't have any of it. How you achieve this wealth and affluence does not matter to anyone, what they are interested in is the money. Now let me ask you again, as you entered Lagos through the expressway, what did you see boldly written at the entrance? "This is Lagos", hmm. If you go to other states in the nation, what you see is "Welcome to Imo state", "Welcome to River state", "Welcome to Abia state", "Welcome to Delta state". But in Lagos, it's different, it is "This is Lagos". What do you think this means? It means shine your eyes immediately you enter Lagos or else the city will swallow you up.'

'I definitely don't belong here at all o!' screamed Gwen. 'Be quiet,' retorted Yewande. 'Who do you think enjoys the filthy life here? But it's the way of the world. It seems as if money now rules the world notwithstanding how it is made, o ga' o!' (a Yoruba word which Gwen has now picked up by association since coming to Lagos which literally means 'it's tough')

'This invitation for lunch and all of that, is it not an exploitative way of misusing desperate young people trying to fulfil their dreams as young, up-and-coming graduates?'

'What experience do you have, then?' asked Yewande. 'Who is your godfather? Do you have any connections in the upper echelon of the Nigerian society? Are you a close ally of any politician, governor, senator, or member of the House of Representatives?' she asked.

'Who then do you have to assist you? Is your uncle an oil magnate or a heavy-duty chief executive of a bank?'

'In the absence of that, you use what you have to get what you want.'

'Meaning?' asked Gwen.

'Ms Gwen Mudiaga, meaning that you are a survivor and because you are a survivor in the unfortunate circumstance of not being born with a silver spoon in your mouth, you must survive using what you were born with—which is a silver endowment, not silver spoon.'

'What? What did you just say?' Gwen asked in astonishment. 'Exactly what you heard. I am not speaking German, Gwen Mudiaga. Don't sound like a naive old maid.'

'What! Yewande, in answer to your question, I have God,' mumbled Gwen grudgingly. My Bible says that they that know their God shall be strong and shall do exploits.'

'But God helps those who help themselves,' Yewande replied sharply in a bid to justify the advice she gave to Gwen.

Immediately after this eye-opening intimate conversation with Yewande, the whole answer to the question about Yewande's photograph with the same very old man whom Gwen sighted in her office premises came to mind.

'Yewande, I thought you are a born-again Christian, you were the leader of a very strong Christian association during our university days.'

'I still am a born-again Christian' replied Yewande. 'Nothing has changed my faith in God, but I believe that God helps those who help themselves in this day and time, my sister.'

'What does the Bible then teach you about adultery and fornication?' asked Gwen, determined to now make Yewande have a change of heart.

'Oh please, Pastor Gwen, leave your preaching for another day,' said Yewande, almost sounding irritable. 'I beg I am famished, I need to grab something to eat from the kitchen.' As Yewande walked to the kitchen, Gwen stared at her big backside as she rolled it left, right, left, right, left, right.

'This explains it then,' she thought to herself; her friend whom she thought was a good Christian woman was living a double-standard life.

'Where is the old-time religious ethos?' Gwen snorted, almost to herself.

Since she had come to live with Yewande in her family home, no Sunday morning passed without them attending church. Yewande was the leader of the choir in her church, the House of Praise and Salvation, founded by Reverend Soji Peters.

Yewande was deeply involved in church activities and paid heavy tithes and offerings in church as part of her religious conviction that the more you give in the house of God, the more you are blessed by God. Yewande was an example of the twenty-first-century born-again Christian who believes so much in the grace of God brought about by the death of Christ on the cross of Calvary, forgetting that this same grace does not exist for sin to abound.

Yewande was a great actress and manipulator. When in church, she was a different person, but outside church activities, she was a go-getter who uses her body to get whatever she wants. Yewande's watchword was 'If you are not born with a silver spoon in your mouth, at least you are born with a silver endowment, so use it.' She was also quite conversant with all Bible verses, from the book of Genesis to Revelation.

Despite her Christian belief and seeming commitment in church, Yewande continued to nurse this watchword at the back of her mind. She indulged in all kinds of practices even though she was a member of the choir with a sonorous voice. When she sang in church, the whole congregation stood still.

Yewande also gave all kinds of expensive gifts to the church in the form of expensive cars, volunteering to give her time to the service of the church also. No Sunday passed by without her coming out to give one testimony or another about God's faithfulness in her life. Despite all of this, she had her dark side.

Marriage was the last thing on Yewande's mind at this stage, even though she was approaching her late thirties. She was too busy frolicking and brewing money. The thought of a biological clock never crossed Yewande's thoughts.

Yewande was older than Gwen. She had attended a polytechnic earlier in life where she attained a higher national diploma (HND) before she decided to acquire a university degree qualification.

Yewande was one of the few people whom Gwen looked up to for motivation during their school days and so to think that she did not really know Yewande's frolicking nature came as a rude shock to her, and at a time when she needed all the moral support and encouragement from Yewande.

'Na wao!' Gwen exclaimed in utter shock and dismay. 'Lagos indeed na wa, I swear!' she murmured.

As the truth about these numerous lunch dates unfolded by the day, Gwen was determined not to entertain or encourage any of these proposals. She kept on turning down every invitation that was outside a formal office interview appointment and screening. 'My body is the temple of the Holy Spirit. I cannot be defiled by these old hags just because I want a job,' she went on. 'They send their children to the best schools in Europe and America and Dubai for their master's and doctorate degrees, while there are executive jobs awaiting them upon their return back to Nigeria, and yet they engage in defiling other people's children, exploiting them for their sexual gratification.'

'I will not be a part of the crowd or one of the Joneses that will make up their statistics,' enthused Gwen. 'I will get a job in God's own time and the job will be based on my merits, not on my physical endowment.'

After resigning to her faith, Gwen kept herself busy in doing research on the Internet to improve on her knowledge and skills. She was hopeful that there must certainly be certain employers who were able to offer her a job without having to invite her to a private lunch.

One Saturday evening, as Gwen lazed around the room she shared with her friend Yewande, she received a message on her FB profile from Judy Anne. 'Gwen darl, howdy?' the message read. 'Howdy, Judy. Long time', she replied to Judy's chat.

'What's up?'

'Nothing, nothing, still job-hunting', replied Gwen. 'Listen, I have been inundated by requests from this old family friend who saw your photo and instantly became attracted to you, should I link him up with you?' asked Judy.

'Is he a Christian?' asked Gwen.

'Yes of course he is. In fact he is actually talking serious o!'

'How do you mean?' asked Gwen.

'He wants to connect with you on FB, please check him out on my profile, and if you think you like him, then you may accept him as your friend and let's see how it goes', advised Judy.

'Okay o! Thanks anyway. Cheers.'

'Speak soon', replied Judy in a typical British manner and she was gone.

'Oh! I forgot to ask his name,' muttered Gwen to herself. 'Anyway, I will wait and see. Perhaps any male who prompts me who is a mutual friend with Judy, I will assume he should be the one.'

****

My mother always gives the best advice.
When I left Puerto Rico to pursue my dreams,
she always supported me and said to me
'I'm never going to cut your wings, so don't let anyone else do
that to you.'
That has been my philosophy through life.
I want to share that valuable lesson with my little girl someday.
—Roselyn Sanchez

****

Days later, Gwen received a friend request from a male called Lawrence Tokunboh (aka Talk on Boy); she suspected this must be the one. Earlier before now, she had gone through Judy's FB profile, painstakingly trying to guess who her secret admirer all the way from the United Kingdom would be.

With all hopes of getting a job fading before her eyes, Gwen felt this could be another answer to her prayers. 'At least if I cannot find a job, let me at least get married,' she thought to herself.

Immediately, she accepted the friend request and, at the same time, sent Judy an inbox message asking her to confirm the name of her secret admirer. 'His name is Lawrence Tokunboh aka Talk on Boy. I see you guys are friends now.'

'Yes, I just accepted his friend request', responded Gwen.

'Good, kudos. I hope you like him as much as he does you.'

'I hope so o! Let's see how it goes. I'm still in Lagos trying to find a job o! This country is tough to the extent that jobs don't come easy if you don't have a godfather on top o! It's so sad.'

'Erm erm, good luck with your search', replied Judy Anne. 'I cannot chat much now, I'm at work.'

'You bet', replied Gwen. 'Hey, I have to go back to my desk now my break time is over', said Judy, 'xoxoxoxoxoxo.'

'What does xoxoxoxox mean, girl?'

'It means "kisses and hugs", my dear. Speak soon.'

'Same here,' replied Gwen, 'thanks.'

Immediately, Gwen received an inbox message from Lawrence: 'Hi, stranger! How are you?' Gwen did not know whether it was right to respond immediately or to just play hard to get in order not to come across as being cheap. She waited for some time, and as she wanted to respond, another inbox message came in: 'Hello, angel, are you still there?'

'Oh hi', she responded,

'It's good to hear from you after such a long time', said Lawrence. 'Same here', replied Gwen.

'Am I allowed to call you G?'

'Please yourself, no problem', Gwen said.

'Okay, how is Nigeria?'

'Fine o.'

'Why do you always end each comment with the word *o*, even on your timeline on Facebook?' asked Lawrence. 'Oh, don't mind me o! That is the way we lay emphasis on words in this part of the world', grinned Gwen.

'Really?' asked Lawrence. 'Yes, really', answered Gwen.

It so happened that immediately after this first contact, it felt so right. It felt as though the two of them had known each other for so long. Lawrence was quite sure he had met the bone of his bones after such a long time of being an old bachelor, having divorced his wife of fifteen years, because of accusations and counter-accusations of infidelity from both parties.

Gwen, for her part, could not decipher what exactly was the driving force behind this seeming attraction and interest which she had developed suddenly for a man whom she had not met in person but whose marriage proposals she had accepted almost immediately he made his intentions known to her. Could her acceptance be out of frustration? Could it be due to the reason that she would relocate to the UK to start a new life? She deeply thought about it, while she heaved a sigh, saying to herself 'Whatever it may be, it has to be for good o!'

'I am a mature man and I am led, I do not have time to waste', retorted Lawrence during one of their now frequent FB chats. 'I know what I want and you are what I want. I want to marry you and bring you to live with me immediately in the UK', said Lawrence.

'Hmm, slow down, slow down, take it easy,' Gwen jokingly replied.

And so within six months of chatting on FB and daily telephone calls, most times from Lawrence, Gwen and Lawrence made arrangements for him to visit Nigeria to meet with Gwen in person and also to make himself known to her folks.

He also constantly sent her money through Western Union for her upkeep. Once Gwen was now sure of steady maintenance money coming from the man she now called her fiancé, she announced to her friend Yewande and her mum that she could not cope with the life in Lagos. 'This Lagos na wao!' she said to Yewande. 'I cannot cope. It's just too fast and too rugged for me, you know I am a village girl from the countryside.'

'So what do you intend to do?' asked Yewande.

'Go back to Delta state of course,' Gwen replied quickly in a matter-of-fact manner.

At this time, she contemplated whether she should reveal the detail about her marriage proposal coming from someone based in the UK. She then remembered advice from Aunty Ogbeyanu, who said not to ever involve any of her friends whom she knows to be wayward, in any of her constructive relationships which she discerned might lead to marriage. She could hear Aunty Ogbeyanu saying, 'Don't be naive with friends, especially the ones you know are in the world. They have their ways and don't have conscience and can discourage you from getting married or even discourage any man who truly wants to be serious with you, because of their lifestyle.'

'I will be going back to Delta on Saturday before my money runs out. I also miss my mum and siblings and they will be worried about me,' said Gwen.

'Okay o, no problem, I'm here any day as a friend when you need me, trust me,' said Yewande. 'I will be travelling to Abuja on that same Saturday; I might as well give you a lift to Benin on my way.'

'Okay, no problem. Thank you so much for your hospitality. You are a lifesaver,' Gwen said while standing close to Yewande with an outstretched hand; the two ladies then hugged each other.

'I am already missing you,' said Yewande to Gwen. 'My mum is so boring and she sleeps so early, you cannot have a full conversation with her or even watch a movie with her from start to finish without hearing her snoring away loudly.'

'I will be back again before you know it. Remember I still have some of my job applications which are still pending and I await a response from the potential employers soon. Please keep me posted once you receive any feedback from any one of them. I have used your home address as my contact address. I trust that you will not fail me.'

'Certainly not, fingers crossed, I am your BFF,' replied Yewande.

Chapter Fourteen

This life, which had been the tomb of his virtue and of his honour,
is but a walking shadow,
a poor player, that struts and frets his hour upon the stage,
And then is heard no more;
It is a tale told by an idiot,
Full of sound and fury, signifying nothing.
—William Shakespeare

The meeting between Lawrence Tokunboh and Gwendolyn Mudiaga was magical. They felt so comfortable in each other's presence. It was love at first sight. If there were any misgivings in Gwen's heart before, it was time to shed them off.

Lawrence was just the kind of man she dreamed about. He was dashingly handsome and stunningly rugged at the same time. She loved the way he casually wore his jean trousers and Ralph Lauren T-shirt. It made him look exquisitely sculptured. She also loved the smell of his aftershave and his perfume, which he usually dabbed luxuriously all over him. Aramis—yes, it was Aramis cologne. The thought of his boyish looks also kept her awake all night.

She could not imagine anything better and to top up the icing on her cake, she would be travelling to join him in the UK. This could be an opportunity for her to end the sufferings of her mum and other siblings, she kept thinking to herself. Maybe this dark unspoken loneliness which had eaten her up all these years would finally give way to complete happiness and fulfilment in the white man's land.

There was, however, one big hurdle to cross. How was she going to tell her husband-to-be that she had been raised by a single parent and that her father Chief Mudiaga had never been a part of her life? What about the incident of rape she experienced during a religious riot while at university in the northern part of Nigeria? What if this man rejected her upon return to the UK just because she had been raised by a single parent? She pondered on her life and all the shenanigans of her upbringing. 'If he truly loves me, he will accept me for who I am,' she tried to convince herself.

'I am an accident waiting to happen, huh?' she said to herself. 'Let's see where this takes us.'

'It's not like most of my friends who claim to be raised by both parents are any better morally than me anyway. I have been raised by a strong, confident, morally upright, and disciplined single woman, I am solid.' She tried to comfort herself with these thoughts while bracing herself for the challenges ahead of her. 'Everyone has their little demon which they face sometimes in life, I will gallantly face mine and conquer it,' she grimaced, almost shouting out loud to herself and for the first time exuding a dangerous self-confidence despite herself.

'Is it Louisa whose mum continuously cheats on her dad? Or is it Aunt Amaka, Judy's aunty whose marriage has broken down irreconcilably and yet she and her husband still live together under the same roof? I'm yet to see any one of them who are more decent morally than me. Take for example Yewande, whose mum continuously changes men like she is changing wrappers, one month after her husband died, and yet she claims to miss her husband sorely each day.

'My family background notwithstanding, there are people I know, a lot of things which these people do which I cannot indulge in. I have been raised by a mother with a heart of gold who, despite being unlucky in her relationship with men, is an epitome of goodness and kindness, and good morals and family values. Where I suffered rejection by a father who did not care about me or who did not want to accept his parental responsibility, my mother accepted me. Where I would have lacked financial support or risked being fostered or adopted out because of my father's rejection, she accepted me and single-handedly raised not just me but my siblings, doing the work of two people successfully. Where

I would have suffered lack, she provided for me, she made me feel that I can be somebody in life. Her determination to see me succeed even spurred me on the more.'

While Gwen was busy consoling herself on her background and family, little did she know that her husband-to-be, Lawrence also has his own story about life's challenges and how he and his mum suffered at the hands of a violent father, leading to him being taken into care despite his mother's determination to raise him by herself.

Lawrence was raised in an abusive environment, and because of incidents of domestic violence, he and his siblings were taken into foster care and later raised by foster parents. His brother suffered both physical and sexual abuse in the foster home where he was placed. This affected their relationship till date. Lawrence was able to, however, take hold of his life when he turned eighteen years of age. He came back to his mother and went through college and university, graduating finally with a second-class upper division.

'Why could they not help my family to resolve the incidents of domestic violence rather than take us away from both parents?' he sometimes asked himself.

'They should at least have given us to my mum and given her all the moral, physical, and financial support she needed to raise her children, rather than taking us completely away to be raised by strangers who were not interested in our future, our heritage, and our background.

'They only succeeded in raising children who are broken, who feel rejected and left alone in a world, just like the one seen in the TV series *Tracy Beaker*. I wish I could turn back the hands of the clock to allow me ample time to be raised in a home where my mum and dad doted on me. Why should children suffer just because two adults are having a fight?'

Each time Lawrence went down memory lane, he became heavy with emotions. The effect that years of abuse and rejection had on him was concealed in him for over two decades, only to manifest itself as a destructive demon later in his marital life, years after he had been married to his wife Gwendolyn.

He was, however, grateful that when he turned eighteen years of age, he was able to reconnect with his mother, a reunion that brought about memories of the dark, lonely, and painful nights he and his siblings spent in the homes of complete strangers. Lawrence remembered every single bit of the loneliness, the feeling of rejection, the unanswered questions, the hurt and sometimes resentment all mixed into one. In all of this, there was also a twist to the relationship Lawrence shared with the woman whom he grew up to know as his mother.

'I must make sure my children do not go through what I have gone through,' he would consciously promise himself.

In the meantime, as part of their marriage engagement and preparation, Lawrence planned to visit Gwen's mum, and this visit to Mum Chinua was smooth and easy sailing. They took to each other immediately once they met. However, because of Lawrence's English accent, Chinua kept on asking her daughter in Igbo, 'Osi gini?' meaning 'What did he say?' She kept on saying, 'Oji imi na su oyibo' (he uses his nostrils to speak English). 'Do you understand all of what he is saying?' asked Chinua. 'Of course now,' replied Gwen proudly. 'He is speaking Queen's English. I thought you said you attended Ovim girls' secondary school and you were taught by white missionaries,' Gwen asked her mum.

'Yes of course I did but this one is different o! Nwa na su oyibo' (meaning 'this young child speaks too much good English).

'I hope he will not use Queen's English to kill my daughter Gwen in the white man's land,' she joked while laughing hilariously. You could sense her joy, happiness, and fulfilment at this major family achievement. She also remembered once when she and her daughters attended a family friend's daughter's wedding. They were all fully involved in helping this family to cook, and carry out other tedious household chores which such an important ceremony involves. Chinua was surprised when the bride's mum turned round to her daughter Gwendolyn and cynically asked, 'When are you and your sisters ever going to get married or are you all treading in your mother's footsteps?' Unknown to this family friend, Chinua was within earshot of this vile comment coming from a person she called a friend. Trust Chinua on that day to give this woman a full load of her mind and what she thought about her. After this incident, Chinua ceased visiting this woman despite accepting her apology reluctantly on that day.

Lawrence on his own understood that Chinua did not become a single parent by choice but by circumstance; having been partly raised by a single mother himself, he knew what his mum sacrificed to see him through school up till university. He also remembered vividly the days when his mum would go without food, fasting and praying for him to be successful in life, also the days when she would use her last savings to make sure that he buys his textbooks and other course materials.

School days, in the mind of Lawrence, were traumatic. He remembered how he felt annoyed and angry each parent evening, especially when he saw others of his classmates attending these evenings with their mum and dad. It made him feel lonely and sad and angry. His dad was never there for him and his mum and he used to wonder why until the secret of his past came calling, when his father took ill and he opted to offer him one of his kidneys.

My mother, who sat and washed my infant head
When sleeping on my cradle bed,
And prayer of sweet affection shed,
My mother . . .
When pain and sickness made me cry,
Who gazed upon my heavy eyes
And wept for fear that I should die
My mother . . .

Who taught my infant lips to pray
And love God's holy book and day
And walk in wisdom pleasant way?
My mother
And can I ever cease to be
Affectionate and kind to thee
Who wast so very kind to me
My mother?
Ah, no! the thought I cannot bear
And if God please my life to spare
I hope I shall reward thy care
My mother.

When thou art feeble, old and grey
My healthy arm shall be thy stay,
And I will soothe thy pains away
My mother.

—Ann Taylor

Each time Lawrence remembered this poem by Ann Taylor, it made him feel nostalgic, despite his difficult upbringing, he loved his mum unconditionally.

Lawrence Tokunboh's visit to Nigeria was a pleasant one; he had a nice time with the whole family and promised to come back the next year with some members of his family and friends to perform the marriage rites. He knew he had a strong connection with Nigeria and was even convinced upon his first visit. It was difficult to do anything at this stage because he had promised his mother never to discuss this family secret until after she passed on. Little did Lawrence know that it wouldn't take so long a time before such a time came to pass. Lawrence's visit to Nigeria also reminded him of his brother who was sent back to Nigeria to live with their mother's brother once they noticed he showed signs that like her, he was a person with bipolar affective disorder. They did not want to be embarrassed by his condition and so they bundled him back to the village, where he was hidden away completely until he finally died in a farm on one occasion when he followed his uncle to his farmland in the village, to cultivate his farm. He died unsung and unmourned just because he had this condition regarded as a disgrace and a stigma to his family. 'How I wish I knew the route to the village where he was buried,' thought Lawrence to himself. 'I would have at least gone there to lay a wreath as a mark of respect to his memory.'

'Why are you soliloquizing?' questioned Gwen. 'Really, am I?' responded Lawrence quietly, not in the least prepared to take Gwen into the pains and regrets suffered by him and other members of his family.

As Lawrence prepared to return, back to the UK, different parcels were wrapped up for him to take back. 'I eat out most times,' he laughed, 'I can't cook. Don't worry, perhaps when Gwen joins me, you will have loads and loads of time to send some of these goodies to us. I love your jollof rice,' he said to Chinua thankfully.

Once Lawrence returned to England, serious preparations were put in place for his traditional marriage to his wife-to-be Gwen, whom he hoped would join him in the United Kingdom immediately after their traditional marriage Igba Nkwu wine-carrying. Lawrence struggled with the pronunciation of *Igba Nkwu*; he never stopped pronouncing it as 'ebuku', causing everyone around him to laugh until tears came out of their eyes.

Lawrence spearheaded all the financial demands which the marriage involved. A list of all items required for the traditional marriage was sent to him via email. It involved a long list as follows: 5 cartons of hot drink, 5 cartons of red wine, 5 cartons of white wine, 1 bag of traditional kola nut, 1 bag of garden egg, 1 bag of bitter cola, 2 boxes of wrapper and head tie, 5 pairs of shoes, 2 George wrappers for Chinua, 10 yards of lace for Chinua, 5 head ties (Hayes), N100,000 cash for the purchase of gold jewellery for bride-to-be, N50,000 cash for other miscellaneous expenses incurred for the traditional wedding, N250,000 for live band.

All arrangements were in top gear three months later when Lawrence Tokunboh returned to marry his wife. Unfortunately, despite expectations that he would be coming with his mother, this was not to be, because of her ill health. Lawrence's mum had only recently been diagnosed with ovarian cancer which, according to her medical consultants, had already started spreading. She was billed to start her chemo session immediately and was preoccupied with doing everything the doctors and consultants had told her to do. She had been given six months to live but did not disclose this to her son as she did not want to upset him. 'Each time I feel I already have it, life turns out to play a fast one on me,' she cried on their way home one evening after attending hospital together, and they were driving back home in her son's PT Cruiser.

'Don't say that, Mum, you will definitely pull through,' Lawrence tried to encourage his mum despite being filled with fear, anxiety, and the knowledge that his mum would not be able to travel with him to attend his wedding. 'It is well,' said Lawrence. 'Mum, it could have been worse. I know of a Nigerian woman in our neighbourhood years ago who was diagnosed with cancer, she worked so hard in this country and was able to buy two properties. All of her properties were completely paid off. She worked round the clock to the extent that she hardly had time for any relationship with either male partners or even members of her family in Africa. During the time she was alive, she would hoard all kinds of household stuff in her house and would not receive guests or encourage anyone to visit her. No family member of hers knew anything about her and she lived a solitary life. She also died without a will, and at the time she died, another neighbour who thought she was smart took over this woman's estate even though they are not related. Till date, all properties and money left in the bank by this deceased woman were taken over by this neighbour because of the carelessness of this woman when she was alive. Marie—that was her name. She led a solitary life and carelessly did not think that she would die one day. If she had remembered death, perhaps she would have planned how her estranged family members in Africa should inherit her estate, or even made a will passing her estate to any charity of her choice. At the time this woman died, she never had anyone to confide in. Lawrence, when I heard Marie's story, I immediately contacted a lawyer who drafted a will on my behalf. Please, in case I am not able to survive, I have a will in place. Find my solicitors on Google; I have lodged my last will and testament with them, you are my son, no matter what they say and always remember that I love you.'

As Lawrence's mum continued with her narration, there was sudden silence between the two of them; you could have cut it with a knife. 'Nothing is going to happen to you, Mum,' Lawrence told his mum in between sobs; he could not at this time control himself. He let the steam out, and as the tears streamed down his face, he felt a blindness, on the motorway. Suddenly his view became blurred, but he instantly gained control while holding firmly to the steering of his car. The remaining part of their journey home that evening was spent in thoughtful unspoken words and deep silence.

Lawrence travelled to Nigeria with some few friends and his mum's elder sister Aunty Julie. Aunty Julie made sure everyone coming from London had the same *aso ebi* uniform, which was worn as a mark of solidarity and friendship and love for the couples.

All other items needed for the ceremony were brought in from the UK. The church wedding also took place immediately the next weekend, and after they took a short break on their honeymoon in one of the five-star hotels in Lagos, arrangements were now made to process all travel documents for Gwen to join Lawrence in the UK.

An agent assisted them to fill out the application form which was later submitted with two passport photos of Gwen, her brand-new Nigerian passport, marriage photos, and other documents provided by Lawrence in form of his twelve months' bank statements, twelve months' payslips, P60, mortgage statement showing he is a homeowner in the UK, and a certified copy of his British passport, amongst others. At first the entry clearance visa was turned down and the reason given was that Lawrence and Gwen could not show proof of maintaining contact prior to their marriage.

'Haba! Proof of maintaining contact kwa!' exclaimed Gwen. 'This is a man who calls me every other day with his international call card. He has thrown all the cards away in the bin, how do they want him to carry over 100 used cards to Nigeria biko nunu! Please pardon me!'

'My enemies are at it again,' said Chinua stoically, 'but you know what? I shall defeat them. You must go to this London o! I will pray and fast, until this visa is granted to you.'

After Lawrence sought the advice of a lawyer, he was now advised appropriately on how to establish contact with his wife. He called her on his landline at least once a week and this registered in his phone bill, which he gathered over the months and included in his fresh application for his wife. He was also advised by his lawyer to wait for some time before lodging the fresh application, which they did. Gwen was then subsequently granted entry clearance visa to join her husband in the UK.

When Lawrence heard about the success of this application, he asked her how many years were granted, and Gwen replied five years. 'Five years? I thought they said it was two years probationary period,' he mumbled. 'Yes it used to be,' Gwen replied confidently, pretending now to have a little knowledge of the UK immigration rules. 'The law has changed now, and so they no longer issue two years but five years. The lawyer explained to me that part of the reason is to see the subsistence of the marriage relationship within this period of five years.'

'I will come and pick you up, I'm checking online now to see if there is any cheap flight. It will be too daunting for you if I leave you to travel alone seeing as this will be your first time.'

'Oh, babes, thank you so much.'

'Babes?' questioned Lawrence. 'I told you, I really don't like that pet name. If you call me babes, when you now have my children, what will they be called?'

'Oh, sorry, babes—erm erm, sorry, honey,' quipped Gwen, sheepishly struggling to get used to the new name 'honey'.

'That's better, I prefer you calling me your honey, it sounds quite romantic and makes me believe I am the only honey in your cuppa.'

'What's cuppa?'

'Sorry, I meant your cup of tea,' he chuckled.

After Gwen was granted an entry clearance visa to join her husband in the UK, she returned briefly to see her mum in Delta state, and prayers were said for her and her husband. She was also escorted to the airport in Lagos with *atilogu* dancers making their full presence on that day to celebrate their marriage and send her off to the UK.

'Remember me and your siblings, my daughter. Remember who raised you o. Remember that the queen of England, despite her beauty and wealth, is still under a man o. Do not let my enemies laugh at me. Your marriage must work and it must be successful, and my God will lead you to the white man's land and you shall prosper.' These were the powerful prayers said by Chinua for her daughter Gwen.

'I will miss you.' They both almost said this simultaneously to each other as they hugged and cried while embracing each other. 'Do not forget the God you have always known and served,' Chinua advised her daughter. 'That God that saw me and you through the trials of life, that same God is taking you on another journey and will not forsake you, my daughter. Stay away from bad friends o! I hear that the white man allows women so much freedom which sometimes gets to their heads. Don't call police on your husband o, we forbid it! Marriage is not a bed of roses but you have gone through nursery, primary school, secondary school, and university and succeeded, you did not drop out, so you must not drop out from this school of marriage. 'Dibe ndidi', marriage is patience.'

'Thank you, Mummy Chinua,' said Gwen hurriedly before boarding the cab that took her straight to the motor park to Lagos where she will board her plane to the UK.

Yewande was on the ground in Lagos to assist them and to make their journey quite memorable. 'Oh, gal, na wao!' Yewande spoke in pidgin. She sobbed as they approached Murtala Mohammed International Airport in Lagos.

Despite her kindness, Yewande never stopped flirting around Lawrence. She would do anything during the short period they were together to stand up and exhibit her backside, rolling her eyes up and down oblivious of Gwen's presence.

'I wonder what he sees in this plain-looking girl,' Yewande thought to herself as she suddenly became engrossed in her thoughts, making her recoil suddenly while not engaging in the laughter and jokes shared by the newly married couple.

'A penny for your thoughts,' whispered Gwen. 'Erm, erm—yes, plain-looking, yes,' stuttered Yewande. 'What is plain-looking?' asked Gwen. 'Oh sorry, I just drifted off, don't mind me at all.' Yewande beguiled her thoughts with these excuses, stood up, and suddenly excused herself from their presence.

'I don't know what it is but I just don't fancy this your friend.'

'How do you mean?' asked Gwen. As Lawrence tried to explain what he meant, Yewande casually strolled in and took her seat close to Lawrence, avoiding the empty seat close to her friend Gwen. At this time, she smelled different and it was obvious that she freshened up and topped up another perfume and brushed her hair, which at this time was loosely spreading all over her face and neck.

'Passengers for flight AB00456 to London Heathrow, please, could you start boarding from gate E.'

As they heard the public announcement at the departure lounge, they knew it was time to say goodbye to Yewande, who at this time was off her face on drink. 'Here is my card.' Yewande stretched forward her hands and tried to hand her business card to Lawrence. 'What's that?' he asked. 'Pass it on to my wife, please.' He shoved her off while briskly walking towards Gwen and holding her hands, beckoning that they rush off.

'You for stay back small now, ah ah, wetin,' she moaned. 'Na so the marriage done dey do you?' Yewande chuckled in pidgin. Gwen, who all this while kept mute all through the drive to the airport and even beyond, understood that there was always a dark side to her friend Yewande. If she noticed her friend's flirtatious behaviour towards her husband, she at least did not show it. She knew there was more for her to bother about. Here she was an unemployed graduate who struggled to find a job but could not because of her solid religious upbringing. Now she was flying on an international plane with a man she could now boldly call her own. She had also not even entered a local plane before, she thought deeply, not sure of what would befall her once she started living under the same roof with Lawrence. 'I hope his mum likes me,' she whispered to herself.

'Huh?' asked Yewande. 'What did you say?' At this time, Yewande thought Gwen was talking to her.

'I am not talking to you, we need to rush and board immediately before it's too late.'

'Too late ke,' responded Yewande, 'we are one hour early. Your flight leaves at 6 p.m., it's 5 p.m. by my time now.'

'Who told you that?' asked Gwen. 'My flight leaves now, did you not listen to the public announcement system?'

'Bye, Yewande,' Lawrence smiled coyly in his boyish manner. 'Bye,' Yewande answered. 'Take care of my friend o!'

'Perhaps you may want to come with us, to be doubly sure that your friend will be taken care of.'

'Ah, this man, you have bad mouth o! I thought you are my brother.'

'Bye, Yewande,' shouted Gwen quickly. 'Honey, let's go, we are running late.' She rushed to hug her friend Yewande, who at this time was shedding tears. It was, however, not clear whether her tears arose out of a frustration that she could not end up enticing Lawrence or whether it was based on pure love for a friend whom she would miss dearly.

As Yewande found her way back to the car park on her way back home, she thought of the last time she escorted a cousin of hers to this same airport. This cousin of hers owed her some money from a business deal handed over to Yewande which she completed and added her own profit; it then turned out that her cousin traced the home address of every single debtor who owed them money, collected all money owed, including the additional profit meant for Yewande, and till date did not mention anything about her actions. Yewande vividly remembered how when she saw her cousin to the airport on her trip to Europe, she started crying as they approached the airport; she was actually crying because she knew that she would miss her cousin so much, having been not just a cousin to her but a close friend and confidant. To Yewande's chagrin, immediately the cousin who at this time was in the car with her, saw her crying, she screamed hysterically, 'Why are you crying, why are you crying, is it money? Money. Money', it actually dawned on Yewande that her cousin was referring to the money which she took from Yewande without sharing part of the profit with her, despite the fact that Yewande sold most of the these wares to her customers using her time and resources.

As Yewande thought of this, she sighed to herself, 'Life, oh life, and to think that at the time this actually happened, I thought I was the one at fault. Life is survival of the fittest. This silly Britico man who calls himself my friend's husband, God has saved him today. Tomorrow is another day. He will fall into my trap some other day,' Yewande promised herself and whether this promise was kept is something which is left to be imagined.

As Gwen boarded the international flight to London, she could not believe her luck. She had a mind set on what she would achieve in the white man's land. However, while on board the plane, as much as she tried to take her mind off the phobia of flying, she could not help but show her naivety as the plane taxied down the runway to take off.

'This is Sabena Airways flight AB000456 to Heathrow . . .' As Gwen listened to this announcement, she drifted off into sleep only to be woken up one hour later by her husband, who at this time had ordered some snacks and drinks on board the plane for both of them. 'You okay?' he asked. 'Oh yes,' she responded. 'I am a bit nervous though, this is the first international flight I have ever boarded and I am trying to get used to the luxury,' Gwen said in her matter-of-fact manner. 'Never mind, you will be fine, make yourself comfortable and relax, you are with your husband, remember?' She looked at him and smiled heartily while he smiled back and held her hands. 'You know, your mum,' he went on, 'your mum is an amazing woman. Do you realise that most of all the traditional stuff requested by your dad and other chiefs during the traditional marriage was somehow waived by your mother. She is so understanding and supportive. Such women are hard to find these days. I remember in England when I attended a friend's marriage engagement, the wife's mother almost sent my friend and his family to the Bank of England vault that night, because of her very high demand and insatiable greed for money. I could not cope with that at all.'

The remaining part of the flight to London was spent quietly in unspoken words as these two newly-weds held hands as a sign of reassurance of their love for each other.

****

Chapter Fifteen

<u>Welcome to London</u>

As they drove home from Heathrow Airport, it suddenly dawned on Gwen that indeed this was going to be a new life and a new environment and community for her. She needed to learn the lifestyle, their food, sometimes the cockney English and the different accents within this community.

Gwen enjoyed the multicultural society of London. In all her life, she had never seen so many people from different races and colours living together so peacefully amongst themselves without any fear of intimidation.

One thing that also struck Gwen which she found even more fascinating was the fact that all the streets in London were lit up, the roads were too smooth without bumps, and there were also police cars with their siren bleeping as they drove past the streets. She noticed the right-hand-driven cars and found that quite intriguing.

She imagined herself driving on such a busy street at night all alone after having mastered the routes, and this thought almost made her breathless with a cacophonic mixture of anxiety and fear.

Aside from the fact that the community had facilities and infrastructure, she however noticed a kind of loneliness and stand-offish behaviour of people in the community. Everybody sort of minded their own business and they spoke through their nostrils. Gwen had an expectation that once they landed, they would continue to have visitors who would come in to congratulate them having been newly married, but there were none.

They had been back now for one week, and the only person who called the house was her friend Judy, who promised to come over to see her once she was off work.

She was amazed at her friend's structured pattern of life and was disappointed. 'Et tu, Brute?' she mimicked. What kind of work would prevent a long-time friend from taking time to see her friend who had only just arrived in town? 'Na wao!' she exclaimed in pidgin English.

This was Judy who was so close to her she could not believe that Judy would stay back in her home for one day without rushing to see her, knowing that she was in town and also having only been recently married to a friend whom she introduced to her.

The feeling of loneliness was also nothing compared to the constant concerns she noticed people had in the community. Words she heard people mention each time over the phone or in conversation were bills, mortgage, work shifts. They also talked about the weather, which she later found out was something quite huge within the community.

'Na wa for dis London people o!' Gwen exclaimed to herself. 'Babes, babes,' she called out to her new husband. 'Please, I need to call my mum in Nigeria. Babes!' No answer. She walked straight to the telephone in the living room, sat down nicely, and started dialling.

'The number you have called is not recognised, please check the number and dial again . . .' This was the automated response from the phone company BT.

'Aha, what is wrong with this phone? Babes!' Then suddenly Lawrence walked out of the bathroom into the living room and sighted his wife dialling an international number with the house phone. 'What are you doing?' he asked her sternly.

'I have been calling you, babes, where were you? I want to call Nigeria, I'm bored already.'

'How can you be bored when am here with you, huh? You are bored because you insist on calling me babes. You don't call Nigeria using the landline, that is pretty expensive. Once I step out later, I will buy you an international call card, it's just £5.00 and you can at least speak with your mum and siblings for as long as twenty minutes or even more.'

'Oh! Okay. I didn't know that. Was that why the phone kept on saying, "Your call cannot be completed, please hang up and try again?"'

'No, it could be because you have not added the country code, that must be why, and also, I barred all international calls from my landline, making it difficult for anyone to call an international number from my landline.'

'Na wa o. This is a new school o.'

'What's that?' asked Lawrence. 'I mean, I am learning really fast in this your country o,' she said amidst laughter by both of them. 'Obodo oyibo, here I am,' she jokingly screamed out.

Hours later, Lawrence went out to the newsagents to purchase an international call card. 'Do you want to come with me?' he asked Gwen. 'Oh no, I am cold, go alone.'

'I will run along then, but I thought if you come with me perhaps I can teach you how to charge the gas and electricity at the news agents when I am not around.'

'Please, my husband, leave it for some other day, there is a whole lot to learn.'

'Okay then, if you say so, will be back.' Lawrence was back in a jiffy. 'Here is the international call card.' Lawrence handed this over and taught Gwen how to scratch it off with a coin and proceeded to teach her how to call with the PIN number. As this was done, Gwen heard the automated voice instructing her on what to do and she became amazed. 'Aha! This woman speaking has so much time o,' she said. 'Please type in your number, your credit is £5, please enter the number you wish to dial. Na wao! Is this her full-time job?' Lawrence could not stop laughing at Gwen's innocent genuine comments and intrigues over the western technologies which she was now being exposed to. He laughed and called her a bush girl.

Gwen spent more than thirty minutes on the phone, talking to her mother Chinua. Chinua also asked her why Judy had not been to see her. She then told her mum that the life in the UK is completely different from the life in Nigeria. 'The life here requires careful planning, Mama,' she said. 'Judy has to plan to take time off work before she can come over to visit me. She also has to notify me and my husband in advance to make sure the arrangement is convenient also for the two of us.'

'So you mean when you have your child and I want to visit you in the white man's land, I will have to get permission?' asked Chinua.

'Mama, this place na wao! You cannot just visit people the way you like as we do it back home in Nigeria. You have to call them to let them know you are coming. Even when you visit people, they are not obliged to accommodate or feed you. It has to be something planned over a period of time. The only language they talk about here is bills, bills, bills. It looks as if people live their lives here to pay bills. Judy cannot visit me because she is working and, until she is off work, cannot visit me.

'My own beloved husband,' she whispered, 'my husband hardly stays at home. He works round the clock. His mother has also not visited us since we came back from Nigeria. She is too tired and we will be at her place every other weekend, that's when we can visit. I have, however, spoken to her on the phone several times and I think we both have struck the chord of friendship and mutual respect.

'Mama, this place is lonely o! I don't even know who our neighbours are. Everybody minds their business and they all seem to talk through their nostrils and they are very slim. It looks as if they don't eat food at all. They look like osisi ukazi, strands of a vegetable plant. I hear some of them live on just plain nuts and raw vegetables. Each time in the morning, you see them in piles, running. They call it jogging, and each of them wears this type of tracksuit sold in Oshodi market with canvas, sweating it out. I also noticed that some of them block their ears with two plugs and could get knocked down by a car, na wao!

'Mama, you need to come and see for yourself, all the streets are lighted up at night and the roads are quite smooth. Once it's 6 p.m., everywhere becomes pitch-dark. Beke bu agbara,' literally meaning the white man is a terrestrial spirit, a word commonly used amongst the Igbos to emphasise the civilisation and advancement of the white man.

'If only my husband will allow me to wash my clothes and his clothes with my hands ye kwe modidi, it will be bearable for me, but no, he insists it is faster with the washing machine, which spins and spins and spins non-stop, squeezing all colour and good quality of my linen fabrics to shreds.

'Mama, Mama, someone is speaking on the other side of the phone saying my credit is finishing, it looks like someone has tapped my phone, I will call you later.'

'Babes, babes!' As Gwen called out for her husband, she heard him laughing aloud. 'Why are you laughing? What is funny?' Lawrence then told her no one tapped her phone—that the voice she heard while on the phone was only warning her that her credit had run out.

'Now, Mrs Lawrence,' he mused, 'have I not told you not to call me babes?'

'Oh, sorry, my king,' Gwen answered.

Subsequent days in London found Gwen even getting more amazed at events and occurrences. The diversity of the community was something she found quite interesting. She looked forward to each passing day. There were people from all over the continent of Africa and Europe all living in London. There were Asians, people from the Caribbean, people from the Philippines, China, Nigeria, Ghana, Cameroon, Sierra Leone, Congo, Brazil, Ethiopia, Kenya, Zimbabwe, South Africa, Singapore, United Arab Emirates, so many beautiful people. She never saw so many people living together peacefully like this before, Gwen thought to herself. She would, however, later discover that amidst this diversity, there were also issues that had to do with cultural differences. There were also serious issues dwelling amongst people in diaspora who are envious of one another and therefore compete amongst themselves as to who succeeds better than the other, leading to a spirit of rivalry, lack of genuine love, and sometimes loneliness and unhealthy rivalry and competition.

Lawrence was fantastic during the first two years of their marriage. He made sure that he took Gwen everywhere she wanted to go to. He registered her with his own family doctor and she was issued a new NHS card.

Lawrence also encouraged his wife Gwen to get her National Insurance number at the Department of Works and Pension. As she did not want to be staying idle at home, she kept on pestering him to allow her find a job even if it was a part-time job.

'Okay, I know where you can find a job. I will buy you Guardian society on Wednesday on my way from work so we can search for a job. The thing is, you do not have any UK experience and so it will be difficult for you to be offered a decent job at this stage. I would rather you attend college or university to get some UK qualifications, and after that, you can start searching for a job.'

Gwen stared at her husband in disbelief. 'So what happens to me while I'm attending these courses, I will just be here not earning any money while you pay all the bills? No, it cannot happen, my friend Judy advised me the other day that it is best that couples in this country work together in unity, to avoid any form of resentment. If you continue to work and I then continue to stay at home while all the financial burden is placed on you, this may lead to resentment and frustration, considering the way life is run in this part of the world. I've been told there is nothing like 'sole provider', this syndrome died with the colonial masters in Africa o!

'I am ready to work. My friend has told me how to get a voluntary job where I can work for free for six months, and after that, I can get a reference from these people. She told me the place is in All Gate.'

'All Gate? Where is that in London?' mused Lawrence. 'Oh, do you mean Aldgate? It must be Aldgate. So when are you billed to go there?'

'Judy promised to get me the application form from another friend of hers this weekend when she comes to visit again. There is another job which she mentioned, she said the place is called We Care, where I can do some menial jobs there and be paid substantial amount.'

'Gwendolyn,' chipped in Lawrence, 'there is nowhere called We Care in the whole of the United Kingdom. What is wrong with your memory? You seem to be pronouncing these names as if you have gone bonkers, if it's not All Gate, it is Egiware instead of Edgware, or Lechester instead of Leicester. The other day you pronounced Surrey as Sureh!'

'Can you pronounce any African word?' asked Gwen. 'Okay, let me give you the simplest African word to pronounce, if you get it right, I will give you one hundred naira.'

'One hundred naira? Where do you think you are, Nigeria? Blimey.'

'Okay, pronounce the name Ikemefuna.' Lawrence sighed heavily and said, 'Aikemefun!'

'HA ha ha!' laughed Gwen. 'you see how difficult it is now?, you must commend me for even pronouncing these English words properly even though English is not my first language. You lose, I win,' she cracked, to Lawrence's chagrin.

'Oh, you mean IKEA?'

'Yes, IKEA.'

'What job can you do there anyway?' asked Lawrence. 'I will clarify with Judy when she visits, but I think I prefer that in Aldgate as it will assist you with what you want to study later in this country.'

'Why is it that the way people pronounce things in this country is different?' asked Gwen. 'You pronounce Egiware as Edgware, Surikeys as Surrey Quays, Sorry as Surrey, Lewis Ham as Lewisham, Leicester as Lester, 'Isn't it?' as 'Innit?', 'Are you all right?' as 'You'rright?', butter as burrer, water as warra.'

'How did you hear all this pronunciation?' asked Lawrence surprisingly.

'Of course on TV, that's all I do when you go out to work.'

'Hmm, my lovely wife is really catching up fast,' joked Lawrence.

'What church do you attend here?' asked Gwen.

'Church?'

'Yes, church.'

'You know I work most weekends and anytime I am off work, I either rest or attend the Church of England down the street where we live.'

'I thought you told me you were born-again?'

'Of course I am born-again, but I am a staunch member of the Church of England.'

'I will really love to attend any of the Pentecostal churches close by if I have my way, just to see the difference between the ones here and the ones in Nigeria. I will ask Judy when she visits again.'

As promised, Judy visited that weekend and brought a copy of an application form which they filled together, with Judy doing most of the writing. 'How is marriage life treating you?' Judy asked her friend. 'Fine,' responded Gwen, 'but I am bored. I need a job. I need to take care of my mother and younger siblings back home in Nigeria. It's been seven months now since I came to this UK. To say I am disillusioned is an understatement. I promised my poor mum and siblings that immediately I come in, I will turn their lives around. They have held on to that promise tenaciously, bombarding me with telephone calls each day and every day, sometimes crying over the phone, thinking I have abandoned them just because I am now in a comfort zone—the white man's land.'

'My daughter,' said Chinua. 'You are my hope now, you know I am getting old and cannot really work hard the way I used to, since my business got burnt. I could not recover and West African Intercontinental Bank are at my back, sending me letters every day to come and pay up my debt. I have a major concern because I have mortgaged my land to get that loan and they have my land documents. They sold off my neighbours' house the other day and I need you to please come to my aid to pay back this loan.' As Chinua narrated this to Gwen, her daughter, she burst into tears.

'I understand, Ma, but I don't have a job just yet, this place is not what people back home think it is. Money don't come easy in this part of the world. The truth is that you still have to work as hard as you do anywhere else in the world to make ends meet. It is also not automatic, you have to go through a process of getting good advisers to show you the right way to go, get a job, and get a career by getting additional qualification and UK experience before you can say you have found your feet.'

'I will do whatever it takes to help my mother, because a promise is a debt,' said Gwen. 'Are there no other menial jobs that I can start with that can at least pay me a meagre wage pending when I get a better one? I can add my voluntary job with a paid job and just juggle between the two.' Judy promised to carry out some further search and information regarding anywhere she could find a quick job.

Eight weeks later, Gwen got a job after searching tremendously in all the daily newspapers—Guardian Society. She started working in a care home as a support worker. Her job included assisting people with dual diagnosis (people with alcohol and drug problems) to run their daily lives. This, however, was not automatic as she had to attend a one-month course where she was taught manual handling and other nitty-gritty of working in a care home. She was also issued a moving and handling certificate. Her husband Lawrence paid for the course, a payment which included a CRB check which was carried out and uniforms were handed to her. Gwen hated the uniform; it made her look too serious, she thought to herself.

On her first day at work, she enjoyed the work environment, the gigantic building in a nice posh area in London. What she did not enjoy, however, was the shift pattern of the job. She did both morning and evening shifts which meant she either had to wake up as early as 5.00 a.m. to travel all the way to work in the freezing cold winter. She preferred the evening shift but also had misgivings about having to get home late at night, not sure of the safety when at times she found herself alone at the bus stop waiting for the bus to come. Another interesting aspect of her bus journeys was the fact that she wondered how the buses kept to time. At each bus stop, each time she waited for her bus, she always saw one or two people, reading the map at the bus stop and she thought to herself, 'How do they understand the reading of this map? I really don't get it.'

She noticed that all the buses were numbered and each had its different routes and timings. She preferred to sit at the topmost upper deck of bus 53 each time she was on her way to work. It gave her an ample view of the beautiful city which had suddenly become her own city.

One cold lonely night, at about 10.30 p.m., Gwen had a close shave with a street mugger who tried to grab her bag from her at the bus stop. She was so fortunate that night because immediately this hooded guy plunged at her, she pulled back her handbag from him forcefully and saw the bus approaching; she jumped into the bus on the wrong side, where passengers were alighting and started shouting 'Ole ole, thief thief' while the young hooded man fizzled away into the dark lonely park directly opposite the bus stop, like a whirlwind.

At this point, Gwen did not realise she took the wrong bus heading to a different route. Once she realised, she asked a gentleman on the bus where she could alight and get another bus; this gentleman, who had a cockney accent kept on answering by nodding his head continuously, and when he finally spoke, he kept on saying, 'Huh? Huh? Huh?' as if to say, 'I don't understand what you are saying.'

Gwen felt a little flustered and embarrassed by not just the response of this man but also his lack of willingness to help her, seeing she was only asking for directions.

Immediately, this same man stood up from where he was sitting and walked back to the back seat, ignoring her further. As Gwen looked towards this man, she saw an elderly woman who might be in her early sixties smiling in a friendly way and beckoning to her to come over. Gwen walked back to this woman and almost tripped as the double-decker bus stopped at another bus stop, allowing more passengers to alight from the bus.

'Se kosi?' This elderly woman asked her in a language she recognised as Yoruba. Even though she was not Yoruba, she understood that this woman was from Africa—Nigeria, for that matter—and immediately she felt a sense of belonging. 'I have a bit of a problem, ma, I think I missed my way by getting into the wrong bus, ma.'

'Where are you going, my daughter?' she asked.

'I am going to Sorry Keys.'

'Do you mean Surrey Quays? It is called Surrey Quays, my daughter, not Sorry Keys.'

'Oh, okay, ma, thank you, ma.'

'I think you must have taken the wrong bus o! You should be on the other side of the road, not on the side where you took the bus. You have to get down at the next bus stop, cross to the other side and then look out for the right bus going to Surrey Quays.'

'Thank you so much, ma.'

'Ose, my dear,' grinned the elderly woman satisfactorily.

As Gwen alighted from the bus at the next bus stop, she kept on thinking to herself how it was that the traffic rules here were the other way round; you had to always keep left unlike what was obtainable in Nigeria. She also thought about the elderly woman who gave her directions in the bus. She noticed vividly that despite her age, this woman had a beautiful gold diamond-crusted ring on her fingers. 'These are the lucky ones,' she thought to herself. 'My mother Chinua has been so unlucky in her relationship with men, even though this woman may not be totally or completely better than my mother in character, looks, her perspective of life, or her morals. Being married and staying married takes a whole lot,' she thought to herself.

'Beauty is just about 10 per cent of what it takes. Character may be 50 per cent but the remaining 40 per cent may have to do with destiny, God, and a stint of good luck. I will do everything within my power to make sure my marriage works, just to prove a point that something good can also come from a child raised by a single mother contrary to what society believes,' Gwen thought to herself in a matter-of-fact manner.

Pim! Pim! Pim! Pim! Pim! Pim! Gwen suddenly heard the screech of a car and a loud horn blasting across the road as she tried to cross to the other side of the road to catch the correct bus. 'What the heck! Are you crazy? Have you lost your mind?' She heard the driver swearing and screaming at the top of his voice as he drove past.

She ran quickly to the other side and tried to wave at the driver, apologising, but he was gone. She shivered in the cold, more out of fright, despite the chilly weather, than out of the effect of the cold weather.

As Gwen waited for her bus, she suddenly remembered to check her phone and she saw twenty missed calls, ten text messages from her husband Lawrence. One of the text messages read 'Honey, where are you? Are you okay? I'm worried about you, please call me as soon as you get this message.'

She tried to call him back and the phone was engaged. Five minutes later, a call came through from Lawrence and she answered. He was fuming on the other end. 'Where are you?' he asked.

'I am on my way. I got lost, had a near miss with a thief, ran into the wrong bus, heading back home now.'

'Okay then, you better be careful, this is why I asked you to stay at home for long until you become accustomed to the streets of London. London is tough just like any other major cosmopolitan city around the world.'

'Where are you now, are you almost home?'

'I don't think so because I just got on the bus now,' responded Gwen rather irritably despite her husband's show of genuine concern.

'Let me know when you are almost home, I will come pick you up from the bus stop, the one close to the Texaco gas station.'

'Okay, thanks, will do,' replied Gwen thankfully.

As the bus lazily drove down the lighted streets of South East London, through East Street, Walworth Road, down Elephant and Castle Tube Station, Gwen drifted off to sleep; she was quite tired now as she had done a long day working back to back twelve hours non-stop with a one-hour break in between. She had calculated to herself that this would be the best way of achieving two things at the same time, if she did four long days in her regular job and then three days in her voluntary job. She worked seven days a week, sometimes taking off days on Sundays to attend church with her husband who had a regular nine-to-five job with the local council and a part-time weekend job.

When Gwen got home on this day, Lawrence searched through the map and looked for alternative train routes which, according to him, were faster and safer for her.

Travelling by train was another great and exhilarating experience for Gwendolyn Mudiaga. She referred to the Oyster card as world-class technology of the white man. Sometimes rather than simply calling it an Oyster card, she preferred to say, 'the Oyster card and its magic'.

'How did these people do these things even?' she asked herself.

As she tried to pass through the barriers, she was reminded to touch in and touch out by the station attendant. 'Touch out kwa?' she said bemusedly. 'First it was an escalator playing around with my head when I tried to use the wrong one and met with a deadlock, now it's touch in, touch out, okay o!'

Even though she had so much to master with her Tube journeys, she enjoyed it more and found it more straightforward, quicker, and less tiring. Each time she embarked on her journey to work, she would always recite Psalm 91 as the thought of the train travelling underground made her quite apprehensive; the more she travelled by train, the more she became afraid. She did not understand how humans commuted each day underground and still had a full supply of oxygen, without getting suffocated. 'Hmm, anya furum ihe. My eyes have seen a lot'—she was referring to her experiences in London.

****

To Gwen, her new job as a support worker was a source of financial relief for her and her extended family back home; she would send money home to her mother on a monthly basis. She placed her on a monthly maintenance of N20,000, which increased later to N50,000 as the months progressed and she started saving some money also. She also sent clothes, jewellery, and shoes to her family once she knew of anyone who was travelling back home.

She once had a bad experience with a friend whom she reconnected with upon her visit to the UK. She bought two suitcases of clothes and shoes and handed them to this friend to pass on to her mother and siblings but till date, those things never got to her family and every attempt made by Gwen to contact her friend was frustrated.

Once she called her friend's number and heard the voice of a lady—a voice she recognised as her friend's voice, having been acquainted with her since their primary school days. Immediately she started asking why the two suitcases never got to her family, the lady on the other end changed to a foreign accent saying, 'Wrong number please.'

Gwen had learnt a lesson through this, not to trust a person just based on the number of years she had known that person, as they may have changed over the years because of life's struggles, new relationships and new beliefs, and challenges of life.

Seven months after Gwen started working with her employers, she started facing problems of racial discrimination. This was the second time she would experience this since her relocation to the UK. The first experience was when she was ignored by a passenger in a bus, whom she asked questions about her bus route when she boarded the wrong bus on her way home. This same passenger also changed seats once Gwen sat close to him.

One day as Gwen was on an afternoon shift with one of her white colleagues, it was time to prepare lunch for the residents and she entered the fully furnished kitchen. She met her colleague Chloe bringing out ingredients from the two-door American-style fridge. Gwen had checked the menu for that day and knew they were to prepare jacket potatoes served with tuna and vegetable salad. Earlier during that shift, her colleague had all the while ignored her or even feigned not understanding her each time she spoke by saying, 'Huh? Huh? Huh? I can't hear you, Gwen, you know you have got an accent, don't you?'

'Of course I agree I've got accent, this is part of my identity, you have got accent also, have you not?' Immediately Gwen gave this response, Chloe turned away from her in anger and walked briskly away, avoiding any further contact with Gwen the remaining part of the shift.

As Gwen travelled by train back home on that day, she was so scared. She almost fell off the escalator as she approached the wrong side moving downwards. She sighted a teenage girl who tried to laugh while another woman pulled this girl out of the way. Gwen got the message and turned round into the right escalator taking her upwards. As she got to the edge of this escalator, she practically jumped out, almost skidding off balance.

'How they put these machineries in place still beats me,' she said to herself. Immediately she heard 'The next station is Elephant and Castle, please mind the gap between the train and the station.'

As she prepared to alight off the train, she kept on wondering why that station was named after an elephant. 'I will ask my husband once I get home,' she promised herself. 'I hope I will not forget the name, I will use *hippopotamus* to remember the name.'

The next day upon resuming her shift, she walked down the hallway and as she entered the kitchen, Chloe immediately shut the fridge as if she noticed the entrance of a contagious germ disease flying in. 'I need to have a word with you, please,' she said curtly with an assured air of superiority.

'Okay, hope no problem, just wait for me, let me go and piss.'

'Piss?' You are swearing, Gwen, that is foul language, and people who work here are not allowed to swear, and more so, this is an environment where vulnerable people are rehabilitated and rehoused, it is unacceptable for you to keep using swear words in this environment.'

'I did not know that the word *piss* is linked to swearing o! I'm sorry, will be back.' Gwen rushed off to the restroom and came back five minutes later. 'Ehen, you said you wanted to see me.'

'Yeees! Pardon me, but what I want to say to you is that I will rather prefer to cook the residents' meal alone, seeing that you are not used to most of the menu and the ingredients used. The last time I cooked with you, you seemed lost and did not know how to prepare a simple jacket potato. You also asked me where the jacket to the potato was, I thought that was unbelievable and haven't even mentioned your naivety to the manager just yet. While I prepare dinner, you could go do other things.'

Gwen then answered, 'I may not be used to the ingredients or the food, but I am willing to learn if you teach me. Seeing that I was not employed as a cook, neither am I a chef, you cannot stop me from joining you to cook in this kitchen, a small girl like you, when I qualified from the university, I'm sure you were still running around in nappies. Do you know I am a graduate of a notable university in Africa?' Gwen ranted and ranted, and suddenly noticed that her colleague Chloe turned completely pale and was agitated. She ran out of the kitchen in fright, thinking that Gwen would hurt her because of the aggression she exhibited. At the back of her mind, she thought perhaps Gwen had some mental health problems and must have lost it. She didn't know anyone could express their anger with so much aggression.

Gwen was very happy on that day that she asserted herself. She thought to herself that she made her husband proud by asserting herself. 'This little girl born yesterday, coming to tell me what to do, can you imagine the effrontery?' She could not wait for her break time to call to speak to her husband and her best friend Judy—these were people who had warned her in advance of some of the challenges she might face at her place of work.

During her break time, Gwen called her husband Lawrence to let him know what transpired between her and her colleague Chloe, but his phone went straight into voice mail. She immediately called her friend Judy and heard a message at the other end: 'The subscriber voicemail is full.'

'Aha, subscriber ke,' she thought to herself and as she looked down on her phone then noticed that she had dialled the wrong number. 'Mseeeeeew,' she sighed to herself. 'I don't need this at all.' Gwen immediately called her friend again, and she picked up the phone. 'Have been trying to call you, oh madam.' Judy jokingly sighed. Madam was a name she chose to call Gwen anytime she wanted to pull her leg while pretending to be formal and respectful. 'I have been calling you myself, Judy, thank God I got you.'

'Are you okay?' Judy asked.

'Wish I was,' she replied. 'It's one little girl here at my workplace trying to wind me up, can you imagine?'

'What happened?'

'Since the first day this girl set eyes on me, she has been cold towards me. I tried to ignore her because I know why I am here, but no, she will not let me be. Today she actually called me aside and tried to order me around, telling me I should not cook residents' food with her. She did not just stop there but went on to remind me that the last time I prepared residents' dinner with her, I showed a naivety that was paralleled with ignorance and my lack of understanding of the ingredients and menu. Trust me now, when I started with her, she ran out of the kitchen and became so scared.'

'You have to be patient with your work colleagues. London is a leveller, no one respects age or qualifications, especially when it's not gained within the UK. People rise through the ranks and become managers and supervisors. You upset people even more by telling them you are overqualified for your job and then you make yourself a target. What matters here is the skill and experience on the job over the years,' chuckled Judy as she struggled between laughter and her ability to address such an important issue.

'Gwen, you will encounter even worse things at your place of work. You are lucky that your colleague was diplomatic in her approach and did not say whatever she said in the presence of other colleagues to embarrass you.'

'The worst-case scenario you may sometimes come across will be people from your African origin who will gang up against you to make sure you are sacked. We get this every day in different workplaces in the UK. This is the way of the world here in the UK, the African diasporans are quite competitive and envious of one another for reasons best known to them, and what other nationalities do is to take undue advantage of this, because a house divided against itself cannot stand, if you know what I mean.

'One thing I will advise you, however, is not to raise your voice when you try to put your case across. Be assertive but not aggressive. I will see you next weekend, okay? Bye.'

'Thanks, Judy. Bye, then.'

'Tell Lawrence I was here and I met him sleeping, later he will complain I don't visit old man,' giggled Judy.

'Haba, who are you calling, old man, is it my Okor?' (*Okor* meant husband.) 'You must be dreaming, please get a life, you are jealous,' joked Gwen in return.

After Judy hung up, Gwen sat down to play back the incident between her and Chloe. When she got home that day after her second encounter with Chloe at work, she narrated the whole incident to her husband, and unlike Judy, he advised Gwen to stop working and instead concentrate on her voluntary work. 'Why should I stop working? Tell me. I have to work, you cannot be paying all the bills while I sit down and enjoy all the luxury of life. It's quite unfair. I am an adult and must take a bit of responsibility on my own. Working is part of life,' she said.

'Okay, no worries, but please be careful and do not overreact so that you are not misinterpreted.'

'Okay, I'll try, my husband.'

As she thought of the love, happiness, and support she had received from Lawrence since joining him in the UK, she missed him suddenly, and so walked straight into their bedroom, where Lawrence was lying down, pretending to be sleeping. 'Come here,' Lawrence beckoned Gwen to join him in bed and as she tucked herself into the luxurious silk duvet cover, he held her closely to his hairy chest while kissing her all over. He then stretched out his hands and turned off the bedside lamp.

'Thank you for the love and understanding you have shown me as a husband. I love you,' Gwen whispered into her husband's ears while nibbling gently at his cheek, running her hands along his torso. 'I miss you,' continued Gwen.

'But I'm here with you and I love you too,' whispered Lawrence. 'I loved you from the first time I set eyes on your photos, despite not having met you in person. Imagine a person returning from a long journey that is thirsty and finally being offered water to drink. The feeling of relief and satisfaction such a person feels cannot be compared to what I feel about you,' continued Lawrence in his usual husky voice.

'Hmm, you're making my head swell,' grinned Gwen while at the same time wondering how Lawrence managed to have a clean, fresh breath any time of the day, whether awake or asleep. Gwen was however jostled out of her thoughts as Lawrence pulled her closer to him while caressing her body all over, gently penetrating her while she let out silent groans in excitement and pleasure. 'You are always wet,' he moaned. 'I love it.' As he felt her warm wetness inside, he continued his gentle strokes until they both reached orgasm and drifted off to sleep.

****

A New Dawn

The next day at work, Gwen noticed that her colleague Chloe called in sick. After that day, the office rota was also amended several times. At first she thought it was a coincidence but later she realised that whenever she was put down to work with Chloe, she would call in sick, leaving her to work with a locum staff who had to be called to fill in that shift at short notice.

Gwen was not bothered by this seeming avoidance by her colleague. 'It's up to her, if she chooses not to work with me, she is the one that has a problem, not me.' Unknown to Gwen, however, Chloe had an ace up her sleeve. She took time to make up stories and deliberate lies against Gwen in a bid to make sure that Gwen got sacked.

Weeks later, after the encounter with Chloe, Gwen was invited by her manager Annabel to what the manager called an informal grievance meeting, where a complaint was lodged against her that she was heard swearing at a colleague while working and also heard shouting inappropriately at that same colleague who happened to be from an African country. This same colleague, Boma, was also a person determined to gang up with others to bear false witness against Gwen.

Immediately Gwen knew who this colleague was, she tried to give an account of what transpired with Chloe and another male colleague.

Surprisingly, her manager went on to say to her that indeed she did not see anything wrong if Chloe suggested to her that she preferred to cook dinner alone, because it was a choice. When Gwen tried to question why this should be, the manager did not sound convincing, saying that was just what it was. Days ran into weeks, weeks into months, and it was quite clear that Gwen was unhappy each time she went to work. As time went on, what seemed like a subtle discomfort at work became a major concern as other colleagues would ignore her at work, even when she said hello or good morning.

It seemed like a gang-up or something planned. She could not really place it but knew something was wrong. One day as they attended a meeting together with other work colleagues, she tried to speak up as part of her contribution to an idea raised about a service user's daily care plan during the meeting. As she spoke up, all she heard was 'Huh huh? Huh? What did you say?' One of her colleagues, Nick, now said to her, 'You have got accent.' This direct attack on Gwen infuriated her, and she reacted immediately by shouting back 'You have got an accent also, don't you think so?' Immediately after this response, the whole meeting room became silent as everyone looked from left to right, wondering how she was so bold to be able to express herself back, despite her seeming naive and unassuming nature and demeanour. Gwen was even more infuriated on this day, considering that she had not spoken a word or made any contribution thirty minutes after the meeting commenced. All her other white colleagues sat together on a separate leather settee, while she was offered a single sofa to sit on. She felt so alone and this made her for the first time feel like abandoning every other thing and returning to Africa.

Gwen stood up and ran into the nearest bathroom, shut the door behind her, and started sobbing. She sobbed and sobbed, not quite sure what she was sobbing about. She sobbed about the loneliness she felt, having left home for the first time.

She missed her mother and siblings so much, her poor mother who struggled single-handedly to raise her and her siblings without any help or assistance, her siblings whose hope had been placed in her. She sobbed about the culture shock, the loneliness, not being able to visit people or freely talk to neighbours or friends the way she was used to in Nigeria. She remembered the frequent unannounced visits from family and friends to her home; she missed her mother's tales by moonlight and her stories about the Nigerian civil war. She sobbed about the lifestyle which she thought was so straightjacketed, a lifestyle where all people talked about was the weather, their bills, their mortgage and career.

She sobbed and sobbed, remembering that she only met her husband in person just once before she said 'I do', not having courted with him for a long time. She was not quite sure if the acceptance of marriage was borne out of love for her husband or out of desperation to be married to prove a point that she had accomplished this aspect of life despite being raised by a single parent, or out of the desperation to travel abroad in order to be able to rescue her family from the cold hands of poverty. 'I think I love him now—that's what really matters. He is kind to me and I feel really safe and secure with him,' she tried to reassure herself. For the first time in her life, a man was showing her love and attention, the kind of love and attention she never received from her father Chief Mudiaga. The thought of her father and the rejection experienced by her and her mother came rushing back all over again, and she felt sick and suddenly started shivering.

Gwen continued sobbing because she had concealed this heaviness of heart for such a long time. All of these sober reflections happened in a short while, and then suddenly, she heard a knock on the door which rudely took her from the subconscious to the conscious. 'Who is it?' she asked.

'It's me,' she heard the voice of one of her male colleagues, Matt, calling out from the outside. 'It's me, Gwen.'

'Oh, Matt,' Gwen called out, trying to conceal the heaviness in her voice, 'I won't be long.' This was the only staff toilet, used by all members of staff, both male and female, and she need not waste too much time any longer here, despite herself. She then stood up from the toilet seat, turned to the washbasin in the toilet sink and turned on the tap while she ran the cold water over her face. She wiped her face with the tissue, took a deep breath, and walked out of the restroom. Fortunately for her, Matt wasn't standing out there as she envisaged; she quickly rushed back to her desk, took her bag, dashed into the toilet the second time to freshen up her make-up.

As she proceeded out of the toilet, she felt a sharp pang of pain in her lower abdomen; she locked the door tightly with the latch at the back, sat on the toilet bowl to do the number two. The lasagne meal she had was definitely coming back to request her hands in 'friendship'. She was not used to this meal and it was now taking its toll on her. As she pushed, her stomach made noises. Tears slowly gushed out from her eyes, which at this time had turned red. The sound coming from the bathroom became too much, and Gwen decided to turn the tap on to downplay the loud, embarrassing sound. 'Oh dear,' she thought, 'this sound will definitely embarrass me today.'

When she finished, she flushed the toilet twice and checked to make sure there was no trace of any urine or human waste. She particularly remembered being given a query once when her manager reported that one of her colleagues confirmed that after Gwen used the toilet, she noticed that the toilet was not properly flushed as there was still human waste around the toilet bowl.

When she came out finally, Matt was already heading home—he just gave her thumbs-up and a wink and then whispered, 'Goodbye, see you tomorrow' while speeding off to his car parked outside the office building. 'Bye,' murmured Gwen, looking round and sniffing the environment, wondering if Matt perceived or inhaled any bad odour coming from the toilet which she had just 'bombed', in her exact words.

Gwen continued to dread going back to work; it persisted each day and every day. The aggression and unfair treatment at work continued to the extent that it started affecting her emotionally. She became always tearful, lost appetite, snapped at everything, and could no longer concentrate on her work. She mentioned this to another colleague at work where she normally did her part-time voluntary work and was advised to visit any citizens' advice bureau to seek advice on what her position was. She also visited her general practitioner who signed her off sick. She then took time off work and was sending sick notes weekly to her employer. This later changed to monthly sick notes as her condition worsened. Several times, she received telephone calls from her head office, asking her where she lived as they wanted to send HR personnel to visit her at home. She, however, turned down this offer as she was not sure why they wanted to visit her at home. She was also invited to see their occupational health personnel in order that an assessment of her health condition could be made by them and a report given to management. Once when Gwen visited the occupational health officer, she was astonished at this woman's reaction to her health situation. Despite explaining everything she was going through, the occupational health worker carelessly retorted, 'Your game is up, you better pack it in.' Gwen left her on that day feeling worse off and quite unsupported. She cried and cried on her way back home.

Once Gwen instructed a representative to contact her employers, she also gave a standing instruction that she should not be contacted directly anymore as she felt too sick to be burdened with an additional work problem. A couple of weeks after she instructed a representative to contact her employers, she received a letter from her employers offering her a certain amount of money in a compromise agreement. Gwen spoke extensively with both her representatives and ACAS on her position and rights before she finally accepted this money and signed off the compromise agreement, one of the conditions of which was the fact that she would not continue to be employed by her employers and would not institute any further legal actions against them in the future once she had accepted the offer of money given to her.

It was too much for her to take; she became quite emotional, and this even affected her relationship with her husband. She was advised to call ACAS to seek advice which she did; she also took additional advice from her representative. After weighing all her options, she decided it was not worth going back to a job where she would have to continuously watch her back all the time. She could be grassed up and put in serious trouble by her colleagues; it was time to take the money and move on with life.

Immediately after Gwen was paid this lump sum of money, she computed the equivalence of this money in naira and saw herself as a millionaire. 'So this is why everyone who stays abroad can become a millionaire in a short time, because of the value of the pounds,' Gwen thought to herself. 'I am a millionaire, I am a millionaire, who wants to be a millionaire, Gwen wants to be a millionaire,' she mimicked after a popular UK TV series. 'For the first time in my life, I am a millionaire.'

Once the cheque was paid into her account, she decided to send some bulk money home to her mum immediately. Her mum Chinua was full of thanks and blessings. She kept on singing in Igbo, 'Onye ge lem nka mobugunwa, onye gelem nka mobugunwa?' (Who will take care of me in my old age apart from my children?)

'Mama Chinua, don't worry. I will also send some wrappers and Georges soon, okay? I will get them from Liverpool street market where you can buy most African attires,' Chinua promised, and reassured her mum again.

After their first wedding anniversary, Gwen started becoming worried that she could not get pregnant. 'I thought doctors always advised that two years was the maximum for couples?' Lawrence mumbled once she expressed her concerns to him.

'Says who?' answered Gwen. 'I really want a child. I will have to see my GP.'

After Gwen booked an appointment to see her GP, all necessary tests were carried out on her and due referrals made to make sure that her fallopian tubes and ovaries were fine. Once all of these tests came out negative, she was also told that her womb was inverted, which was quite unusual but of little significance as far as childbearing was concerned. She was asked to rest a lot and to add a lot of fruits and vegetables to her daily diet. Advice was also given to her to watch out and understand her period of ovulation as this would be the best time to meet with her husband. 'Why don't you prescribe me Clomid?' asked Gwen. 'Clomid? How did you know about Clomid?' asked her GP. 'A friend of mine had twins after being prescribed this drug, she waited for seven years without conceiving and once she was placed on this drug, she conceived.'

'Hmm,' sighed her GP, Dr Michaels Togher. 'Clomid is just not any drug and I cannot prescribe it to you because you have no need for it. There are severe health risks which you can experience if such a drug is abused. You may experience ectopic pregnancy and other complications also, so be careful.'

When Gwen got home from the surgery, she relayed her conversation with her family doctor to her husband Lawrence. 'I don't know why you worry so much,' said her husband Lawrence. 'We have only been married twelve months now and I know everything is fine. I told you before that that job of yours is too stressful and I am grateful that it's all come to an end now, you need to stay at home and rest—that's all.'

True to what Lawrence said, three months after resting, Gwen became pregnant with her first child.

When she announced to her husband that she was pregnant, he was over the moon. 'This calls for celebration and a short holiday,' he said to her. He was so happy and ecstatic that he almost screamed down the whole house. 'So I am at last going to be a father,' he said. 'Yes of course,' said his wife Gwen. They held hands and looked into each other's eyes while Lawrence whispered sweet nothings into her ears, rubbing his crotch in between her navel and upper abdomen, an action which tickled Gwen tremendously causing her to laugh hysterically.

After losing her part-time job, Gwen was now determined to concentrate on something more professional and so she added a day to the three days she covered in her voluntary job. She worked so hard that whenever she returned home, her feet hurt so badly.

When Gwen was in the second trimester, one day while sitting at home alone, Gwen felt a warm sensation and at once rushed into the toilet to observe her knickers. She spotted blood in her knickers and also felt there was no movement around her stomach area. She hadn't felt her unborn baby for some time. She was not too sure why she would be bleeding; her husband had always been extra gentle with her since she announced that she was pregnant.

She discussed this with her husband, who then advised that she visit the hospital instantly the next day. She looked up the number in her maternity logbook and was asked to come in first thing in the morning for a scan. Once the scan was carried out, it was revealed to Gwen that the foetus had died in her womb. She was also advised to call a family member immediately to help take her home as she might not be in a right frame of mind to withstand the sad news all alone. Gwen immediately called her husband Lawrence, who drove down instantly to the hospital to take her home.

Once the news was made known to Lawrence, he took it stoically in his stride while consoling his wife with the words 'Never mind, we will have more children in God's own time.' Despite his words of consolation, he felt a deep sense of guilt as they drove home together on that day, heartbroken with a deep sense of loss and sadness.

'Maybe, just maybe, if I had not been working so hard, waking up early every morning and going to work, maybe if I had heeded your advice, I would not have lost this baby,' she thought to herself. 'You don't want to kill yourself by blaming yourself over anything,' said Lawrence.

'What will be, will be. Que sera sera. Remember we are Christians and in God's own time, he will bless us with not just one child but children, trust me. There is so much in my loins that I have to give, trust me,' he stammered slightly, not quite sure whether these words were wrongly said out of context.

Immediately Gwen heard this comment, she was not quite sure whether to laugh or cry the more. Lawrence had a way of making a very bad situation seem less hurtful as he used his sense of humour to reduce any pain or feeling of loss or regret.

Gwen found herself between the devil and the deep blue sea after she lost her baby eleven weeks after she was confirmed pregnant.

She, however, managed to return to her voluntary work a couple of days later. 'If I continue to stay at home, loneliness will kill me,' she said to her husband. 'I don't want to sit here alone, watching the Jerry Springer and Maury show and afterwards cry myself to sleep. No way, I will go out there and work to make something out of my life. I know who I am.'

As things bounced back to normal after Gwen's miscarriage, time continued to heal their wound as they started enjoying each other's company once again.

Chapter Sixteen

One bright summer evening, Judy called her friend Gwen to announce to her that she would be getting married to her partner of three years. Everyone was happy and over the moon. All through the later part of that year, arrangements were geared towards making the wedding one of the best talked about in town.

Judy's mother, in her usual way, had a list of friends and socialites she wanted to invite to her daughter's wedding. Judy, on the other hand, preferred a quiet ceremony involving very close family members and long-time friends. A balance was now struck between her mother's needs and her own choice as the bride-to-be.

Judy purchased her wedding gown from a reputable shop known for stocking beautiful wedding gowns and accessories based along Walworth Road in South East London.

The reception was quite exotic and exclusive and it was a strictly by-invitation kind of ceremony. Judy chose the music 'It's nobody's business how I live my life' for the bride and groom's first dance and first official assignment whilst they fed each other.

The wedding day came in all its glory and splendour; it was an opportunity for Judy's parents to show off their make-believe closeness. What came as a surprise to Judy and a few friends and family members who knew this family so well were the comments made by Judy's mother as parting words of advice to her daughter and son-in-law.

When asked to pray for the newly wedded couples, she said, 'I pray that your marriage will be like that of me and your father, you will be

221

married together for thirty years, forty years, sixty years and will see your children's children. Amen.'

Reflecting on her mum's prayers, Judy was not sure whether to cry or to laugh at that instant. She saw the deception, the lies and dishonesty that were filling up that prayer. When everyone said 'Amen', Judy actually did not because she saw no reason to. Judy knew that even though her mum and dad lived together under the same roof, they had separate lives. There was a mutual arrangement which allowed each of them to feel comfortable doing things their way without feeling accountable to each other. This was definitely not the kind of marriage Judy prayed for, because it was a marriage of convenience and her mum and dad were deceiving the whole world.

Five years after Judy's wedding to her husband, serious problems ensued as her mother always intruded in their married life. She would continuously remind Judy that she could swear on her life that it was because of 'paper', meaning immigration papers (British passport)—that was why Judy's husband married her.

'If he married me for paper, then why did I marry him, Mum?' Judy would ask. 'I keep saying this when two adults are in a relationship, they must have made up their mind to get married because of what they have seen in each other. People still get married outside the UK for a reason, either because they are attracted to each other physically or because they are sexually compatible or have perceived that they can take on life's challenges together as a couple in order to be successful in life.'

Judy knew what she wanted and went for it, undermining her mother's misgivings about her husband's genuine intentions towards their marriage. That explained the choice of music during her wedding: 'It's nobody's business how I live my life . . .'

Despite this persistent intrusion, Judy and her husband managed to pull through for four years, and after this period, he lost his job and became very unbearable blaming Judy for all his bad luck. 'If I brought you bad luck, at least I assisted you with your immigration papers, now you can travel, you can work and can do whatever you like. I know, as people have already said, you will leave me one day, but you know what? I really do not care, do as you please.' Judy would go on and on, moaning about how she was sure she would be abandoned by her husband. She also started thinking like her mum after she had been brainwashed into thinking that once her husband became British, he would abandon his responsibilities.

Five years into her daughter's marriage, Judy's mother encouraged her to move in with them, an idea which her husband rebuffed completely, which added to her resentment.

'You have to move into our home with your husband,' Judy's mum commanded over the phone.

'Why?'

'Why not, Judy? We have a six-bedroom house that is empty, it will not be a bad idea if you and your husband move in with us, seeing that presently he does not have any job, that saves you a lot of expenses.'

'Mum, I will call you later after I have discussed this with him.'

I hope he will buy this brilliant idea seeing that I will also be saving a lot of money from my transport fare as I work very close to my mum's, thought Judy.

When Judy told her husband of this new offer, he was furious. 'What does your mum take me for?' he asked. 'Why should I leave my home as a man and move in with her and her husband? I am an African man and cannot do that at all. Your mum is too domineering and overbearing. For how long will I continue with this interference just because she feels it was through you that I got my settlement status in the UK? One thing people like you and your mum do not know is that even a guy who had the intention to use you may end up getting stuck by your kindness. Nothing attracts a man more than the kindness of a woman. If perhaps you have decided to join your mum rather than concentrating on our relationship, I wish you luck.'

Once Judy and her husband had a fracas, and she called her parents on the phone, crying and moaning. Two hours later, her home was filled up with her family members who waged war against her husband, calling him all kinds of names like illegal immigrant, user, slacker, gold-digger. Judy's father also threatened that he would fall upon him like an iroko tree if he ever caused his daughter pain again in the future.

This continuous family fracas and extended family intervention continued even after this couple had children. It was one problem or the other, with Judy not being able to cook the traditional African meal which was her husband's favourite and the additional continuous interference of Judy's mother in the marriage relationship. This interference was so bad to the extent that their first daughter's christening took place at Judy's mother's church upon her insistence.

According to Judy's mother, because it was through her daughter that he got his stay in the UK, he must be subservient to her daughter all through the duration of the marriage. Some days, Judy's mum would call them for a family meeting, requesting that her daughter's husband should gather his family to come to her home to beg her and apologise to her sometimes even when there was nothing to apologise for. This melodrama of begging and controlling behaviour became a pattern as it took place several times until one summer when Kel called her bluff, writing boldly on their bedroom door 'enough is enough nobody can dictate my happiness, not even my status in the UK, I am somebody, an African prince'.

'Despite Kel's determination not to be intimidated by his wife's family members, he however followed his mum to Judy's parents' home upon insistence, to make peace with them. Kel's mother, who came in from Africa, insisted that they should go to enable her see this woman who has given her son and his wife hell for so long.

When they arrived at Judy's parents' home, the whole problem began in earnest as Judy's mum spoke of how she has been disrespected continuously by Kel despite his poor immigration status. At this stage, Kel's mum then asked, 'Is it the immigration issue that is the point here or the marriage relationship?'

'I don't know you from Adam and Eve,' said Judy's mum to Kel's mum as a heated conversation ensued. 'To answer your question, yes, immigration status is part of the relationship because it was the main reason why your son married my beautiful daughter,' replied Judy's mum. 'What is your son's qualification? Eh? You say he has a degree in Nigeria, do you realise this degree is not recognised in this country? Even if it is recognised, it will be an equivalent of an A level qualification.'

At this point, Kel's mum could not take the direct insult and demeaning statements anymore. 'So what was your daughter's motive for marrying my own son?' Kel's mum asked. 'Are young people not supposed to meet and fall in love irrespective of their social class, ethnic origin, educational qualification, or immigration status? Have you tried to ask your daughter what she found interesting in my son? Are you aware that my son accepted your daughter despite her shortcomings when she led an unacceptable life sleeping with people who have the same status as her and yet they failed to commit to the relationship?

'Are you aware of NARIC assessment of overseas qualification, which indeed proves that my son's certificate as a university graduate is acceptable in the UK? At least my son did not attend a school where he will have to access an open-book exam, he worked hard each day during his university days in Nigeria and came out tops with a second-class upper division. Do you know the son of whom you are berating?' asked Kel's mum.

'If these two love each other, why not leave them to live their life, huh? When you and your husband came into this land over forty-five years ago, did you have British passports then? No! So you have suddenly forgotten your roots and where you come from? Please, one thing you should remember is the fact that my son is not hungry, his family home in Africa is not driving him, and he is the son of a well-notable chief and justice of the peace in Africa. You all here live a false life, and I hear there is nothing to show with this passport you boast with. You have been here all these years and could not use this passport constructively to gain some qualification and a good career, and yet you boast each day about holding a passport that the whole world respects. It is what you make out of the passport that is more important, not the passport itself. If not for the greedy leaders we have in Africa who give a bad image of that country, you should be proud and happy that my son asked for your daughter's hand in marriage.

'Did your daughter tell you she has not been able to cook one single African dish for her African husband, yet she is of African origin? What did you do these past forty-five years in the white man's land? You failed to teach your children about your African culture, you failed to take them back to Africa to know your roots and where you come from. You fail to even teach them how to eat or prepare your African dishes. My son has become so thin because of starvation from your daughter. What have you taught your daughter? How to order food from restaurants Mondays through Fridays, how not to be respectful, how to watch movies and soaps like *EastEnders* and *Coronation Street* all day long without embracing changes which affects her as a person of African origin. Your daughter cannot even carry out simple domestic chores, leaving my son to do practically everything. Don't you think that is a flaw my son also accepted because he loves her?

'You failed to teach your daughter your African language and culture. I have a nephew in America married to a white American, and she has visited Nigeria more than ten times since he married her. Your daughter speaks through her nose and doesn't want to hear anything African, and yet she is one of us. I pity you and your daughter, wake up from your slumber, and hey, the world has moved on. Nigeria is the fastest growing economy. Please don't look down on us.'

When Kel's mum finished this speech, so to say, you could hear a pin drop in the room. There was total silence. However, this long speech from Kel's mum even infuriated Judy's mum the more, because she seemed to think at the back of her mind that she had the four aces.

'How dare you talk to me like that?' she screamed at the top of her voice. At this time, she was holding a bottle of cognac which was half filled. 'How dare you? Do you know what it means to help someone in this country? Do you think this is Nigeria? I have been in this country for over forty-five years and will tell you more. Do you know what I and my husband suffered before we got settled in this country?' she further ranted.

'Oh, so because you and your husband suffered for years, every other person must suffer double before they can settle? You sure have a long way to go and are so myopic in your thinking. Take your daughter and tell her to eat her British passport, when was the first time you took them home to Africa or spoke to them about your country or its history and rich heritage? My advice to you is to visit Nigeria more often and acquaint yourself with what people are achieving, perhaps that will help you to understand better, and help to change your view about Africa. Forget what you see in the press, face the reality of situation,' advised Kel's mum.

'Don't allow this marriage between your son and my daughter to be like the disastrous marriage of Mr and Mrs Fredericks Omu oh!' spat out Judy's mum. 'What did you say? Are you threatening me? Okay, since you want to threaten me, I will show you today.' Kel's mum took off her gele from her head, tied it round her waist, and swung her hand towards Judy's mum, inviting her to a free-for-all fight. Within a twinkle of what seemed like a minute, Judy's mum took the bottle of cognac, smashed it on the centre glass table, and plunged directly towards Kel's mother. As these two elderly women scratched each other's faces, they were now separated while breathing hard and cursing.

This fight was even made worse by the unreasonableness of Judy's dad, who cursed and swore at everyone. 'Kel! Kel! Kel!' he ranted, how many times have I called you? I will fall on top of you like an iroko tree if you maltreat my daughter.'

This imbroglio brought about a serious problem between Judy and Kel. At this time, Judy supported her parents' actions and did not see anything wrong in what they did. As far as she was concerned, she had the upper hand because she it was who supported Kel to help him regularise his stay in the UK.

'I am not returning to that house until you and your foul-mouthed mother have come to apologise and beg my parents,' Judy boasted while hitting her fists on her chest.

'Apologise over what?' asked Kel. 'You ask me over what with that display of disrespect that your mother showed to my mother? Oh really? Okay, wait for us, then. We will come and prostrate ourselves to your family soon, okay?' replied Kel.

Kel made up his mind there and then that he could not be a slave to his wife; the marriage was definitely not working because of the fact that Judy and all her family members were still holding on to the fact that because she supported his application for a settled status in the UK, he remained indebted to her and her family all his life. There was too much family intervention and bickering.

He truly loved her, but she saw his immigration status and the fact that he was not British-born as a reason to continue to dictate the pace of their relationship. 'I have some friends who are married to white English girls whose ancestors are English and do not have any connection to any other ethnicity. Once they get married to an African man, they are so excited themselves about learning the culture, the history and even suggest to their spouses to take them back to Africa. Why my wife and her family decide to live in denial of their African roots and heritage still beats my imagination,' said Kel. 'Since I got married to my wife, I have been doing the cooking because she cannot cook, she prefers to buy takeaways each day and when I insist that we must cook, she reminds me that this is not Africa. She forgets that some of the best chefs in the world are English. Yet this woman is raised by two parents who, rather than teach her the right thing, only concentrated more on teaching her how to feel superior to others who are of African origin.

'I will leave her, I have tried, Chikena!' he spoke in Hausa. 'I have tried haba! Her oyibo don too much and this will be her undoing make she go marry her passport then am gone.'

He decided to leave her, but before he did that, he advised his mum to cut short her trip to the UK and return to Nigeria. Once his mother was out of the way, he gave Judy an ultimatum: to return home with their two daughters, who at that time had been enrolled in a school close to where Judy's parents lived.

She insisted that he and his mother must come over to prostrate themselves to her parents and to give a verbal undertaking that they will always recognise the fact that they are superior in the relationship because they it was who gave him settlement status in the UK. She would never set foot in the house until all of this was accomplished. While she was still waiting for that apology, Kel left her, never to return.

And so it was that Judy made a choice to marry without understanding first of all why she got into that relationship. She wanted to be married because all her friends were getting married. When she could not get anyone within her class—as she would usually put it whenever she was having issues with Kel—she decided to 'manage' Kel. She also took additional steps and made another decision to become a single parent despite finding love, just because she allowed her husband's immigration status to continuously dictate the pace of their relationship years after he had been settled and even naturalised as a British citizen.

Perhaps if she knew and understood why she got married in the first place, the immigration status of her husband Kel would not have been an issue strong enough to dictate the pace of their relationship. She would have understood that even if she and Kel were born British, they could still have other issues which might crop up during their relationship because a marriage relationship involves two consenting adults who have agreed to come together despite their differences, on a neutral platform of love because they want to be with each other. Till death do them part.

'Indeed it has come to my realisation that love, beauty, and a red passport are not what dictate a happy marriage,' said Kel. 'I love to eat my African food like eba and egusi soup, dodo and plantain, rice and stew, yam pottage, ewedu and amala, jollof rice—not once in all my years of marriage did this woman I call my wife make any effort to learn how to prepare any of these meals at least to make me happy. All I hear since we got married is "I gave you paper", "I gave you paper." Even before my paper came out it was "Come and take now, I will not file for you. You will suffer in this country until you get frustrated and return to Africa where you came from."

'Judy even wrote to the immigration twice, advising them to cancel my settlement status but unfortunately, this did not take place as they later found out it was a genuine marriage and not a marriage of convenience. Haba! Paper is not the kingdom of God as this woman thinks in her heart. She used it as a tool of control and this badly affected the marriage relationship. Judy unfortunately never gave me the chance to prove my love to her.

'She continued to play God with this paper thing until I developed a thick skin. Haba, my own fellow black discriminating against me in our marriage because of my immigration status, na wao! Nna men!

'I have managed to also meet other men and women who suffered the same fate at the hands of their spouses,' explained Kel. 'Upon carefully considering their position, they revealed to me that they would still have been married to their spouses today, if she had accepted them and everything that came with them rather than judging them based on their status and their nationality.'

****

Don't follow any advice, no matter how good,
until you feel as deeply in your spirit as you think in your mind
that the counsel is wise.
—Joan Rivers

****

Immediately Gwen heard about the problems faced by Judy in her marriage, she arranged to see her in a neutral place as she did not want to visit her at her parents' home, because of the kind of advice she planned to give her. 'I do not want any disruption.'

Gwen had also noticed that the few times she visited Judy's home, the look in Judy's parents' eyes spoke millions of words. If interpreted, they looked down on her, as if to say, 'Here we go again, another scrounger from Africa!'

'I know they also see me as that local Nigerian girl with a strong Nigerian accent, and so they will not want to take my advice to their daughter seriously.'

'Judy, can we meet on Saturday in McDonald's restaurant close to the A13?' Gwen suggested.

'Why?' Judy asked.

'You know why, Judy, I need to talk to you privately, will 2.30 p.m. be convenient for you? At 2.30 promptly, then. I don't want African time.'

'Okie-dokie,' replied Judy.

Till date, Gwen could not lay her hands on or make any sense out of the reason why Judy's marriage failed. 'Judy,' she said to her friend when they finally met, 'I thought the gap year you spent in Nigeria had a heavy impact on the way you see and interpret life. Life is not all about your red passport, you know, that is not what brings happiness. You know I will not tell you lies. You had Kel all round your fingers, he was a good man, he cooked for you because you could not cook those African dishes, he washed and hoovered, all he ever complained of was the fact that you allowed too much family interference in your relationship. You always saw him as a second-class citizen even though he is your husband, just because he was not born in the UK.

'I warned you but you would not listen. Your mum and dad have lived their lives and more importantly, an African man is an African man even if you are the one providing the money, he still wants to be seen as one who calls the shots. Not in a bad way, but in a respectful way.

'You keep talking about helping him with his immigration papers, have you thought of why you accepted him yourself? He accepted you also even though you cannot cook. This aspect of not being able to cook, what culture is that? I ask this because I have seen girls who are 100 per cent born and bred in this country, their parents also born and bred in this country, but they can cook all English dishes and even more. Not being able to cook, therefore, especially as a grown woman, is not a culture but a lifestyle you have chosen yourself. Perhaps you should have married a man who himself enjoys eating out 24/7—that way, there will not be any problems as the two of you will be able to adjust.'

Gwen continued, 'Despite having helped him with his immigration status, you did not know when to stop, you kept on rubbing it in his face and allowing your family to see him as a second-class citizen, forever accusing him that he came into the relationship to regularise his stay and that once he had achieved that, he would leave.

'I hear you even asked his mum once whether she uses china dishes to eat in Africa, and she gave you the answer you deserved, saying to you that the choice of china dishes she had used, you could not now afford it because it was the type manufactured exclusively even before your mum met your dad. I heard you took offence at that response, interpreting it to mean that she insinuated through her response that your parents could not afford expensive chinaware. What you don't seem to realise, Judy, is that not all Africans are impoverished. Not all Africans are naive and timid. Just like what we have here also, there are very poor Africans, middle-class Africans, and very wealthy and affluent Africans. You have seen all of this with your own eyes during the period you came to stay with your aunt. I thought that experience would have changed your perception of Africa. We don't live on top of trees as I hear some naive people still imagine we do.

'What you have with Kel is a relationship and so please respect that relationship. Do not introduce cankerworms into it by continuously reminding him that you are the boss wife because you supported him to regularise his stay. If you do not support him, then you could as well travel back with him to live in Africa, it's as simple as that. This guy loves you, relationships still break down each day even with people of same nationality. I wonder what married couples outside this country use against themselves each day. Do they say, "Oh, you married me because of my money" or do they say, "You married me because of my beauty" or "You married me because you love me." What do people think they marry others for?

You have two daughters with Kel and he adores them so much. Allow them to share their lives with their father and please don't deprive them that golden opportunity even if you decide not to return to your matrimonial home.

Immediately, Judy spoke out, 'Please change the topic, Gwen, you don't know these African men. My parents are right, they come in under different disguises and once they get that kpali,' (literally meaning paper) 'you then see their true colour.'

'Are you then saying to me that there are no genuine men who get married for the genuine reason of love? For example, me and my husband? I know at the time I married my husband, I could really not place or define exactly what I wanted, but since being married to him, I have come to respect and love him even more, not because he made me move to the UK but because of the love, respect, and kindness he has shown me. If my husband decides to change today and I leave him because of bad treatment from him, will he then go all out to say because he gave me kpali, I have left him? I'm sure he will be sincere enough to state categorically how he contributed to the failure of the relationship.'

Gwen went on and on. 'How are you going to cope with your daughters alone now? The school runs, the parents' evenings, and other social functions like taking them out to swimming and karate classes?'

'Never mind,' said Judy. 'Once I return to work, I shall enrol them in an after-school club where they can stay up to 6.00 p.m. and then I will pick them up. What you don't understand, Gwen, is that the social security system even helps me more as a single parent. I will be entitled to financial support from them to help towards my child care and so that will not be a problem.'

'Oh, I see,' continued Gwen. 'Is this one of the reasons why you want out, then? For its financial gain?'

'Oh no, don't be silly, not at all,' said Judy.

'I ask because I have heard of women who prefer to remain single just because they are told they stand to gain more financially by being single parents. Is this a plague or plain madness in the name of civilisation? What happens after they have all the money and no one to talk to after their kids have left home, eh?' cried Gwen.

Judy did not truly understand why her marriage broke up, but what she failed to understand till date was the fact that she contributed massively to the breakdown of her marriage. As the years rolled by, however, upon careful consideration of her actions, she started feeling really guilty and vulnerable, knowing that it would need a lot of getting used to, to get into a new relationship where she would enjoy the privileges she enjoyed while with Kel.

Kel had since moved on after two years of having to file a divorce petition, which involved a lot of rancour and physical confrontation from Judy's family. Each time there was a court hearing during the divorce proceedings and the financial dispute resolution, they were all in full attendance, issuing all kinds of threats on Kel.

Chapter Seventeen

Matrimonial Rights of Estate

Judy's family were misled into believing that their daughter owned all of the family estate because she it was who gave her ex-husband Kel the right to reside in the UK. It was also their daughter's name that was in the title deed of their two properties. One of the properties was bought by Judy before she became married to Kel and the other was bought after their marriage. Judy contributed more deposit to the second purchase than Kel, and to them, he should be left with nothing, as according to them, he came with nothing.

Unfortunately, most of the advice given to Judy and her extended family members by their solicitors remained ignored, and they attended these court hearings with so much dexterity and determination to see him leave the marriage with nothing.

During one of the court hearings, Judy said to the presiding judge, 'He used me, I am the one who gave him papers in this country and I bought my first home before we got married, he did not contribute to the deposit and so should not be given anything.'

The judge then asked, 'Did he live at that same address when you got married?'

'Yes, your honour,' she replied.

'Was he married to you at the time ownership of the property still continued?'

'Yes, sir.'

'Then that property is regarded as matrimonial property irrespective of any contribution he may have or may not have made. It does not matter whether he did not have a job for a long time. He may have not contributed financially but supported you emotionally and physically on the home front, that too is calculated as his own contribution. I think your lawyer should have enlightened you on this, but just for argument's sake, I will summarise what should have been done differently before marriage, which is you should have drafted a prenuptial agreement or put a will in place with a codicil clearly stating that should you be married in the future, your marriage will not be deemed to nullify the contents of your already written will.'

After the case was further adjourned that day, on their way out of the court premises, shouts of 'Ole, barawo! Ole, barawo! Scrounger! Parasite!' filled the air. 'You are despicable,' said Judy to Kel. 'You better move on and leave what I have worked for with me, or else you will not see your daughters again after this case. I will make sure you suffer, you are just despicable.'

Judy knew how very attached emotionally Kel was to his daughters, and she wanted to pull this string to hurt him further. Upon hearing these threats from his estranged wife, Kel became very worried and anxious. He did not blink an eye all through the night. The next day, he called his representatives to book an appointment to seek further advice on his position.

'What do I do? Judy has threatened that I leave everything to her, or else she will stop me from seeing my daughters . . . She has asked me to sign off all my matrimonial rights to our two properties over to her, saying that once I do that, she will ask her solicitors to draw up a consent order allowing me access to my children as many times as I can cope with.'

'Is she trying to blackmail you then?' asked Kel's solicitor. 'We can also apply to the courts for a right of access to your daughters should you wish to do so.'

'How does this work?' Kel asked.

'We will first of all make a proposal to her through her representative, requesting that mediation take place so that both parties can agree on what days you can have access to your daughters for them to be released to you either during weekdays or weekends. What you need to do is to let me know which days will be convenient for you, depending on your schedule and your ex-wife's schedule and availability. Once both parties are in agreement, then we shall draw up a consent order signed by both parties and their representatives which will be binding on all. Usually, failure to abide by the consent order will be interpreted as contempt of court, with serious consequences including a fine.'

'Why do women think they can use their children to spite and hurt their husbands once there is a crack in their relationships, even when the situation is such that they are the ones opting out of the relationship?'

'Well, it is a weapon used to spite the men, especially when the woman is hurt and she is losing out. In some cases, the woman may feel hurt that she has been cheated upon and, as a tool for revenge, withhold her children from her husband to express her bitterness. Some also dread the fact that if their children are accessed by their husband, this may expose the children to the other woman, whom they see as an enemy. Another reason may be as a result of the loss and hopelessness they feel upon losing their husbands to another woman, and so they hold on to their children as the only source of hope, succour, and happiness, using everything possible to incite the children against their father, just to be able to be the only one in the children's lives.'

Such was the case with Kel and Judy. Kel has not seen his daughters for the past fifteen months. At first she allowed him calls to speak to them twice every week, then she became agitated and advised him to buy their own phone so he can contact them directly, as she was not ready to be 'your receptionist who picks up your calls for your daughters.'

'Kel Ebube, buy your daughters a phone and please stop calling my number, I find you quite annoying.'

Kel was happy with this arrangement as he did not want to have anything to do with her insults and vile tongue. He immediately bought his daughter a Blackberry phone, which he took to school to hand to her. She was over the moon once her head teacher called to inform her that her daddy was around to see her. He handed over the phone to her on that day and said to her, 'No matter what happens, always know that Daddy loves you.'

The purchase of this phone made life bearable for Kel as he would call his daughters after school to speak to them and they would be on the phone several times on end.

Suddenly one day, Kel called his daughter's number and there was no sound at the other end; he noticed it was not ringing. He also called

Judy's number and noticed that his number had been blocked and he could not reach any one of them. He started panicking and did not know what to do. He called a close cousin of Judy who, all through the relationship, was against the maltreatment which was meted out to Kel because of his status. 'Have you heard from your cousin for a while?' he asked. 'Yes, I was with them last night. Any problem, I hope you are okay?'

'Yes, I am,' answered Kel. He then told this cousin how he could not reach his daughters and Judy on the phone.

'Don't mind that girl, so she carried out her threat. She boasted yesterday that she would stop her daughters from further speaking to you and that she would also block you from her phone so you cannot reach her. Judy still has not learnt from her silly mistake. She keeps listening to her parents, who are giving her negative advice, it's such a pity.'

Kel later learnt that part of Judy's frustration was her disillusionment from the fact that since becoming single again out of choice, she had met with all kinds of subtle criticisms and negativities from family members (those same family members who encouraged her to leave her husband), friends, and acquaintances.

And so the battle for the family estate and the custody of both children continued between Judy and Kel. Kel struggled, through his solicitors, to gain supervised contacts pending further investigations on the allegations made by Judy against him that he had been violent towards her in the presence of the two children.

As the months rolled by, Judy noticed a pattern each time she was approached by members of the opposite sex. Once she revealed to them that she had two daughters, she noticed that their countenance changed and they never warmed up to her again.

Once she had this man who was all over her for months on end. They finally hooked up during lunch, and the two of them stopped to have a drink at a local bar close to her office. Once she told this young man about her daughters, he abruptly stopped any more contacts with her and even changed his number. The ones who wanted the relationship, upon being told she had two children, only wanted one thing, which was to get into her knickers.

Judy continued to ponder, 'Why are people so sceptical about a single woman who has children, without asking to know the circumstances within which she became single?' Judy sometimes pondered on this. 'The society all over tends to have a single story about single parents. There is a notion that every single parent is immoral, loose, not capable of keeping her home, and therefore cannot raise successful children within the community. Anyone who has raised children on their own knows that it is a tough job and involves serious responsibility and so why does society place such a stigma on single parents? Why do they always think the children of single parents will end up selling drugs on the street or are always the ones scrounging off the government?

'The question now is that it is said that in times of austerity, the phrase "single mother" is often treated as if it is synonymous with "socially irresponsible" or that charming label "scrounger"? Why can it not be synonymous with people like the president of the United States, Obama, and Oprah Winfrey. These are two successful people raised by single parents,' continued Judy.

'I even hear that in the United States, it is even worse as every single mother is seen as a stripper, prostitute, while national reports into crimes' statistics are often juxtaposed with statistics on single-parent families. Without tacitly trying to encourage a one-parent home over two, there are just as well some single parents who became single out of the tragedies of life, or out of necessity, having been in an abusive relationship, or indeed out of wrong choices which they may later have repented from and determined to turn over a new leaf in life. All of these are also single parents along with the widowed, the divorced. This same label which is seen as exclusively reserved for shaming people who dared to procreate out of wedlock, at the same time not minding that every single mother has a different story, which is now made a single story without having to hear each out or whether each wanted to regularly reveal personal details about their life to strangers and the whole world alike. Indeed from the little I have experienced now, anyone who has single-handedly raised children knows and understands that it is far from a walk in the park.

'As a single parent now, I understand that we are dedicated, conscientious people who try to do right things despite the crippling social discrimination. Does it then mean that being raised by a single mum and later being taken and sent to a foster home therefore makes Lawrence—Gwen's husband—an unsuitable husband? Hmm, what a shame.' As Judy asked aloud, she heard her doorbell chiming and she slowly walked to the door to see who it was. It was her mum.

'Mum, you didn't call to say you will be coming'.

'I know,' responded her mum matter-of-factly. 'I thought of you last night and thought I should stop by to see how you are and also to see my granddaughters.'

'Well, you have come at a wrong time, Mum, because I am not in the mood at all, I need to be left alone. I've only just picked up your granddaughters from school and need time to be on my own so I can think straight for once.'

'That is part of the reason why I am here,' replied Judy's mum. 'It's been two years now, I have been waiting, hoping, and praying.'

'About what?' asked Judy.

'You know it is seen as unnatural, you know a lot of people think that single parents are bringing down the morals of the nation. I don't want you to be part of those statistics. You know I am an elder in the church, and you know the societal perceptions of single parents and the perceived deficits attached to them by society. There is internalized negative stereotype which can lead to low self-worth, they never look at the strengths and positives at all, so you have to do something, and fast too.'

'Oh, so now you know, when you have succeeded in ruining my marriage, now you want me to start off a new one on a rebound?'

'Not really, but I am just reminding you to come out of this comfort zone which you built for yourself years ago.'

'I am already outside my comfort zone, Mum. I now wear many hats, all thanks to you and Dad, I work hard and prioritize, I am strong-willed, independent, and hard-working, I sacrifice a lot to be a good mother, even though I miss the positive male influence that my ex-husband Kel would have had on our children, but hey, what do I do if my relationship failed than to learn lessons from it and then move on. People now see me as part of the norm in the society and I am now part of statistics and history, rather than seeing my status as part of the result of either bad judgement, accidental pregnancy, rape, sudden death of spouse, or even abusive relationship rather than playing the blame game of hurriedly drawing a conclusion that I am one of those women who are fighting for women's liberation and therefore highly opinionated, strong-willed and a person who deliberately wants to raise children on her own as a mark of independence and liberation.

'I now balance roles. I now provide financial and emotional support for my two children, manage work and family-life demands. I provide physical/emotional/spiritual support for my children. My nurturing skills have improved tremendously, and my ability to multitask, and parental and life skills. Mum, I have my regrets, but hey, do not make a conscious effort to perpetuate the existing stigmas attached to single parenting. Rather, try and self-reflect on biases and assumptions around what constitutes a healthy family. Thank you.'

After Judy's mum left her home on that day, she hurriedly rushed to pick her two girls, served them dinner, gave them a wash, and tucked them into bed. She now made herself a hot cup of chocolate drink while reflecting on her relationship with her estranged husband Kel.

WHY MARRY JUDY?- IMMIGRATION PSYCHOSIS.

His name is Kelly but I call him Kel—that's the way I prefer to refer to him, different from every other person. I am not the type of a lover cut out for frivolities attached to endearments like babes, honey, sweetheart, or darling. In fact, growing up, I never heard my mum call my dad anything more than his native African name and sometimes she called him *ikporosi inemem*; this last name Ikporosi Inemem as much as most of us children did not know till date its full meaning, but while in Nigeria for my gap year, I managed to find out its meaning and concluded that this could have been a nickname used by my mum whenever she wanted to tease my dad about his promiscuous lifestyle. I was told the literary meaning of *ikporosi inemem* in Igbo language is 'you are undoing yourself'.

It was difficult to learn anything relating to a healthy and respectable relationship as far as my family setting was concerned. There were accusations and counter-accusations. Once, my mum came home fuming, with her hands akimbo, waiting for my dad to get back. According to her, she saw him with a young girl, young enough to be one of his daughters, in a nearby African restaurant. According to Mum, Dad doted on this girl as if nothing else mattered in the world to him, and this girl in return took undue advantage of this and kept on ordering for all kinds of delicacies in the menu list, causing even the waitress who was attending to them to chuckle with laughter which drew my mum's attention to them. My mum had gone to eat at this same African restaurant with business partners when she saw my dad and this girl. My dad ended up not coming home that night, and when he eventually came back the next day, he did not show any remorse as he countered every one of my mum's accusations with his own version of accusations against her.

'Mum, I thought you told us that you were out in the African restaurant with your business partners?' asked Judy. 'Ehen,' retorted my mum sharply, 'when I said business partners, I did not specify whether they were male or female, did I?' she asked.

'Male or female indeed,' replied Dad, 'how many of you were there on that day? Tell your daughter, won't you?'

'Ononadi achodi. You are married but still searching. You want to be a man, don't you? You want to wear the trousers in this relationship but you cannot. In our African culture, when a man cheats on his wife, it is acceptable within the society, however, when a woman is seen to cheat, the society frowns against it. You are only disgracing yourself, not me. A married woman attending such a restaurant at that time of the night with three different men all shared amongst you and your two other shameless friends who also claim to be married women.' Judy played back in her mind how the heated conversation between her mum and dad ensued: 'I was not sure whether Dad took time to lecture Mum on her moralities on that day more out of a feeling of guilt rather than a determination to make sure that morality is seen as a virtue and a stringent teaching in the Bible.

Despite being raised in a dysfunctional home such as the one occupied by Mum and Dad, I still saw myself as someone who would get married one day and thereafter live happily ever after with my future husband. My own case, therefore, cannot be said to be that of "like mother, like daughter".

'My relationship with Kel started on a sour note as my parents gave him hell. After two years of courtship, Kel proposed to me, and upon making an arrangement to introduce him to my family, he visited my mum and dad in our family home on this fateful day. Before he came to our home on that day, we were already seated, and surprisingly, my dad and mum had invited two of our extended family members to this meeting.

'As Kel came in, he greeted everyone and took a seat close to where I was sitting pretty. I remember it was my dad who started the conversation by asking him what part of Nigeria he came from, and once Kel replied, he went on and on, reminding him of how my family was from a royal family, how I am a princess and the granddaughter of a king. At the back of my mind, I actually saw myself sitting close to this large African king dressed in his African regalia. My dad went on and on, and further asked Kel what his qualifications were. He said he had a first degree from one of the universities in Nigeria. Then my dad did the most despicable thing, he said, "All these degrees that you people get from your country in Africa, it is just equivalent to an NVQ here in the UK. You and my daughter are not on the same level, as you can see. You need to go back to school, get some UK qualification, find a job, get a home of your own, and then at that stage, you can now come in to make your intentions known to me, should you still be interested in my daughter." He went on to also ask Kel about his family background. "Where are your mum and dad?"

"'In Nigeria," said Kel.

"'Are they still together?"

"'No, they are divorced," answered Kel.

"'Okay, no daughter of mine will marry a man who is from a broken home. There is too much to take in from you, as a matter of fact. No paper, no qualification, from a dysfunctional family, and now this . . ." After this long speech, Kel did an amazing thing. He said, "Thank you, sir" to my dad, stood up, shook hands with my other family members, and set out to leave. I immediately ran after him, pleading for him not to take my dad or anything he said on that day to heart. I thought my dad was so hypocritical in his speech on that day anyway. How could he who, even though he lives with my mum, runs his life separate from her? How can he then be the one to question others about their lifestyles despite the fact that he is also guilty of such conduct, despite hiding under the canopy of being married? Which amongst them is best known to be morally upright, then: the married couples who live their lives cheating on each other, or the single parents who hardly ever go on a date but who have been labelled by society as being promiscuous as a result of their single status?

'In all of these shenanigans, it took another eighteen months before wedding plans came to fruition as I stood my ground that this was the man I wanted to marry. Marriage to Kel did not in any way deter my parents from their controlling attitude. Instead, it worsened it completely. They would find a reason to always remind Kel that it was through me that he got his permission to remain in the UK. They would tell anyone that cared to listen how Kel would be sent back to Nigeria any day he dared misbehave or treat me badly. My dad always used the words "I will fall on you like an iroko tree" meaning he would deal with Kel, to ward Kel off from misbehaving or treating me unfairly.

'When I had my first child, I stayed in the hospital for two days and once I was discharged, my mum insisted that I follow her home to enable her to take care of me and my newborn baby. According to her, it would save her the inconveniences of having to travel from Nottingham to Dulwich in London, where we lived. At first, we did not read any meanings into this as we thought this was the reasonable thing to do. One week, however, progressed to one month, one month to one year, and I ended up spending the whole one year of my maternity period in my parents' home. I started thinking that my mum was only using me to fill the gap that her husband's absence created since at this time, she was all alone at home while my dad kept on in his old ways. He would usually say to her, "I told you that what goes up must come down, you are an old woman now, no man wants you even if you are sold for twopence."

'Fourteen months after the birth of my first child, I still did not see anything wrong in my actions as I continued living with my parents in my family home while my husband would travel almost every day from work to visit me and our daughter. One day, he insisted that we must go back home with him and there was a serious argument as my mum gave one reason or the other why I should continue to stay back. My husband Kel blatantly turned down all excuses and insisted that we must return home with him that night. We packed all our personal belongings haphazardly and followed him in the car. Because of this, a battle line was again drawn between mum and Kel. She would not want to have anything to do with him after that day. She made a series of complaints against him to dad. And each day continued to fuel accusations against him. Mum would also call me, and during each telephone call, she deliberately talked down on Kel, calling him a user and an impersonator. Till date, I never really understood why my mum called Kel an impersonator. "Whom did he impersonate?" I would usually ask Mum, not quite sure whether this was the appropriate word she meant to use or whether it was a slip of the tongue. "Whom did he not impersonate?" she would reply. "Everything under the sun has been impersonated by this man you call your husband." She would go on and on.

'At first I made up my mind that I would stick by my man no matter what; I even decided to stay completely away from my extended family for a period of six months without visiting them or allowing them to visit me. I feigned being very busy as I wanted to be left alone. Mum went everywhere telling people how very disrespectful Kel was, how he seemed to forget that it was through her daughter—referring to me—that he now had the right to reside in the UK. On one occasion, Kel had to ask them during a family meeting which they arranged, whether they were not originally from Africa themselves and why were they so fake and living in denial despite having relocated to the UK at a very mature age when they should have inculcated some of the African culture which should make them able to accept others having been in that same position when they originally came into this country.

"How dare you? You see this boy, he does not have any fear or respect at all, despite all that my daughter has done for him. I will make sure he goes back to that his country so that he will later appreciate my daughter if given an opportunity again." My mum and dad would go on and on about how I saved Kel's life by giving settlement status. It never ended, from day 1 of the relationship till the end of the relationship, they kept on like that, sounding like a broken record until Kel became thick-skinned and started reminding them of their African roots, which they seem to have forgotten.

"'Have you thought of what the advantage also that my marriage to your daughter Judy has brought to her?" he asked on one occasion when they started addressing him on how I was his saviour and messiah. "Do you realise that Judy and I are in this together and that we could be in another country and still be married irrespective of our nationalities? Is this all you have to offer your children? Your daughter cannot cook any proper meal. She cannot tidy up, she does not understand the African culture despite having roots in Africa, there is basically nothing connecting to Africa that you have taught her from the language, the name, food, to the attire to the mannerism and level of respect for elders, to the solid belief in extended family system. Nothing. At what age did you come into the UK? By my calculation twenty-five years or twenty-seven years, this means that you have also lived half of your adult years in Africa and yet you seem to have forgotten your roots.

"'Why don't you sometimes copy the Asians who, despite the numbers of years spent in the UK, make it a point of duty to teach their children their culture and their heritage? Most of their children born in the UK also speak Punjabi or Hudu language, why can you not emulate these good qualities of these people?" he screamed out.

"'Na wao! So because I marry Britico I no go drink water drop cup again. Every day, you want to call olopa police on me. I no fit talk for my house again. After all, I pay most of the bills in this house. I also do all the shopping and all the cooking without complaining. Are you saying there is nothing good about me just because of red p? I no understand dis kind people o!"

'These were Kel's statements when he really got annoyed with the constant nagging, not basically from me but from mum and dad. I wouldn't say I actually know how I got initiated into their line of thinking. I suddenly started bullying Kel. I became highly suspicious, questioning his every move and not allowing him to contact his family or even have a relationship with them. This and many more became part of the irony which led to my separation and subsequent divorce.

'At the time Kel and I were divorcing, I had been advised by my parents to call the police on him so he would be sent out of the family home. This was a family home we both built together with almost 60 per cent of the deposit money used for the purchase having been provided by Kel and 40 per cent by me. Mum advised me to throw him out and also to insist that should he not sign off and relinquish all his rights to this property, I will get the authorities involved to withdraw his papers. Such a wicked plot between Mum and Dad, however, did not hold water as far as Kel was concerned because at this stage, he had sought advice from an appropriate source, and his adviser told him that as far as he already has his British passport, this cannot be revoked except on grounds of criminal involvement or if I could prove that the marriage is a sham. I could definitely not prove this. We were married for seven years and had a lot of financial ties and commitment together. I should have known better. Because after Kel moved out, he stopped paying the mortgage after sometime as he could not cope with paying rent in the apartment where he now lived and also paying the mortgage of the family home. I sought advice from the citizens advice bureau, who advised me that because Kel's name is still in the property, it would be difficult to carry out a mesne test on my behalf alone. They wanted to know whether Kel was in full-time employment and how much he earned.

'Apart from this issue of mortgage payment, I was also faced with the issue of child support. Several times, I had a shouting bout with Kel, who would not pick up my phone call anytime he was with his new partner. Sometimes, I would call him more than five times before finally leaving a text message. 'Call me please if you can,' I would text him, and then suddenly receive a response: 'I am busy right now.' This was the kind of life in which I now found myself because of very poor advice and lack of direction by Mum and Dad. As bad as this experience may have been and despite the hard lessons learnt, I have come out a better person at the end of the day. Since my divorce came through, I have tried to deliberate on the role I played in contributing to my divorce. In the past, I used to lay all the blame on Kel, saying he only came into the relationship to enable him reside in the UK lawfully, through me. He never loved or respected me; neither did he have any iota of respect for my parents. However, upon careful consideration of incidents that occurred during the tenure of our marriage, I have come to accept that 60 per cent of the reasons why the marriage could not sustain itself were because in the first place, I did not understand why I was getting married. I was not prepared for the responsibilities that come with marriage. My mum never sat me down to give me good counsel or indeed prepare me for this very important aspect of my life. First and foremost, I may be British but of African origin. Understanding my African origin/roots, my culture, language, food, and customs would have helped me a great deal to understand my people. I would have understood Kel perhaps even better, knowing why he did some of the things he did as a result of the African culture, not because he is a bad person. I grew up in a culture where, as a child, I was allowed to do whatever pleased me, however I felt like doing it, and I made crucial decisions myself without any interventions by my mum and dad. Despite spending twelve months in Africa during my gap years, that period did not help to inculcate in me the totality of the African culture. If therefore I made up my mind to marry someone of African origin, I should have taken extra steps to make sure I understood his culture and the traditions of his people. I should have travelled to Africa more often with him to meet with his family and to learn their ways as his people automatically became my people. I should have given Kel a chance rather than continuously questioning his sincerity and commitment to our relationship. If I did not think he was getting into the relationship with a genuine intention, I should as well have not bothered to accept

to marry him or any other who did not have a settled status in the UK.
I should have married a full born-and-bred British citizen to avoid all of
this razzmatazz.

'My parents, most especially my mum, did not help matters. Most
of the things I learnt about keeping a home were learnt from my aunt
whom I lived with in Nigeria. My mum did not find time to prepare me
for marriage. She was too busy. I also learnt a lot from my friend Gwen's
mum, even better than I did from my own mum. Yet people in the
society would give my mum more respect than they were wont to give to
Gwen's mum because of her single status.'

As Judy continued to ponder on her life, her thoughts went back to
her friend's mother in Nigeria—Mummy Chinua. 'An amazing woman,'
she thought to herself. The music "Sweet Mother" by Prince Nico and
his Rocafil Jazz—a popular music band in Nigeria in the '80s—could
not overemphasise the role played by single mothers, like Gwen's mother,
who suffered and toiled tirelessly to put food on their children's tables
single-handedly without the support of the father of these children either
financially, emotionally, and through their physical presence.'

'Oh dear, I have not heard from Gwen for some time, let me call her
now and get her mum's number, I need to speak to Gwen's mum.'

'Hello, Gwen, hello,' Judy called out once Gwen's telephone started
ringing. 'I know she will be dancing to the ringtone now rather than
rushing to pick up the phone to enable her to speak with the person on
the other end.'

'Hiya,' called out Gwen from the other end, 'you all right? Hmm, you
have turned into Oyinbo o!'

'Hiya, init, you all right. Biko, tell me what's new.'

'Nothing o,' said Gwen, 'I just came back from work and am
relaxing. This man is giving me real problems o, I cannot tell you lies.

'What do you mean?' asked Judy.

'What else, it's Lawrence o!' chipped in Gwen, 'I don't understand
him at all. I hope I have not made a mistake. It's been over eight years
now we have been married; there is nothing to show for it in the form
of successes because of this man's stubbornness. 'Let's go for IVF, no,
let's go for surrogacy, no', now let's go for adoption,' it then becomes
whether his mother purposely adopted him out, and so he is justified
adopting children of his own. He never stopped reminding me of how he
suffered in foster care and how a child is best placed with their parents.

His mother's illness was really telling on him. She was presently in respite, and each time he became withdrawn and soliloquized on his own.'

'Gwen, one crazy thing about Africans and Africa is that once there is a problem about having children, the society automatically blames the woman even if it's the man that has the problem. Have you two gone to see your consultants?'

'Several times, and you will not believe what nonsense this man tells anyone or everyone who cares to listen including the receptionists at the GP surgery. He will tell them that the problem is from me not from him because he already has two children of his own from previous failed relationships. This man never told me he has two children. Part of my fault, anyway, I should have taken my time to carry out research on him to know who I was getting married to before saying "I do" to him just because he had come to ask for my hand in marriage from London. I accepted him hook, line, and sinker.'

'Oh, I'm so sorry to hear this, I'm sorry I did not tell you about Lawrence's two children. We agreed that he is best placed to tell you himself,' Judy tried to explain herself, sounding quite guilty.

'That's not even a problem at this stage, as the saying goes, it will be too late to cry when the head is off. I sensed trouble once we landed at the airport. He suggested that we take the train home and I insisted I was not doing any such thing. Haba! I had four suitcases and told him that, but he waved it aside and explained to me how quite economical it is while also saving energy and pollution. Judy, this man is a bit queer and a freak. He is also very obsessed with cleanliness to the extent that I am beginning to wonder whether something is wrong. I cannot get into our bedroom once I walk into the house from outside, I will have to take my shower first. According to him, there is pollution everywhere in the buses and trains and the women's breasts smell.'

'What do you mean?' asked Judy.

'Yes o, this is what I am going through oh! I am taking it easy with him because I know he has been very kind to me in the past. I know all marriages have their own downside. I have to support him through this, more importantly he needs me now that his mum is in respite.'

As Gwen was speaking on the phone, Lawrence walked in and immediately asked her, 'Who are you on the phone with, Gwendolyn?' He only called her full name when he was upset with her. 'It's Judy.'

'Which Judy?'

'Judy your friend, our mutual friend.'

'Mseeeeeeeeew,' he sighed, 'you have to minimise the way you relate with that lady, you know.'

'How do you mean?' asked Gwen.

'You know she is a single mum now, and you should not be making friends with such a lady because you are married.'

'How can you want to put a label on her suddenly just because she is divorced from her husband?'

'Don't be naive,' Lawrence said, 'nothing good comes from people like that.'

'Haba, Lawrence, but she used to be one of your best friends. What, what has changed?'

'The thing that has changed, Gwen, is that she has failed in the most important journey of life, which is marriage, and as such, every other quality she may have had is automatically insignificant.'

'You have just told a single story,' said Gwen, 'a single story of a marriage that failed but could be restored, a single story of just an aspect of life's journey where Judy did not succeed, which may not be a complete and total interpretation of a failure in all other ramifications of life. Have you thought of other areas where she has excelled? In fact since her divorce from her husband, she has single-handedly raised her two children, carrying on the double responsibility of a mother and a father while at the same time depriving herself of any fun, leisure, or relaxation. You are here judging her but you have been given a second chance but have failed to give her that same opportunity you are enjoying.' At this time, Gwen became quite agitated at Lawrence's unreasonableness and effrontery, at the way he casted aspersions at Judy despite having experienced two failed marriages himself. 'Na wao! This is a case of a kettle calling a pot black.'

'Ah! Ah! Oh my God, ah! I feel really sick, just a minute.' Gwen rushed into the bathroom. Suddenly, Lawrence heard the shrill sound of someone sick in the bathroom; he rushed to the door and met it unlocked. 'You all right?' Totally oblivious of his presence, she continued vomiting. He watched her as she laid her head in the sink, retching painfully. It was as though every single bit of what she had inside her stomach was being forced out of her involuntarily. He noticed tears coming out of her eyes and her eyes became quite red. As he held her from behind, he could feel her warm helpless body shaking in a spasm. 'Are you sure you are okay? I need to take you immediately to A & E.'

'I'll be fine, don't worry,' answered Gwen weakly. 'Go get something to eat.'

'No, don't be silly, I cannot leave you like this, let's go and see a doctor, the earlier the better. As he tried to convince her to see the doctor, he moved forwards, ran the cold water over her face, and asked Gwen to run some into her mouth so as to rinse off any remaining sick which might have been left over inside her mouth. He then used the blue flannel on the towel rail to gently wipe her oval face while holding her close to him. Immediately, she started laughing despite herself, as she felt something warm from his groin as he pressed his manhood close to her lower belly. 'I just want to lie down,' she whispered. 'Okay, that's fine by me,' he concurred, understanding where this would lead to. As he took Gwen into the bedroom, he helped her to undress while stroking and caressing her full breast. All the while, she shut her eyes enjoying the touch of his hands. She could feel a wild wetness which had become a part of what she enjoyed each time they were engaged in foreplay.

His breathing became quicker, as he held her in his hands, kissed her passionately while thrusting himself into her as if he wanted to be swallowed by the passion and rhythm of her love.

'You are already wet,' he whispered to her. 'I love you,' he said. 'Love you too,' she whispered sweetly. As they enjoyed each other's warmth, little did they know that their prayers had been answered until the next morning when a test was carried out on Gwen and it was announced that she was five weeks pregnant.

'You're joking! Tell me it's real,' Lawrence screamed once the test was confirmed positive and the doctor announced that Gwen was pregnant.

All arrangements were in full gear from day one for the arrival of Gwen's long-awaited baby. Everything was fine with her all through during the second trimester into her pregnancy; she started experiencing some hormonal and physical changes which saw her being admitted into hospital several times. Gwen also became anaemic during this period. She once swooped and fell down in Borough high street on her way home and was rushed to Guy's and St Thomas's hospital.

Baby Shower

When Gwen was thirty-four weeks pregnant, Judy and other friends of hers organised a baby shower on her behalf. Several gifts were bought and there was plenty to eat and drink. Unfortunately, as she went in to use the restroom, she started feeling an unusual warmness around her lap; she quickly rushed in and opened up her legs to have a view and what she saw sent quivers down her spine. She screamed so loud that she blacked out and was rushed to the hospital where an emergency caesarean was carried out on her, according to the doctors, to save her and her baby as her amniotic fluid had broken and her baby was at risk if nothing was done to bring it out.

At exactly 9 p.m. that evening, Gwen was delivered of a bouncing baby boy who weighed 3.5 kilograms.

'Why do these women leave their babies in the baby cot in hospitals at night?' asked Gwen. 'Will they not have a need to breastfeed their babies at night? Na wao.'

'It is believed that this prepares the babies for a level of independence when they return home. Once a baby is too attached to his mum's hands, it becomes a problem to detach as the mother spends most of the time carrying this baby, leaving other house chores to suffer.'

'Okay oh, Oyibo always does their things differently. If I was at home in Africa, I would be fed with hot pepper soup, hot tea, or hot custard or pap because it is believed that this hot menu will help the remaining blood in my body flow out easily, avoiding any form of haemorrhage or internal bleeding. I, however, don't understand why I am served with a jar of cold water with ice cubes each single morning and I am expected to actually drink it. Don't they think the cold water can make my blood congeal and cause me to fall ill?' asked Gwen. 'Please I want to go home.'

'Yes, I have been told that you will be discharged tomorrow,' said Lawrence excitedly in high expectation.

After Gwen was discharged from hospital, she and the baby were driven home by Lawrence, who came to meet her in the hospital ward early enough to meet with the doctor during the morning ward round.

As they got home, Lawrence quickly came out from the driver side and picked up the baby, opened the door, and led Gwen in while trotting behind her with his head down in a sober manner. Gwen noticed this calm, calculated, and sad look but thought it must be because he was tired after having been visiting her in hospital every other day for the past three days.

As they got in and shut the door, he placed the baby, who was now sleeping, in his cot. Immediately, he turned back, walked towards Gwen, and made an announcement. 'Gwen, my mum passed on yesterday! My mum passed on yesterday!'

'What?' screamed Gwen. 'Why did you not tell me? Oh dear.' She held him as he rushed towards her and held her while he broke down and cried like a baby. Lawrence tried to explain in between sobs the reason why he did not want to break the bad news, seeing that she had not recovered fully after her surgery.

'She is gone,' he said, 'she is gone, she left without saying goodbye, she left me.' He sobbed, holding tightly to Gwen while the two of them sobbed together non-stop for over ten minutes, until they heard the shrieking sound of the baby crying for attention.

The End

****

Once upon a time, there was an island where all the human feelings lived: Happiness, Sadness, Knowledge, and all of the others, including Love.

One day, it was announced to the feelings that the island would sink, so all constructed boats and left, except for Love.

Love was the only one who stayed. Love wanted to hold out until the last possible moment.

When the island had almost sunk, Love decided to ask for help.

Richness was passing by Love in a grand boat; Love said, 'Richness, can you take me with you?'

Richness answered, 'No, I can't, there is a lot of gold and silver in my boat. There is no place here for you.'

Love decided to ask Vanity, who was also passing by in a beautiful vessel. 'Vanity, please help me!'

'I can't help you, Love. You are all wet and might damage my expensive boat,' Vanity answered.

Sadness was close by, so Love asked, 'Sadness, let me go with you.'

'Oh . . . Love, I am so sad that I need to be by myself!'

Happiness passed by Love too but she was so happy that she did not even hear when Love called out for help.

Suddenly, there was a voice.

'Come, Love, I will take you.'

It was an elder. So blessed and overjoyed, Love even forgot to ask the elder where they were going.

When they arrived at the dry land, the elder went her own way.

Realizing how much was owed, Love asked Knowledge, another elder, 'Who helped me?'

'It was Time.' Knowledge answered.

'Time?' asked Love. 'But why did Time help me?'

Knowledge smiled with deep wisdom and answered, 'Because only Time is capable of understanding how valuable Love is.'

—Unknown